IT WAS A FALSE ACCUSATION . . . FROM A MAN WHO BETRAYED HER TRUST BUT SHE WOULD NOT LET THE INSULT PASS . . .

Dorothea could see that one of the comte's eyes was nearly swollen shut, and a small trickle of blood had dried beside his lip, but her pity was not roused by his plight. Still holding Martha tightly, she went over to where the comte stood. In her towering anger, she longed to do or say something that would wound him as much as he had wounded her through Martha—her own child. But she could think of nothing but a feeble insult.

"You despicable excuse for a man," she spat at him. "How low you are, to take advantage of the country that has sheltered you, and to betray the trust of people who offered you their friendship." She could keep her anger in check no longer and lifted her free hand to slap him across his no-longer-handsome face. But she stopped her swing an inch short of his cheek, ashamed of herself for taking advantage of his helplessness.

He smiled sardonically down at her, his eyes glittering with unfathomable emotion. "Ah, *ma chérie*, is that any way to treat a . . . *former* intimate friend? I can understand your jealousy when I was so fickle as to run off with Maria Madalena, but you were never one to have such a hard touch. Your caresses were much more gentle when we spent those long hours together in your sister's house. . . ."

Dorothea

Dorothea
Catherine Moorhouse

A Dell/Banbury Book

Published by
Banbury Books, Inc.
37 West Avenue
Wayne, Pennsylvania 19087

Dell ® 681510, Dell Publishing Co., Inc.

ISBN: 0-440-01986-9

Printed in the United States of America

1991 EDITION
LEISURE ENTERTAINMENT SERVICE CO., INC.

Chapter 1

"How you can be such an ingrate after all I have done for you, I cannot fathom, Dorothea," Miss Letitia Grayson declared, glaring at her hapless companion. "Must I remind you, missy, that I took you in, out of pure Christian charity and familial duty, and have generously fed and clothed you these four years? And now you have the temerity to have refused my simple request that you sing for my guests last evening." Her jowls quivered with outrage at the memory of the girl's perfidy. "Not that I personally like to hear your caterwauling, but you know that Mrs. Barnett and Lady Silverton consider any social gathering to be sadly lacking in *ton* if no young lady makes an exhibition of herself. Well, I give you fair warning, if you play this shabby trick on me again, I shall throw you out, see if I don't, duty or not!" The pendulous jowls and censorious tongue ceased their wagging more or less simultaneously, as Miss Grayson turned her attention to her lap dog, Clarissa, with a marked increase in warmth and decrease in sense.

Dorothea Sandham was not at all displeased at taking a secondary position to the overstuffed pug. With

1

a heartfelt sigh, she released the breath she had held ever since the older woman's reference to "caterwauling," and silently prayed that Clarissa might perform some unspeakable act which would supersede her own offense. The likelihood of this occurring was not great, as the pug's lethargy was exceeded only by that of its owner. More than once Dorothea had marveled at the resemblance between Miss Grayson and the odious animal, particularly when both were left panting by some minor exertion, or when they glared at her in concert over some real or imagined offense.

Miss Grayson's allusion to the time which Dorothea had spent in the unenviable position of poor relation-cum-unpaid companion failed to arouse the appropriate feeling of gratitude in the girl's breast. Instead, she stared bleakly down at the threadbare, ill-fitting brown stuff gown that was one of the "generous contributions" cited by Miss Grayson. The outmoded dress did little to enhance her appearance and the four years with Miss Grayson since her parents' death had done even less. Her cousin's constant nagging made every meal an ordeal. As a result, the young woman was too slender to be considered a beauty, a fact which Miss Grayson reveled in pointing out.

Now the hazel eyes seemed too large in the thin face and the fine nose and cheekbones almost too prominent. The thick dark auburn hair that had once hung heavily to her waist was pulled severely back and covered by a cap, which her cousin insisted was more appropriate to her station in life.

As she listlessly fingered her drab and faded skirts, Dorothea pondered her depressed past and even more depressing future. These reflections raised a spark of rebellion and spurred her into an attempt to defend her behavior of the previous evening.

"But you know what a punishment it is for me to appear before company, cousin. I find it impossible to perform in front of strangers with any degree of composure." She raised her hazel eyes in mute appeal, though she knew it was hopeless to expect compassion from a woman whose only passions in life centered on her dining table and her drooling pug.

"Don't try to cozen me, my girl. You deliberately disobeyed me just to make me look ridiculous before my guests. I recommend that you think over what you owe to me, and next time I expect compliance."

"But with Sir William there," Thea protested, "I thought you did not really wish me to sing. Don't you remember the last time? You took me to task for 'showing off' before that gentleman."

Miss Grayson shifted her considerable bulk in her Chinese Chippendale chair, which creaked ominously. "And so you were, shamelessly gazing at him as you sang. The poor man is quite unaccustomed to such barefaced pursuit, and it quite overset his equipoise."

"But I wasn't even aware I was looking at him! I was minding my notes and thought only of the music."

"A likely story. And you needn't think to entrap a husband through such brazen stratagems. Any agitation on my dear Sir William's part surely arose from his chronic dyspepsia. You may be certain that he is as permanently confirmed a bachelor as I am a maiden, and though he greatly enjoys my company, we shall *never* marry." She patted her sparse grey curls with one plump hand, and obviously waited to be contradicted.

Dorothea disobliged her, lost in her own thoughts on the absent gentleman, a thin, gouty specimen, who barely reached Miss Grayson's chins. She smiled in spite of herself at Miss Grayson's absurd accusations and fond hopes, but then her smile faded. Perhaps the accusations were not so absurd. After all, if she did undertake to "entrap" the kindly old man into marriage, at least she would escape the unkindly old lady who glowered at her over Clarissa's beribboned head.

Avoiding Miss Grayson's eye, Thea picked up her cup and walked to the silver coffeepot on the sideboard, where she stood for a moment listening to her cousin coo idiocies into Clarissa's ear and thinking with repugnance of the prospect of a loveless marriage. Not without some pain, she recalled the exceedingly romantic attachment that had marked her own parents' happy, if ill-starred, union. Indeed, as a child, she had selfishly deemed their absorption in one another to be rather excessive. Captain Sandham had always been so engrossed in his adoring wife during his brief visits home that he seldom had much time or affection to lavish on his small daughter.

As for Mamma, the adult Dorothea mused to herself, she lived only for the moments Papa walked through the cottage door and swept her into his arms. Well, for that privilege Martha Sandham had paid dearly. Cast off by her family upon her marriage to a penniless soldier, she had gone from being the petted youngest daughter of Frederick and Georgiana Grayson to being the lonely and impoverished wife of a military man, who, of necessity, spent most of his time away from her and their small daughter. But Thea was convinced that her mother would not have traded their cramped cottage for all the estates of a dukedom.

The tiny home in Dorset, immaculate and snug, had been the only home Thea had known until her

4

mother's death. Captain Sandham had come home from maneuvers when his beloved wife had been brought to bed. When she died, along with her infant son, Mrs. Sandham had left a double bequest to Thea: her gold wedding band and the care of the grieving captain. Thea had had no opportunity to fulfill the latter, for her father had thrown himself into the first major battle of the Peninsular war, dying at Talavera in July of 1809, a few short weeks after his wife's death.

Letitia Grayson, Martha Sandham's distant cousin, had swooped down on Dorothea at a time when she was most alone in the world. With neither father nor mother, no source of income and no employable skills, the future had looked bleak indeed. But if she had viewed Miss Grayson as some variety of fairy godmother, her illusions had been quickly dispelled. Cousin Letitia had pronounced the cozy cottage squalid and Dorothea a country nobody. She had uprooted the grief-stricken girl from the small town in Dorset and set her to work at her home in Bath as a companion. Dorothea's true position in the house was rather lower than that of a scullery maid's in many other establishments, who at least had a wage and an occasional day of freedom.

For Thea, each day was very much like the one that preceded it. Rising promptly at nine a.m., Miss Grayson spent an hour at her toilette, then settled in with Clarissa for a hearty breakfast while she read the Bath *Journal*, concentrating on the births, deaths and marriages. At noon she sallied forth to walk the several blocks to the Pump Room. Dorothea's role in this excursion was to make certain that Clarissa did not exert herself unduly. As the objectionable pug began panting after half a block, this evolved into one of Thea's few diversions. She would place a wager with herself as to whether she would get as far as Matcham's Library before having to pick up Clarissa and carry her. Up to the present her losses far outweighed her wins, but at least it made the walks less monotonous.

Miss Grayson customarily spent an hour at the Pump Room, taking the vile waters and gossiping with her cronies. This was generally the only opportunity Thea had of seeing her own contemporaries, but as she was kept on a short leash by Miss Grayson, she had developed no more than a nodding acquaintance with anyone her own age.

Each afternoon she would read to her cousin from *The Christian Comforter* until the old woman nodded off, at which point Thea would escape to her room for a few moments of well-earned respite. She always made certain to return before Miss Grayson's nap was finished, else she would be subjected to yet another lecture on her ingratitude.

At teatime they either made calls or received them. Thea suspected that Miss Grayson and her friends chose teatime for the majority of their calls so that none of them might be expected to return the more lavish and costly hospitality of dinner engagements.

Infrequently one of these ancient bosom bows would host an evening at home, offering for refreshment dried biscuits, orgeat and ratafia, and for entertainment the hostess' own indifferent performance on the piano or harp. Dorothea trod a fine line at these elderly assemblies. If she remained completely silent and apart, she was castigated for her sullenness. If she entered into conversations with any of the valetudinarian gentlemen at these gatherings, she was accused of forcing herself upon them in an unmaidenly manner.

But what she dreaded most was when her cousin

6

commanded her to sing. Miss Grayson had no pride in Dorothea's fine contralto voice. Rather, as she had often confided to the girl, it was her only available means of retaliation for the tedious hours she had spent at her friends' musical mercy.

In the four years that she had spent in Cousin Letitia's household, Thea had tried to learn what was expected of her, and in general was able to avoid the kind of breakfast scene that she had been subjected to today. Usually Miss Grayson found solace for her displeasure with her companion in her morning paper, but her unabated anger indicated that the obituary column was sadly thin of juicy entries this morning.

It seemed as if Miss Grayson were reading her mind, for that lady, stopping her hand in midstroke over Clarissa's round back, grumbled, "Hmph, died in childbed, did she?" in a satisfied voice.

Dorothea bit her lip and tried to steel herself for yet another lecture by Miss Grayson on the folly, bordering on impropriety, of her mother's becoming with child at the advanced age of thirty-eight. It had been borne in on the girl numerous times that Mrs. Sandham had received something of her just desserts for: 1) her unsuitable marriage, and 2) her lasting fleshly passion for her husband, both of which flew in the face of everything Miss Grayson held dear.

But when Miss Grayson continued, "Well, it serves him right, marrying a foreigner like that," her words threw the girl into confusion.

Whirling to face her long-time tormentor, Thea saw that Miss Grayson's countenance was still buried in the Bath *Journal*.

"I beg your pardon, ma'am, to whom are you referring?"

7

"Sir Tate Bancroft's foreign wife. I don't know how I could have missed the notice in the paper when she died. Why, that was weeks ago! But I suppose, since he was off in Spain or Portugal somewhere, there was no one to see that the notice was published. It was most remiss of his housekeeper, Agatha Whitesley, but then she never did manage things with anything *approaching* efficiency."

"I have never heard you mention the family before."

Miss Grayson's tiny eyes squinted over the top of the newspaper. "Sir Tate is a rackety young man, a soldier, who came into his baronetcy last year after being missing in action in the Peninsula for nearly a twelvemonth. And when he did come back he brought this Portugee creature with him as his wife. I heard she was a beauty, if one likes the type," she said with a disparaging sniff. "His twin sister Adriana also dropped from sight. There were scandalous stories going round about her, let me tell you."

"Ummm," Thea murmured, only half attending. As her cousin's mood was so greatly improved at finding someone she knew, if only by name, in the obituary page, she welcomed the diversion, however morbid. This news, however, seemed to raise more than the usual measure of Miss Grayson's avid interest, and Thea glanced at her cousin with mild curiosity.

"Did you know these people personally, or are you just repeating idle gossip, cousin?"

"Idle gossip? Certainly not! Adriana and Tate were neighbors of mine before I removed permanently to Bath for my spells. They were only children then, and always up to some brand of mischief. Why, they used to steal my peaches and let my geese out of their pens!"

"Did you actually see them do these terrible things?"

Thea asked, enjoying the thought of someone besting Miss Grayson.

"I didn't need to. All I had to do was look at their guilty faces. I was constantly having to drive over to Bancroft Hall and report their misdeeds to their father. He always solemnly promised to give the wretched brats the punishment they deserved, but that did not seem to improve them one jot, as far as I could tell. I don't believe those two ever received one stroke of a stick once I had gone." Miss Grayson fed a morsel of ham to Clarissa and fell silent, seemingly lost in thought. Then her face lit up in a manner which awoke dire apprehension in Miss Sandham.

"Dorothea, tell Burcham to hire a postchaise for the morrow. We are going to Bancroft Hall to offer our condolences. It is the very least I can do. After all, Charlotte Bancroft and I were like *that* as girls," she said, twining one pudgy finger round another.

"But at such a sad time, don't you think that the family should be left to mourn in peace, ma'am? Let the gentleman's mother comfort him. Strangers will only be in the way."

"Charlotte has been dead these twenty years and more," huffed Miss Grayson. "Died in childbed herself after being delivered of the twins, which is doubtless why they were raised in so deplorable a fashion. Charlotte was a woman of strong character and would never have countenanced the rowdy behavior of those two hellions."

In spite of herself, Dorothea's interest was piqued by what she had heard of the twins. She could not help but think that if their mother had survived their birth she might have blighted what seemed to her to be most interesting childhoods. "But what of their father, cousin? Did he have no hand in shaping their characters?"

"Oh, fiddle! Sir Walter was a most peculiar parent, I can assure you. He cared for nothing but his horses, and later in life, those infernal steam machines. In fact it was the machines that ate up most of his fortune, and horses that killed him. He came to grief over a fence. With no mother and a father like that, it's no wonder those two twins turned out so ramshackle. And such an infelicitous marriage as Tate made." Miss Grayson shook her curls emphatically. "Why his wife could not speak a word of English. Not one word! Only that Portugee gobbledygook. A nice replacement for Lady Charlotte! I imagine that the servants have run wild since her arrival last year. Cheating her at every turn, I shouldn't wonder. No, I think it is my duty as an old neighbor to offer to set things to rights."

"But what of Sir Tate's sister? Is it not more appropriate to leave these matters to her?" Thea protested, dreading to be drawn into yet another ludicrous coil at the hands of her cousin, who made a practice of thrusting herself in, unasked and unwanted, and dragging her reluctant companion along.

"Adriana is herself great with child, and having some difficulties, so I hear," Miss Grayson said with relish. "Her husband, Sir Nicholas Laidley, has insisted that she remain at their London townhouse for the rest of her confinement, so as to be close to the finest Harley Street medical men. And would you believe it, having seen her settled in, what does he do but go haring off to parts unknown? Very odd behavior in a man married barely a year. But then, I hear he was always the most unpredictable of lovers. He apparently treated Sophia Wyndham disgracefully, and why a drab little thing like Adriana should expect any better treatment from him is beyond me. Though Tate was no more considerate of *his* wife when she was breeding. I doubt he was even in England when she was confined, and now she's as dead as mutton," she said with ill-concealed satisfaction.

Dorothea raised every objection she could think of to prevent Miss Grayson's carrying out her plan. Despite her arguments, the next morning she was wedged into a hired chaise beside her cousin and the ubiquitous Clarissa, posting up the long hill that led out of Bath.

Miss Grayson spent the entire journey bemoaning the straitened circumstances that prevented her keeping her own chaise and pair. Thea was well aware that her cousin had fallen into a sizable inheritance at a very young age and was exceedingly wealthy. She was just too tight-fisted to lay out the necessary blunt, so she sealed her ears to the complaints of her companion and the yapping of Clarissa and replied with vague murmurs at measured intervals. The majority of her attention was taken up by the pastoral scene unfolding before her, the fields of grain bathed in the shimmering light of midsummer noon.

The time that Thea had spent in Miss Grayson's household had made her earlier years seem a distant, bucolic dream. Although Bath was considered a hopelessly rustic watering place by those accustomed to the bustle of London, it was the largest metropolis that the country-bred girl had ever known and she had sorely missed the long walks of her childhood.

The few glimpses she had had of the countryside around the town had all been on excursions such as this, boxed up in the smallest and least dear carriage that Miss Grayson could find for her condolence calls.

Thea turned her gaze resolutely to the fields of grain, just beginning to ripen to a green-gold, and could almost imagine herself outside the coach and striding along the hedgerows as she had done so long ago in Dorset.

Miss Grayson sighed noisily and took out her black-edged handkerchief, which she reserved for lugubrious outings like this one. Dorothea, watching her companion as she carefully unfolded and refolded the square of cambric, as if planning her show of grief, thought of the young widower she was about to meet. Despite Miss Grayson's heartless version of his plight, Dorothea was struck by sympathy for him, separated from his wife at such a time by his military career. This naturally led her thoughts to her own father, his death at Talavera and the ongoing war in the Peninsula.

As the daughter of a soldier, Dorothea had always taken a lively and personal interest in the progress of England's struggles with Napoleon Bonaparte. Ever since 1808, when Captain Sandham had gone out to Portugal in the forces led by Wellington, or Wellesley as he was then known, she had closely followed the campaign to oust the occupying French. Even now, long after her father's death on the battlefield, she still read every scrap of news she could find about the efforts of Wellington to hound the French forces permanently out of Portugal and dislodge them from Spain.

Indeed, one of the lessons taught her by her sojourn in Bath was that her passionate interest in things military was most unusual for a young lady. Miss Grayson and her circle thought it singular in the extreme that she puzzled over the subtleties of Wellington's strategies. They themselves were far more concerned with pricing ribbons for their caps and in counting the months intervening between marriage vows and child-bed, or in swooping down like vultures on such unhappy mourners as this Tate Bancroft.

Tate Bancroft, she said to herself, wondering what sort of a man he would be. Someone with the pluck, as a lad, to brave Miss Grayson in her peach orchard. Someone with the sense of duty to go off to war when he could just as easily have sold out. Someone who had forsaken hearth and home for the incommodious billets of Portugal.

Her imaginings were brought to an abrupt halt as the chaise turned into an elm-lined avenue that sloped gently downward, providing a glimpse of the manor house below. The large building of golden Bath stone had the graceful lines of the last century and showed no signs of the disrepair that she had been led to expect. In fact, the lawn bordering the sweeping drive and the gardens beyond, all spoke of conscientious and loving care.

It seemed to Dorothea that her cousin had been guilty once more of exaggerating the justified misfortunes of a neighbor she had taken in dislike. She wondered if perhaps the present baronet and his sister had been less mischievous hoydens than Miss Grayson had made them out to be, and were, instead, pattern cards of perfection.

The postchaise rolled to a stop at the front door of the stately hall and Miss Grayson lost no time in calling to the old man she espied trimming the shrubbery to fetch a groom or footman.

The imperious airs of her cousin only heightened the embarrassment of Miss Sandham, as she could easily perceive that this establishment was as far above Miss Grayson's cramped lodgings as Miss Grayson felt her Bath lodgings to be above the cottage which Thea still considered her true home.

What the master of this elegant domain will think of Miss Grayson's presumption, I dare not even speculate, she thought with a frown. And I shall be judged guilty of equally encroaching ways, no doubt. With any luck, this Sir Tate won't admit us, she thought hopefully, as she firmly removed Clarissa from her lap. And even if Miss Grayson does manage to accomplish this, the presence of a dowdy, tongue-tied companion will probably go unnoticed.

A stout-looking groom came to open the door of the chaise, but before he could assist Miss Grayson in descending, no mean feat, Clarissa leaped out of the carriage and disappeared into the shrubbery.

"Clarissa! Come back immediately, I say!" Miss Grayson shrieked, and when her importunings had no appreciable effect, she ordered Dorothea to give chase.

Chapter 2

Dorothea was delighted to go after the delinquent dog and prayed that Clarissa would prove elusive enough to allow her to miss much of the forthcoming interview with the baronet. Parting the shrubbery with her hands, she discovered a gravel path on the other side, and slipped through nearly as effortlessly as Clarissa had done. As she walked down the pathway she felt quite exhilarated at her unexpected freedom. On both sides the dense shrubbery provided a wall of green; there was no possibility of Miss Grayson's forcing her substantial person through the leafy barrier, even if she were likely to make the effort. She could only gain the path by going through the house, where she would surely be detained by servants and the master of the house.

A bubble of laughter rose in Thea's throat and she found herself chuckling out loud with pure elation. The sound of her own laughter was a rare enough one that it brought her almost to a halt, and she looked round to make sure that no one would overhear her mirth.

Ahead of her the inner edge of the walkway was bordered by a low, closely trimmed hedge, beyond which grew a profusion of rosebushes. Their scent and color were almost overwhelming and she stood enraptured, lost in the beauty of the scene, her mission forgotten. A sudden barking from farther along the path prompted her into action once again and she followed the sound into a narrow passage where the hedge had been allowed to grow high and wild on either side. After the brilliance of the midday sun, the dark shadows of this passage nearly blinded her and she emerged on the far side of it at a full run, colliding violently with a man in the bower beyond. Her forehead encountered his chin with such force that she saw the proverbial stars, whereas he apparently saw only red, if his words were any indication.

"Who in the bloody hell are you?" he growled at her as she clutched at him convulsively, trying to clear her head of its pain and vertigo.

"Sir, I . . . I . . ." she gasped, then, lifting her eyes, she saw with a slight shock that the person to whom she clung appeared to be a vagrant who might offer her bodily harm. His brown curls were wildly disheveled, his clothing looked as though it had been slept in and his scowling grey eyes were red-rimmed as though from lack of sleep or inebriation or both. Closer examination overruled her first fear, however. No hedgebird ever wore such a well-cut jacket, nor lounged at ease in a gentleman's garden in broad daylight. Still, she quivered with apprehension seeing that, whoever he was, he was more than a trifle disguised. Although, in truth, it was difficult to judge of the matter, as the full glass of spirits which he had held in his hand had been a casualty of their collision and the contents had been liberally splashed over her own gown.

With as much dignity as she could summon, Dorothea straightened up and released the crumpled lapels of the raven-black frock coat. "I am merely in pursuit of a dog, sir. If you would kindly tell me which way the creature has gone, I will be on my way."

"Surely you don't mean to tell me that that disgustingly mollycoddled specimen belongs to you!" The grey eyes flicked over her as if she were even more repugnant than the specimen under discussion.

Dorothea opened her mouth to tell this insulting lout in no uncertain terms that she owed him no explanations that she knew of, when a man appeared in the arbor carrying a silver salver upon which rested the distinctive calling card of Miss Letitia Grayson. Apart from the fact that she knew Miss Grayson was in the house, Dorothea would have recognized the card anyway, for it bore not only the names of Miss Letitia and Miss Clarissa Grayson, but was embellished with a portrait of the latter, in sepia tones.

The gentleman placed the bottle of brandy he had been holding on a nearby stone bench and glowered at the bit of pasteboard. Dorothea sank onto the bench beside it. She had formed the most lowering conviction that this wild-eyed, disheveled "lout" was none other than the widowed baronet himself. She watched, speechless with mortification, as with clear loathing he read the inscription aloud.

"As if I didn't have enough grief to bear; now that old witch has insinuated herself into my drawing room. Wants to satisfy her ghoulish curiosity, I expect. Well, by hell, I'll not be gawked at by that harpy. Tell her I'm not at home, Parker, or tell her I've blown my brains out. She'd enjoy that no end, and it's not far off the mark, if a bit premature. That is, if the French oblige

17

with a musket ball. What the devil is wrong with you, man?"

The elderly butler, who had been repeatedly clearing his throat and rolling his eyes at Thea in a marked manner, instantly subsided. "If I might be so bold as to inform you, Sir Tate," he said with great dignity, "this young, er, person, accompanied Miss Grayson here." He fixed a doleful eye on the girl, whose delicate white countenance became deeply flushed.

The baronet also turned his eye on the discomfitted young woman.

"You came here in the company of that vicious gabble-monger? The devil you say! I suppose this means that I shall be forced to face her." The grey eyes that had flashed with anger were once again dull and lifeless, and Thea felt a pang of sympathy for him.

"Not on my account, I assure you, sir," she spoke as she rose to her feet, sending her head painfully spinning once again. "I did my best to dissuade her from intruding on your . . . grief, but as I am only her poor relation, my words carried no weight whatsoever. However, I must find that dratted beast or Miss Grayson will never leave the premises, whether or not she succeeds in flushing you out."

Sir Tate looked at Dorothea for a moment, but she had the feeling that he looked straight through her. For her part, however, she was seeing him with distressing clarity. Despite the droop of his broad shoulders, she could discern a fine physique. The deep-set grey eyes held a profound sadness and his face was a study of bitterness. As the baronet ran the long fingers of one hand through his tousled curls, Thea felt a wave of tenderness wash over her. More than anything else she longed to gather him into her arms and comfort him as she would a sobbing child.

The realization of the impropriety of this impulse brought the hot color once again to her cheeks and dispelled the last vestiges of dizziness. Hoping to conceal her agitation, Dorothea began calling for Clarissa and searching the hedge for the recalcitrant animal.

She tracked the sound of muffled yelps to a sheltered place behind a group of rosebushes only to discover that Clarissa was not alone. She was, in fact, in a most compromising position with a mongrel male dog of dubious antecedents. She grabbed Clarissa away and pinioned the squirming pug to her side, admonishing her in what she hoped was a creditable imitation of Miss Grayson's voice. "Cla-ris-sa, my girl, whatever would your mistress say. Indulging in the sins of the flesh at the first opportunity. It bespeaks a lamentable lack of breeding, you know."

To her intense embarrassment she heard the baronet's voice immediately behind her, as he consulted with the butler. With a fervent hope that they had not been witness to Clarissa's fall from grace, and with a muddled notion of making an apology, she turned around and self-consciously interrupted their whispered conversation. "And now, Parker," she said, "if you will show me how to get back to my cousin, I shall do my best to rid you of her, with no one the wiser."

"I think you are overlooking one rather important factor, Miss. . . ?"

"Sandham." Dorothea reluctantly raised her eyes to the baronet's face.

"Miss Sandham. And that is that you bear the redolent evidence of our encounter." For an instant, something very like laughter glinted in those grey eyes, and Thea was possessed of a wish to have met him under happier circumstances. As she gazed up into his eyes, she saw the curtain of sadness descend once more. In a weary voice, he said, "If you think you can explain away how you came to be soaked in spirits, I am, of course, perfectly willing to allow you to help me avoid seeing your mistress. It is up to you, madam, to decide the best course."

"Parker," Dorothea said firmly, "would you please tell Miss Grayson that although Sir Tate is not at home, you did manage to find Clarissa and me, and that we will meet her at the carriage?"

After the butler had left them, Dorothea clutched Clarissa snugly to her side and prepared to depart back down the garden path, but a sudden impulse made her address her silent host.

"For my part in this conspiracy of silence I do exact a price, however," she said, trying to keep her tone light, although her request was to be deadly serious.

The baronet scrutinized her as though for the first time, taking in the shabby gown and severe cap. "Certainly. I expected as much," he said contemptuously. "After all, an impoverished spinster in your circumstances must make a living." He pulled a small leather purse from his pocket.

"Don't be insulting. I don't want your money." Thea's voice was as haughty as her injured pride could make it. "But you must give me your word of honor . . ."

"My word of honor? What are you babbling on about now? I am in no mood . . ."

"Your word of honor," she went on briskly, not daring to look at him, "that you will stop talking of, or even thinking of, ending your own life. I never knew your young wife, but it is my estimation that she was a person of exceptional courage to uproot herself from the country of her birth to start a new life in a foreign land. I don't believe that she would ever countenance so cowardly an act as suicide."

"You go too far, madam, and your advice is facile," he replied in arctic accents. "Just what do you pretend to know of my wife. Or for that matter, of my grief."

"Only what I learned through losing my mother, father and infant brother all in the space of a month. And, I regret to tell you that my father, just as you, deliberately sought death on the battlefield and was signally successful in his aim. As for my brother, of course he was but a newborn babe, but still I felt his loss, just as you doubtless feel the loss of your child."

"No, I . . ." he started to say, then, when his voice broke, he stopped speaking and plucked aimlessly at a yellow rose.

"Well, I expect that after all is said and done, it was best in both cases that the infants died with their mothers. I know that was what I felt about my little brother, for even during the few days that he lived, my father refused to acknowledge his existence, holding him accountable somehow for the death of Mamma. It was so unfair, and so heartbreaking."

She saw a shadow pass over the features of the gentleman, and suddenly realized how she must be wounding him. This jarred her into chattering out an apology for her foolishness. The last thing she wished was to add to his suffering.

"I can't think why I went on and on like that, it is not my usual mode of speaking, I do assure you. You must think me worse than Cousin Letitia. Do forgive me for speaking so plainly, Sir Tate."

21

"Nonsense, Miss Sandham. You owe me no apologies. And now, if you will excuse me, I have little taste for company just now." He made a slight bow, and turned away from her, picking up the decanter of spirits from the stone bench in a determined manner that made Thea realize that her words had accomplished nothing. He had the air of a man seeking oblivion and perdition, in that order, and she felt powerless to stop him from finding either.

Blindly she whirled, and shifting Clarissa to her other arm, started back up the path toward the house, praying that before she burst into tears she might find the break in the shrubbery through which she had entered. To her growing frustration, the hedge continued uniformly impenetrable and she found her composure slipping from her as she fumbled down the leafy corridor seeking a way out.

She quickly dashed the tears of anger and frustration from her eyes, however, when she heard the stentorian tones of Miss Grayson coming down the pathway toward her.

"Parker, come along, and don't try to gull me with some farrago of nonsense about Tate being from home. I'll just see for myself if he is in the garden."

At these words, the girl looked wildly about her, hoping to discover an avenue of escape, but then resigning herself to the inevitable, she walked calmly toward her cousin. Her brain was awhirl with possible explanations and excuses, but none was required, for Miss Grayson herself wrested the pug and the conversation from her hands.

"Poor little puppykins, were you frightened without me? Dorothea, I am most vexed with you. I have been prostrate with worry over Clarissa, convinced as I was that she had fallen over the haha, and here I find you idling the afternoon away with no thought for my poor nerves." She paused for a dramatic sniff in illustration of her shattered emotions, and unhappily for Thea, the result of this was a look of genuine horror.

"Do-ro-the-a! You smell like a tavern wench! I am utterly appalled. You know my sentiments on these things, and you have flagrantly disregarded my convictions by imbibing spirits. Well, I suppose it was only to be expected from a young woman of your parentage. One weakness of the flesh is as bad as another. But this time you have overstepped yourself, my girl. It shall be the streets for you . . ."

But Miss Grayson was cut off in mid-harangue by Sir Tate Bancroft, who stepped out from the bower and addressed her.

"Miss Grayson, what a surprise to find you in the neighborhood again," he said, directing an ironic glance at Thea, who marveled at the convincing, though cool, welcome he had managed when she knew his real feelings. Her cousin crunched down the gravel to seize the young man's hand and wring it vigorously.

"Ah, Tate, I have come, posthaste, to succor you in your hour of tribulation. I simply could not stay away, poor motherless boy that you are. But I can see how hopelessly muddled your household is by this terrible tragedy. Why, even your own butler did not know your whereabouts, and the cucumber sandwiches served to me by your cook while I was waiting for my darling Clarissa to be found were dreadfully stale and dry. But then, it is only natural. Foreigners simply don't know how to handle our English servants."

Thea, deeply mortified at her cousin's indelicacy,

tried to change the subject by remarking on the loveliness of the roses in the bower.

The baronet looked grateful for her tactful intercession. "Actually, all the credit for the roses belongs to my twin sister, Adriana, who spent most of last summer slaving away in the garden. It had fallen into a sad state over the years because of my father's, er, unusual habits."

A snort issued from Miss Grayson at these seemingly innocuous words. "Unusual habits! I should say. Sir Walter spent every pence he had on fast horses and cock-eyed inventions. If I told him once, I told him a hundred times . . ."

"What an unusual color this one is, Sir Tate. What is the name of this variety?" Dorothea broke in, earning a baleful stare from Miss Grayson.

With a face purpled in fury the old woman cut off the baronet's civil reply by barking out, "And what do you propose to do about your daughter, Tate?"

His only reply was a negligible shrug of his broad shoulders.

A dreadful suspicion crept into Dorothea's mind and she blurted out, "What do you mean, cousin?"

"While I was left cooling my heels in the drawing room I happened to look into the hall, where I found Agatha Whitesley passing by. She was the governess employed by Sir Walter to see to the twins' upbringing, not that she ever had the slightest control over them." Miss Grayson paused dramatically to ascertain what effect her disparaging remarks might have had on Sir Tate, but he had once again seemingly retreated into a bleak world of his own.

To Thea's mounting discomfort, her cousin continued in a stage whisper. "At any rate, Miss Whitesley informed me that the infant did not die and, all things considered"—at this she shot a look pregnant with meaning at the unheeding Tate—"is in remarkably good condition, except for being colicky and jaundiced."

Thea tried desperately to recall what exactly she had said on just this subject to Sir Tate, and felt a mixture of embarrassment at her mistake and anger at his allowing her to believe that the child had not survived.

"Agatha also told me that she is totally beside herself with worry. It is imperative that she leave at once to be with Adriana, who is having such difficulties with her own delicate condition. But the baby is too frail to travel as yet, and Tate is bullheadedly determined to set off for Portugal," Miss Grayson said with palpable pleasure in the distressing situation. A certain self-satisfaction settled over her porcine countenance as she leaned toward the young man and, laying one pudgy hand on his sleeve, demanded again to know his plans for his daughter.

Sir Tate roused himself enough to respond to the pressure of her grasp. "I haven't any particular plans, if you must know. Surely the servants can mind it in my absence," he finally flung at her, his patience at an end.

"I don't think that is good enough. What if you should be struck down in battle? Rather a haphazard way to provide for your daughter's future." The small eyes glittered brightly from the folds of flesh and the normally strident voice dripped with honeyed tones. "Now, Tate, my dear, I would be only too happy to help you out of your dilemma by moving in here and taking charge of everything. You need a mature, responsible woman to oversee matters, and I am prepared to make the sacrifice."

Thea had a disturbing vision of an entrenched Miss

Grayson as a permanent fixture of this grand old home, and a shiver of revulsion ran up her spine.

"I couldn't ask it of you, Miss Grayson. Why, I might be gone for years and . . ."

"It is only my Christian duty, Tate, and naturally, I would be prepared to step aside instantly when you find a stepmother for the little mite, though, of course, that will surely be a good, long while." She smirked a little.

"And I would ask that you draw up a legal document giving me full rein in case of your demise, so that I am able to bring up your little girl in the proper manner. I'm sure you wouldn't want her to turn out a hoyden like Adriana. No, I'll keep a close eye on her, you may rest assured."

Sir Tate visibly flinched. "I somehow doubt that my notion of the 'proper manner' of raising her would tally with yours, madam. And in any case, I could not impose on your . . . good nature. You have been most helpful in reminding me where my duty lies, however. I suppose it would be irresponsible of me to leave for the Peninsula without making legal provisions for its future."

With a sharp pain Thea recalled his words about killing himself and was filled with compassion for him and empathy for the baby girl whom he was abandoning.

She saw the two before her almost as figures in an illustrated fairy tale. Sir Tate, wrapt in an unhappy vision of a bleak future, appeared completely unaware of the presence of Miss Grayson, the dragon coiled in anticipation of taking over the future of the child and this noble estate. The halls which had once rung with the irrepressible laughter of the youthful Tate Bancroft and his twin sister would be cloaked in the repressive gloom of the mean-spirited old lady. The vision of this man's daughter coming of age under the supervision of Miss Grayson brought Thea to the point of intervention, like some mythic Saint George charging in to protect the innocent. Fortunately the baronet bore little real resemblance to a maiden in distress, for before she could open her mouth and issue the warning, to her surprise, the gentleman once again began to speak of the subject, in a taut, flat voice. The mention of her own name brought her back to reality.

"I regard your visit, along with Miss Sandham, to be positively providential. You have been of immense help and shown me what I should do."

Miss Grayson smoothed down Clarissa's coat smugly. "Then I shall move in directly. The chaise can return to Bath for our possessions."

"No, you don't understand, madam. As I said before, I couldn't bring myself to make you stay, but you spoke good sense about providing a stepmother for the child. Miss Sandham? From what I overheard in the garden, you are currently without a post, is that correct?"

Dorothea stood as if turned to stone. "I fear you are correct, yes, sir," she whispered.

"Then I would like to offer you a post, effective immediately, as stepmother to the infant."

Dorothea's eyes flew to the baronet's face, but it was so impassive that she could not believe what she had heard. Indeed, she was about to conclude that she had imagined his words, when Miss Grayson spluttered into speech.

"B-but that is outrageous! Tate, I would not have believed this, even of you. I should have warned you, Dorothea, that this boy is forever playing pranks on unsuspecting victims, but I would have supposed him to be beyond such infamous tricks at his age, especially during a time of mourning. But this is very bad of you, Tate," she said, reproving him directly. "Making game of Dorothea in this insulting manner. Though it is perfectly obvious that she will never attract a suitor, skin and bones as she is, I think it most unhandsome of you to put her to the blush with your satirical mockery."

The gentleman ignored the old woman's scolding as though she were an insignificant insect. Instead, his steady gaze never left Thea's face.

"It is not a jest, Miss Sandham, I assure you. I am much in earnest. If you agree, I shall procure a special license so that we may marry tonight. Then I shall be free to go back to Portugal on the morrow, with a clear conscience."

Miss Grayson looked apoplectic. Her bosom heaved and her voice shook with rage. "If this is a joke, sir, it is in extremely poor taste. Now, I must insist that you cease this nonsense on the instant. It is simply incredible that you hold your guests up to ridicule, especially when we have come out of the goodness of our hearts to help you through this desolate time. Well, I, for one, shall not stay to be further insulted. Come, Dorothea." She wheeled and stalked away in high dudgeon.

In something of a daze, the girl started to follow Miss Grayson's retreating back, but the touch of the baronet's hand on her arm stopped her.

"Miss Sandham," he said, in a voice roughened by emotion, or drink, or both, "I ask that you seriously consider my offer. You have much to gain by it, and nothing whatsoever to lose, except, perhaps, the companionship of your cousin."

Dorothea struggled to form an answer, but fearing that he was only making fun of her, as Miss Grayson had said, could not utter a word. With her thoughts in chaos, she searched his countenance for evidence of his sincerity.

He turned away and kicked at the gravel, for all the world, thought the young woman, like a small boy thwarted of his heart's desire. But how absurd, she reminded herself sternly. It has nothing to do with the desire of his heart. He has made this preposterous offer merely to salve his conscience.

Still studying the gravel walk, the baronet continued in a wooden voice, "You needn't worry, you know, that it would be anything but a union in name only. And, if the French prove accommodating, you will not be burdened with a husband for long, even *in absentia*. Now, wouldn't you like to become a wealthy widow?"

As though already facing the enemy on the field of battle, he turned and met Thea's searching gaze. When she continued silent, he went doggedly on. "Of course, after I die, the baronetcy will go to a distant cousin, and though you would have to leave Bancroft Hall, you will still remain Lady Bancroft. Since my income derives largely from unentailed business ventures of my father, you would want for nothing. I believe that you could still clear five thousand per annum, not counting . . ."

"Stop, please," Dorothea cried, finally goaded into speech. "If I *were* to agree to this mad scheme, it would not be for the money, it would only be so that I might look after the little girl."

"Then you do agree to this . . . proposition?" he said in a voice utterly devoid of feeling.

"Will I have a free hand with the baby? And may I be guaranteed that if I become her mother, I shall not have her taken from me later on? It would be too much for me to bear if I had to lose someone else I had come to love."

"It seems to me that you are caviling over trifles, Miss Sandham. Will you or won't you marry me? A simple yes or no is all I require."

"There is nothing simple about this transaction, Sir Tate, but, yes, I will mother your child, and try to make up to her what she has been deprived of—loving parents." She peered into his face, trying to read his thoughts, but saw nothing except relief in his grey eyes.

With a formal bow, he acknowledged her acceptance, then began instructing her as to what must be done.

He might just as well have been dickering over the purchase of a horse, for all the emotion he feels over this, she thought ruefully, and then decided she probably didn't even rouse the interest he would have felt in the acquisition of a thoroughbred. I would guess that I am more on the level of a sway-backed plough horse in such a comparison. "Well, at least I'm unharnessed from Cousin Letitia," she murmured with a half-smile.

"I beg your pardon?" Sir Tate snapped, irritated by the interruption.

Dorothea, giddy at the rapid series of events that had turned her life topsy-turvy, felt a hysterical giggle rising in her throat. She managed to disguise it with a cough and forced herself to listen to his instructions with strict and sober concentration.

"As I said before," he went on gravely, "I must be off immediately to see to the license. You may have the ineffable pleasure of informing Miss Grayson of your decision, much as it would gratify me to put a spoke in her wheel myself. Then you may go to the house and ask Aggie, that is, Miss Whitesley, to see to the washing of your, er, garment. It looks to me entirely too much like what I used to see on the old peasant widows in the Portuguese villages. And while this is hardly a romantic occasion, I would think even an old gown of Adriana's would be more appropriate for the wedding ceremony than that awful sack," he growled, and, turning on his heel, strode away without another word.

Chapter 3

With a sensation of total unreality, Dorothea walked
down the path and through great good luck was able to
find the break in the foliage through which she had
chased Clarissa, a lifetime before. Her skirt caught on
one of the lower branches, and as she bent to untangle
it, the realization swept over her that before the day
was done, the shrubbery and the rose bower, which
were really all that she had seen at close quarters of Sir
Tate's estate, would officially be under her charge, as
mistress of Bancroft Hall. Her hands started shaking so
violently that she could not loosen the fabric from the
hedge, as she reminded herself that the supervision of
the garden was as nothing next to her real responsibility: Sir Tate's tiny, defenseless daughter. She felt a great
tenderness bloom inside her and an equally great resolution that nothing was going to stand in the way of
making the babe happy and healthy.

This served to calm and strengthen her and she
unhesitatingly seized the ugly cloth and ripped it away
from the thorns which bound it. Holding the tattered
hem in one hand, she walked resolutely toward the
chaise.

Dorothea

Miss Grayson greeted her with a torrent of ill-humor. "And what kept you so long, missy. I must say that I think I have been treated badly enough already today, without having to sit around in a smelly, sweltering chaise, waiting for you. Now just jump in and we'll be off. I have no desire to stay where I am so obviously not wanted," the woman huffed and fanned herself vigorously with a hideous chicken-skin fan.

"Cousin Letitia," Thea replied calmly, "I must inform you that I have accepted Sir Tate's offer of marriage."

The chicken-skin fan slipped out of sight and Miss Grayson's eyes appeared ready to pop from her head. "What did you say?" she gasped.

"I said that I am going to marry Sir Tate," Dorothea enunciated slowly and clearly, greatly enjoying Miss Grayson's evident shock.

"Well, if this isn't the outside of enough! First I take you in off the streets, rescue you from penury, and treat you as I would my own daughter, and this is how you reward me? By abandoning me to my solitude without so much as a by-your-leave? Humph! I suppose breeding will tell. Your mother was a mutton-headed little idiot, whose carnal lust caused her to disregard her duty to her family. Now here you are, doing the same thing."

"Carnal lust has nothing whatsoever to do with it, cousin," Dorothea said with a sigh. "But I know that you are dying to spread the tale of my perfidy, so I won't delay you further. I shall send someone for my things as soon as possible."

"They shall find them in the street, where I should have left you!" Miss Grayson spat out.

"And where you had already told me I was going,

if you will recall. It was you, strictly speaking, who cast
me off, not the other way around. And, by the way, I
should have Clarissa checked by Mr. Cotter, if I were
you. She may be in pup. When I found her she was
with a very . . . er . . . attentive male," Thea said
with mock alarm.

"Not *my* Clarissa! She has far too much regard for
me ever to engage in sordid affairs of the flesh. Not like
some." And on that scathing note, Letitia Grayson called
to the postilion to start his horses, and with nose held
high, rode away.

Dorothea watched the chaise drive through the gates
with rising excitement. She even went so far as to
dance a few steps of a country dance and hum a few
bars of one of the Scottish ditties that she used to sing
with her mother. Her little celebration ground to a
quick halt, however, when she heard someone address
her in a disapproving tone.

"Miss Sandham, I presume?"

She froze in midstep, painfully aware of the awkwardness of her situation, and looking round, saw that
the speaker was a tall, spare woman of uncertain age,
clad in a plain black bombazine gown. Dorothea made
the woman a slight curtsy, her high spirits thoroughly
scuttled by the sober countenance before her.

"Yes, I am Dorothea Sandham."

"I am Agatha Whitesley. Tate has told me of his,
er, intentions, and directed me to find you here." The
woman looked at her sternly, but when Thea started to
thank her, she held up her hand for silence. "I don't
wish you to misunderstand me, Miss Sandham. I think
that Tate is being far too precipitate in this, as in
everything he does. He has, however, told me why he
has chosen you for what he calls this 'post.' "

Dorothea, having a fairly good idea of what these reasons were, still felt most uncomfortable at the prospect of hearing them enumerated, but listened intently, nevertheless.

"After all, as Tate says, Miss Grayson is such a stickler for propriety, that any companion of hers must be a respectable young woman. Furthermore, anyone who could survive any length of time in Letitia's employ must be hardworking and healthy as a horse, or so he reasons."

So, thought Dorothea, my self-comparison with horse trading was not so far from his views of the matter, after all. I wonder that he did not check my teeth and withers.

"Besides," Miss Whitesley continued, "it is also true that the last thing Tate needs is a raving beauty for a wife. If you were one of *those*, you might dally with admirers and ignore the baby."

Dorothea longed to ask if this last was also Tate's own assessment of her, but feared that the answer would be yes, so refrained.

Miss Whitesley's expression softened. "I suppose Tate's reasons for this marriage are, in reality, just as sound as some boyish infatuation. In any case, now that his mind is made up, nothing I could say to try and convince him to change it would have the slightest effect. So I am resigned to this foolhardy plan, and will say nothing except, 'Welcome to Bancroft Hall.' "

"Miss Whitesley, I'm sure that this all seems most irregular and, as you say, foolhardy to you. In your position I would have the same reservations. Even in my own position, I must admit to some, but please believe me that my major concern is the same as yours," Dorothea said earnestly, leaning forward a little.

Miss Whitesley drew herself up and inquired what she meant.

"I mean the baby, of course. I only agreed to this so that I might help the little mite."

The old governess shook her head sadly. "Ah, yes, the poor little darling. I've been worried to death about her. We have had a parade of wet nurses through the nursery but have found none whose nourishment seems to satisfy the tiny thing. She came so early, you know, and even suckling at the breast tires her. Why we've had to resort to giving her boiled goat's milk from a bottle with a hole in the teat large enough to flow without much effort on her part."

Miss Whitesley turned anguished eyes on her companion. "I don't wish to leave her, but Adriana needs me so, though she writes me not to come. Tate's wife had such an easy time of her pregnancy, I would never have thought that what happened could have. I raised Adriana from infancy, you know, as well as Tate, and I know that she is having difficulties, and I . . ."

The lined face crumpled, and before she quite knew what had happened, Dorothea was leading Miss Whitesley to sit on a stone bench and patting her soothingly on the shoulder.

"Now, now, Miss Whitesley. That is just why I am staying. You may go to your dear Adriana and rest assured that I will take the very best charge of our little . . ."

She stopped and exclaimed, "But I don't even know the baby's name! Sir Tate only referred to her by 'it' and the like. Whatever is she called?"

Miss Whitesley wiped her eyes with a large handkerchief from her reticule and said sorrowfully, "She doesn't even have a name yet. I've been trying to make

Tate decide on one and have her properly christened, but the poor boy has been so distracted since Lady Bancroft's death that nothing has been done. Perhaps *you* could remedy matters. He won't listen to me, and Adriana is too far away to do anything except write letter after letter, which lie unopened and unread on his desk."

"I shall do what I can, but you must know that I have no influence with him at all. After all, we are strangers to one another." They sat for a long moment, each lost in her own thoughts, and then Thea straightened up.

"But what are we doing moping about out here? I want to meet my daughter-to-be." The two rose of one accord and hurried into the house and up to the nursery.

As they tiptoed into the large, sunny room, they found a young nursemaid struggling vainly to introduce a rubber teat into the howling mouth of the tiniest infant Dorothea had ever seen. Without a moment's hesitation she walked up to the nurse and took baby and bottle into her own arms. Sitting down in an old rocking chair, Miss Sandham followed her own instincts and began to sing a lullaby in her rich contralto voice. The infant seemed to be aware of the change and the music, and to the girl's immense delight, stopped crying and began to suck contentedly at the bottle. With some measure of peace established, Thea was able to look closely at the infant she held and she was captivated by what she saw.

Soft, light, downy hair was barely visible on the little head, and the eyes which sought her own were still the muddy blue of early infancy. There was a faint yellow cast to the skin, which worried her, but the features, in Dorothea's estimation, were perfect—delicate and beautifully formed. There were none of the blotches

38

or lumps that she had seen on other, ordinary babies. No, this was no ordinary baby. This was to be her own baby, and her only baby. She tightened her arms around her small burden and found tears welling up in her eyes. She looked at Miss Whitesley and smiled through her tears.

"I shall call her Martha, after my mamma, if Sir Tate doesn't object."

"It's a lovely name. Yes, little Martha. That will do nicely. Now, my dear, I think we had better let Annie here put her into her cradle for a nap. We must get you ready for your wedding."

With great reluctance, Dorothea agreed, but she herself put the baby into the intricately carved cherry cradle, which stood by the window, and drew the curtains. She leaned over and gently kissed the baby's unbelievably soft cheek, then followed Miss Whitesley out of the nursery and down the hall.

As she went along, she began feeling more and more nervous about what she was about to do. Although now that she had seen the baby, wild horses could not have dragged her away, still the reality of the fast-approaching ceremony with a complete stranger was most unsettling.

Miss Whitesley appeared to sense her growing apprehension, and kept up what, in a more frivolous woman, would have been called an endless line of chatter, to soothe the nervous girl. Their way led them through a corridor lined with portraits, and she called Dorothea's attention to various pictures which she thought might interest her.

"That one was done when Adriana and Tate were only six years old. I had the most dreadful time keeping them clean for the posing sessions, and getting them to hold still. And this one was painted just before Tate joined the military, when he was eighteen. Can't you just see how proud he is of his regimentals? It is Adriana's favorite. She says he looks just like Lord Wellington surveying his troops. Tate was always military-mad, you see. From the time he was breeched he longed for a uniform. When he finally talked Sir Walter into purchasing him his colors, he was utterly cock-a-hoop."

"Yes, I can see that in his face. He looks so different now," Dorothea said, and wished that the man she was about to marry was the exultant youth of the painting and not the somber gentleman of the rose bower. But then, a handsome, young, happy-go-lucky Tate Bancroft would never have looked twice at her, much less asked her to contract a marriage, of convenience or otherwise.

The last portrait they came to was of a raven-haired beauty who gazed shyly forth as if a little unsure of her welcome in this hall of Anglo-Saxon ancestors. There could be no doubt that here was the Portuguese bride so mourned by her widower that he could not face life without her, or accept the child whose arrival had cost her her life.

"Is that Lady Bancroft?" Dorothea breathed, and Miss Whitesley nodded, unable to speak.

"What was her name?"

"Mathilde," came the answer, and Dorothea tried to pronounce the name as the governess had: "Ma-teeu-gee. As lovely a name as she was a lady."

Miss Whitesley glanced at the portrait, then looked determinedly away. "And now, we must find you something to wear. Here's Adriana's old room, just across from Tate's chambers. Those two scamps always insisted on the arrangement so that they could conspire across the hallway without my hearing them. My room was up by the nursery, you see."

She led the girl into a room that was cheerful and delightfully decorated in a manner very much to Thea's taste. The sun streaming in through the west-facing window was filtered through the leaves of an ancient elm that stood outside. It gave the room a dappled look of diffuse warmth. With its snowy linen and pale wood, the room had lightness and femininity without the frills that Dorothea had been accustomed to seeing in the homes of Miss Grayson's acquaintances. On the walls were a few portraits of what Thea assumed were Sir Walter and Lady Charlotte in their younger years. And on the mantel over the fireplace hung a miniature of the portrait of the twins in the gallery. The absence of an occupant had not been an excuse for closing off and ignoring this chamber; it showed the same loving care as the rest of the manor house.

When Miss Whitesley spoke, it was in a gentle voice. "Perhaps it would be best if you were to occupy this room, Miss . . ." She broke off and then added in a rush, "May I call you by your Christian name? I feel the awkwardness of this relationship as much as you do."

"Please, call me Thea. No one has since Mamma and Papa died."

"And please call me Aggie," Miss Whitesley responded. "That will put us on a less formal footing, I hope." She crossed to the wardrobe that stood against the wall and began to draw out the small store of pale gowns that were folded neatly on one shelf.

"I'm afraid that much of what Adriana left behind after her marriage would hardly be more suitable for today's occasion than what you are presently wearing."

41

Aggie shook her head in dismay as she unfolded the cambric and muslin garments. Several of the gowns had worn through completely at the elbow or shoulder. Some had been patched, but others had merely been discarded in a state of disrepair.

"You are doubtless right, Aggie, but I would gladly exchange this dreadful object for a muslin, no matter how worn. At least I should not go to my nuptials reeking of brandy."

They found a sprig muslin that was reasonably intact and Dorothea gladly took off her old gown and raised her arms for Miss Whitesley to slip on the new. The seams strained ominously, but held, as the dress was tugged over her slender frame. In the end, however, it was all for nought, as the buttons in the back would not close and the gown fell a full four inches short of Thea's ankles.

Miss Whitesley shook her head grimly. "This will never do. I wouldn't have thought you were much bigger than Adriana, so thin as you are, and that's a shame, you know. You should try to put some flesh on those bones. But we must find something else for you to wear." Aggie's face was creased in thought, but a gleam of inspiration came into the faded eyes and she unexpectedly winked at Thea. "You just stay right here," she said in an undertone. "I'll be back in two shakes of a lamb's tail." And she whisked out of the room with remarkable alacrity.

Chapter 4

Dorothea was still in a state of shock at the turn of events in her life and somehow this sparkling and immaculate chamber did nothing to dispel the dreamlike quality of the day. How different it was from the cramped dark hole of a room she had occupied at Miss Grayson's.

Sinking onto the bed, she began to hum unconsciously as she folded the shabby pastel dresses that were scattered beside her, but her mind was trying to work itself around the total upheaval in her life. Only yesterday she had stood at the coffeepot in Cousin Letitia's dining room and considered the bleak prospect of a life spent at the beck and call of that termagant. Well, she sighed to herself, with any luck she would not have to see Miss Grayson again, ever.

Finished with the folding, she took the neat stack of clothing to the wardrobe and found the shelf where they had been stored. A pile of rumpled garments in a far corner caught her eye and she knelt to fold them. To her astonishment, they were boy's clothing, breeches, linen, a waistcoat and jacket. They were surely far too small for Sir Tate to have worn at any time in the recent past, and yet they did not appear to be so very out of fashion. She was still puzzling this out when Aggie returned.

The bemused look on Thea's face was so comical that Aggie gave a choked laugh and put down the muslin gown that she was carrying and crossed to take the breeches from Thea's grasp.

"I see you have discovered Adriana's guilty secret. Tsk, tsk. She should have disposed of these a long time ago, but, as you can tell by the gowns, she refuses to throw out anything."

"I'm sorry, Aggie, my brain must be fogged. Do you mean to say that these boy's clothes actually belong to Sir Tate's sister?"

Aggie's face wore a censorious expression. "Yes, indeed, and the scandal it might have caused if anyone had found her out! She and Tate thought it was a high treat to rig Adriana out in this garb and gallop about the countryside, but Adriana carried on the jest far too long." Aggie's voice trailed off, and she looked into Thea's clear hazel eyes, as though trying to make up her mind about something.

"Hmph," she said, settling herself beside Thea on the bed. "I daresay you can keep your own counsel, and it's only fair that you should know something about the family to which you're allying yourself." She plucked at the frill of the dress she had brought with her.

"It was five years ago that Tate went off to fight that monster, Napoleon, in the Peninsula. He came back once in that time and he had changed from the carefree lad who had left into a man of responsibility. In the summer of 1811 we received word that he was missing in action, and presumed dead. Well, Adriana would not believe it—some farradiddle about how she would *know* if her twin were dead. Sir Walter died that same month in a hunting accident and left her in rather straitened circumstances."

"Miss Grayson told me something of the late baronet's eccentric pursuits," Thea interposed.

"That harpy!" sniffed Miss Whitesley. "She would doubtless put the worst construction on poor Sir Walter's choice of investments, which turned out to be wise, after all. But, truth to tell, the house and lands were allowed to fall into sad disrepair. I thank the Lord that those hard times are behind us, although the events of the past month have brought back sad remembrances, I can assure you.

"After Sir Walter's funeral I thought I had convinced Adriana to remove with me to Brighton where my brother had retired to a small cottage, but she had gotten a maggot in her brain about going to find her brother. When she was discovered to have left the house at dead of night, I was frantic. I thought perhaps that grief had driven her to the edge of madness. The grooms that I dispatched returned without any clue to her whereabouts. It had stormed all night long and I had visions of little Adriana drowned in a ditch by the side of the road.

"When I had received no word of her, after many weeks, at last I gave up and joined my brother in Brighton, leaving word with Mr. Broderick, the family solicitor, that any communication he received regarding Miss Adriana was to be forwarded to me there. I tried to couch this message in as ambiguous a fashion as I could manage, but he suspected that there was something most irregular going on."

"But Adriana was right about her brother, was she not?" prodded Thea.

"Oh, yes. However wrong she was in her behavior,

there was no fault in her instinct. Tate had received a serious head wound and had been found wandering about the Portuguese countryside with no memory of who he was or how he had gotten there. It was Mathilde's family that discovered him and took him in, not knowing anything but that he was a foreigner and a gentleman and desperately ill. He was fortunate to be discovered by an aristocratic family with an abhorrence of Napoleon. Otherwise he might have been summarily executed by the French, as he was not in soldier's uniform at the time."

Dorothea's eyes widened. "Sir Tate is a spy?"

"Hush, child, we don't speak of that, even here in England. There are many who would like to see Napoleon succeed, although I trust none are employed at Bancroft Hall."

Thea glanced around her as though expecting the very walls and furniture to conceal listeners, as Aggie continued her tale.

"That was why there was no definite word from the War Ministry. They were reluctant to send searchers after Tate when such action might endanger his life. And that's where Sir Nicholas Laidley came into the picture."

"Do you mean Adriana's husband?"

"He was certainly not her husband at the time," Miss Whitesley huffed in disapproval. "He took her into his household to be a governess for his young cousin and heir, and traveled with her a good deal without a chaperone. It was an extremely compromising position, I fear. If her thoughtless adventures had been discovered by the World, she would not have had a shred of reputation left. Even her position as Lady

Laidley might not redeem her should the truth become known."

Dorothea smiled, thinking how both her bridegroom and his sister had exceeded even Miss Grayson's expectations. That old witch hadn't known the half. And just as well that she hadn't, for it was precisely the sort of tale she would delight in spreading—colored broadly with vicious innuendo. But Thea wished to know more. "How did Sir Tate regain his memory and his home?" she queried.

"That, too, was through the good offices of Sir Nicholas. He and Adriana had made some sort of pact: he would teach her Portuguese in exchange for care of young Harry, his ward and heir, and in the meanwhile, pull what strings he could in Whitehall to find Tate. In the end, he had to go to Portugal himself to bring the lad back. By that time, Tate was head over ears in love with poor little Mathilde and nothing would do but that he bring her back to England."

She paused pensively and looked at the watch that she wore pinned to her dress. "Oh, merciful heavens, will you look at the time! And here I've been bending your ear for this half hour and more." She took Thea's thin hand in her own and looked into the serious hazel eyes. "You won't mention what I have told you outside this room, will you? There are lives that might be endangered by such loose talk." There was entreaty in the faded blue eyes.

"You may trust me not to breathe a word to anyone," Thea promised, returning the grasp of the strong fingers. "Now, we must find an appropriate gown. That is, if you can pry this inappropriate one from me."

With Aggie's help the girl wriggled her way out of

the dress, then glanced at the small picture of the twins on the chamber wall.

"How I wish I might have met Adriana and Tate several years ago under happier circumstances," she burst out impulsively. "They sound so vital and courageous. I feel a veritable craven by comparison."

Agatha Whitesley sniffed audibly. "Adriana's courage consists largely of the total lack of a sense of propriety. I could never make her listen to reason. And I wouldn't belittle your own brand of courage, either, my dear. This situation that you are entering could bring you great unhappiness. Are you certain that you have made the right choice? I shall tell you now that I feel it is the right choice for the child and for Adriana's sake, so close to her time and fretting herself to flinders over Tate. And with Sir Nicholas gone back into God knows what danger. Yet, I cannot be convinced that this arrangement will benefit you in the end. I am not thinking of Tate now, for in his present condition, he may do something irretrievably foolish, and his marriage to you will make no difference one way or another. But if he dies in battle you will be a widow with a child not your own."

"I already consider Martha my own child and I intend to treat her as such," Thea said indignantly.

"Now, my dear, don't fly up into the boughs. I saw how you and that babe took to each other. It confirmed my opinion that this step would be in the best interest of the child. But have you considered what your position will be when Tate comes back, when the war is finally over? That is, if he survives."

This reference to an uncertain future was only an echo of the thoughts that, thus far, Thea had resolutely consigned to the very back of her consciousness. The image of the dejected and caustic baronet was an unsettling one, and one, she was forced to admit, that provoked a disturbing set of unfamiliar emotions. To think of him as setting off for untold dangers and possibly death was an idea that aroused her pity and dismay. But to think of him as returning to her, handsome, young—and still in mourning for Mathilde—was so daunting a prospect that, were she to consider it probable, she would doubtless abandon the whole idea of this makeshift marriage.

Some of this uncertainty colored her voice as she answered, "Oh, Aggie, I haven't thought that far ahead. I jumped at Sir Tate's offer because of the child." Thea glanced at her hands, folded tightly in her lap. "And, I shall be frank with you, to escape the clutches of Miss Grayson. I daresay it would be prudent to back down, but in the first place I could not abandon little Martha, and, in the second," she smiled ruefully, "I have no home to return to."

Miss Whitesley shook her head in sympathy. "How that Grayson creature could sleep nights for the disgraceful way she has treated you is a mystery to me," she said tartly, holding the white muslin out for Thea to slip into. "If you only knew what a thorn she was in my side when she lived nearby. Always carrying tales about the twins to their papa, and she especially adored it when what she had to report reflected badly on me. And then, when she herself becomes responsible for a young person, she treats her like a dog."

Thea smiled. "Actually, that isn't quite true. I fear that Clarissa was treated far better than I ever was. Not that I coveted her lofty position. Can you imagine how lowering it would be to be fawned over by Cousin Letitia?"

"Yes, I suppose you are right. I can't say I would particularly relish that myself. Now we'll just pull this down," Aggie indicated the gown that was resting on Thea's shoulders, "and we'll see how it fits."

With Aggie's help Thea adjusted the muslin gown around the bodice and did up the tiny seed pearl buttons at the neckline. Although plain, the gown's elegant lines indicated the hand of a fashionable modiste. It fit to perfection, except for length. Aggie, inspecting the hem, declared that it could easily be let down the necessary inch or two, and began to snip at the stitching with a pair of scissors she had brought with her.

Still surprised at the excellence of the fit, Thea inquired, "Wherever did this gown come from?" When she received no reply, she peered closely into the older woman's face. "Oh, Aggie, no. This dress didn't belong to . . ."

"Yes, it did, to Mathilde, but I'll have no argument from you. It's the only dress in the house that will do."

At Thea's continued protestation, Aggie made an impatient gesture. "You needn't think that you'll be stepping into her shoes, for they would never fit you, she was such a pocket Venus, her feet were exceedingly tiny. In truth, my dear, Mathilde wore this gown but once. When some wine spilled on the sleeve, she relegated it to the back of her closet and never wore it again. I feel certain that Tate will not recognize it."

It was apparent that Thea remained unconvinced. Miss Whitesley got up slowly from the low stool where she had been sitting and took the limp hand of the younger woman in her own. She found the words of assurance that Thea needed to hear. "Mathilde would have been the first to thank you for the love and care you bring to her child." Then her tone once more became brisk. "Now, let us hear no more about it."

Aggie had finished tearing out the hem and stood back to inspect her handiwork. "It's still a bit on the short side, but I daresay it will pass muster. I'll just give this to Betty to turn up and press. In the meantime, you just take off that ridiculous cap and brush out your hair. It's a lovely color, but we could find a style that's a bit more becoming than those tight braids. I trust that the cap was Miss Grayson's idea of how to keep a young person in her place. She should be pilloried for insisting on it."

Aggie bustled out of the room and was back before Thea had time to think. By now an enormous lethargy had engulfed her and she felt as though she stood apart from the passive doll who was being dressed and bathed and coiffed by the commanding Aggie and her minion. The gown, with no noticeable signs of alteration, was again slipped over her head and the pearl buttons fastened. Her long auburn hair was brushed out amidst clucks by Aggie and admiring sighs by the housemaid, Betty, and redressed in soft waves about her face and a loose knot in the back.

At last her two attendants seemed satisfied with their handiwork and turned her about to view herself in the full-length glass.

"There now, you look more like a bride and less like a clapperdudgeon," declared Aggie.

"Oh, yes, miss, you look pretty as a picture," echoed Betty.

Miss Whitesley gave the housemaid a quelling look and she bowed her way out of the room like a frightened mouse. Thea stood transfixed by her image in the mirror.

Dorothea

With the new hairstyle, an elegant gown, with her only ornament her mother's gold wedding ring worn on a chain around her neck, and the faint flush of excitement, she was remarkably transformed from the drudge she had last beheld in a mirror into a passably lovely bride!

Aggie's voice awoke her from her befuddled state. "Such a pity about that wine stain on the sleeve, but then that accounts for Mathilde's only wearing it once." She frowned in concern, then her expression lightened. "Oh, I know how we shall conceal the stain. You shall wear this blue silk shawl."

Miss Whitesley slipped the azure fringed shawl from around her shoulders. "Tate brought it for me from Portugal. It's light as a feather and you'll scarcely feel it, though you don't really need a shawl in all this heat. If you drape it just so . . . there . . . no one will be the wiser, least of all Tate. He never pays much attention to what anyone wears, especially in mufti."

"I pray you are right, and I thank you for the loan of your shawl." Thea gave a short, ironical laugh. "It will be my 'borrowed and blue,' and my dear mamma's ring is my 'something old.' Now all I lack is the 'something new.' But then, I would think that the baby fulfills that requirement for me. Do you"—she nearly choked on the words—"do you think it is time to go down?"

"Oh, dear, yes it is," Miss Whitesley answered, once again checking her small watch. "But wait here, I shall go before you and try to convince Tate that we would be more comfortable in the rose garden. The air in the drawing room is so close, with only the French doors to admit a breeze. We shall all be in a lather because of the ceremony as it is—we don't need smothering as well. Besides, the bower is a lovely setting for a wedding, no matter what the circumstances," she added.

Dorothea's eyes suddenly filled with tears, and she found herself enveloped in a sympathetic hug.

"Don't worry, my dear," Miss Whitesley whispered in her ear. "I shall help you all I can, and I'm sure that Adriana will, too, once she comes to know you. I'll send a footman to fetch you when they're ready below." And with a final pat, Miss Whitesley left the bedchamber in a rustle of bombazine.

Chapter 5

Dorothea turned back to re-examine herself in the mirror. Was this really happening to her? Had it been only yesterday that she had considered and rejected the thought of a loveless marriage with old Sir William? And here she was, rushing pell-mell into something which might turn out far worse than the desiccated companionship which Sir William might have offered. How would she be able to endure marriage to a man bent on making her into a widow at the earliest possible moment? And what would become of her if he lived through the remainder of the war? Her head still whirled with these and other considerations when she heard a light tap at the door.

" 'Tis time, Miss Sandham," a deep male voice said. She opened the door, expecting to find the footman promised by Miss Whitesley. Instead she found herself face to face with a young gentleman in the uniform of the Fifth Cavalry. His dark hair was swept back from a high forehead, and the blue eyes set under arched brows regarded her with some consternation. The scarlet of his tunic was almost the same shade as his complexion and he looked as though the collar of his immaculate uniform was about to choke him. One arm was in a sling and the other held stiffly at his side.

"You aren't the footman, are you?" she stammered out, aware immediately of how idiotic she must sound.

"N-no," the young officer said haltingly. "I'm Captain Robin Wynne. I'm a friend of Tate's and just arrived this afternoon on a condolence visit and now I've been pressed into service, as it were."

"What do you mean?"

"If you will allow it, I'm to give you away. There was no one else, you see. Tate was all for doing without anyone, but Miss Whitesley insisted. And . . . and . . . I also brought you this."

From behind his back he brought out a small bouquet of exquisite flowers from the garden. "I hope you don't mind. I just picked a few posies for you . . . every bride deserves some flowers to carry, in spite of what Tate says." As Captain Wynne spoke, his voice dropped lower and lower, until at the end he was barely whispering. Dorothea, herself in agonies of embarrassment, realized that if anything, he was as nonplussed as she was, pitchforked into an awkward situation.

"Thank you, Captain. It was kind of you to think of it," she said gently, taking the nosegay from him and burying her face in the blossoms. When she looked up, she was startled to see that he was regarding her with something very like admiration in his bright blue eyes. Apart from the rheumy glances of Sir William, no gentleman had ever taken any particular notice of her before, and once more she was plunged into confusion.

"H-have you known Sir Tate long, Captain?" she asked hesitantly, trying to regain her composure.

"Ever since '08, when we both joined the Fifth Regiment. We've been thick as thieves ever since. Of course, I haven't seen quite so much of him in the last year, since he got himself legshackled to Mathilde, but then . . ." he trailed off, blushing furiously. "My cursed tongue . . . I fear that I am no ladies' man, and I always say the wrong thing when forced into conversation with a woman."

Dorothea looked up at him sympathetically. "Captain Wynne, this conversation is taking place under such odd circumstances that nothing either of us says could possibly salvage it. So, let's just make the best of things and don't you fret about offending me. I've been wonderfully hardened to all manner of offenses by living four years with an expert in the field. You couldn't possibly hold a candle to my Cousin Letitia, when it comes to adding insult to injury."

All that her sally accomplished was a heightened gleam in Captain Wynne's eye. He seemed prepared to stand looking at her with approbation for the rest of the evening. She finally cleared her throat and gently reminded the bemused gentleman that they were wanted belowstairs.

"Oh, the deuce, pardon me, ma'am, but I had quite forgotten what we were about. Shall we go? The vicar and Tate and Miss Whitesley are, I believe, in the garden."

He proffered his good arm, and Dorothea, feeling lightheaded, gratefully clung to him for moral as well as physical support as they descended the stairs. She retraced the path of her morning's adventures, out the French doors of the drawing room and down the garden walkway. In spite of the heat of the evening, a breeze had sprung up, which carried fluttering rose petals, for all the world, she thought, like an invisible bridemaiden scattering flowers before her.

"Would you mind giving my arm a pinch, Captain," she whispered. "I cannot believe that this is truly happening to me. Or are you too a creation of my fevered imagination?"

"Oh, I couldn't do that, Miss Sandham. But you have my word that you are quite awake. Though I'd go bail that Tate is sleepwalking from the way he looks and acts. Just look at him standing there so stiff and still. Poor fellow—he is inconsolable."

She did look, though to lift her eyes and meet the dull, almost accusing gaze of her bridegroom at the end of the gravel path was one of the most difficult feats she had ever undertaken.

In a silence broken only by the sound of their footsteps, Thea and her escort came into the rose bower and took up their places as indicated by the portly gentleman in clerical garb who was obviously the vicar.

When the two principals were properly arranged, the clergyman opened his black book and began to intone the marriage ceremony.

At his words Dorothea felt a wave of panic sweep over her, and almost without knowing what she did, cried out, "But where is Martha? Shouldn't she be here?"

"I beg your pardon, madam?" said the vicar, taken aback by the untoward interruption.

"What are you talking about, Miss Sandham?" Tate growled, looking angrily down at her from his superior height. "If you had someone you wished to have present, you should have told me before so that I might have had her notified. It's late in the day to be wishing for the support of friends. May we not simply go on with the ceremony and then you may fill the house with your acquaintance in my absence." Turning away from the silent group, he stalked over to one of the stone benches and stood with one foot on it in a posture of impatience.

Dorothea stood her ground against his anger. "No, no, I mean your daughter, Sir Tate. I call her Martha and I want her with us. Indeed, I insist upon it."

"What a piece of nonsense. This is enough of an ordeal without dragging in a screaming infant."

"Sir Tate, that baby is the *raison d'être* for this ceremony and I think it will be important to her when she is older, to know that she was present when I became her stepmother. Please. I'll see that she does not fuss."

"Tate," Miss Whitesley chimed in, "Dorothea is quite right. I shall go get your daughter and be back in a trice. Mr. Stevens," she said to the vicar, "don't you dare say another word until I return." And shaking her finger at the startled man, she hastened away.

They all stood round awkwardly during the interval of Miss Whitesley's absence, with Tate glaring at everyone else by turns, and Dorothea tensely chattering with the vicar and Captain Wynne about the beauties of the garden.

At length, the black-clad minister drew her aside and earnestly inquired if she really wished to go through with the marriage.

"After all, as I told Sir Tate, it is most unwise for him to be taking a wife on the spur of the moment, with his first buried little more than a fortnight ago."

"I realize that, sir, and I know that it must seem peculiar to you. But I have my reasons for marrying Sir Tate, and . . . here she is!" she said, smiling, as Aggie reappeared in the garden carrying the tiny baby.

"Ah, yes, the young . . . the very young . . . lady

of the household. She looks to be a veritable rosebud herself."

"Exactly. Vicar, is there any reason I cannot hold Martha during the ceremony? After all, she is the cement for this absurd union."

"Well, I have never seen it done in exactly that fashion, but I don't believe there is anything in the Bible that expressly forbids it."

Dorothea went up to Aggie and gently took the child into her arms, then walked back to Tate's side. For his part, he steadfastly looked the other way, as if even to look upon the child somehow renewed his grief and pain. The vicar cleared his throat and continued with the vows, and things went smoothly along, accompanied by minute coos from the baby, until they reached the blessing of the ring.

When Mr. Stevens asked for the wedding ring, a look of alarm passed over Captain Wynne's face. He looked wildly at the baronet, who seemed equally at a loss. It was perfectly clear that neither of the gentlemen had thought to procure a ring for the ceremony.

Dorothea, feeling strangely calmed by the warm bundle she held close to her breast, spoke up. "I have a ring here," she said quietly, and pulled the gold chain from the bodice of her white gown. "Miss Whitesley, if you would assist me . . ."

She dared not look at her groom as he took the ring from her nerveless hand and slipped it over her third finger, left hand. His touch alone stirred an unwonted reaction and she saw that her hand trembled noticeably.

"Such a resourceful young woman," he whispered. "Or were you so reluctant to be an ape-leader that you bring a wedding ring wherever you go, just in case someone proposes?"

The sarcasm in his voice pained her more than she would have deemed possible. That he thought she had resigned herself to a life in spinsterhood infuriated her, but she consoled herself by fixing her gaze on the baby she held, an action that calmed the quivering of her limbs.

At that point the attention of the nuptial party was diverted by the arrival on the scene of the same stray male dog who had been so besotted with Clarissa. His shaggy brown hair nearly covered one eye, giving his face a slightly rakish air. To Thea he seemed a most perceptive creature, winking and grinning at the foolish humans in the rose bower.

When Miss Whitesley bristled and tried to shoo the animal away, Thea stopped her. "After all, ma'am, if it weren't for that creature, none of this would be happening. Surely he deserves an invitation to the . . . er . . . festivities."

"If you please, madam, we are not quite finished," the clergyman sniffed icily.

"I'm so sorry. Please proceed," Dorothea said, trying to stifle a fit of wildly inappropriate giggles. This regrettable tendency became nearly uncontrollable when the clergyman did proceed.

Mr. Stevens chose that moment in the ceremony to deliver a little homily on the lusts of the flesh and the cleaving together of man and wife in extremely graphic terms, while the mongrel dog chose the same moment to lie down beneath a rose bush and rest his unkempt head on his paws with what sounded for all the world like a sigh of utter satisfaction. As Thea could not easily apply the vicar's advice to herself and her bridegroom, all that she could envision was the romantic interlude she had interrupted between Clarissa and her reprobate swain that morning. That the vicar's words should apply to the mutual attraction of two canines struck her as exceedingly amusing. Fortunately, before she disgraced herself by exploding into laughter, the minister mumbled the final words which bound her in matrimony to the stranger at her side.

At the exact moment that Mr. Stevens directed Sir Tate to kiss his bride, however, the heavens opened in a torrential downpour. It seemed to Thea as if it were a divine comment on the completion of their sacramental travesty, or perhaps on the deplorable lack of gravity on the part of the bride.

In any event, grateful for an excuse to avoid the charade of a nuptial embrace, Dorothea hugged the baby to her and ran for the house. She did not stop until she reached the nursery, where she changed the child into dry clothing and sat down in the cherry rocking chair to feed her and lull her to sleep. Her heart was still thudding so violently from her emotional upheaval and physical exertions that she wondered it didn't frighten the baby, it sounded so thunderous in her own ears.

"Dorothea, you may kiss your daughter," she murmured, deliberately paraphrasing the closing words of the clergyman in the garden. "After all, my little pumpkin, 'twas for you that I went through that sham, so you are the one I shall kiss in order to seal the bargain." She brushed her lips over the soft, downy pate, and sighed into the child's tiny, perfect ear. "You are my daughter now, Martha, and I shall see that you grow into a young woman who is well able to look after herself. No, you shall never be subjected to a Cousin

Letitia's vagaries, and Lord knows, you shall never be shut out by the consuming passion your parents hold for one another," she said ruefully. "And, I promise you with all my heart that you shall never have to marry for the sake of convenience. You shall have a handsome prince of a husband, who adores you . . ."

"And shall live happily ever after, no doubt." A deep voice finished for her in scathing tones. She turned her head and saw that her husband was standing in the nursery door, looking most unlike a happy bridegroom.

She lay a finger to her lips to caution him into silence, and carefully carried her sleeping burden to the cradle. There she remained, looking down with a sense of wonder at the baby, trying to grasp the reality that she was really to mother the tiny creature lying there. "Most women have nine full months to prepare themselves for motherhood," she said softly, more to herself than to the man who stood behind her. "And I had considerably less than nine hours to do so." She straightened up and walked toward the door, expecting that he would move to one side to allow her to pass. Instead, he remained exactly where he was, frowning into nothingness, as if unaware of her movement toward him.

She was finally compelled to address him directly, seeing that he made no motion. "If you will excuse me, sir . . ."

"Of course, I'll excuse you, but I warn you as well. Don't you go filling my daughter's head with ridiculous delusions about handsome princes and living happily ever after. That is only a fairy tale. No one should expect the impossible, and 'happily ever after' only happens in womanish books. I can certainly testify to that."

Dorothea

"I scarcely think we need discuss this here and now," she replied, leading the way out into the hall. "It's early days yet to worry about what the child hears from me about her future, and when you have recovered a little from your terrible loss, perhaps you will see things differently and allow your daughter to indulge in a little maidenly dreaming."

"What a lot of drivel you talk, and hypocritical drivel at that. Just exactly what became of *your* maidenly dreams of bliss, Miss Sand . . . my dear wife?" He made the endearment sound like a curse.

"You are ungenerous, sir. I see no need to discuss the subject further."

"There are other subjects, however, that we must discuss, my dear wife, before I depart. If you will follow me . . ." The baronet moved toward the door to the chamber across the hall from her own, but they were interrupted by the clearing of a throat behind them. The butler had approached so silently that neither had been aware of his presence.

"My lady, dinner is served in the dining parlor," he pronounced with grave dignity. "And may I take this opportunity to offer my felicitations, as well as those of the entire staff."

"Don't be absurd, Parker," Tate growled, then spoke woodenly to Thea. "I daresay that matters can wait until after the nuptial feast." He turned abruptly and brushed past the butler, who still stood in the corridor.

Dorothea, against all reason and logic, felt quite offended at her groom's cavalier attitude and surprised herself, the butler and her bridegroom, by graciously thanking Parker for his good wishes and smiling warmly at the old man. He bowed and beamed back at her as she followed the retreating back of her oblivious husband down the stairs to her wedding dinner, which, under the circumstance, promised to be a miserable failure.

Nervously taking her place at one end of the table, Dorothea quickly perceived that the servants had done their best to do honor to their new mistress. The cook had procured a brace of quails and had served them up with a sweet grape sauce, the trout tasted as though it had just leapt from a nearby brook into the frying pan, and the young vegetables were all elegantly prepared and presented.

In spite of the efforts of the staff, however, Thea might just as well have been eating sawdust. Glancing nervously under her lashes at her three companions, she judged that they felt much the same. Her bridegroom sat sullen and silent during most of the removes and the groomsman grew more tongue-tied with each glass of wine. It was difficult to discern whether the flush that periodically swept the latter's countenance was a result of the champagne that he was downing at regular intervals, or the obvious embarrassment he felt each time he was surprised in the act of admiring the bride.

Thea sighed and turned her attention to some remark of Miss Whitesley's. The burden of civil conversation had fallen on their shoulders, as their two male companions were singularly unable or unwilling to participate. As a result, the bulk of their exchange consisted of Aggie's giving the new Lady Bancroft sundry information about the practicalities of running Bancroft Hall.

Even this seemingly innocent exchange was not without its pitfalls, however. Many of the questions

Dorothea asked of her informant brought forth uncomfortable pauses. From these, nearly as much as from the eventual answers which Miss Whitesley supplied, Dorothea began to sense that Miss Grayson had not been so very far off the mark when she had apostrophised Mathilde as a less than successful housekeeper. Though, of course, Aggie did not say it in so many words, it appeared that Dorothea's predecessor had been more ornamental than efficient in her role as chatelaine to this grand old manor house.

Given the company and the occasion, it was with marked relief that the young woman discovered one area of housekeeping in which Mathilde had excelled—overseeing the succession houses.

"Which was hardly to be wondered at," Miss Whitesley confided, "for her father, the Conde de Vasconcellos, owns hundreds of vineyards in Portugal. Mathilde used to hear all the details of cultivation, and to travel about with her papa to oversee the vintage. Yes, she had a true knack for growing things, and the succession houses flourished last year under her direction." She smiled in fond reminiscence, then, glancing uneasily at Tate, whose countenance was positively stony, she changed the subject. "Now, as to handling the cook, my dear, you must always remember to . . ."

"Please, Aggie, spare us any more of these domestic trivialities," Tate interjected. "Surely you can wait until Robin and I are gone before unburdening yourself to . . . to . . ." He broke off and frowned. "Confound it, I don't even know her Christian name."

"What? Why, Tate, she said it loud and clear during the ceremony, and what's more, you yourself said, 'I, Tate, take thee, Dorothea . . .' but then, I suppose you have been so distracted that the words flew right out of your head. Dorothea is your new wife's name, and a beautiful one it is, too."

"Gift of God," Robin Wynne burst out, then, seeing everyone look at him in astonishment, he took another swallow of wine before finding the nerve to proceed. "Gift of God. Dorothea means gift of God. From the Greek, you know."

"Yes, *I* know, Robin, having had Greek drubbed into me from infancy by my father. But I never knew you to look into a Greek grammar, all the years I've known you. Your vast knowledge does amaze me," Tate said sarcastically.

"Well, she *is* a gift straight from Providence, Tate, for all you make game of it," Aggie protested. "Where would we be without her I shudder to think. I must leave at the earliest possible moment to join Adriana in London. She needs me with her for her confinement."

"Your presence didn't do a jot of good for Mathilde, did it?" Tate asked bitterly. "I pray your company will bring about a happier outcome with Adriana." He turned from Miss Whitesley to Dorothea. "The women in my family seem to be cursed unlucky in their child-bearing. First my mother, then my wife, and next, perhaps, my twin. Just be grateful you will never face their fate, Dorothea."

Cheeks aflame, Thea dropped her eyes to her wine-glass and was relieved to hear Captain Wynne shyly change the subject.

"This champagne is excellent, Tate," he remarked, his speech slightly slurred by the glasses of excellent champagne he had imbibed. "Wherever did you get it? It's getting devilish hard to procure decent stuff, with the blockade and all."

"You forget, Robin. My wife's . . . that is, my *first*

wife's father is a wine producer of some note. He insisted on sending over a substantial dowry for Mathilde." The baronet lowered his bleak gaze to his empty plate and his voice broke. He cleared his throat before continuing in a strained manner. "Much of the dowry was in bottles. The wines his vineyards did not produce, he traded for, so as to provide me with a complete wine cellar. Sent it over by private vessel, swearing that Napoleon himself couldn't keep him from properly dowering his only child upon her marriage with her 'dashing English soldier.' What a supreme irony this all is—drinking to the health of Mathilde's successor in her father's wine." He raised his glass to Dorothea, then drained it.

The captain looked even more bemused and seemed to be attempting to work through a puzzle aloud, with wits clouded by wine. "But if the conde has private ships at his disposal," he said slowly, in a tone of wonder, "why did he not come himself when Mathilde . . ." He paused, aghast at his own words.

Miss Whitesley, with a worried look at her former charge, answered the captain. "Because the condessa herself had been dangerously ill, and the conde could not leave her. If you could but see the heartbreaking letters the two of them have sent. Naturally, I can't read a word of them. They are, of course, in Portuguese, but I could see the tear stains on the paper, and they're the same in any language. And I know they are wild to see their little granddaughter. The one word I could easily make out was *bebé*, which was scattered throughout every letter. If that's not Portuguese for 'baby,' I'll eat my cap."

Mention of the child roused Thea out of her embarrassed silence into stiff speech. "Speaking of the *bebé*, Sir Tate, I think it is most important that we have her christened before you leave."

Aggie harrumphed her agreement. "Should have been done long since, as I have been telling you, Tate."

"I don't know why you need my presence for that. Can't you just arrange to have the vicar do it after we leave?"

"It is only fitting that you be here, Tate," began Miss Whitesley.

"You are, after all, the father, sir," Dorothea said, goaded by his disinterest into an uncharacteristically shrill tone, which quite drowned out the other woman's quiet remonstrance. "And it *is* important that you lend your presence to this important ceremony. It is bad enough that you are abandoning your tiny daughter to the care of a stranger, but now you are trying to escape even this small duty regarding the poor little girl." She looked at him defiantly.

"Never let it be said that I shirk my duty." He nodded his head mockingly in her direction, in a caricature of a bow. "But I have higher duties to attend to and must leave on the morrow. There simply is no time to sprinkle the brat."

"I'm sure that the vicar would be more than happy to return and perform the ceremony for us this evening," Thea retorted. "It is early yet, and after the peculiarities of the other ritual he has been called on to carry out for us today, I doubt that he will balk at a hasty christening."

"No, indeed, and I think it is an excellent notion. May I fetch him, Tate?" Aggie asked eagerly.

"I suppose so, though it does seem a lot of fuss and bother over nothing," he said grudgingly, which sent

Miss Whitesley flying from the room with remarkable speed for a woman of her years and dignity.

Captain Wynne struggled to his feet. "I think it would be best if Miss Whitesley were to have my escort," he blurted out. "Frightful weather out there, you know. I'll just run along and see to the hitching of the carriage. If you'll excuse me," and before either Thea or Tate could respond and urge him to remain, he, too, had removed himself from their presence.

Chapter 6

Left alone with her husband, Dorothea felt her customary shyness return, but she nevertheless forced herself to raise one more issue. "Before the others return with Mr. Stevens, Sir Tate, we must discuss the child's name."

"Suit yourself," Tate drawled in a bored tone, reaching once more for the wine decanter. "I have no preference. Anything will do, except its mother's name."

"I had thought to name her Martha, after my own mother, if you have no objections," she ventured.

"I trust you are not deaf, Miss . . . er . . . Dorothea. I have said that any name save one will do. If I recall, you had already begun to call her by that name before ever asking for my consent."

This obvious dismissal of herself and of his own child made her ache with helpless fury and she longed to pitch her wine in his face. But time was too short to indulge herself so, and she merely asked him, coolly, what it was he had wished to discuss before Parker announced dinner.

Tate looked at her as though she were not there. The grey eyes seemed to have trouble bringing her into focus.

"Well, what is it?" she inquired again, taking courage from another sip of wine.

At length Tate replied, speaking in a weary monotone, as though he were reading off a list of laundry or other ineffably boring items.

"First of all, I shall instruct my solicitor, Mr. Broderick, to draw up a new will which will include you, and also arrange for a marital settlement which will provide you with a competency when I am dead."

Her eyes flew to his face in concern, and she desperately cast about for words to plead with him not to follow her father's fatal example. He gave her no opportunity to say anything, however, plunging doggedly on with his discourse.

"Broderick will also draw up the necessary papers to make you co-guardian with Nick Laidley, Adriana's husband, and Captain Wynne."

"Co-guardian? But what of our agreement that I was to have full responsibility for the child?"

"Oh, that is all very well for an infant, but later on a masculine hand will be required. Though I do wish I could be here to see old Nick and Robin coming over the heavy guardians with a flighty miss." A half-smile came over his face, but Dorothea was too enraged to appreciate the change of expression. She sat stock still, fighting to control her anger at his having gone back on his word.

"Until the child is eighteen, you *will* be in full command, then Nick and Robin will take over. After all, what would a woman like you know about maneuvering a young heiress into a suitable marriage?"

"What, indeed," she said acidly.

He ignored her reply, and went on to explain in detail when and how she would be receiving monies from Broderick, then he paused and glanced at her sidelong.

"Incidentally, I want it clearly understood that I expect you to be discreet in your behavior. Should there be any scandal on your part, Broderick will be authorized to remove you from your guardianship. Is that clear?"

"Perfectly. And, of course, that means that should Captain Wynne or your brother-in-law also blot the family escutcheon, they would naturally also be removed, as a polluting influence?"

"It is not at all the same thing, as you are quite aware."

"No, I am not aware that is so, and I heartily resent your implication that I am unworthy of your trust merely because I am a woman."

"And my wife."

"Yes, your wife, at least in the eyes of the world. But it is not too late to remedy that misconception and end this charade by annulling the marriage."

"Are you threatening me?"

"No, I am merely saying that if you do not give me sole guardianship of your daughter, as you led me to believe would be the case, I will resign this 'post,' and if that means annulment, so be it. I have been harried and hounded for the past four years, and I will not place myself in a situation in which I shall be constantly watched and judged for my moral fitness. Either you take me on trust, or not at all."

This speech, made in ringing tones, caused the baronet to whirl in surprise and examine her closely. Finally he shrugged and turned away. "I have little desire for a termagant wife, but you do have me at *point non plus*. To nullify our union would take more time than I care to spend in England, or anywhere, at present. And even after annulment, I would be back where I started, with no one to look after the brat but servants." He considered in silence. "All right, I agree to your terms, but I must exact your solemn oath not to besmirch the family name with scandal. After all, I know nothing of you, nor your character."

Angry words swarmed to Dorothea's lips, but she said nothing. It was a small price to pay, after all: vowing not to do something she wouldn't do anyway.

"Very well, sir, I do so promise." She pushed her chair back and rose to leave, unable to stand the look of desolation on the baronet's face any longer. "If you will excuse me, sir," she murmured, "I shall see that Martha is readied for her christening." She walked out of the dining parlor, feeling his eyes, grey and critical, burning into her back.

She ran upstairs to the nursery, and finding the infant still sound asleep, satisfied herself as best she could by selecting an embroidered gown and cap for the baby to wear for the ritual, and instructing Annie to dress and bring the child downstairs within the hour.

With a last fond look at the sleeping infant, she left the nursery and descended the staircase to the corridor below. She stood for a moment in uncertainty, wondering where she could go until Aggie and Captain Wynne returned with the vicar. The last thing she desired was further conversation with her husband, so she turned into the small sitting room at the opposite end of the corridor.

It was a charming room, done up delightfully in rose and tan. The chairs were dainty and covered with frilly chintz, but appeared comfortable. Lining all but a few of the shelves were mementos of a childhood completely alien to Thea's experience. Dolls of every size and color and hand-carved trinkets had all been maintained with loving care. Other shelves held worn volumes, books that appeared to have been read and reread often. Their Portuguese titles confirmed her guess that this had been Mathilde's boudoir. On one wall hung a small portrait of a dignified couple, and on another was a stringed instrument which Thea had no trouble in recognizing as a guitar, though she had seen one only in a picture.

She made a circuit of the room and examined the dolls carefully. Most were as perfect in their porcelain beauty as the portrait of Mathilde she had seen in the gallery. She thumbed through a few of the books she found, but could not understand any of the printed words.

Taking the guitar down from the wall, she marveled at the workmanship in the rosewood instrument, which was inlaid with ebony and mother-of-pearl. It was exquisite. She sat down in one of the soft chairs and gave the strings a light strum, grimacing at the result. Tentatively she picked out a melody on one string, an experiment which proved more successful.

After several attempts to puzzle out a melody, an old ballad which had been a favorite of her father's, she gained sufficient mastery over one of the strings to produce a recognizable air. The lilting cadence of the music carried her beyond her skill on the unfamiliar instrument, and she let the guitar rest on her lap unplucked as she threw herself into her song. Her dark contralto filled the little room, and conjured up in her mind the image of her parents. Even as she sang, she pictured the two singing the melancholy duet and gazing soulfully into one another's eyes, oblivious to their daughter.

> "Fare thee well, my dear, I must be gone
>   and leave thee for a while
> If I roam away, I'll come back again
>   If I roam ten thousand miles, my dear,
>   though I roam ten thousand miles."

By the time she arrived at the final stanza, the numbing effect had run its course, and she felt the irony of the words with painful clarity.

> "O yonder sits that little turtle dove,
>   he doth sit on yonder high tree.
> A-making a moan for the loss of his love,
>   as I will do for thee, my dear,
>   as I will do for thee."

The last note faded away, but before she had quite caught her breath again, the door to the small parlor flew open, revealing the taut, white face of Tate Bancroft.

Dorothea was so startled that she jumped several inches off her seat, and the guitar began to slide from her lap. Just in time, she caught it, but in so doing, the silken shawl which she had so carefully worn over the telltale stain slipped to the floor. Unaware of this, she smiled impulsively at her successful catch and exclaimed, "You gave me such a turn, sir! But no harm is done, after all."

Her engaging smile was quickly erased by his response.

"By what right . . . by what right, do you dare to play Mathilde's *violão*?" he spat out.

It seemed to Dorothea, mesmerized by his accusing words and her own sense of guilt, that his grey eyes darkened with emotion. She was unable to form a reply and stood mutely clutching the guitar as if to shield herself behind it, staring into his grim countenance.

He removed the guitar from her grasp and gently laid it in a velvet-lined leather case. With the extreme care of a parent putting a sleeping child into its cradle, he placed the case in a large carved chest, then straightened up. "And that dress . . ." his voice thickened with fury as he advanced toward her.

Fortunately Miss Whitesley came into the room at that moment and, hearing Tate's words, she took up the cudgels on Dorothea's behalf.

" 'Twas the only thing we could find for her to wear, Tate. Don't take on so. Would you have had her stand up with you in her own old dress, reeking of brandy? Now, do set aside your anger and beg Thea's pardon like a gentleman for losing your temper."

There was a long, painful silence, broken only by Miss Whitesley's clucks of disapproval. Then, primming her lips, she said severely, "Tate, I am disappointed in you. Surely I taught you better manners than this. But I suppose that now you are a man it is for you to decide how ill you treat other people." She sighed and glanced at the still shaken Dorothea.

"The vicar is waiting in the drawing room with Captain Wynne, and Annie is coming down with Martha directly. Shall we join them there?"

When neither of the two spoke or moved, one from outrage and one from embarrassment, Miss Whitesley apparently felt sterner measures were called for.

"Tate, offer your arm to Dorothea, and escort her to the drawing room this instant, or I shall be forced to send for Miss Grayson. It's obvious that what you young people need to bully you into proper behavior is a merciless witch of a woman, unhampered by manners or scruples. I am sadly hamstrung by such humane considerations. Therefore, it appears that Letitia Grayson's presence is required."

"Miss Whitesley . . . Aggie . . . you wouldn't really bring Cousin Letitia . . ." Dorothea exclaimed, shocked at the thought of seeing her late, unlamented employer again so soon, or ever, for that matter.

"She would do no such thing, the old fraud. Blackmail is neither scrupulous nor mannerly," Tate growled.

"If you cannot bring yourself to apologize for your ungentlemanly behavior, then just march straight to the drawing room, Tate. But I had not thought you to be so callous," Miss Whitesley admonished with a reproachful look, but the apparently unrepentant young man made no move to leave.

"I-I'm sorry," Thea stammered out, feeling that she was in the wrong, in spite of Miss Whitesley's defenses.

Sir Tate did not answer her, but came toward her in a determined manner that made her flinch away instinctively. He stopped directly in front of her and shook his head. "Afraid, dear wife? I'm shocked at your lack of backbone. Don't you know that Bancroft women are traditionally full of pluck? Famous for it. You must cultivate a little courage, to live up to the name. In name only, of course."

"I'm sure you will find me sufficiently stouthearted to fulfill the duties of my post, Sir Tate. After all, were I as timorous as you think me, I would hardly have accepted your peculiar offer," she protested.

Tate shrugged. "Well, you need not be troubled

by my presence much longer," he reminded her. "I shall oblige your whim in regards to this christening foolishness, but you should know, both of you, that I have decided to leave directly after it is finished."

"Tonight? But Tate, it is nearly dark now, and with no moon, and the roads all muddy from today's rainstorm, you cannot possibly reach town tonight!" Aggie expostulated.

"Yes, but at the very least I shall be away from here," he said, and flung out of the room.

Miss Whitesley was the first to speak. "You must forgive him, my dear. He's not himself."

Dorothea shrugged and gave a wry smile. "I don't even know what 'being himself' entails, Aggie. For all I know he's always like this."

"It was the guitar, I'm afraid. We had just returned with Mr. Stevens and had gone to the drawing room to join Tate when you started playing on the guitar and we could hear it. Mathilde was most particular about not letting anyone else touch the thing—treated it like a child, she did, a spoiled child at that. And when we heard the music, well, though I knew it couldn't be Mathilde, it even gave me a start. As for Tate, I have never seen such an expression on his face. We had to bury her before he returned, you see, so he never saw her after . . ."

"But surely neither of you seriously thought that my fumbling attempts to play could be . . ." Dorothea broke off, horrified at the bumblebroth which she had caused by her innocent music-making.

"Not really, but the shock of hearing the guitar again, coupled with sight of that unfortunate stain, well, I fear it has quite overset dear Tate. But, it isn't your fault. How could you have known? Cheer up, my dear, after all, we've a christening to tend to. There—I think I hear our baby crying."

Martha's distant screams caused the girl to catapult to the door. "Good Lord, all we need now is for Martha to estrange her father even more by crying her head off the first time he holds her in his arms. Come on, Aggie," she said impatiently.

Miss Whitesley smiled indulgently at her and the two hastened to the drawing room. The tableau that met their eyes would have been amusing if it had not been so heart-rending.

Captain Wynne and the vicar were feverishly attempting to soothe the frantic baby, awkwardly clutched by the reluctant father, by cooing and playing peek-a-boo through their fingers. When Sir Tate caught sight of Dorothea, he uttered an exasperated "Here!" and thrust the child into her willing arms, then proceeded to rail against the young servant who had left him saddled with the child while she ran upstairs for a forgotten cap.

"That wretched girl forced me to take the brat and it screamed the moment I took hold. I shall sack that irresponsible wench for this," he muttered, pacing the floor in his irritation.

"Don't be a fool. Annie is an excellent nursemaid and must certainly stay to help me in this ludicrous 'post' I have so rashly undertaken. After all, she only made a perfectly natural error in judging that a father would not object to holding his own child." She left off what looked to be a fruitless attempt to scold her husband into proper regard for his daughter and concentrated on calming the daughter herself.

"There, there, lovey. It's all right, quite all right. Papa doesn't *mean* to be beastly." When her words failed of their purpose, she fell back on what had worked before, and began once again to sing the old lullaby, without any thought for the audience listening to her and thus without any of her customary shyness in singing before others. To her great relief, the baby's screams subsided into sobs, and then, miraculously dwindled into an occasional hiccough. By the time that the breathless Annie rushed in and tied the lace cap on the infant, everything was remarkably serene.

"If you are quite ready, my lady," the vicar said hesitantly.

"Certainly, Mr. Stevens," she answered in a whisper, not wishing to disturb the baby, who had dozed off obligingly in her arms.

"What is the child to be called?" he asked softly, as they moved into a line before him.

"Martha. Martha Bancroft, if you please," she replied in low tones, not daring to look at her husband, who stood rigidly beside her.

"And the second name?"

Silence met this query and Dorothea waited quietly. It was up to the father to come up with another name. She did not want to overstep the bounds of her new position, as she feared she had already done by suggesting her mother's name in the first place. Besides, she thought to herself, perhaps this will force him to acknowledge his bond with Martha, make him give some thought to her. As the silence lengthened, however, everyone began shifting uneasily.

It was Captain Wynne who finally spoke up. "Well, I think it would be fitting to name her after your mother, Tate. What was her Christian name?"

"Charlotte," the baronet replied in a colorless tone.

"And is that what you wish to use for a second name, Sir Tate?" the vicar prodded. He seemed to be losing some of his composure. "You must decide before we can proceed," he fussed.

"It will do as well as any, I daresay. Anything to get this over with. I must leave for town before the light is completely gone."

"Come, Tate, we've already lost the light and . . ." Captain Wynne began, but his mild protests were loudly overridden by the vicar's vociferous exclamations.

"Leave for London? In all this dirt? You'll be mired before you reach the crossroads! The three of us could barely get through from the vicarage. Why, you'll be spattered terribly, and . . ."

"Believe me, Vicar, I have faced worse perils than a little mud. Are you with me, Robin? If not, I'll go by myself." Tate shot a questioning look at his friend, who shrugged good-humoredly, then nodded in agreement.

"Now that we have settled the business of a middle name, Mr. Stevens, will you kindly proceed with this . . . er . . . ceremony?" Tate directed brusquely.

Mr. Stevens regarded the assembled group as though they were all candidates for bedlam. "Certainly, Sir Tate," he said. "I take it Miss Whitesley and the captain are to stand as godparents?"

"Yes, yes. Look, Stevens, can't you make haste?"

"I shall do my best, Sir Tate. Now if you will give me the child, Lady Bancroft, we shall start." He launched into a long, droning recitation which, to Dorothea, and doubtless to the man beside her, seemed endless.

When it was finally over, Thea took the child from the vicar, who took his leave, cautioning Tate once more about the mud as he went out. Dorothea barely noticed his departure, so engrossed was she in her child. "Good night, little Martha Charlotte Bancroft," she whispered, tenderly kissing the baby before surrendering it to the nursemaid.

Sir Tate watched in silence as Annie bore the baby away, then, turning abruptly he addressed his old governess. "This is good-bye, Aggie. Take care of Adriana for me and try to forget the awful tripe I threw at·you before."

"Oh, Tate, my dearest boy. Be careful out there. We need you—all of us. Adriana, and Martha, and . . ."

"Don't be silly, Aggie. You'll be fine," he said gruffly, then gave the elderly woman a warm hug.

Captain Wynne came up to Dorothea and made an awkward bow. "I hope to have the good fortune of seeing you again, ma'am," he said. "And I shall do what I can to calm Tate down before he leaves England for the field." Then, struck by a sudden inspiration, he blushed even deeper red than before. "Tate," he called across to his friend, "may I kiss your bride? Strictly within the bounds of tradition, and all that."

Tate turned away from Miss Whitesley. When his eyes met Thea's, she was perplexed to see an accusing expression in their depths.

He shrugged negligently. "Of course, Robin. It makes no difference to me, one way or the other." Still, he watched closely as the slender soldier gingerly brushed her cheek with his lips and stepped back in agonies of bashfulness.

Aggie's penetrating whisper came to Dorothea's ears, as she stood watching Captain Wynne start for the door.

"It's only appropriate, Tate, for you to kiss her, too. You never did at the wedding because of the rain, and I think you should."

"Don't be a gudgeon, Aggie," he said in a withering tone. "Neither of us wishes it in the least, and it would only be another empty gesture in this day of empty gestures."

Suddenly Dorothea was struck by the very upsetting realization that he was wrong. Though he is unerringly accurate as to his own reluctance, I would like it above all things to be kissed by that infuriating man, she thought, with a visible start.

"There, you see, she is horrified by the very thought, and so am I," Tate continued, "but to satisfy you I will be civil in taking my leave."

He came over to where Dorothea stood, shivering with her unruly emotions. "Madam, I bid you farewell. Ours has been a short, but . . . interesting, er . . . courtship. But, as you know, duty calls."

"Sir Tate," she said, fighting her impulse to fall upon his neck and beg him to be careful, "I shall not fail you. You may rest assured that Martha will be well cared for, and dearly loved." To her great discomfiture, her eyes rebelled against her will and lingered regrettably on his lips so close to hers. She heard discreet rustling in the background and the shutting of the door, and realized that Aggie and Captain Wynne had tactfully left them alone.

That her husband was also aware of this she read in the frown which brought his mouth into an unyielding line. "It seems that they are expecting us to play out an affecting scene of marital leavetaking. Well, we mustn't disappoint them," Sir Tate said.

To her astonishment, with an expression of fierce resolve on his countenance, he seized her in his arms and kissed her, deeply, passionately, with nothing whatever of tenderness or love and much of anger and desperation.

Dorothea at first struggled to free herself from this humiliating embrace. Though she had thought it was what she wanted, in reality she recognized it as the insult that it was. What should have been a joy was only a punishment and she knew he was somehow taking out his frustration on the nearest helpless object. But as the embrace lengthened, she found her own outrage melting away, and, unbelievably, her body seemed to be taking on a life of its own. When at last he lifted his face from hers, she discovered to her chagrin that she was clinging to him like a limpet.

They stood motionless in each other's arms until Dorothea finally dared to open her eyes, feeling terribly vulnerable and exposed. Tate looked stunned for an instant, then the mask of bitterness returned and he removed her arms from his neck and stepped away.

"So the prim Miss Sandham is not the stick she has made herself out to be, spinster's caps notwithstanding. I can't say that the discovery is comforting. I fear that your promises to keep the family name spotless might well crumble if and when any other stranger makes such an advance on your virtue. After all, if you are so . . . yielding with someone who has made his lack of interest crystal clear, what on earth will you do when presented with a real beau?" he said sarcastically.

Once again, with no conscious decision on Dorothea's part, her body acted on its own. Her hand came up and roundly slapped the gentleman's mocking face.

Dorothea

"I think we have taken leave enough of each other, not to mention our senses, Sir Tate. Good-bye," she contrived to say with some degree of calm, then, turning on her heel, she bolted from the room and sought her chamber for a long, and, she felt, richly deserved session of crying.

Chapter 7

The next morning a timid knocking on her chamber door brought Thea awake with a start. Before she quite realized where she was, she called out, "Yes, cousin, I shall take Clarissa for her walk directly."

There was a pause, then the servant girl called back in respectful accents, "Lady Bancroft, I have your breakfast tray. May I enter?" Dorothea sat up instantly, shaking her head to clear the cobwebs. So it hadn't been a dream after all.

"Of course, come in, Betty. Forgive me for keeping you waiting," she said, pulling on a dressing gown, which the resourceful Miss Whitesley had unearthed from Tate's youthful castoffs.

Betty entered, bearing a lightweight tray, covered with a snow-white cloth and heaped with steaming food. There were eggs and ham and toasted bread and coffee, all piping hot and smelling heavenly. In one corner of the tray was a small crystal vase with a barely opened yellow rosebud. At Thea's dumbstruck stare, Betty laughed. "It's your breakfast, madam, courtesy of Mr. Parker, him not knowin' when you might waken."

When Thea continued to stare, Betty put the tray

on the dressing table and steered her seemingly witless mistress back to the bed, where she plumped the pillows and gently forced Thea back under the coverlet. She then dashed out into the corridor and returned with a pitcher of hot water, which she left beside the bowl on the dressing table.

Betty tactfully exited before Thea recovered her powers of speech. Breakfast in bed only reinforced the dreamlike quality of the day before. In all her twenty and a half years, Thea had never been served a meal in bed. And what was more, she realized that she was exceedingly hungry. The atmosphere at last night's "wedding feast" had made the act of eating almost as much a strain as it had been at Miss Grayson's. She dove into the hot breakfast and devoured it ravenously. As she licked the dripping butter from the last wedge of toast, she sank back against the pillows and a small laugh escaped her lips.

Small wonder it all seemed like a dream, she reflected, looking about her at the bright, cheerful room. Yesterday when I awoke it was in a bed half this size, in a room a quarter this size. This morning I am married into the baronetage, the mother of a bouncing baby girl and the mistress of all I behold. Quite a step up in the world. She snuggled down into the snowy sheets.

If anything, she was struck by how much it resembled a plot from a Gothic romance, such as had been her secret delight while suffering through the years with her cousin. I shall see to it that Martha and I turn out the heroines of the piece, if it's the last thing I do.

With a contented sigh, she set aside the tray, threw back the light comforter and began to change out of the dressing gown, slipping into the old dress that she had worn yesterday on her arrival at Bancroft Hall.

It had been laundered, and while it still bore the traces of a brandy stain, it at least smelled of lavender rather than spirits.

Taking up the silver-backed brush that lay on the dresser and seating herself before the looking glass, she began to brush her hair out from its single nighttime braid. She was arrested by her own pale reflection, which in the light of day revealed large hazel eyes still heavy from the tears of the night before, a small straight nose and a generous mouth that had been forced into an unnatural primness in the past few years, but which now smiled impishly at its owner. The rich auburn hair framed the thin face becomingly, but Thea found little comfort in her own appearance.

"I must say, Lady Bancroft, that you don't look the least like a heroine. While you are mercifully free of freckles, an unforgivable affliction in anyone aspiring to heroic stature, you are hardly the requisite raving beauty. Though, now that I think of it, that nice young man, Captain Wynne, paid you the compliment of looking at you as though you were. Whereas your esteemed husband only looked at you as if to determine that you don't have two heads. Not a pleasant experience on the whole."

Not surprisingly, these reflections reminded her of her final moments in the company of Sir Tate and she watched the color flood her cheeks at the recollection of his callous embrace. Even more disturbing, moreover, was the remembrance of her own unexpected and unconscionable response. However, it was much easier, and certainly much more satisfying, to heap abuse on the absent baronet.

How dared he, she thought. No man of honor would have insulted me so. It speaks of a sad lack of breeding, to take advantage of what *I*, at least, consider a strictly business relationship. Well, I know nothing of him, after all. Perhaps he treats all his business acquaintances so.

Trying to make light of what had been a most unsettling episode did much to improve her state of mind, though she could not entirely erase it from her memory. She finished plaiting her hair in its two thick braids, wound it rapidly into a coil at the back of her neck, jabbed in hairpins to secure it and turned to shake a finger at herself in the glass.

"Now, no more romantic nonsense, my girl. You have a great responsibility to fulfill now, and coming all over missish about trifles will accomplish nothing."

Out of longstanding habit, she quickly straightened the bedclothes on her bed and carried her breakfast tray downstairs. As she entered the cavernous kitchen, she found only one person there, Parker, who was finishing a solitary breakfast. When he saw her, he stood up respectfully, then his eyes widened in surprise as he took in what she was about.

"My lady, surely you should leave that to the servants," he said faintly.

"I suppose you are right, Parker," she replied, smiling, "but old habits die hard, and I was used to taking care of myself at Cousin Letitia's. It was a rare treat for me this morning, I can assure you, to be treated like a princess. If my doing for myself upsets you, I will, of course, allow myself to be pampered, but I'm afraid I shall feel most uncomfortable as the grande dame," she confided.

As this was said with a great deal of good humor, the elderly servant smiled back and made a slight bow.

"If there is anything one can do to help, madam, you need only ask."

"Thank you, Parker, I appreciate your help. Now, where can I find Miss Whitesley at this hour, do you suppose?"

"Doubtless she is in the nursery, madam. I believe she spent the night there. Annie was down for the infant's milk a few minutes ago and said the poor little mite cried far into the night and neither she nor Miss Whitesley got a speck of sleep."

"Oh, no, how dreadful! They should have wakened me to help! I shall ring a rare peal over Miss Whitesley for this. She should not wear herself into a frazzle doing what I have pledged to do. I expect you to help me in this too, Parker."

"Until she departs, I shall be your faithful eyes and ears, and notify you whenever Miss Whitesley is overzealous in the nursery."

"Thank you," Thea said warmly, as she started for the nursery, "but I trust that it will not be for long."

When she opened the nursery door, she found Aggie sound asleep in the rocking chair, with the sleeping baby on her lap. Dorothea shook her head, smiling, and eased the child out of the old woman's arms and into her cradle without waking her. When she walked back to the rocker she gently shook Miss Whitesley awake.

"Aggie," she urged in a soft voice, "you must go to your room and get into a proper bed. I am most displeased with you for playing this trick on me. Surely I ought to have been summoned if anything was amiss with Martha. You are a dear to go through this for me, but no more, do you hear?" she scolded gently.

"Oh . . . Thea." Miss Whitesley shook her head as though to dispel the clouds of sleep. "What time is it?"

"Well past time for you to be in your bed. Annie and I can take over the nursery duties now. I shall see you at nuncheon, and not before."

"But . . ."

"No buts." Dorothea was firm as she drew Miss Whitesley to her feet and began steering her toward the door. "Off you go."

She watched the woman drag herself slowly down the hall to her own room, then turned all her attention to the peacefully sleeping child. Martha lay on her stomach in the cradle, one small fist clenched close to her cheek, the other arm extended. She looked for all the world like a miniature fencer. The fine hair on the top of the perfectly shaped head seemed to have almost no color, and certainly no length, but Thea smoothed it anyway, and felt a surge of warmth at the feel of the fragile body that was now her responsibility. This must have been what Aggie had felt when Tate and Adriana had been put in her care some twenty-five years earlier.

She took Aggie's place in the rocker and sat with her eyes riveted to the small figure in the cradle, certain that she would never tire of the sight. She watched fascinated as the baby's eyelids fluttered in her sleep, wondering what the child could be dreaming about.

Later on, when the baby awoke, Thea was even more enthralled. The tiny fingers gripping hers moved her nearly to tears of joy and her happiness was complete when the baby's blue eyes seemed to meet hers with recognition.

"I know it is only foolishness, Martha, but I think you know me, don't you, my lamb. I'm your new mamma, and we are going to be so happy together,"

Thea said, punctuating her promises with kisses and cuddling the warm little body affectionately.

The morning passed quickly for Dorothea, playing and talking with the infant, and when she met with Miss Whitesley over luncheon trays in the garden, she could contain her excitement no longer and chattered on and on about the newfound joys of motherhood.

"That feeling will depart soon enough, when you have paced the nursery floor at three in the morning, trying to quiet her, my dear. Though we may bless our lucky stars that she isn't twins, like her father and Adriana. I really had my hands full with those two. Just as one would finally get to sleep, the other would awaken and start in. And it didn't cease when they outgrew their cradles, either. If one wasn't up to some sort of caper the other was. Yes, the nursery was a lively enough place in those days."

She paused, her eyes focused far in the distance, then recalling herself, she went on. "And speaking of Adriana, I truly must leave today, though I know it must seem to you like desertion. No matter what terrible things Tate said yesterday, my place is with her during her travail. Do you think you can carry on without me now, my dear?"

"It certainly will not be easy, ma'am. You are a great source of strength. But with Parker to guide me through the running of the house and Annie to help care for Martha and me, we shall muddle, and puddle, along well enough," Thea replied, giving Miss Whitesley's hand a reassuring pat.

The conversation turned to more mundane matters, the details of the housekeeping and overseeing the staff and keeping the large house running smoothly. After dispensing a great deal of useful advice and information, Miss Whitesley beamed confidently down on Dorothea.

"Don't worry, my girl. Bancroft Hall can practically run itself. Parker knows his business thoroughly and is a dab hand at turning Cook up sweet after one of her fusses. Annie is a capable nurse and abigail, though not one of your fashionable London servants, and is as diligent as the day is long. So if you have any questions at all, you can rely on their answers. And, just between the two of us, poor Mathilde never really did much but play her guitar and look beautiful. A charming girl, but not what I would call energetic, like Adriana."

"I am looking forward immensely to making the acquaintance of Sir Tate's twin," Thea said warmly. "I only hope that she does not take me for an adventuress." A small crease of worry appeared between the finely arched brows.

"Ha!" exclaimed Miss Whitesley. "That young scapegrace hasn't a leg to stand on in that department, I assure you. And even if she were in a position to throw stones at you, she wouldn't, believe me. And besides, I shall tell her plainly that your only interest in the union was the baby. As I told you before, she herself came to love her future husband after coming to care for his ward, Harry. She'll understand."

"But the cases are not at all alike, ma'am. Sir Tate and I . . ."

Aggie interrupted before Thea could elaborate on the gulf that separated the two marriages.

"You two eventually will do extremely well together, mark my words. Mathilde was a captivating child, but it is my belief that if Tate had spent less time in Portugal and more at Bancroft Hall, some of the charm might have worn a bit thin." Aggie sighed. "I don't like to speak of Mathilde in this way, and it is unfair to make comparisons, but knowing you for just one short day convinces me that you will make Tate exactly the sort of wife he needs."

These confidences, though surely intended to bolster Dorothea's spirits, had just the opposite effect.

"If you mean that I fit all his requirements for this 'post' you are quite right. Someone firmly on the shelf, drab enough to be a safe guardian of the family hearth and honor, and someone who knows her place. A fairly accurate description of Dorothea Sand . . . Bancroft, don't you think?" She made a mocking curtsy. "I shall do my best to carry out my part of this business bargain, but don't, pray, saddle me with any of your tottyheaded notions of roseate bliss with Sir Tate. I have no such intentions, and neither does he."

Aggie stirred her cold tea around in her cup. "More's the pity, I say." She stood and shook out her skirts. "If you have no more questions, I think I shall get to my packing so that I may leave this afternoon."

She crunched up the garden pathway and disappeared behind the curve of the hedgerow.

Thea sat down on the marble bench next to the green archway and considered Aggie's words, wondering where this impetuous marriage might lead her. She tried to take a dispassionate view of the possibilities by once again taking up the comparison with a Gothic novel.

The bereaved widower gone off to possible death or disfigurement in war, daring the Fates that had taken his young wife to take him as well fit the Gothic formula, she reflected wistfully. In all self-respecting fairy tales the heroine found some way to secure the love of the handsome prince. "Well, perhaps my domestic abilities, calm good sense and maternal instincts will do the trick," she said aloud with a mirthless laugh.

"That would certainly be a new twist on the old tale, my girl, to win the heart of the hero through motherly love rather than ethereal beauty. And just what sort of mother will you turn out to be if you become all atwitter every time someone mentions your husband's name . . ."

Her soliloquy was cut short by the sound of a rustling in the bushes behind her. She had no desire for anyone to eavesdrop on what she considered "lunatic ravings."

"Who is there?" she asked uncertainly. When no one answered, she stood up and called, much more resolutely, "Don't you know it is a crime to trespass? Now, show yourself this instant, or I shall send for the footmen to take you before the magistrate."

Still no one came into view, though the bushes continued to shake in an ominous fashion. Thea felt a momentary shiver of apprehension, but calmed herself in her usual fashion by making light of her fears. There had to be some humor in this situation, she thought. After all, if I were the heroine of a Gothic piece, I would take this opportunity to swoon gracefully into the arms of a conveniently passing gentleman, who would fall in love with my plain, but character-laden exterior, sensing instinctively the poetic beauty of my soul.

"As that would only land me in a bed of thorns rather than a hero's embrace," she sighed, "I suppose I shall have to investigate this intruder myself."

She marched resolutely to the spot where the shrubs were shaking most violently and spoke in the gruffest tones she could muster. "Come out . . ." her voice broke in a squeak, but she cleared it and started over. "Come out at once," she commanded, "or you shall answer to the master!"

With trembling hands she parted the bushes, only to discover that her intruder was not standing opposite her at eye level, but was digging himself a hole under the shrubbery. He raised his shaggy head and cocked it at a crazy angle, panting after his exertions. It was none other than Clarissa's seducer, looking even more unkempt than he had the day before. A night spent in the rain had improved neither his appearance nor his aroma.

"Well, old fellow," said Thea with a broad grin, relieved that her trespasser was so innocuous. "I can hardly kick you off the property, can I? If it weren't for you I wouldn't be here, but back in Bath taking your lady love for her constitutional."

The mongrel did not stir from his hole in the hedge, but his matted tail wagged slightly, carving a faint path in the damp earth. When Thea approached a little closer, the dog moved away, exactly the same distance.

"I can see that you have not always had the kindest of attentions, my friend," said the girl. "I understand your sentiments exactly. Any attempt at reasoning on my part will get me nowhere. It seems that I must resort to bribery."

It took quite a bit of coaxing, but after twenty minutes of soothing words and blandishments and arm-wearying offers of scraps from the luncheon plates, Thea had the animal eating at her feet.

Sitting on the stone bench, she fed him absent-mindedly and rubbed a spot behind his ears, which he couldn't reach himself. When Thea stopped to eye his shaggy face consideringly, he pressed his head heavily onto her knees. After it became apparent that the trick of pushing against her leg was not going to work, the dog stood on his hind legs, put his large dirty front paws on her lap and attempted to lick her face.

Laughing, she pushed him away, and overcome by a wayward impulse, addressed him directly. "How would you like to be adopted, my gallant admirer, my *cicibeo*? After all, in this day and age, no lady's home is complete without one, and I fear that you are the closest I shall come to that appurtenance." She paused in thought. "I believe I shall call you Lovelace. Surely you remember him from your reading? He was the amorous gentleman who seduced the fair Clarissa Harlowe in Mr. Samuel Richardson's book of the same title. When I think of our first encounter there seems to be no other name for you. And it fits you so well, too—a less-loved animal would be hard to find. But we shall soon remedy that."

She stood and brushed the muddy paw prints from her skirts as best she could. "Come, Lovelace. Let's find you a bath and something more substantial to eat." With the dog close on her heels, she made her way into the house and rang for Parker.

When the elderly butler came into the drawing room and discovered the disreputable dog roaming about and investigating every corner of the room, his eyes widened in horror, though his face retained its accustomary calm.

"My apologies, my lady. I have no idea how that disgusting creature got in here. I shall see to its removal at once," he said, advancing resolutely toward the animal. Lovelace, sensing where his security lay, made a beeline for Thea's skirts and placed his new mistress firmly between himself and the butler.

Thea smiled apologetically. "No, no, Parker. That is not why I rang. This . . . er . . . fine fellow is my new lap dog, Lovelace, and I want you to see that he has a bath and a good meal directly."

Parker stared at her as if he could not believe his ears. "I beg your pardon, my lady. Did you say 'lap dog'?" he faltered.

"Yes," she laughed, "although I rather doubt he would fit on my lap, if the truth be known. However, I am already exceedingly attached to him, and he is, I believe, equally taken with me. Surely you must see that separation now would be unthinkable."

"Unthinkable," echoed Parker, hollowly. "Very well, my lady. I shall take him to the kitchen for the footboy to wash."

"And feed. Don't forget to give him his nuncheon, Parker. A healthy specimen such as Lovelace surely has a large appetite."

"Quite." Parker gingerly approached the dog, his mouth twitching in distaste. "Now, if you will please follow me," he said stiffly. Lovelace peered apprehensively out at him from behind Thea's dress.

"I suppose you had best send to the village for a leather collar, too. Otherwise there will be no way to control him. Meanwhile, I shall just have to chastise him into obedience. Lovelace, go! Go, I say!" She pointed toward the door and Lovelace, to Parker's astonishment, slunk through it to the hall. Without another word, the butler followed the animal out, and shut the door behind him in a marked manner.

A twinkle came into Thea's eye as she pictured the scene which Lovelace's entry into the kitchen would occasion. If Cook were as temperamental as rumored, it would require all of Aggie's diplomatic skills to bring her round after the dog's appearance in her domain.

With a sudden start she remembered that Miss Whitesley would be leaving for London within the hour, and if any diplomacy were required, it must come from the new Lady Bancroft.

Chapter 8

Dorothea made her way slowly up the stairs and along the corridor to Miss Whitesley's quarters, where that redoubtable lady was putting the final touches on her packing. From what Thea could see, it consisted of layer upon layer of black bombazine in a commodious portmanteau.

When the elderly woman looked up and saw Thea standing there, she shook her head sadly. "If only I could stay and go at the same time," she said, her eyes filling with tears.

"You mustn't worry too much about Martha and me, you know. We'll get along famously," Thea assured her.

"I know that, my dear, but I just wish that circumstances were otherwise . . ."

"Of course, as do I. But they aren't. And as for companionship, if you must know, I have already acquired a most amusing admirer."

Aggie's face took on a severe expression, as Thea, reading the censorious frown accurately, went on, "High stickler that you are, Aggie, you would find him even more disreputable than does Parker, redolent as he is of nights spent in the rain and years spent without bathing. Oh, Aggie, your expression is priceless!" she whooped. "It is Clarissa's beau and our uninvited guest. I've taken the liberty of christening him Lovelace, without Mr. Stevens' aid. I seem to be making a career of this naming business. Perhaps I should set up in competition with the parson."

They shared a chuckle, but Thea found that her humor and confidence evaporated when Aggie closed the lid of her portmanteau firmly. It was very difficult to feel optimistic and assured facing the hard reality of her ally's departure.

"Oh, Aggie," she quavered. "What shall I do without you?"

"Now, now, my dear," soothed Miss Whitesley, in her turn. "You shall do very well on your own. And after all, you now have a protector of sorts. But I expect you to write every week to tell us how you go on, and how Martha is doing."

Thea earnestly promised to do so as she accompanied the older woman down the stairs and out to the waiting carriage. There she looked on in growing agitation as the footman loaded the portmanteau and then helped Miss Whitesley to her seat inside. When the coachman climbed to his lofty perch, the finality of Miss Whitesley's departure descended on the girl. In near panic she watched the black lacquered vehicle round the bend in the drive and disappear behind the stand of elms that signaled the edge of the home wood.

Standing on the broad flagstone steps, Dorothea tried to subdue her apprehension, but with little success. How on earth am I going to cope with a child who screams all night, she thought frantically. Annie is a good girl, but has no great talent for quieting the child.

If only there were some way I could tire Martha out so that she would be exhausted enough to sleep through the night.

With a sigh she shaded her eyes with one hand and peered down the drive where the chaise had gone. Part of her envied the woman who was riding away from these heavy responsibilities behind the team of glossy chestnuts.

This notion sparked the germ of an idea and she went indoors with renewed courage to seek the opinion of Parker. He came to her in the drawing room and she was relieved to see no evidence of lasting umbrage over Lovelace. Cook, however, was another matter; the butler reported that he had barely managed to calm that woman's wounded sensibilities.

"You don't think there has been any permanent damage done to her pride, do you, Parker?" Thea asked.

"Not at all, my lady. The animal is no longer in the kitchen, but in the breakfast room with Robert. After their departure, Mrs. Keighley's humor is much improved."

"I daresay it is. Well, if my lap dog is presentable, I shall go and fetch him." As Parker bowed and prepared to leave, she stopped him. "Excuse me, Parker, there's one more thing. Do you know if there might be any vehicle like a pony cart in the stables? And a pony, of course, or some gentle animal, which I might drive?"

Parker paused a moment in thought, then said, "I believe there is an old cart, which Master Tate and Miss Adriana used to drive about. As for a pony, you'd best ask Joss, the head groom. There were ponies, of course, when the two of them were just children, but that was many years ago." The butler was too well trained to betray any curiosity as to what the new

103

mistress might want with these relics of her husband's childhood. And Thea was not about to reveal her scheme until she could be assured that it would solve her problem.

Before going to the stables she stopped in the morning room to collect Lovelace and relieve Robert of his thankless task. When she opened the door, the animal bounded from Robert's grasp to her side and fell fawning at her feet.

"You don't have to abase yourself with me, Lovelace. Simple obedience is all I require." Thea addressed him after Robert had departed with a sigh of very apparent relief. If the bath had improved Lovelace's aroma appreciably, it had done little for his appearance and less for his manners. He looked to be a combination of several country breeds: part hound, part sheepdog, part spaniel. Dorothea judged his color to be naturally muddy since most of the dirt that had matted his coat was now gone. When he stood, after Robert's exit, he came about to Thea's knee.

Apparently Robert had had some problems with the animal, for he had tied a piece of clothesline about Lovelace's neck to prevent any irredeemable accidents. Now this trailed behind him as he accompanied Thea on her way to the stables. He was sufficiently enamored of her that he was not about to stray far from her side.

She had to ask the way to the stables from one of the gardeners. "It seems strange, Lovelace, that I am now mistress here and I have to ask directions of the servants in order to find my way about. Surely most brides are given tours of their prospective domains by their bridegrooms. But then, we all know that I am not at all like most brides, don't we?" she said wistfully.

When they arrived at the stables, Lovelace let his nose lead him about as he made the acquaintance of the animals there and Thea introduced herself to this whole new group of the staff of Bancroft Hall.

To her delight, Joseph assured her that he had just the animal for her to use with the pony cart. It was not a pony, but a small horse, called Bessie, who was broken to harness and extremely gentle. Bidding him to hitch up the animal to the pony cart, and calling to the exploring Lovelace, she returned to the hall, where Martha had just finished her afternoon feeding.

While Thea dressed the baby in a loose gown and pretty bonnet, she directed Annie to pad a box with blankets and meet her at the front of the house. Then she carried the baby downstairs and, with the box firmly anchored on the cart seat beside her, drove off to explore the countryside, Lovelace coursing alongside the cart.

"If the combination of jouncing around, gallons of fresh air and an endless variety of sights doesn't wear this baby out, nothing will," she confided to Lovelace. Glancing down at Martha, she noticed with satisfaction that the child was peering about her with bright blue eyes, and there were no signs of colicky fussing.

That night proved the efficacy of Dorothea's plan. Martha fell asleep straightaway and, for the first time, slept until morning without waking. Delighted with her success, Thea made the cart outings part of the baby's regular routine. They served the triple purpose of stimulating the infant, exercising the dog and introducing the new Lady Bancroft to the entire neighborhood. She found that in spite of the odd circumstances surrounding her hasty marriage, her nearest neighbors warmly welcomed her impromptu visits.

105

As the days grew warmer, she began to dispense with some of the baby's blankets. In time, both she and Martha were going about without bonnets, and by the end of the second week the baby had exchanged her yellow hue for rosy cheeks. Dorothea also bloomed in the sunshine, her face glowing with health and her hair growing sun-streaked.

Annie, while pleased at the former, looked askance at the latter's unladylike tan. " 'Tain't proper, my lady. Your gallivanting about the countryside with that awful dog without a bonnet or a groom. Really, madam . . ."

"Now, now, Annie. Lovelace would look silly in my bonnet, anyway."

"Why, madam, I didn't mean the dog should be wearing a bonnet, and why you do insist on twisting my words around until I don't know what I'm about, I shall never know."

"But you must admit, Annie," said Thea, "that I do know what I'm about. Don't you think it is much better to have Martha sleep peacefully through the night?"

"Of course, my lady, but . . ."

"But . . . stop worrying, my girl. I have everything under control." No sooner were the words out of Thea's mouth than a knock came at the nursery door.

"My lady," Parker said as he entered, "there is a person below asking for you. A foreign person, I believe."

"Perhaps it is someone with a message from the master," Thea exclaimed. "I shall be down at once."

She flew to her room to tidy her hair, but was too impatient to do more than tuck a few of the more unruly strands into place. Her heart was pounding furiously at the thought that her husband might have sent someone with word of his safety, or—she refused to dwell on the possibility—the opposite. Running downstairs pell-mell, she threw open the drawing room doors and catapulted breathlessly into the room in a manner most deplorable in a young woman of good breeding.

Her headlong dash was brought up short by the sight of her visitor, who was far from the military messenger that she had anticipated. Instead, she saw a tiny, ramrod-straight woman of uncertain age, dressed in mourning from head to toe and veiled in black lace.

"I am Lady Bancroft," Thea was finally able to gasp, when she at last caught her breath. "What is it you wish of me?"

"I am Senhora Seraphim. The Conde de Vasconcellos sent me to care for his granddaughter," the woman said in a heavily accented voice, then gave up on what was obviously a prepared memorized speech. "And if *you* are truly the . . . the . . ." she groped for the correct word, then fell into what was her native tongue, "*madrasta* to the *bebé*, then I think it is very good thing I am here."

Thea stood for a few moments, thunderstruck. At last, speaking slowly, she asked about the senhora's journey to England.

"It was most . . . interesting, my lady," she said coldly. "There was a . . . blockade. Is that the correct word? We depart at night and were fired upon."

" 'Blockade' certainly sounds like the right word. How dangerous for you! You must have been very frightened."

"It was no worse than the war itself. In Portugal we have had many years of war. One grows accustomed."

Dorothea thought that she could never "grow accustomed" to living in fear as the conde's family seemed to have done.

"Have you been in the conde's employ long?" she asked.

"But naturally, my lady." The senhora seemed astonished at the depths of this Englishwoman's ignorance. "I was governess and then *dama de companhia* to Mathilde before her *impetuoso* marriage to Sir Tate." She shook her head significantly. "It was not good, that marriage, not good for my little Mathilde. She should have married Senhor Gades, as the conde and condessa had planned. But instead, she must follow her English soldier to this England." Implicit in this statement was the senhora's conviction that Mathilde might be alive today if she had not been so foolish as to fall in love with a heathenish Englishman.

The lady stood up and announced her intention to see the infant immediately.

Dorothea sighed and rose to her feet. Leading the way upstairs to the nursery, she wondered how this rigidly formal woman would adjust to Bancroft Hall. While unbending convictions might be an asset while in a state of siege, they could create numerous problems in the bucolic atmosphere of Wiltshire.

Dorothea could tell that from the moment the senhora set foot in the nursery she declared it to be her territory, although not in so many words, of course. Her English, though fluent, was not up to such colloquialisms, but her attitude was distinctly one of command, like a general surveying his troops, thought Dorothea. It was also apparent from the first that if the nursery was the battleground, Dona Dorotéia, as the senhora referred to her, was the enemy.

Senhora Seraphim took charge of Martha with a vengeance, wresting her from Annie's arms where she was pacifically taking a bottle, and assuring herself that the child was clean and well-nourished. Naturally enough, at this interruption of her meal, Martha set up a healthy squall, and since the senhora insisted on inspecting before the meal could be continued, all three women were subjected to the cries of frustration for a good quarter-hour before Martha was returned to Annie's charge. The senhora was nothing if not thorough. It took another few minutes before the screaming infant could be calmed enough to take the bottle once again.

Each scream from Martha seemed to pierce Thea to the heart. The child had been so good in the past month that she and Annie had seldom heard her cry. Senhora Seraphim did not even appear to hear the wails as she declared in a mix of English and Portuguese that her charge looked healthy, *mais ou menos*, but would need some strict discipline if she were not to become hopelessly spoiled. She issued the statement that the sooner she was given complete control of the nursery, the better it would be for all concerned, then stalked from the room, leaving Thea bristling with indignation and Annie quaking with awe.

When the two met again over dinner, the senhora wasted no time in giving Dorothea a very detailed list of items she felt were sadly lacking in the child's wardrobe and the nursery. As these consisted primarily of items that would deck Martha out like a doll, Thea half-heartedly said she would see to their purchase with no intention of doing so.

"But, no, Dona Dorotéia, it is not necessary. The condessa and I have seen to it that these necessities were sent along. It is only to wait for the carriage from the post house tomorrow. All will be complete then."

Thea's heart sank. Any objections that she raised were very politely and firmly argued away. This woman was an irresistible force, with experience, strong conviction and the condessa on her side.

The only thing with which the senhora found no fault was the choice of a name for the child, which she pronounced "Marta" in the Portuguese fashion.

Dorothea sought vainly for some other neutral topic. "You must have spent a great deal of time with Sir Tate and Mathilde as a chaperone before they were wed," she ventured, hoping to avoid yet another confrontation, and perhaps to gain some insight into the young woman who had been her predecessor.

"I was with Mathilde when she found Sir Tate wandering about like an *idiota*, a *bobo*. He had no mind, no memory. Mathilde did not know what language he spoke, but I recognize it at once as English. I know, too, what danger there is in this." She looked over her shoulder in much the same way that Thea had when Aggie had told her of Tate's activities in the Peninsula. "He wears no uniform, you see. An Englishman in this part of the country, and no sign of the soldier about him—this means only one thing." She shook her head ominously.

"I was in favor of leaving him where he was, but my Mathilde would not hear of it. She had always a soft heart for a lost creature. I wish I had never listened to her pleading." The old woman's voice cracked, but she quickly regained her iron composure. "But she had always a mind of her own, as well. She insisted we send for the servants to carry the poor *ofendido* back to the *castello*. And she took care of him. I do not wonder that he came to love her. She was an angel. And so delicately raised."

By this time, Thea had had a sufficiency of the senhora's companionship. She showed the elderly woman to the quarters formerly occupied by Miss Whitesley, hoping that when Aggie returned from London, as she must do at some time, Senhora Seraphim would consider her own presence unnecessary. But Thea could not feel very optimistic about this possibility.

She retired to her room, and after plaiting her hair into its long braid, lay in bed waiting for sleep. Since the advent of the daily rides in the pony cart she had had no problem falling asleep; just like Martha she thrived and grew exhausted on the doses of fresh air and exercise. She had viewed the summer that stretched before her as a pleasant round of outdoor activity. But this new development in their lives loomed with alarming proportions, dispelling sleep and causing Thea her first bout of insomnia since her wedding night.

When she did fall asleep it was to dream fitfully of her absent husband and Mathilde. It was not a flesh-and-blood woman who haunted her dreams, however, but a one-dimensional painted image, who wore a halo, like a figure in a religious painting. The action of the dream was confusing, involving Lovelace, Clarissa and Miss Grayson, in a repetition of their wedding day roles. The sequence of events on that day repeated itself with one disturbing exception. When Thea was swept into her husband's arms for that final unnerving embrace, the haloed icon of Mathilde, with its serene, doll-like expression, inserted itself between them, leaving Dorothea fuming helplessly on the sidelines.

Beside her, grinning hugely and foolishly was Seraphim, who gloated, "You see, it is just as I said, my Mathilde *is* an angel."

Dorothea

This bewildering dream recurred several times, until Thea could stand it no longer. At five-thirty she arose and made herself ready to face the day and what it might bring in the way of confrontations with Senhora Seraphim.

Chapter 9

As it transpired most of her worst fears about Senhora Seraphim were realized. The older woman seemed constantly to be comparing her with Mathilde and finding her sadly wanting. Not only had her predecessor been a beautiful and charming child, but she had grown, without blemish, into an angelic adolescent and perfect young woman. Even taking into consideration the senhora's understandable bias, Thea's meager self-confidence wore thin under the torrent of the senhora's reminiscences.

Even worse was the realization that had she had the perfection to compete with the first Lady Bancroft, in the eyes of Senhora Seraphim she would be forever an interloper. Sir Tate, of course, came in for his share of the blame. It was, naturally, unforgivable for him to have married again so soon, with Mathilde barely in her grave. None of Thea's explanations of the marriage for the sake of the child carried any weight with Seraphim. She soon gave up trying and accepted the condemnation which seemed to be her lot.

"The supreme irony of this, you realize," she confided to Lovelace one afternoon in the garden, where

113

she often sought refuge from Seraphim's importuning, "is that if the senhora had only appeared on the scene a month earlier to take charge of Martha, there would have been no marriage for her to rail against." Lovelace licked her hand in sympathy.

"I dread to think what will happen if . . . that is, when, Sir Tate returns, Lovelace. The woman goes on and on about her adored Mathilde, and I fear that if she continues in this vein to him it will stir up memories that are better buried."

But the biggest problem with the senhora arose over the care of Martha. It was clear from the outset that there was a philosophical gulf about the raising of children between the two women that no amount of rational discussion could bridge.

The pony cart became the first, but by no means the last, bone of domestic and maternal contention between the two. The very first morning when Thea came downstairs with the baby in her arms and the dog at her heels for her daily drive, she was waylaid on the front steps by the senhora.

"And where do you go with Martinha?" demanded the older woman, using the Portuguese diminutive for Martha. She cast a suspicious eye on the waiting cart.

Dorothea, thinking that a cheerful approach might be the most effective antidote to the woman's poisonous presence, gaily exclaimed, "We are having our morning ride. I think today we will go to visit one of the old cottagers, who has some lambkins. Martha loves watching them at play."

Senhora Seraphim drew herself up, and for a woman of exceedingly short stature, managed to exude a great deal of outrage. "Am I to comprehend, Dona, that you are solely riding that *carreta?*"

"Why, yes, we go every day. Martha so enjoys the sights, and the sunshine. And the fresh air and the excitement of bouncing along the lane seem to help her sleep." She swept past the other woman and installed the baby in her anchored box on the seat and climbed in beside her.

However soothing the cart ride might be for Martha, it had the exact opposite effect on the baby's newest protectress.

"But you have no *accompanhante*! And the *bebé* . . . just see how she is uncovered! *Nossa, Senhora!*" she exclaimed, and although the exact meaning of the Portuguese words escaped Dorothea, there was no mistaking the sentiment behind them.

In spite of Senhora Seraphim's obvious objections, Dorothea took up the reins. "Senhora, you must, er . . . comprehend that things are decidedly different here in England."

"Then all ladies go without *accompanhante*?" The black eyes screwed up in patent disbelief. "*Que barbarismo!*"

"One woman's barbarism is another's delight, Senhora," Dorothea said with a shrug. Then, preferring an invigorating ride to a lengthy self-defense, she nodded and drove away, with a silent prayer that the foreign lady would not happen to exchange her views with Annie. Despite her thorough Englishness, Annie certainly shared most of them.

From that day on, she found that every time she went to collect Martha for her cart ride, the old woman seemed to deliberately arrange lengthy delays, in increasingly blatant attempts to prevent Thea from taking the child on the objectionable outings.

Sometimes Seraphim would have fed the child long

before the usual hour and rocked her to sleep, while she plied her endless needle. Other times Dorothea would find the child in the middle of a long and unnecessarily thorough bath.

After a series of such stratagems, all unsuccessful in their object, Seraphim seemed to bow to defeat. In truth, however, she merely became more subtle in her tactics. Whenever Dorothea came for the child she would find the infant wrapped so tightly in exquisitely embroidered covers that she was as immobile as a China doll. Seraphim had explained that unless this was done, the baby's limbs would bow out. She herself had performed this office for Mathilde and had had her reward: Mathilde's limbs had been as lovely and straight as any in the land. Dorothea's arguments against this treatment fell on deaf ears.

The garments that the senhora used for swaddling had been lovingly embroidered by the condessa and had run the dangers of the blockade with Seraphim, so that Thea was at first reluctant to object and stir up yet another conflict. But gradually she took to loosening the wraps during the ride, then to unwrapping Martha's legs, and finally to bringing along some loose clothes and effecting a complete change as soon as they were out of sight of the house. Before returning the baby to Seraphim, however, she would always rewrap her, murmuring apologies to the wriggling Martha for subjecting her to the ridiculous charade. If one combatant could wage a war of subtlety, she reasoned, so could the other, so long as the baby was not made too unhappy by the battles that were being waged over her.

One unseasonably warm June afternoon Thea drove Bessie to the banks of a cheerful little stream that ran through the home wood and along the border of the property. She had often brought Martha and Lovelace to this spot for picnics. Martha seemed fascinated by the variety of wild flowers and butterflies, and Lovelace derived endless satisfaction from trying to catch Sir Tate's trout. As his method was to leap into the stream with all four paws extended, he had never succeeded in his aim.

Martha's Portuguese clothes lay in a neatly folded pile in the cart and she rolled about nearly naked on the blanket, wearing only a sundress that Thea had contrived from one of the baby's old nightgowns that the senhora had destined for the dustbin. So delighted was Thea in watching the baby stretch her tan little arms in freedom that she was unaware that a thunderstorm approached until the first raindrop hit her squarely on the nose. By the time she caught Bessie's bridle, whistled for the wide-ranging Lovelace and folded the blanket, the storm broke over them. In spite of Bessie's fastest shuffle, when they reached the front door of the manor house, horse, dog, baby and driver were thoroughly drenched.

Both baby and dog found the situation hilarious. Martha laughed each time a raindrop splashed on her and seemed to think the thunder was a concert arranged for her benefit; while Lovelace jumped into every puddle on the road and then shook himself dry before running ahead to the next one. Thea only hoped that she could get the baby up to the nursery and back into her fancy dress before being spotted by the senhora.

After handing the reins over to one of the footmen, she dashed into the hall, only to be halted in her tracks by the shocked accents of Senhora Seraphim.

"Dona Dorotéia!" she exclaimed. "What have you done to Marta? How wet she is! And where are her clothes? I knew you to be a woman *sem graça*, and a total *ignorante* about *bebés*, but I cannot allow you to expose Marta to dangerous illness! I shall write to the condessa about this!" Snatching the infant from Dorothea, Senhora Seraphim stalked away.

For her part, Dorothea did some stalking as well, straight to the library for pen and paper. Tears of anger and frustration stung her eyes, and she dashed them away with the back of her hand. One of the conditions of her marriage had been total responsibility for the child and now it seemed that all her authority was being eroded in a way that she was helpless to prevent. As an emissary from Martha's grandparents, the senhora was more certain of her position than was the parvenu wife.

"Senhora Seraphim is not the only one who can write an angry letter," she muttered to Lovelace, who responded by shaking his wet coat all over the library carpet. All the frustration that she had experienced at the hands of the Portuguese woman spilled over and she dashed off a missive to her husband, the first time she had attempted to communicate with him. After all, he had made no request that she report on her activities, or Martha's progress, and from what Miss Whitesley had told her of his secret work, it was highly unlikely that the post would reach him. But at least she would try.

"Dear Sir Tate," she wrote.

"I am writing you to tell you of some very unsettling developments here, in the person of one Senhora Seraphim. She arrived, unheralded, some time ago, and has proceeded to undermine all my efforts with Martha by insisting upon antediluvian dictates on child-raising.

118

I will not bore or burden you with the particulars, but I do ask that you write to the conde and condessa explaining to them that I am responsible for the child and thus must make decisions about her upbringing as I see fit.

Martha, by the way, is thriving, in spite of Seraphim's efforts to turn her into a poppet, and is rolling over by herself, an act of sheer genius in one her age. I promise you that if I am able to proceed with her unimpeded, you will have a daughter of whom you will be justifiably proud.

I hope that this letter finds you in safety and that you are running no unnecessary risks.

> Your obedient, etc., etc.
> Dorothea Bancroft"

She read over her words and felt it a pity that she must be so formal and distant with the man who was, after all, her husband. "Ah, Lovelace, we are in such a coil. I only hope that Tate receives this—and deigns to reply before matters get to a worse pass." She folded the sheet and, using the wax and seal she found in the desk drawer, closed and directed it to her husband, care of the ministry in London which seemed to oversee his journeys.

For several days, she watched the post like a bird looking for crumbs, although she realized the absurdity of expecting to hear anything soon, if at all. To her delight, however, the very day that she resigned herself to not hearing anything brought the delivery of two letters of unusual interest, though neither was from Sir Tate.

One was very neat and officially directed, and she opened it first. It was from a Mr. Broderick, London solicitor for the Bancroft family, who informed her that her husband had been to visit his legal establishment on his way through town en route to the Peninsula.

"You may imagine my surprise, indeed, I may say, my shock, upon being informed by Sir Tate that he had taken another wife upon the very heels of Lady Bancroft's death. As I make it a policy of being completely honest with all my clients, I feel it my duty to inform you that I feared he had been taken in by an Adventuress and that it would be simplicity itself to have the marriage annulled under such circumstances. Sir Tate assured me that this was not at all the case, and that you were a sedate young woman who is old for your years, not a society beauty who would shirk Duty for Pleasure."

Dorothea paused and reread the paragraph, feeling not entirely flattered by Sir Tate's description. Then, shaking her head at her idiotish reactions, she perused the rest of the letter, which dealt with financial arrangements. "Well, Lovelace, it appears that the master is far more generous with his money than he is with his compliments," she said, scratching the dog's ear, which always reduced him to ecstasy. The marriage settlement, which would be hers to keep no matter what transpired, seemed to her a small fortune in itself and, in addition, there was a substantial allowance to be paid quarterly. Compared to her previous existence with Miss Grayson, she would be living like a queen.

Why, then, should she feel this curious sinking feeling every time anyone so much as mentioned the name of her so open-handed husband?

She purposefully set aside this thought, and the letter, and turned to the other letter.

"Dear Dorothea," she read,

"Aggie has done nothing but chatter about you since arriving here, and I am all eagerness to meet you. I do hope that you will come to town as soon as is practicable with little Martha and make a long stay with me. The infernal accoucheur has insisted that I make an invalid out of myself until my confinement or he'll 'not answer for the consequences.' I have told him that the only consequence I am certain of at present if I do follow his orders to the letter is that I shall be brought to Bedlam before I ever am brought to bed.

My husband's six-year-old ward, Harry, who lives with us, is in an even more advanced state of boredom than I. It would be an act of mercy if you could come soon, for we desperately need a new face here. And, of course, I quite long to see the newest face in the family (for the moment), baby Martha. Most of one whole floor of our townhouse is used for a nursery, or soon will be. It has several separate rooms as well as a large playroom/schoolroom. My new niece (how nice that sounds) can be easily housed, even after her *enormous* new cousin arrives, if ever!

When Tate was here I did mention having you visit and he raised no particular objec-

tion. I almost wish he had. Any show of emotion
would be preferable to his listless melancholy.
I fear you have linked yourself with a most
unhappy family just now! Tate stuck in the
dismals and me stuck to my sofa. Please come.

> Your sister,
> Adriana Laidley"

Mr. Broderick's stuffy message Dorothea buried in
a bottom drawer of the library desk, but Adriana's she
folded and stuck in her reticule. During the next few
days, whenever she felt in need of a little cheer, which
was often, she took it out and read it and considered
whether or not Martha could bear the journey as yet.
The warm, chatty letter was a comforting beacon of
proffered friendship in the midst of a veritable sea of
difficulties, all caused directly or indirectly by Senhora
Seraphim.

It quickly became apparent that the old woman's
disdain for things English did not stop at the nursery
door, but extended over the entire house. Unbeknownst
to Thea, the erstwhile governess even invaded the cook's
domain, offering scathing criticism of English cuisine,
which set up Mrs. Keighley's back and required all of
Parker's unflappable tact to restore tranquility.. If she
had been able to understand the language in which the
disparagements were muttered, not all of the butler's
efforts would have smoothed her ruffled feathers. But
the ultimate crime in Cook's eyes was the senhora's
attempt to fix meals for herself and Martha that con-
formed to her Portuguese notions of proper cookery.

The tensions which this had created belowstairs
were withheld from Dorothea. The servants, all very
fond of their new mistress and well aware of the antag-

onism that had arisen between the two women, were in tacit agreement not to burden her with any more difficulties. However, the turmoil that the senhora had created in the kitchen burst into view one evening when Thea was playing hostess with a modest dinner for the vicar and his unmarried older sister, who kept house for him at the vicarage.

As it was the first time that Dorothea had essayed into the social fray, she was quite nervous about it, though it was only a small endeavor, which a more experienced hostess would have considered paltry. Still, she did want to show the vicar some appreciation for his professional services, rendered on the fateful day, now seemingly an eternity ago, when he had married her to Tate.

Miss Stevens bore a striking, if unfortunate, resemblance to her portly, middle-aged brother, yet had the airs and dress of a woman half her age. Her hair was an unconvincing shade of yellow, cropped and coiled into ringlets and pulled back from her forehead by a series of coral bows. Her pink gown, with its frills and flounces, would have been most becoming on a slim debutante, but Miss Stevens was neither slender nor seventeen. From the moment she set eyes on Thea, she fixed the girl with an icy stare, and though she smiled and did the polite, her true feelings barbed every honeyed remark. It took an effort of will for Thea to maintain her composure under the barrage of impertinent questions, salted with sly looks, posed by Miss Stevens.

The vicar, on the other hand, was the soul of pompous amiability. Taking one look at Thea's burnished copper curls, the recently fleshed out figure and the rosy glow of good health, he put himself out to be as charming as his sense of his own worth would permit.

After half an hour of defending herself against Miss Stevens' barbed queries and Mr. Stevens' flattering attentions, Thea was happy to take her guests into the dining room. In her earlier discussions with Cook and Parker, they had decided on seven o'clock as the time to begin serving dinner. It was five past the hour when the three sat down at the magnificent mahogany table.

Miss Stevens continued her catechism as she sipped her tepid water and unfolded her napkin. It was as clear as the crystal goblets on the spotless linen tablecloth that she disapproved of everything about the new Lady Bancroft.

"And just where did your mother come from, Lady Bancroft? I myself am personally acquainted with almost all branches of the Grayson lineage. Your dear cousin, Letitia, was one of my greatest friends before her removal to Bath, but I don't believe I ever heard her mention your name."

"We were doubtless beneath her notice, Miss Stevens. I, for one, never knew of *her* existence until she transported me to Bath after the death of my parents," Dorothea replied absently, wondering when Parker would appear with the soup course.

As though in answer to her unspoken question, the butler entered the room. When she noticed the absence of a soup tureen, coupled with the expression of harassment on the elderly man's face, Thea felt her heart turn over.

"Forgive me, madam," he said forlornly. "But there is a bit of a problem in the kitchen."

Dorothea bit her lip in vexation, then quietly excusing herself to her curious guests, followed the butler into the hall.

"What is it, Parker?"

"That Seraphim creature, madam. She has spoilt the soup by putting in some heathen peppers while Cook's back was turned. Cook is in a rare high taking— even higher than usual. She refuses to set foot back in the kitchen and is proclaiming to all the staff that this is sabotage."

Thea gave a rueful laugh. "Cook is probably right, though it would never do to say so. Well, send Seraphim to me in the morning room, and assure Mrs. Keighley that this will never happen again."

He hurried off and Dorothea paced the hall, feeling ready to burst into tears. I expected that my situation here would be complicated by Mathilde's shadow, she thought bitterly, but I certainly did not anticipate that my entire existence would be blighted by Mathilde's childhood nurse. It is simply too much! Her reflections continued in this vein as she awaited Seraphim's presence in the morning room.

The object of her ire came into the room, sat down and, without a word or a flicker of her eyelids, took out her everlasting needlework.

Controlling her temper with an effort, Thea marched over to the sofa. "Senhora Seraphim, I cannot allow you to disrupt my kitchen in this way. What on earth prompted you to put peppers into the soup?"

"*Sopa*? Ha! This *sopa* was fit only for *porcos*—as you say, 'peegs.' It was *repulsiva*. I could not allow such stuff to be fed to guests in the house of my Mathilde."

Thea forced herself to count each and every one of her fingers before trusting herself to speak in anything but an unladylike screech.

"Senhora, you must realize that this is no longer the home of your Mathilde! It is *my* home, and I am

125

mistress here. And if my cook fixes *sopa,* I mean soup, for my guests, it is not your affair what it tastes like. I *must* insist that you stay out of the kitchen from now on. Otherwise, my husband will see that you are sent back to Portugal, at once."

A half smile played about the thin mouth of the old woman, and with an unmistakable glitter of triumph in the black eyes, she drew a sheet of folded paper from her workbag.

"Ah, but I do not think that Sir Tate would do such a thing. The condessa has written that Sir Tate has sent a letter to the conde saying he is most grateful to them for sending me to England. He also expressed hope that I will raise Martinha into a woman as *sensível* and *adorável* as his beloved Mathilde."

Dorothea felt as though someone had suddenly whisked the superb Aubusson carpet out from beneath her feet. Was it possible that Seraphim could be telling the truth? The smug set of the woman's head was a clear indication that she felt herself firmly entrenched in a position of authority.

The girl longed to snatch the closely written sheet from the black-mitted hand, but refrained. After all, the Portuguese words would convey little sense to her. Instead she clenched her hands together, and, taking a deep breath, addressed her companion with a dignified calm that she was far from feeling.

"Whether that is true or not remains to be seen, Senhora Seraphim, but the fact remains that you do *not* have a free hand in the kitchen, and any further interference with the cook will get you nowhere but back to Portugal."

Dorothea swung round and started back to the dining room. Pausing outside the door, she rummaged through her reticule for her handkerchief, and her hand came into contact with Adriana's creased letter. Just the touch reminded her that she did have one powerful potential ally left to her, and in the heat of the moment she decided that she would do just as Adriana asked.

She swept into the dining room just as Robert arrived with the controversial soup. As she sat down, she beamed at her guests and said, "Do forgive me, dear ma'am, 'twas but a trifle, but you know how it is, settling disputes among the servants. This soup is a Portuguese delicacy and, I believe, quite popular with Lord Wellington."

At the mention of the war hero's name, Miss Stevens' face was wreathed in smiles. "Doubtless Tate has supped with the glorious Earl on this fine broth. I am all eagerness to try it," she gushed, and instructed Robert to fill her bowl to the very top. At the first whiff of the peppers, she recoiled, but was quick to make a recovery, and smiled sweetly to cover her shock.

Her histrionic abilities, however, were no match for the peppers. The first sip created a fit of coughing that lasted several minutes, which was finally eased after three full glasses of water.

"Lord Wellington must have a stomach of iron to enjoy such a dish!" she croaked in a strangled voice, while she wiped her streaming eyes with a napkin.

"The Earl is known for his courage. Perhaps it extends to culinary matters as well," replied Dorothea, who had herself barely touched Senhora Seraphim's concoction, her appetite taken away by Miss Stevens' reference to her Sir Tate.

"I would say that our new Lady Bancroft has considerable courage herself, in enduring the redoubtable Portugee senhora," interjected the vicar. "The village

has been humming with tales of her mischief-making."
He ventured a wink at Dorothea, who was mercifully
oblivious to his flat-footed attempts at gallantry. In fact,
she was so overwrought by her encounter with Seraphim, and so buoyed by her decision to go to Adriana,
that she virtually chattered during the whole of the
meal. Her excitement was so apparent that at the end
of the evening, when all three retired to the drawing
room, the vicar having no taste for a postprandial cigar,
Miss Stevens remarked on it with a knowing smile.

"My dear Lady Bancroft, I must tell you that you are
quite different from the subdued, spiritless being I had
been led to expect from my brother. It's obvious to me,
also, that he was completely mistaken when he said that
you and Sir Tate are barely acquaintances. Why, every
time his name was mentioned this evening you positively glowed with emotion. So touching. And when I
saw you merely toying with that . . . er . . . unusual
soup, I asked myself, Cora, I said, could it be that Lady
Bancroft's lack of appetite arises from some, shall we
say, more interesting condition?" she asked archly. "I
do pride myself on being the first to perceive these
things, it's quite uncanny, really. Why, I was the first
to notice when Lady Bancroft, that is, Lady *Mathilde*
Bancroft, was increasing. In fact, I believe that 'twas I
who first broke the news to dear Sir Tate. Such a pity
he isn't here so that I might perform the same office
for you." She paused, disconsolate, then brightened. "I
know, I shall write at once to dear Letitia. After all, she
is your cousin."

Horrified at the fantastic direction Miss Stevens'
thoughts were taking her, Dorothea stuttered and demurred, but in vain. She directed a pleading glance at
the vicar, who merely patted her hand with a knowing

smile. With her back to the wall, she blurted out that such a thing was impossible.

Both her visitors were visibly taken aback by her blunt denial. More than anything else, Dorothea wished her words unsaid. With Miss Stevens' wagging tongue at work it would not be long before the entire neighborhood (and through Miss Grayson, the entire *haut ton*) would know that the Bancroft/Sandham union was not only unexpected and unsuitable, but unconsummated as well.

Searching desperately for a change of subject, Dorothea summoned up all the enthusiasm she could and announced her plans to visit Adriana in London, but even this attempt fell short of her hopes.

"But, do you really think you should take the baby on such a journey at so young an age? Of course," Miss Stevens added coyly, "we maidens have little notion of how to raise offspring, but I would think that since Sir Tate left you to look after the child, you should stay quietly here at Bancroft Hall and not hare off to town."

"As you say, Sir Tate left the child to my care, and it is my judgment that we would both be happier with her Aunt Adriana. Besides, Dr. Hawk thinks I have worked miracles with Martha. He says she is a very different being from the sickly, yellowed infant he brought into the world," Dorothea said distantly.

At the mention of the doctor, a subtle change came over Miss Stevens' face. "Dr. Hawk is modest in the extreme, and it is so like him to ascribe credit to others when it is himself who has wrought the miracles."

"It matters not whose care has put the roses in her cheeks. The important thing is that she is robust enough to go to London, and go she shall," Thea repeated emphatically. Her haughty manner had the desired effect of prompting her two guests to set down their teacups and rise to leave.

Thea managed to thank the two for the pleasure of their company as they stood on the broad stone steps leading down to the drive and waited for their gig to be brought round from the stables. Somehow she kept her manner conventionally polite despite her burning desire to be rid of them.

"Oh, we are so delighted to oblige," Miss Stevens twittered. "There are so few people of any real breeding here in the country with whom we can dine with any degree of gentility. And now here you are abandoning us for the more tempting attractions of London. Such a pity."

"You misunderstand, ma'am. I go to town out of duty, not pleasure. Adriana tells me that she needs me and is longing to see Martha."

Miss Stevens sniffed audibly, and the vicar shook an admonitory finger at her. "Now, Cora, it is, after all, none of your affair if Lady Bancroft takes her step-daughter to London. I'm sure that Sir Tate has every confidence that his wife can avoid the evil temptations which shall beset her there, and that she will protect his child at any cost."

Miss Stevens spun round to face her brother, obviously so angry at his flank attack that she forgot where she was and who was there.

"But you yourself said it was a patched-up hasty affair, and that you had never been so shocked in your life. Mathilde scarcely cold and . . ."

"Thank you once again for coming, Miss Stevens," Dorothea interrupted with glacial calm. "I do hope you suffer no lasting ill effects from the soup."

This shifted the lady's attention from the Bancroft marriage to the far more absorbing topic of her own digestion, and she wondered again how the dear Lord Wellington could stomach the brew, until she was finally shepherded out by her sheepish brother.

Chapter 10

As soon as the two had departed, Dorothea went to the library and rang for Robert. When the young footman arrived, she requested him to bring her the best bottle of champagne from the cellar, two glasses and Lovelace. She choked back a slightly hysterical giggle at the look of blank puzzlement in the footman's face. However curious Robert might have been, he returned promptly with a dusty bottle, two crystal goblets and Lovelace following on his heels. After opening the bottle, he lingered hopefully, but Thea grew impatient and dismissed him.

"You may go now, Robert," she said firmly, and his face fell. When the door closed she picked up the bottle and poured out a generous glass for herself and one for Lovelace. Hers she lifted into the air in salute, and his she placed on the floor.

"Lovelace, my friend, I propose a toast, to Adriana Laidley. May she prove a strong ally and a delightful sister and together may we confound our enemies!"

After several swallows of the superb sparkling wine, she felt immeasurably revived. Suddenly she was struck by the utter absurdity of the evening. "Lovelace," she confided, "if only you had been there to witness my social triumph." She raised her glass to the light and contemplated the stream of tiny bubbles climbing upward in the wine.

"First there was Miss Stevens' barely concealed aversion. Oh, she tried to hide it behind cloying statements, but each sweet turn of phrase held a hook. Then her brother, the good parson, uttering clumsy compliments and gazing at me with those bovine eyes." Lovelace leaned his head heavily on her knee, as though in agreement.

She ignored his bid for affection and continued her list of the evening's disasters. "Then dear Cora had the unmitigated gall to suggest that I might be in the family way. As you and I know, such a circumstance is thoroughly out of the question, unless it may be accomplished by a very brief, very insulting embrace, which I still blush to remember." With a conscious effort she put the discomfiting memory aside.

"It is all Tate's fault after all. I should never have agreed to this ludicrous arrangement. Then I should not have been subjected to Miss Stevens' censure, nor to her brother's heavy-handed flattery, nor to Senhora Seraphim's autocratic disruption of Martha's life and my own. *Sopa* for *porcos*, indeed, Lovelace. Can you imagine Cook's face when the first pepper surfaced in the soup kettle?" She began to laugh uncontrollably and fell back on the sofa, while the dog, as if catching her hilarity, jumped up on the sofa beside her and barked.

She pushed him away, but relented, and with a faraway expression in her eyes, stroked his head. "But if I hadn't married Sir Tate," she mumbled, through a yawn, "I would never have had the inestimable joy of my daughter, Martha, nor the boon companionship of my good friend Lovelace, nor the support and, I hope, friendship of my sister Adriana . . . who has invited us . . . in warmest . . ." Exhaustion overcame her and her eyes closed.

When Robert came in half an hour later, that was where he found her, curled up sound asleep with a smile on her face nearly as beatific as that on the dog passed out on the carpet beside her.

Late the next afternoon, Dorothea watched, fascinated, as the sights of suburban London rolled by the window of the chaise. Somehow, in none of her girlhood daydreams of visiting the glorious capital had she ever envisioned herself sitting next to a frowning elderly foreigner or under a squirming infant stepdaughter. It would be hard to say which of the two is more dampening, she thought with a chuckle.

For the senhora's disapproval of the cart outings were dwarfed by her explosion of outrage when she had learned of the proposed trip to London. Even after an exhausting morning of packing and afternoon of travel, the Portuguese woman had plenty of energy left for diatribes. She repeatedly pointed out the unsurpassed folly of dragging the infant away from Bancroft Hall and into the noise and confusion of city life, a fate which, nevertheless, the old woman had insisted on sharing.

Dorothea, for the most part, listened to the endless scolding in silence, but finally was roused to answer. "Yes, Senhora, I am fully aware that the blessed Mathilde never left her parents' *casa* until she married, but this blessed babe is not Mathilde, and this is not Portugal."

"But the conde . . ."

"Please, Senhora," Dorothea said, wearily shifting

135

the sleeping baby to her other arm, "let us cry truce with one another. We are come to London because Sir Tate's sister has need of us. And Martha has borne the journey admirably well, you must admit it." As if to prove her stepmother's point, the baby awoke and smiled.

"You see? She is pleased as punch to be going to town, aren't you, lovey?" She turned the child so that Senhora Seraphim could see the baby's face, knowing full well that nothing would stir her companion out of the sulks as effectively as the sight of "Martinha's" pink and white countenance.

On a sudden inspiration, she asked, "Would you like to hold her now, Senhora? My arms are all pins and needles."

The Portuguese woman looked at her blankly. "Peens and needles? Oh, I comprehend, Dona. In Portuguese when this happens to the limbs we say they are *formigar*—are with ants."

"How amusing and how accurate a phrase. That is exactly what it feels like! My arms feel as if they house entire anthills at present." To the utter amazement of both ladies, they shared a laugh over the downy head of the oblivious child, as Dorothea passed her over to the other woman. The momentary truce and the anticipation of securing an ally in her sister-in-law sent Thea's spirits soaring. She started enumerating all the wonderful things they would do in London, punctuating each item with a light kiss on Martha's tiny nose.

"And we shall go with your Cousin Harry to see the lion at the Royal Menagerie, and the legendary horses at Astley's, and we shall ride every day in Hyde Park in an open carriage, and you, my dear Martha, shall be the toast of the town."

Senhora Seraphim's smile disappeared as quickly

as it had appeared, and her customary frown spread over her face. "But surely you do not pretend to do such frivolous things, Dona. Is the family not . . . bah . . . how do you say . . . *de luto* for poor Mathilde? In *seclusão . . . por amor de Deus.*"

"*Seclusão?* Seclusion? You must mean mourning. Why, yes, of course adults observe mourning here, but as for children, why, what harm is there in letting them enjoy their little pastimes?"

Her answer from Senhora Seraphim was a muttered imprecation about the barbarous English, and the two were returned to their old state of mutual hostility by the time the chaise stopped in front of the elegant townhouse belonging to Nicholas and Adriana Laidley.

They were met at the door by a surprised Miss Whitesley, who was immediately all aflutter to see the baby. "Why, I never expected to see you so soon!" she exclaimed. "When Adriana mentioned that she had invited you to come to London and to bring Martha, I never thought that you would arrive within the fortnight! And you must be Seraphim. Tate wrote us that you were coming to help. Let me see the baby!"

During all of Aggie's exclamations over their sudden appearance, and Dorothea's murmured responses, Senhora Seraphim had hugged the baby tightly to her chest. When Aggie reached out her arms for the child, the senhora drew back and tightened her hold. But when the sharp black eyes met Aggie's faded blue ones, they seemed to recognize a kindred spirit. After a few low-voiced Portuguese endearments and a slight adjustment of the lace blanket, she relinquished Martha to the waiting Miss Whitesley.

As both grey heads nodded and smiled over the

happily cooing baby, Thea marveled at the smooth transfer of power. In spite of the vast differences in their dealings with Martha's stepmother, they hit it off remarkably well with each other. Both were maiden ladies who had nearly single-handedly raised the parents of this tiny child. In a sense, they were the true grandmothers of Martha. Beside this common bond, all differences of language and temperament shrank into insignificance.

When Aggie had completed her inspection of the infant and ascertained that all fingers and toes were just as perfect, if slightly larger, as they had been six weeks earlier, she beamed at Thea and the senhora.

"Between the two of you, Martha seems to be a most contented and healthy specimen. And the journey seems to have done her no harm whatsoever."

Dorothea could not repress a slightly satisfied smile. "I'm so glad that you approve, Aggie. It has not always been the easiest of times at the Hall, and we have missed your support. But now, I insist that you take me to meet my sister-in-law."

"You must be as eager to meet Adriana as she is to meet you. She has talked of nothing else since receiving your note. She is, of course, confined to her bed on doctor's orders, but is allowed as many visitors as she wishes. Just now she is teaching Harry the finer points of Casino. He is already familiar with the rudiments. I have no doubt that she would rather make your acquaintance."

Still cradling little Martha in her arms, Aggie led the way up the broad, but steep, flight of stairs. All the way up Thea could hear the sound of a low adult voice and a high-pitched child's prattle raised in lighthearted argument.

"No, Harry, you know as well as I do that you do not receive an automatic three points for that two. That is the two of clubs and Little Casino is the two of spades, and you know the difference by now, so don't try to gammon me. And besides, you cannot make points on it, because, aha! I have the two of spades myself. So there!"

"You're a reg'lar Captain Sharp, A."

"What was that! What did you call me? You seem to have a sad lack of conduct or respect for your elders, young man. I see that I shall have to punish you. Take that!" and Harry's frantic giggles ensued, only to be cut short.

Both the very pregnant woman and the squirming child on the enormous bed were stopped, open-mouthed in surprise, at the sight of the visitors. For her part, Thea was equally astonished at the strong resemblance between her husband and his twin sister. Here were the same unruly brown curls and dark-fringed grey eyes, although Adriana's twinkled with a gaiety that Thea had never seen in her husband's eyes, and the smile on Adriana's lips was a far cry from Tate's frowns. So this is what he would look like under happier circumstances, Dorothea thought.

But these reflections were all swept away by Adriana's demand that Aggie bring the baby for her to hold, and by Harry's insistence that he be allowed to hold his new relation as well.

"Not just yet, Harry," Adriana admonished him gently. "First you must wash your hands, then sit quietly in a chair, and then maybe Aggie will permit you to hold her. See how tiny she is. She is very, very fragile and you must be very, very careful with her." She handed the baby back to Miss Whitesley and suggested to her ward, "For now, Harry, why don't you lead the way to the nursery and help Aggie and the senhora to settle down in there, while I make your Aunt Thea's acquaintance."

Harry bounded from the bed and skipped on ahead, chattering happily, "Aggie, do you think Martha would like to ride my pony? I can teach her to play ball . . ."

Aggie's response was lost, along with the rest of Harry's suggestions for Martha's entertainment, but the two ladies who remained behind exchanged knowing looks. "That is a very winning little boy," Dorothea remarked.

"In more ways than one," Adriana smiled wryly. "He's beginning to beat me at cards, a circumstance which I take in very bad grace."

She patted the bed and bade Thea sit down for a nice coze, while she regarded her closely. "From what Aggie told me, I know you have a heart of gold. And the color of your hair, why it is perfectly lovely, all that red-gold."

Unaccustomed to compliments of any kind, Dorothea flushed as she replied, "And you are so like Tate, it quite takes one's breath away. Of course, I knew you were twins, but I didn't expect . . . the same hair, and eyes, and yet you are so pretty, while he is so . . ." She blushed even deeper and averted her eyes from Adriana's searching look.

"Incorrigible?" Adriana prompted with a smile. "Impossible? Provoking? Or is 'handsome' the word you seek? He is certainly all of those things. Tell me, Thea, if I may call you that, is it true that you knew Tate but a few minutes before agreeing to become his wife?"

Dorothea nodded mutely.

"La, how romantical. When I first met Nick, all he

140

wanted me to become was a sort of nursemaid to Harry. And all he gave me in exchange for my services were lessons in Portuguese."

"Perhaps that was just his way of keeping you near him," Dorothea said. "That sounds romantical enough to me."

Adriana smiled enigmatically and changed the subject. "And how do you like Bancroft Hall?"

"It is lovely, but, well, there is something which has puzzled me ever since I arrived there," Thea said hesitantly.

"If you are going to tell me that you have discovered a delicious secret passage or horrid ruin in the garden, please spare me. I tried for years to find such things and would be crushed by your success where I failed."

"No, nothing like that. It's just that, well, Miss Grayson told me that your father spent his entire fortune on what she called 'unusual habits.' But Bancroft Hall shows no sign of penury. It is the epitome of elegance. Where did the money come from to make it so?"

"Oddly enough, from this horrible war," Adriana said with a twisted grin. "As Napoleon himself has pronounced, 'An army travels on its belly,' and one of my father's protégés developed a method of preserving foodstuffs in tinned cylinders for the soldiers. It is sobering to reflect that without this terrible conflict, our family fortunes would not have been recouped. But then, Tate would not have disappeared in Portugal, and I would not have met Nicholas, or Tate his Mathilde, or . . ."

Dorothea completed the sentence, ". . . and she

would not have died bearing Martha, and I would not be here."

"And now here we are, sisters. Well, it is not the first time that Tate has sprung an unknown lady on me as a sister, but I pray it is the last." Before Dorothea could reply, Adriana briskly asked if it was her first visit to the metropolis.

"Yes, I have lived only in the country until now, except for the last four years in Bath."

"Ah, yes, with dear Miss Grayson. You need tell me nothing about that old horror. I had a sufficiency of encounters with her myself as a girl to sympathize with your plight. To be doomed to live with her—why, I cannot conceive of such a miserable existence."

"It certainly was an education in human nature, at the very least. After Cousin Letitia, the rest of humanity is sheer amiability. Except possibly Senhora Seraphim."

Adriana's eyes widened. "I thought that I detected a bit of tension between the two of you. Tell me about it."

Dorothea, thrilled to have a sympathetic listener, unburdened herself thoroughly on the subject of the Portuguese governess and the problems she had brought to Bancroft Hall. By the time she reached the episode of the *"sopa* for *porcos,"* she felt that here was a sister indeed, and the two of them burst into gales of laughter, which left them with streaming eyes.

Impulsively Thea leaned over and gave Adriana a warm hug. "I know I shall love having you for my sister."

"And I you, Dorothea. I must confess that, fond as I was of Mathilde, I never felt that we had much in common. Her English was of the sketchiest, poor thing, and she never could appreciate my puns. I only hope that they do not stretch your tolerance to the extreme. The story of your drunken revels shared with the dog makes me feel that we are meant to be true sisters. I would dearly love to meet your pot-companion."

"Actually, that is easily achieved, Adriana. I took the liberty of bringing Lovelace with me. He rode all the way in the luggage cart with Annie, Martha's nurse and my abigail. I hoped he might be of use in diverting Harry. And Annie herself will be a lively companion."

"A stroke of utter genius. You must introduce Harry to Lovelace immediately. But first, we must send for my mantua-maker and order you some new clothes. Unless my eyes deceive me, that is an old one of Mathilde's and not at all becoming."

"But . . ." Thea began to protest.

"No buts, Dorothea. You must not object to my amusing myself by refurbishing you. I have precious little else to do in my present state, and I can hardly derive enjoyment from dressing myself these days." She ruefully indicated her swelling body and laughed. "A riding habit, a morning gown or two, and, of course, an evening *toilette*. Something subdued, for mourning, nothing to draw attention. But we must make haste in procuring the evening dress. Then you can come with me to Lady Flemming's musicale on Friday evening."

"But you said you were not to leave your sofa, Adriana. I won't have you risking complications on my account. Besides, with Mathilde's death only a few months past, I would feel most uncomfortable going out in society. Heaven knows I feel uncomfortable enough on any account."

"I suppose it is too soon to go into society as a general rule, but this is a special occasion. A concert to benefit a cause for which I have a special interest: widows and orphans of our soldiers. You see, I feel so helpless sitting here while Nick and Tate are out in the Peninsula risking their lives."

"Yes, I know what you mean, as I am such an orphan myself, though not, I pray, a widow. But what about the doctor's orders?"

"Oh, I shall sit quietly on a sofa in Lady Flemming's drawing room, I solemnly promise. And we shall go by chair to the very door. Dr. Collins shall never know."

"Very well, then, let us go. But I warn you, I shall be a quivering mass of nerves all evening."

"Yes, rather like sitting on a powderkeg, isn't it? But it is as nothing compared with what our husbands face every day."

Dorothea's face turned sober. "But just as dangerous, Adriana. Don't belittle the risk."

"But at least *we* are not likely to be guillotined as spies if we make a false move, though, frankly, I sometimes feel that way."

Dorothea was mystified by this speech, but before she could demand an explanation, Harry burst into the room and Adriana dispatched them to meet Lovelace.

Chapter 11

Harry chattered away to Thea as they went along to the mews where she hoped to find Lovelace.

"That new baby is so small and weak, she can't even sit up. I don't believe I was ever that small, no matter what Aggie and that awful Senhora Sera . . . Sera . . . I can't say her name, but she does not seem at all friendly to me. And I think she hates England, which seems a sort of traitor thing to do after all we are doing in her country. But she likes Cousin Nicklas and Uncle Tate, so she can't hate England all that much, I think."

Then he frowned in deep concentration. "Who is this Mr. Lovelace?" he whispered loudly.

"You shall know soon enough. He's a rather rough character, but a reliable friend. I think you two will like each other enormously."

It took a while to track the dog down, but they finally ran him to earth in the stables where the coach that had brought their luggage from Bancroft Hall was being unhitched.

Harry and Lovelace wasted no time in cementing their friendship. The dog leapt around until Harry found a stick for him to fetch and they both wore themselves out in the small park that was the centerpiece of Portman Square. When both dog and boy were panting from their exertions and a bowl of water had been procured for the former and a glass of lemon squash for the latter, Harry seated himself next to Thea on the wrought-iron settle while Lovelace stretched himself protectively at their feet.

"It looks to me as though you and Lovelace are already the best of friends," Thea ventured to observe.

"Oh, yes, he's a prime 'un. I don't have a dog at home. I had an old cat, but she died. I do have a pony named Harney. I fell off him when I tried to take a jump once and desiccated this bone, here,"—he indicated his collarbone, and Thea assumed that he meant "dislocated," since the article in question did not appear shriveled and sere.

"That was when Adriana's cousin, Adrian, was my tutor. Adriana's a trump, up to everything, but I rather miss Adrian. He's the one who taught me my letters and how to ride and send my heart over and not fear any raspers. But he left for the colonies years ago, when I was just a child. Adriana is all right, but since she has gotten so fat, she must just lie about in bed. Aggie says she is increasing, whatever that means, but Adriana says that she will soon have a baby. Will the baby be like Martha, do you think?" He turned his big blue eyes on Thea, who assured him that there was every possibility that Adriana's baby would be very much like Martha, only, of course, much smaller.

Harry scoffed at this notion. "I don't think anyone could be smaller than Martha." He paused for a moment, then looked at Thea speculatively. "Will you explain something to me?"

Thea felt her heart sink, fearing that Harry would inquire as to how a baby could have gotten into Adriana's belly or some such matter of curiosity that she felt ill-equipped to answer. But she put on a brave face and said, "Certainly, if I can. What do you wish to know?"

"What has become of Aunt Mathilde? Aggie has told me some whisker about the angels taking her up to heaven, but I know that there are no angels, because my Cousin Nicklas says so. I think that Adriana must know what has become of her, but Aggie made me promise, word of a Laidley, not to ask Adriana anything about it—I think it's because of this increasing business— and now you are my new aunt and married to my sort-of Uncle Tate and I just wonder what happened to Aunt Mathilde." Harry ran out of breath at the end of this very elaborate question and waited expectantly for an answer, while Thea searched for some way to explain the true nature of the situation to him.

"Well, Harry, do you remember when your cat died? What happened to her?" she asked.

"Oh, she just kind of went to sleep one night and never woke up. And there was an old stud that died, too, at the stables, the same way. Is that what happened to Aunt Mathilde?" Harry's eyes were wide with amazement.

"Almost, but not quite. You know that your Aunt Mathilde wasn't *very* old, like your dog or the horse, but sometimes people, and animals, too, get sick and no one can make them better, and it's just like when they get so old. They die. And the people who love them are very sad, because they will never see them again. I believe that that is why Aggie didn't want you to say anything to Adriana, because thinking of Mathilde would make her sad. And that is why the senhora is bad-tempered sometimes, too, because she loved your Aunt Mathilde more than any of us, except perhaps your Uncle Tate. He loved her very, very much."

"Oh," said Harry, quiet for a moment while he chewed over this morsel of information. "I daresay that is what happened to my mother. I think I remember someone telling me that she had died, but I don't remember her at all." His eyes lit up in sudden excitement. "That makes Martha a whole lot like me, doesn't it? Both our mothers are dead and neither of us can remember our real mothers."

"Perhaps you could appoint yourself Martha's guardian, Harry, and take care of her when you can."

"Just like my Cousin Nicklas did with me!" Harry exclaimed. "That's capital! You know, Aunt Thea, I really miss Cousin Nicklas and Uncle Tate, too. I wish that old Napoleon and all the French soldiers would just get out of the Peninsula soon so that they can both come home."

"So do I, Harry, so do I," Thea said disjointedly, giving him a hug.

Any further confidences were cut short by the sound of Miss Whitesley's voice calling from the house. With a start, Thea realized that it was nearly dusk and probably well past Harry's bedtime, and that she was starving. Harry shyly took her hand and led her back to the house, Lovelace gamboling on ahead. Aggie separated them at the door and sent Harry to his dinner and bed, Lovelace to the library and Thea to the dining room, where a cold meal awaited her.

In all, Thea reflected as she settled that night between clean starched sheets in the chamber which adjoined Adriana's, this may turn out to be the happiest time since my odd wedding. And she drifted off into peaceful, dreamless sleep.

As Dorothea had hoped, removing to London did blunt the conflict with Seraphim over Martha. What had been a personal crusade by Mathilde's friend against an interloping foreign *madrasta*, was transformed into a set of loose generational alliances, with Seraphim and Agatha Whitesley ranged against Dorothea and Adriana. These battle lines were blurred somewhat by the fact that Adriana spoke Portuguese, albeit rudimentarily, as a result of her lessons with Sir Nicholas. Senhora Seraphim was so pleased to find someone with some understanding of her language that she forgave much of Adriana's misguided notions on childrearing. Though disagreements still occurred with predictable regularity, they were resolved with a degree of amiability that would have been impossible for the new Lady Bancroft and the old Portuguese governess had they remained at Bancroft Hall.

With Adriana's enthusiastic support, for instance, Dorothea was allowed to take Martha with her with minimal opposition when she took Harry on many of their outings.

Harry delighted in showing his new friend his "special fav'rite" spots in the next few days. He had visited these sights on several occasions with Jem, the elderly coachman who adored Harry nearly as much as Harry idolized him. Chief among Harry's favorites was the Royal Menagerie, whose wild beasts held endless fascination for the boy, though Thea could see that the lion was a rather moth-eaten specimen, and the tiger was virtually toothless. For her part, Thea was so happy to be away from the tensions of her battle of wills with

Senhora Seraphim that she would have accompanied Harry almost anywhere.

Several times a day she visited Adriana's chamber and they talked and talked. Both were so starved for the friendship of a peer that they felt they could not talk enough. Adriana told Thea about her childhood escapades with Tate, and the father whom they loved dearly and the mother they never knew. If Adriana noticed the slight blush that rose to Thea's cheek each time Tate's name was mentioned, or the avidity with which she listened to tales of their misspent youth, she made no remark.

Thea recounted her own happy, if impoverished girlhood and described the parents whose love for each other was, in a sense, a passion fatal to them both.

Together they pored over a map of Portugal and, with the latest newspaper propped beside them on the bed, tried to calculate the possible whereabouts of both their husbands. Beyond this shared concern, they also discovered other common interests: both were avid novel readers and great admirers of the works of Miss Austen. Adriana would read aloud from that lady's entertaining volumes, while Mademoiselle Arlette, the mantua-maker, duly measured and fitted Thea for the gowns that her sister had ordered.

Thea found the experience of being poked with pins and told to hold still through it uncomfortable in the extreme, but the exclamations of delight at her form and face that issued from the French-named but Cockney-accented Arlette merely added to her discomfort.

By the day of Lady Flemming's musicale, Mademoiselle Arlette had turned out two morning dresses and a rust-colored riding habit as well as the simple evening gown for the event itself.

When Thea emerged from the skillful hands of Monsieur Louis, Adriana's coiffeur, late that afternoon and slipped into her new gown, she saw a virtual stranger in the looking glass.

The jonquil silk was cut in a very plain style, with the merest suggestion of a frill given by the pleating over the bosom, in the puff sleeves and around the hem of the gown. White satin slippers and kid gloves completed the picture.

But the real change went far beyond her attire. Her hair was like the polished copper of a new-minted penny, and piled high on her head with a spill of curls over one bare shoulder. The soft hazel eyes that had seemed so huge in the thin, pale face on her wedding day now glowed warmly with excitement, and the healthy color in her cheeks caused her to remark to Lovelace, who sat panting in the heat, "If I were given to self-aggrandizement, my friend, I might say that I look reasonably attractive tonight." In fact, she looked stunning, but she was not accustomed to rate herself so highly.

She hastened downstairs for a quick dinner with Adriana and found her sister in exceptionally good looks herself. Adriana's gown of half-mourning was of dove-grey silk, shot with silver thread. Mademoiselle Arlette had done a masterful job of disguising Adriana's advanced stage of pregnancy by designing the gown with folds gathered thickly under her swelling bosom, which softened the outline of what was beneath.

"Adriana, you look like a goddess of fertility, quite as striking as some of the statuary Harry and I saw at Lord Elgin's."

Adriana grinned. "But surely not so scandalously unclothed. Though you will meet some ladies of fashion tonight who *are*, or at least damp their muslin gowns to achieve that effect. In fact, you will be meeting many noted members of the *haut ton*, though, truth to tell, they are mostly noted for their folly and vapidity."

"Who will the performers be?"

"Ah, therein lies a tale. For the most part they are well-intentioned, well-connected, ill-trained amateurs. I do hope your ear is as wooden as mine, else you are like to suffer a thousand agonies."

"Then suffer I shall, for my one area of proficiency is music. Situated as we were, my mother could afford me no better entertainment or education than singing. Still, I am looking forward to it. It couldn't possibly be worse than some of the wobbly grande dames we used to hear in the upper rooms in Bath on concert nights."

"I can well imagine," Adriana said with a grimace. "But at least it provides me with an adequate excuse for escaping from my bedchamber for the evening. Do you realize that this is the first meal I have eaten at a table in over a month. But enough of this idle chatter, let us finish our meal and make our departure."

They made quick work of the delicacies that Sir Nicholas' French chef placed before them, and with Aggie's cautioning farewell ringing in their ears, made their way to the waiting sedan chairs that would take them to the evening's entertainment.

By the time the two emerged from their chairs and slowly climbed the marble stairs at Lady Flemming's townhouse, they were in a fever of excitement and nerves. When the stately butler announced to the assembled crowd inside the drawing room that Lady Laidley and Lady Bancroft were arrived, they were so

lost to propriety as to giggle at the dignified pro-
nouncement.

They managed to rein in their high spirits in time
to find seats toward the middle of the room before a
doughty matron encrusted with diamonds stood and
imperiously clapped her gloved and beringed hands
together for attention.

"Ladies and gentlemen, welcome to our benefit.
Tonight we are fortunate to have many exceptional
performers, and one in particular whom I am certain
will delight you. Someone so charming, so genteel, so
talented, with such a glorious voice, that you will be
enchanted, or perhaps I should say, *enchantés.*"

Dorothea felt a slight nudge in her side and saw
Adriana nod imperceptibly towards a stout dowager
preening herself at the side of the area cleared for the
piano.

Both were surprised when Lady Flemming, with a
slight curtsy and evident awe, announced, "Monsieur
le Comte Henri Philippe de Blanchard."

The singer who took up his position next to the
ornate pianoforte bore no resemblance to the overbear-
ing soprano they had expected. The Comte de Blanchard
was an extraordinarily good-looking young man of about
average height. With black curls done à la Brutus, and
blazing dark eyes, he appeared the very epitome of a
Byronic hero. The only flaw in this image was that Lord
Byron himself was notoriously casual when it came to
matters of fashion, whereas the Comte de Blanchard
gave every indication of a fastidiousness that stopped
just short of dandyism. All this was lost on Thea, whose
experience of the fashionable world was so limited. But
a trained eye would have detected the hand of the
fashionable men's clothier Mr. Stultz in the cut of the

single-breasted jacket of blue Bath superfine and the touch of a master valet in the intricate folds of the mathematical tie.

When the comte began to sing, he could have been wearing sackcloth and ashes for all that Thea was aware. He had a rich, well-schooled baritone which filled the large salon and thrilled the girl deeply. Not since the death of her father had she heard such a stirring voice, and, she was forced to admit, even his pleasing tenor could not hold a candle to the comte's deep voice.

In the middle of his second song, his black eyes met hers and he began to direct each verse, like a caress, directly to the embarrassed girl. Under his frankly admiring gaze, she felt a slow flush rise from her neck and across her cheeks. She looked away, only to find herself staring into the accusing eyes of Miss Letitia Grayson. Cousin Letitia is the very last person I expected to see in town, she thought in some agitation. What could possibly have brought her to London?

As her cousin's malicious gaze raked her up and down, noting, no doubt, the vast improvement in her face, figure and dress, then darted to the comte, a look of satisfaction came over the mean features, and Thea began to feel ill. During the next two songs Miss Grayson's piercing scrutiny alternated between the singer's handsome face and Dorothea's burning countenance.

When he had finished and accepted the ardent applause of the audience, the young Frenchman seated himself on the side in the first row, while the other members of the *ton* with pretensions to talent made their appearances on the stage.

Though Dorothea was relieved to be spared further embarrassment by the comte, she found his successors offered torture of another variety. There was a steady stream of bellowing sopranos and contraltos, schoolroom misses with no talent but five years of piano or harp lessons behind them, middle-aged macaronis with faint tenor bleats, and no sign of respite. And running a constant accompaniment through it all was the twittering of the debutantes in the seats in front of them, who giggled together while casting die-away looks from behind their fans at the handsome Frenchman.

To their growing dismay, he paid them absolutely no mind. Instead, he divided his attention between two objects. One was an imagined spot on his immaculate evening pump, which apparently gave him a great deal of pain whenever a performer hit a false note. The other was Dorothea, who sank lower and lower into her seat whenever she felt his soulful eyes upon her.

It was becoming very warm in the drawing room and Thea's embarrassment was gradually giving way to yawns, which she was hard put to stifle. As for Adriana, she had fallen completely asleep on her sofa. As an interminable aria done by an ancient tenor drew to its overdue ending, Thea sat up a little straighter in her chair and made a creditable attempt to keep her eyelids from shutting altogether.

The applause which followed the aging dandy's performance was more vigorous than that for the last several artistes, as it appeared that the musicale was at last drawing to a close.

Thea watched with a great sense of relief as Lady Flemming stood up, thinking that a valediction was most welcome. "Ladies and gentlemen, I wish to announce that the money you have donated this evening totals more than five thousand pounds and I wish to thank all of you for coming. I especially wish to extend my gratitude to all of our wonderful performers tonight. But before we finish, I would like to ask if there is any performer who has not had a chance to please us? I want everyone of talent to have an opportunity to participate."

Miss Letitia Grayson lumbered to her feet and a sigh ran round the crowd at the prospect of having to sit through yet another elderly soprano's warbles. Dorothea, frozen in horror, was under no such misapprehension.

"Lady Flemming, Lady Flemming. My young cousin, Lady Bancroft, sings delightfully, and is here with us tonight."

"Lady Bancroft?" Lady Flemming said with a frown. "But I thought she die . . . ."

"She did. This is her successor, my cousin Dorothea." With a sweeping gesture followed by every eye, Miss Grayson extended her hand toward Dorothea, who wanted to crawl beneath her chair.

"But how splendid! Do come up and sing, Lady Bancroft," Lady Flemming cooed.

Dorothea looked desperately around her for rescue. This simply could not be happening. Perhaps she had fallen asleep like Adriana, for this was the stuff of nightmares.

"Lady Bancroft?" again the hostess asked.

"B-but, I have nothing prepared! And no accompanist. Truly, you must excuse me."

"I'm sure that Cousin Dorothea would not wish everyone to think her ungenerous and selfish, that she refuses to sing for the sake of the widows and orphans," Miss Grayson said sweetly.

Stung by these malicious words, Dorothea stood

156

up. "Very well, but it shall be nothing grand. Only a ballad."

She stumbled toward the piano, and when she turned round to the sea of interested faces, she found herself addressed by the handsome Comte de Blanchard.

"Madame, if you would allow me, I should be enchanted to accompany you."

"But I haven't any music," she whispered, painfully aware that they were the cynosure of all eyes. "I am just going to sing 'The Turtle Dove.'"

"So sad a song for so lovely a young lady. Yes, I know it well enough to see you through." He bowed gracefully and sat down at the pianoforte and skillfully played an introduction.

Dorothea felt as if her mouth had turned to cotton and her knees to jelly, but a reproachful glance at the self-satisfied malevolent countenance of Miss Grayson was enough to infuse her with determination to sing her best. She fixed her eyes on an elaborate chandelier at the other end of the room, took a deep breath and sang.

Chapter 12

To Thea's immeasurable relief, she was in excellent voice and she was aware of a rustling sound as several hundred people leaned forward to listen. By the time she reached the final, haunting stanza, she found the courage to lower her gaze from the crystal and candles. To her astonishment she saw that many of the ladies were groping for handkerchiefs to wipe tears from their streaming eyes.

The applause was thunderous, and blushing deeply, she held out her hand to the gentleman at the instrument, to share the accolades with him. The comte, instead of merely bowing to the cheering audience, took her hand and put his lips to it.

Startled, she looked at him, only to look as quickly away when she saw that his eyes were riveted to hers.

"Thank you," she murmured to him, and began to return to her chair. Once again, however, he caught her hand and prevented her moving away. The applause continued, unabated, and he bade her curtsy to her admirers. Still holding her hand, he also took a bow.

Dorothea was at a loss as to what to do. She did

not wish to shake off his grasp in front of everyone, yet to stand hand in hand with a perfect stranger was surely not acceptable behavior, either. She was rescued from her quandary when the hostess came up to kiss each of them on the cheek. The comte promptly, if reluctantly, released her.

"My dear Lady Bancroft, we are all simply devastated. Such an appropriate song for the widows, too. Thank you so much. And now," she said, turning to the audience, "our musicale is ended. But unless I miss my guess, this beautiful young lady's musical career is just beginning." She led the applause once again, until the people started to rise, some to leave and others to pay their compliments to Dorothea and the other performers.

Before Dorothea could gracefully leave Lady Flemming and the comte, they were joined by Miss Grayson.

"So, here you are in town, Dorothea. What a surprise! I had thought you permanently fixed at Bancroft Hall, given the peculiar circumstances of your marriage."

At this statement, the comte cocked an inquisitive eye at the elderly spinster and seemed about to pursue the matter, but he quickly returned his gaze to the much more pleasing face of Lady Bancroft.

"What ecstasy to hear you sing!" he exclaimed. "Tell me, my lady, with whom do you study the voice?"

"Oh, I have never had any formal training," she demurred. "What little I know of singing, I learned from my mamma before she died."

Miss Grayson snorted audibly at the mention of Mrs. Sandham. "I have had a most intriguing letter from Cora Stevens, Dorothea," she observed acidly, barely suppressing a smile.

"And how is Clarissa, cousin?" Dorothea shot back.

"I do hope she suffered no lasting damage from her, er . . . escapade at Bancroft Hall?"

Miss Grayson's countenance suffused with color. "I hold you personally responsible for Clarissa's misfortunes, Dorothea. If you hadn't dallied in the garden with Sir Tate, my poor darling's virtue would be intact."

"Then I take it there is a blessed event in the offing? How lucky for you. I have always thought that with your lap, one lap dog was not nearly enough."

Lady Flemming and the comte followed this exchange with puzzled looks, obviously in the dark as to the identity of Clarissa. To bridge the uncomfortable silence that had fallen between the combatants, Lady Flemming said, "Ah, Letitia, I see that you have come with Sir William Frobisher. Dear Sir William, he's such a delightful creature. In fact, 'tis the *on dit* that you followed him all the way from Bath," she smirked knowingly. "The dear man has been so open-handed with our orphans and widows fund that I must go and thank him personally." She whirled and walked off.

Miss Grayson apparently was not about to let an attractive widow monopolize her sole suitor and she excused herself immediately to follow Lady Flemming. This left Dorothea *tête à tête* with the handsome young Frenchman, whose intent gaze had not left her face.

In seeming disbelief, he asked, "And are you in truth related to that lady?"

"Only distantly," replied Dorothea in a distracted manner. "Now, if you will excuse me, sir, I must rejoin my sister. She will be wondering where I have gone."

"Which is she?" He turned to survey the room through the quizzing glass that he wore on a ribbon round his neck.

"The lady in silver, on the sofa." Thea indicated

the couch where Adriana was now sitting in conversation with an unknown elderly gentleman.

"What is her name?"

"Lady Laidley," Thea answered curtly, anxious to remove herself from his overwhelming presence and make her departure.

"Ah, then she is the wife of the so dashing Sir Nicholas and your husband is the equally mysterious Sir Tate Bancroft." He flashed a brilliant smile in her direction, showing a perfect row of small, white, almost feline teeth. "I have heard," he leaned close to say in a low voice, "that both gentlemen have achieved near-miracles in the struggle to best the Corsican monster in the Peninsular campaign."

"Yes, now if you will . . ."

"And why are your husbands not with you this evening? Are they not worried that their so very beautiful wives will be surrounded by adoring lovers?" he said playfully, but his eyes looked oddly serious.

"They are not here just now, and in any case, neither of us is generally plagued by importunate admirers. Why, Adriana is so besotted with her Nicholas that she would not even notice an adoring lover if she stumbled over him," she said with a smile, moving toward Adriana's sofa.

"And you, madame?"

She looked at him, startled. "I? Why, I . . . I must join my sister on the instant. That she came at all was strictly against the orders of her medical man, and . . . oh, here she is now," she finished weakly as Adriana came up to her with a face wreathed in smiles.

"Dorothea," she said, with an affectionate kiss. "You have certainly kept your light under a bushel. I had no idea you could sing so beautifully. I had dozed

162

off for a moment or two, only to be awakened by your wonderful song. You do the Bancroft name proud, my dear. Music has never been our long suit. Why, in my own case, it isn't even in the pack."

She looked at Dorothea's companion curiously. "And you, sir, were head and shoulders above the rest of the shrieking herd to which we were subjected this evening. But for such a worthy cause, one must be prepared to make some sacrifice."

The comte made her a slight bow and flashed a charming smile. "I thank you for your kind words, my lady. Oddly enough, since I was forced to leave my estates behind in France, I find that the only valuable possession which remains to me is my voice. I am honored to have an opportunity to use it to help succor those who have also suffered at the hands of Bonaparte."

"An admirable sentiment, Monsieur le Comte, and an even more admirable performance. You . . ." She broke off suddenly and brought her hands to her waist.

"Adriana, are you ill?" Dorothea said, looking into her face with concern.

"I do believe, sister mine, that we should return to Portman Square as quickly as possible. I think, though I may be wrong, that a little baronet apparent is about to come into the world." She smiled, albeit nervously, but her fingers clenched the silk of her skirt convulsively.

"Oh, no, Adriana!" Thea exclaimed in alarm. "Our sedan chairs won't be returning for us for another half an hour at the least! I must get a message to Jem Coachman to come for us . . ."

She was interrupted by the comte. "That will not be necessary. My carriage can be at the door in a trice. I insist that you let me take you home."

"You are an angel, monsieur," Dorothea said impulsively, then turned to Adriana, whose countenance was drained of color. "Can you walk to the door, A.? Or shall we carry you?"

"That won't be . . . necessary," Adriana stammered through clenched teeth. "If I could but lean on an arm . . ."

The comte made a move. "You imbecile Englishwomen. Always so stubbornly independent." And without further ceremony, he swept Adriana up in his arms and strode through the crowd to the door, leaving Dorothea to trail behind with a string of murmured "suddenly taken ills" in her own wake.

To her great relief, when the odd threesome arrived at the bottom of the great marble staircase, the comte's carriage was without. The comte barked out directions to his coachman in French, then carefully lifted Adriana inside, helping her to lie down on one seat, and assisted Thea into the opposite seat. He himself mounted to the top of the carriage to sit with his coachman.

Inside the dark vehicle, Dorothea could not see Adriana, but she could hear her occasional gasps, which alarmed her exceedingly.

"Is there anything I can do to make you more comfortable, A.?" she asked nervously.

"Yes, my dear. Could you fix these deuced squabs so that they are behind my head properly?"

"I shall try." She groped around for the offending cushions and arranged them as best she could. As she did so, she was startled to hear Adriana catch her breath and begin what sounded like sobbing.

"There, there, A., don't you worry. You will come through your travail with flying colors and, sooner than you think, you will be the one walking the floor with your little squaller."

"Oh, oh, I'm not crying. I'm laughing. Here we are dashing through the night with an utter stranger, rearranging his squabs with abandon, and I haven't even been properly introduced."

"Nor have I. But he has certainly come to your rescue, and mine earlier in the evening, with inimitable aplomb."

"And with admirably broad shoulders to match. Well, if one must be saved from fates worse than death, it is not entirely undesirable that one is blessed with a handsome deliverer. And speaking of delivery . . ." She gave a little moan. "I think . . . you had better ask the handsome comte to hurry his horses."

Dorothea stood up in the swaying carriage and knocked on the roof as hard as she could, then called, "Make haste, monsieur. Make haste." She heard a shout from above, though the words were garbled, and the swaying became even more violent as her request was met.

To Thea it seemed an eternity before the carriage pulled up in front of the Laidley townhouse. Before the vehicle had come to a complete stop she leaped from it, stumbling slightly and tearing her gown on the handle of the door. Oblivious to this and to the comte's shouts in French, she ran up the stairs and pounded on the oaken door.

When Smithson opened the portal, she gasped out her message. "Send for the doctor immediately. Lady Laidley needs attention . . ."

But before she could elaborate on this breathless request, a cool Gallic voice spoke at her shoulder. "I shall go for the doctor, if you tell me his name and direction."

"Dr. Collins . . . in Harley Street." She turned to him in relief and gave him the number to seek there. "I can't thank you enough."

"Bah! This is not time for gratitude. Here, man, help me carry your mistress into the house," he said to the open-mouthed butler.

The two men gently lifted Adriana down from the carriage and, supporting her between them, carried her up the two flights of stairs and laid her gingerly on her own bed.

"Thank you, monsieur," Adriana sighed, then grimaced as she was enveloped in another pain.

"The doctor will be here directly, madame," he answered with a quick little bow and a glance at the watching Dorothea, and hastened away.

After he had gone, Thea stepped up to the bed and took Adriana's hand. "I shall go for Aggie, now. I'm sure she will be of more use to you than I." She brushed her lips on the pallid forehead and rushed off herself.

She found Aggie in her small room, which adjoined the nursery. The elderly woman was already dressed for bed and was seated in a rocker. She was looking over a volume of improving sermons, her eyeglasses perched precariously on her nose.

"Aggie, it's time, it's time!" was all Dorothea could say.

"Time for what, dearie? Martha has already been fed."

"It's Adriana. It's her time. Come quickly," she exclaimed, then raced back to the master bedroom.

When she reached the chamber where Adriana

166

lay, matters seemed to have taken a turn for the worse, at least to Thea's inexperienced eyes. Adriana was curled up in a ball of tension and her breath came in loud gasps.

"Dear A., can I *do* anything?" Thea wailed, frustrated at her helplessness.

"Just talk to me, Thea," panted Adriana. "I like to hear your voice and know you are here. I am so very glad . . . Oh!" she groaned, involuntarily. A few moments later, when the pain had apparently eased, she continued. "I am so very, very glad that I was able to meet you and 'be-sister' you before . . . this . . ." she stopped again. "And I want . . . want . . . you to promise me, promise . . ."

"Yes, oh, anything, A. What is it?" Thea cried.

"Promise me that if anything should happen to me, you will look after my baby. With Nick and Tate off to war . . . my baby might need you more than we know. And Harry too."

"Of course. I should gladly mother any child of yours, and Harry as well. But I'm sure that will not be necessary. Nothing is going to happen. Ah, good, here is Aggie."

The woman who bustled into the room bore scant resemblance to the Agatha Whitesley they knew. Over her white nightgown she had thrown a dressing gown of the most flamboyant variety—scarlet silk embroidered with a huge purple and gold dragon. Her eyeglasses were askew on her nose, and her hair, unbound, fell to her waist in wild disarray. Even her voice, when she spoke, sounded girlish and piping in her extreme excitement.

"Dorothea, we must get these clothes off her before the doctor arrives. Whatever were you thinking of,

Adriana, going out gallivanting tonight of all nights," she scolded, as the two women began unfastening the numerous hooks at the back of the silver gown. Adriana remained firmly coiled in a ball, which did not simplify their task.

"I hardly planned that my evening of frivolity would end like this, Aggie," Adriana retorted. "And speaking of frivolity, wherever did you get that dressing gown. I am overwhelmed." She directed a speaking glance at Thea.

Aggie bristled. "My brother bought it on one of his Eastern voyages. I only wear it because it is so comfortable. Now, missy, you must stop making game of my attire and try to rest."

"At a time like this?" Adriana laughed weakly. "Now it is you who are jesting." The smile evaporated as another contraction seized her.

The sharp knock on the door that indicated the arrival of the doctor sent Thea hurrying across the room to admit him. As the first person he encountered, she bore the brunt of his displeasure.

"What's this I hear from that young Frenchman," he glowered at her. "Have you two ladies been disobeying my *very strict* orders that Lady Laidley remain in her bed?" He looked about at the evidence of their night of revelry, Adriana's hastily discarded ball gown, Thea's torn, but elegant, silk, and shook his head. "I had expected sterner discipline from you, Miss Whitesley. You seemed a woman of great character, and yet you allowed this ill-judged lark." His voice trailed off as he took in Aggie's resplendent dragons.

Over the governess' outraged protestations, he once more turned his stern gaze on Thea. "I suppose this is all *your* fault, young lady. There were no such carryings on in the past, until you arrived."

Adriana interrupted the doctor with a defense of Thea, but was herself interrupted by another contraction. Aggie took up the cudgels in Dorothea's defense.

"None of this is the girl's fault, Dr. Collins. Adriana would have gone tonight in any case; I don't think any of us could have stopped her, short of physical restraint. Thea is to be thanked for getting her home so promptly."

The physician merely harrumphed and muttered imprecations about the folly of women, but removed himself to Adriana's side to begin his examination. In surprisingly gentle and low tones he asked about the timing of the contractions and then glanced over to Thea, who was still clinging to the doorknob for support.

"Well, young lady, I think you should leave us now," he suggested in a brusque, but not unkind, fashion. "Perhaps you could thank that Frenchie for the service he rendered Adriana this evening. I never could abide the French myself, but it was providential that he was nearby tonight."

Dorothea left Adriana's bedchamber and descended the staircase, wondering what the next few hours would bring to her sister. Lost in her own anxious thoughts, she had nearly forgotten the young Frenchman was waiting for her. Thus, the sound of footsteps coming from the hallway below startled her a little, and she peered down.

In the foyer, the Comte de Blanchard was pacing back and forth, in an unconscious parody of an expectant father. From his hand dangled his quizzing glass on its red silk ribbon, and he nervously twirled it as he walked.

She went up behind him as he made his turn by the large clock. "Monsieur le Comte," she said quietly.

At her words he started slightly, but he quickly recovered his elegant composure and made her a graceful leg.

"My lady, may I inquire how your sister is faring?"

"As well as might be expected, I suppose," she replied vaguely.

"My carriage is outside the door at the ready should it be needed."

"Thank you, sir. You are all generosity, but, though I know little of these things, I deem it highly unlikely that a horse and carriage will be of much use."

"No, I suppose not," he replied with his dazzling smile.

"May I offer you some brandy, sir? Truth to tell, I could do with a little myself, after the trials of this evening."

He smiled at her conspiratorially. "But, of course," he said, and followed her into the small drawing room, where she rang for Smithson.

When the brandy and glasses had been brought to them and Dorothea had poured out two glasses, the comte lifted his.

"To the two most beautiful ladies in London."

"I should think, Comte, that out of common politeness, you might also drink to Adriana and me, and not two beauties with whom we are unacquainted."

"My lady, you do me a grave injustice. It was, naturally, of you and your brave sister that I spoke."

"Hmm, I have always heard that you Frenchmen are gallant, but this surpasses all my expectations," she laughed, only to stop abruptly as the door began to swing open.

170

"Aggie, what is it? How is Adriana? Has anything happened?" she called, but there was no answer.

Puzzled, she crossed the room to admit the new arrival. It was a very forlorn Lovelace who stood outside, regarding her with seeming reproach for taking another as a tippling partner. He entered the room at her heels and when she sat down across from the comte, the dog attached himself to her knee.

"But what is this fellow doing in the house?" asked the comte, eyeing the disreputable creature with alarm. As though in response to this disparaging remark, Lovelace bared his teeth and a growl could be heard deep back in his throat. The comte recoiled slightly and Adriana laid an admonishing hand on Lovelace's head. It was odd for the dog to do such a thing, for he was generally the most friendly of animals. At her touch the growling subsided.

"This, Monsieur le Comte, is my lap dog, Lovelace."

"Ah, you English must have your little jokes on us poor *émigrés*. Always someone is pooling my leg."

Thea choked on her brandy. "Pooling your . . . ? Ah, I see, you mean *pulling* your leg."

She looked up at him impishly, but met only a blank, uncomprehending smile. Lovelace, ignored, wandered disconsolately away.

At the sound of rapid human footsteps approaching the door, Thea froze, and rose to her feet. Her smile vanished, and without thinking, she gripped the comte's arm in apprehension. However, the footsteps went right past the room and on down the corridor.

She released the gentleman's arm and moved to the satinwood table where the decanters stood.

"I cannot bear this suspense," she said brokenly. "Adriana is my only real family, except for little Mar-

171

tha, and I am so terrified lest she die, like my mamma, and hers, and Martha's."

Much to her own embarrassment, she burst into tears, and before she could fumble in her reticule for a handkerchief, she found herself in the comte's arms, his Bath superfine making a rough pillow for her wet cheek.

"There, there, *ma petite*, don't cry, it will be finished soon."

"Th-that's what I'm afraid of," she hiccoughed. A fresh paroxysm of weeping quite overcame her, and instinctively she burrowed her face in his shoulder. He stroked her gently and whispered incomprehensible words of comfort into her tangled hair.

Once again, the sound of footsteps came to them, and Thea, realizing the singularity of her position, moved out of his embrace.

Dashing away her tears as best she could, she looked up at him apologetically. "You must forgive me, monsieur. I quite forgot myself for a moment."

"Think nothing of it, my lady." The comte smoothed out the wrinkles in his fashionable coat with a worried look. "It was my pleasure to be of help. It is not every day that I am permitted to aid a damsel in distress."

"Don't you mean a matron in misfortune?" she said with a watery smile, then she jumped as a knock came on the door.

It was Agatha Whitesley herself, who wore a stunned expression which caused Thea's heart to sink.

"Aggie, what's happened?"

"You'll never guess. I suppose I should have expected it, but . . ."

Dorothea took the woman by the shoulders and gave her a gentle shake. "You must tell me. Is it a boy? Is Adriana all right?"

"Yes, to both questions. Adriana is resting comfortably, and so is her son, and so is her daughter," Aggie finished triumphantly.

"Son . . . and daughter. Twins?"

"Twins. And the doctor never suspected a thing. He is quite mortified. Exactly what happened to Adriana's mamma before her. It quite takes me back, seeing the two little mites in the one cradle. So like Adriana and Tate. I must go tell Seraphim the good news," Aggie said, and turned to go.

After the dragon on Aggie's back disappeared from view, the comte turned to Dorothea.

"I can see I am *de trop* at this joyful moment. Please convey my congratulations to your sister. May I call again to inquire after her health, and yours?"

"Indeed you may, monsieur. And next time, I hope that your call is under more serene circumstances. I must apologize for subjecting you to our family crises."

"To do anything in your service is my greatest pleasure. *Au revoir*, my lady." As he had done at the musicale, which seemed days and days earlier, he took her hand, now ungloved, and pressed his lips to her wrist.

"*Au revoir*," she echoed faintly and watched, dazedly, as he walked from the room.

Chapter 13

The faint sound of infant squalling drew Dorothea out of her distracted state and up the stairs to the nursery. There she found Miss Whitesley and Senhora Seraphim, both with their arms full of the tiniest babies Thea had ever seen. The two women were bathing the twins, who were still suffering from the shock of birth and crying lustily, while Harry looked on, wide-eyed in astonishment. Martha was adding her gurgles to the general uproar, while Lovelace, mercifully, was nowhere to be seen.

Dorothea picked up her stepdaughter, who seemed huge by comparison to the newborns, and carried her over to be properly introduced to her cousins. Martha drooled her appreciation and stretched out her hand, as though in greeting, but was otherwise unmoved by the magnitude of the event.

The little boy looked so forlorn in the midst of all this commotion that Thea invited him along to her chamber. "Come, Harry, I'll tell you a story while I feed Martha. It's a good tale, one that only big boys can understand, not these puny babies."

Harry's face lit up with pleasure that someone still

took on interest in him in the midst of all this "infantry" and followed her docilely into the adjoining room. There she seated him in the rocking chair, allowing him to hold Martha and give her the bottle himself, which delighted him almost as much as the exciting story she spun for him.

When both children were tucked up for the night, she looked in on Adriana but found her sound asleep. As Thea stood by the canopied bed, looking down at her new sister, she felt a great rush of affection, and kissed her gently on the cheek before leaving.

The almost overwhelming fondness that she felt for Adriana still bathed her in a rosy glow as she walked down the hall toward her own chamber. Just before she reached her room, Smithson the butler approached carrying a white envelope in his hand.

"Pardon me, my lady, but this arrived for you while you were out this evening, and with all the excitement, I quite forgot to give it to you. It was brought from Bancroft Hall by the footboy, who was sent there for some fresh fruit from the succession houses. I believe it is from the master."

He gave her a sealed letter, which had the dog-eared appearance of having come a long distance. She carried it into her room, nearly tripping over Lovelace, who was stretched across her threshold. With shaking hands she broke the distinctive seal and by the flickering light of her guttering candle she perused the curt message.

"20 June, 1813

Dear Madam," Tate wrote,
"I received your letter of 29 May only yesterday and am replying in haste to correct

your apparent misunderstanding of your position. Surely I made it clear that the only reason I married you was to avoid the burden of the child's upbringing and not to play referee between the warring factions in my household.

God knows, I have enough to worry about here without your petty grousing. Senhora Seraphim always seemed a level-headed, responsible woman to me, which, it appears, is more than can be said for you. It is unfortunate that she did not arrive a few weeks earlier, and we might have been spared this inconvenient marriage of convenience.

As it is, you must seek to accommodate her as best you can. I shall not be returning to England until after the new year, if at all. Meanwhile, please do not send me any more hysterical complaints.

Tate Bancroft"

Dorothea's first impulse was to tear the paper into shreds. The man was totally devoid of feeling! Could he not see the impossibility of her situation? Though as she read and reread the offensive words, she was forced to admit that since coming to London the Seraphim situation had undergone a considerable metamorphosis. This was of little comfort, given her husband's heartless disregard for his own daughter and heartfelt regret at having remarried.

The letter fell to the floor while her anger and mortification mounted. "Well," she muttered to Lovelace. "I shall show him. I shall see that he eats his cruel words, if it's the last thing I do! 'Inconvenient marriage of convenience,' indeed! 'More than can be said for you'! Just who does he think he is?" Lovelace's floppy tail beat a slow tattoo on the polished floor, but he provided no answers to her question.

She flung off her clothes and splashed cool water on her face, but still her brain raced feverishly, plotting unlikely schemes of revenge against her absent husband, and taking Lovelace deep into her confidence.

Just before she finally fell asleep, however, she resolved not to worry Adriana with the knowledge of just how precariously things stood between Tate and herself.

"Adriana will have her hands full, as it is," she yawned. The dog's only reply was a contented sigh as he stretched himself out full length on her rug.

The next morning, Dorothea slept late, only rousing from her deep slumber when Harry burst into her room and jumped on her bed.

"Aunt Thea, Aunt Thea, there's a stranger here, he talks so funny, and Lovelace bit him on the ankle," he said gleefully.

"What? Oh, no! Who is it, Harry?"

"I don't know. Smithson kept telling him to count, as if that would keep Lovelace away. But old Lovelace didn't care a rap if he counted or not, he just sank in his teeth and . . ."

"Count? Oh, Harry, this is terrible. Is he a foreign gentleman, with black hair?"

"Yes, ma'am."

"You go tell him that I will be right down. And put Lovelace in the mews."

Harry's face fell. "Very well, Aunt Thea, but it was jolly to see! I didn't like this man at all—he kept patting

178

my head and calling me his little cabbage. Ugh! *Cabbage!*" He raced away.

Dorothea threw on her clothes, the old muslin gown of Mathilde's that she had brought from Bancroft Hall, and the slippers that she had worn to last night's ball. She ran a comb through her hair, and feeling rather like something Lovelace had dragged in, went downstairs, dreading what she might find below.

To her surprise, the drawing room was empty, but a considerable noise issuing from the kitchen led her to the correct place. There, seated on a wooden kitchen stool, one ankle and foot stripped bare and soaking in hot water, was the French gentleman of the previous evening. One leg of his yellow pantaloons was rolled up to his knee and a pump of shiny japanned leather lay next to the clocked stocking on the flagstone floor. He was nearly surrounded by a gaggle of servants, all offering medical advice.

As she entered the room, he made a feeble attempt to rise, but she motioned him down and waved away the servants.

"Oh, my dear Comte, I am so sorry that this has happened. I can't think what could have gotten into Lovelace. In general he is so well-behaved!"

"In France an animal so vicious would be destroyed. But I did not come here to talk of that creature. I came only to see my favorite contralto and to ask after her sister." Somehow, such gallantry, coming from someone in such a prosaic position, struck Dorothea as faintly absurd and she smiled.

"Ah, Lady Bancroft, when you look so enchantingly at me you quite take my breath away."

"I hope that will not be the case, Comte. My dog has already nearly taken away your ankle."

She watched him lift his foot from the water and handed him a towel. "It appears that you shall live, monsieur, though I think I should sprinkle the wound with basilicum and wrap it up well."

"You are too kind, madame."

"Not at all, it is the very least I could do. Now, this may sting a little," she said firmly, applying the basilicum powder.

"The only injury you could do me is to my heart, my lady. And you have dealt me a mortal wound."

"I beg you, sir, do not lay any further damages at my door. I am already mortified by what you have suffered at Lovelace's hands . . . or rather, jaws," she replied, marveling once again. Gallantries oozed from the man as easily as the blood oozed from his punctured ankle. It was flattering but slightly ludicrous.

"There, that should do. Now, shall we go to the drawing room and have some coffee?"

"If you could give me your hand, I would find it much easier," he said with another of his brilliant smiles.

"All right." She picked up his shoe and stocking and watched while he stood and tried to straighten his rumpled clothing. From the harassed expression on his face she judged that the rents and wrinkles in his clothing pained him more than the hole in his ankle. He slipped the strap of his pantaloon under his bandaged foot and turned his melting gaze once more on Thea.

She offered him her hand, but instead he draped his arm around her shoulder, and they started out the door. She gave a little shrug instinctively, then reminded herself that the man was truly injured and needed her help. Still, it felt all too much like an embrace for her comfort.

Dorothea seated herself on a brocade sofa in the

drawing room and the comte sat down beside her, while coffee was served to them. When the servant had gone, she turned to offer yet another apology, at which the comte gave a very Gallic shrug.

"*Mais, ce n'est rien*, madame. It is nothing."

"But how can I possibly make amends for this attack, monsieur? At least allow me to buy you some new stockings to replace the ruined pair."

"No, no, I have a much better idea," he said, leaning toward her and looking deeply into her eyes.

For one insane moment, Dorothea sat transfixed, immobilized by the sudden conviction that he was about to claim a kiss as a forfeit.

"Yes, a much, much better idea," he murmured, his lips close to her own. "I shall claim the privilege of giving you singing lessons."

Dorothea's mouth fell open. "You want to give me . . . singing lessons? But I fail to see how that will repay what I owe. It will but sink me further in your debt!"

"Not at all. It would give me immeasurable pleasure to school you . . . in the voice. I myself was fortunate enough to study with the very best teachers in France, and now nothing would please me more than sharing my knowledge with you."

"You have chosen your temptation wisely, monsieur," she said softly, "and I fear I haven't the strength to resist you. Singing has long been my only passion."

"Your only passion?" he inquired.

"Until my marriage, of course," she continued hastily. "Now, of course, I have my stepdaughter to occupy my heart."

"I see, yes, your stepdaughter. And the little boy? He is your *beau-fils*, your stepson?"

181

"Harry?" she smiled fondly. "Why, no, he is Sir Nicholas' ward."

"I am relieved," the comte said with a distinct sigh. "I would hate to think of you forever at *his* tender mercies. The child actually laughed during your dog's attack to my leg. *Laughed!*" He winced in pain, but whether it was his leg or his legwear that grieved him, it would have been hard to say, she thought.

Thea once again apologized for her friends. "Yes, both Harry and Lovelace are rather high-spirited. But Harry does have a reasonable excuse, though it may not seem so to you. You see, with the birth of the twins he has been replaced as his guardian's heir and, what is much worse for him at present, lost his status as the only child in the household. It is not easy for him."

"We shall forget about the naughty boy and the ill-mannered dog for the moment and talk of ourselves." The comte turned the full blaze of his considerable charm upon her. "When may we start the lessons?"

A vision of Tate briefly crossed her mind, but she sternly reminded herself that he could not care less about what she chose to do, and returned the comte's smile with special warmth.

"Very well, if you are certain that is what you wish, let us begin tomorrow." She rose from her seat. "Now, if you will excuse me, Monsieur le Comte, I must go to my sister. I shall see you tomorrow, then?"

"But, of course, *certainement*. Shall we say eleven o'clock?"

"That will be fine."

"*Au revoir, mon petit chou*, my little cabbage."

She paused on her way to the door and wrinkled her nose. "If you please, monsieur, neither Harry nor I has any wish to be your little cabbage."

He grinned, showing his perfect white teeth. "I shall try to remember, *ma belle.*" He bowed, but when he saw that he still held his stocking in his hand, he swiftly straightened up.

His chagrined expression as he quickly stuck the stocking behind him made her laugh and as she mounted to Adriana's chamber a smile still lurked around her mouth. She found her sister sitting up and eating a remarkably hearty breakfast.

"Good morning, Adriana," she said, bending over to kiss her warmly on the cheek. "You have two of the most perfect babies I have ever seen, second and third only to Martha Charlotte Bancroft."

"Which is second and which is third?" Adriana asked mischievously between bites of toast.

Thea considered carefully. "As I have a weakness for Bancroft females, I will place your daughter first, though frankly, I cannot tell them apart when they are clothed," Thea answered, taking a seat on the bed.

"And what of Bancroft men?" demanded Adriana in a teasing voice. And at Thea's slight blush of confusion, she continued playfully, "Of course, he *is* officially a Laidley, which puts a whole other complexion on the matter, in more ways than one. Oh, Thea, you don't know how lovely it is to be able to eat from a breakfast tray without one's middle getting in the way."

"And how lovely it is to see you looking so fit and happy, A." Thea reached out and clasped Adriana's hand in her own.

"You certainly were a slugabed this morning. I myself have been up for simply hours. You should have seen me earlier—trying to breastfeed two babies at once! I felt like nothing so much as an Alderney cow, but I loved it all the same."

183

"You'll never guess who has been to call already this morning, A.," she said.

"The stork?"

"In a way, yes. It was he who delivered you home last night, so that you might deliver here."

"Ah, yes, the handsome young Frenchman, de Blanchard. I am indebted to him."

"I, too. He made my ordeal at the musicale much easier."

Adriana looked troubled. "But how odd that he should come to call, Thea. Do you think he has developed a *tendre* for you?"

"I shouldn't think so, although I suspect he is very adept at the art of dalliance. He just can't help flirting any more than he can help breathing. After all, he *is* French."

"Yes," Adriana said in a considering tone. "I wonder what his reason is for coming to England."

"He said that he has lost all his estates and seems most intent on our besting Bonaparte. Although he does seem elegantly dressed for someone who is living a hand-to-mouth existence. And it certainly costs a pretty penny to keep a coach like his in the metropolis. I have never known anyone so concerned for appearances, particularly his own, as the comte."

"You have never met any of our Pinks of the ton, Thea. No, what troubles me is that here is an able-bodied man enjoying the sybaritic pleasures of London society when he might be of more use on the battlefield. Why should our husbands be risking their lives so that he might regain his wealth, while he himself is safe at Almack's? Or," she added with a grin, "as safe as any eligible bachelor *can* be in the Marriage Mart."

Thea shyly came to the comte's defense. "Perhaps

he fears to lose his head to Madame Guillotine should he be caught on French soil."

"Tate and Nick face the same fate every day, my dear," Adriana chided her gently. "I cannot feel it right that the comte is in England, safe from harm, while they do his fighting for him. However," she shrugged, a twinkle replacing the grave expression in the grey eyes, "I cannot quite imagine our fastidious Frenchman in the middle of a muddy battlefield. He would be so taken up with keeping the dirt from his coat that he would be a sitting duck for Boney's men."

"I'm afraid Lovelace has already taken exception to the comte's mode of dress," Thea smiled. "With his head in danger in France and his leg under attack in England, it's a wonder he doesn't flee to the colonies. Even with its Red Indians, Canada might seem peaceful by comparison."

Adriana, intrigued, demanded to be told the whole story, and her sister willingly obliged. At the end of the tale, both were wiping tears of mirth from their eyes.

"I shall never be able to see the Comte de Blanchard without thinking of Smithson urging him to 'count, count,'" Adriana chuckled. "He must think Harry a most repulsive brat for laughing, but I fear I might have done the same had I been there." The two went off once more into gales of laughter.

"Ah, well," Adriana continued, "the comte *is* charming, and has proved to be most helpful. When I consider that if he had not been at Lady Flemming's last evening, I might have been confined on her sofa in front of a hundred members of the *haut ton*, I shall not question his presence here any further."

"I am glad of that, A.," Thea said with a slight air

of apology, "for the comte has offered to give me lessons in singing. I hope you have no objection."

Adriana peered at her closely, then shrugged. "No, of course not, though it puts us even deeper in his debt. I could almost wish that we did not already owe him so much, for he has the makings of a great figure of fun."

Thea was about to come to the comte's defense once more, but saw the lines of fatigue in Adriana's face. "Now you must get some rest, A. I shall go and fetch Harry for a walk. Poor fellow, he is feeling rather left out of things here."

"I am most grateful to you, too, Thea, for your attentions to the lad. I am rather preoccupied, as you might guess, and for the present, still tied to my bed."

". . . and this time you shall remain so. I don't know about you, but I have no desire to be raked down again by Dr. Collins for disobeying his orders. I'm still quaking from the last trimming he gave me. Though I think he is himself still in shock from seeing Aggie in her oriental splendor." Dorothea laughed and started for the nursery in order to have another glimpse of the new arrivals and their cousin before collecting Harry.

Chapter 14

De Blanchard turned out to be as talented a teacher as he was a performer. Dorothea found the singing lessons with the French count to be enormously stimulating and satisfying, and with her new routine of lessons and practice, coupled with her duties and pleasures as a mother and sister, her days flew by.

Adriana, once she was liberated from her bedchamber by Dr. Collins, enjoyed looking on during the daily lessons.

"The comte's flowery speeches are nearly as entertaining as a play," she said to Dorothea one morning while the two waited for the gentleman to arrive. "And, of course, the singing elevates the drama into opera, giving it an added fillip, as it were."

"I'm glad that you enjoy it, A. It is not often that a rank amateur like me can be considered of operatic caliber."

Adriana chuckled, "The comte certainly seems to relish playing his role as musical *beau ideal*."

"Ah, but you are out there. He is a baritone, not a tenor. Baritones are always the villains of the piece, and he is far too charming for that. Why, he lacks the slightest hint of a menacing scowl or humped back."

"Shh, here he is now," Adriana hissed.

The Comte de Blanchard strode into the drawing room. He does look like the hero making an entrance on the operatic stage, Dorothea thought with amusement.

"My compliments, this wonderful morning, Lady Bancroft, Lady Laidley. I am ever amazed at how lovely you both look at so early an hour."

"You amaze us as well, Comte," murmured Dorothea, glancing sidelong at her sister. "Shall we begin?" She took out her music.

Just then the door flew open and Senhora Seraphim bustled into the room looking very excited. She was so overset that she made no effort to express herself in English. Instead, she addressed Adriana in her own tongue, flailing her hands for emphasis.

Her news must have been something out of the ordinary, for as Adriana replied in her halting Portuguese, she appeared to catch the woman's agitation.

Dorothea moved toward the comte with the intention of apologizing for the interruption, but was checked by the odd expression she discerned on his face. It was a look of deep concentration.

"Do *you* speak Portuguese, Comte?" she asked in some surprise.

"That provincial tongue? Don't be absurd," he said, shaking his head.

Even so, she noticed that once again he appeared to be listening intently to the incomprehensible torrent.

Seraphim finished her impassioned recitation and fluttered away, and Dorothea could contain her curiosity no longer.

"What on earth is going on, Adriana?" she demanded.

Adriana turned with a look of elation on her face. "Wellington has won a great battle. Seraphim heard about it while she was out walking the babies. Word just arrived from the Peninsula and everyone is talking about it."

"Where and when was the battle?" Dorothea asked.

"At Vitória, in Spain, on June 21. They are saying that it means the end of Napoleon's puppet monarchy there. King Joseph, his brother, has decamped," Adriana said triumphantly.

"Does that mean the Peninsular war is ended?" Dorothea inquired anxiously, with the swift realization that this might signal her husband's return.

"Oh, I do hope so," Adriana sang. "Vitória—Victory—the very name sounds hopeful, doesn't it, Comte?"

"One victory does not win a war," de Blanchard said with a slight shrug.

Adriana, nothing daunted, upbraided him for being so pessimistic. Then she was struck by another thought. "Why, June 21 was the date my babies were born, as you, of all people, should remember. I feel sure that is a good omen. I know, I shall give little Mathilde the middle name Vitória in honor of the momentous occasion on her birthdate. What do you think, Thea?"

"I think it is a lovely combination—Mathilde Vitória. I'm sure that Nicholas will be pleased."

A look of worry shadowed Adriana's face. "Oh, I wonder if Nicholas was there, at Vitória. And Tate. What if they were wounded? But then," she assured herself, "their particular duties usually lie far from the thick of the battle."

Uneasy at Adriana's indiscreet references to Tate

189

and Nicholas' secret activities, Dorothea suggested to the comte that they continue with the singing lesson.

He agreed and they returned their attention, or most of it, to the music. Adriana, for her part, solaced her own fears by repairing to the nursery and telling her children the excellent news.

In the days that followed, Thea tried to concentrate as before on her singing, but could not quite dismiss her anxiety over her husband. Still, she could perceive a gradual improvement in her voice. Indeed it was this which attached her to her teacher rather than his endless compliments, which, in truth, rather wearied her.

The only real problem they encountered in the daily sessons was Dorothea's tendency to grow tense every time he touched her, which he did often, especially when Adriana was not in attendance. At first she had demurred at his touch, but he had coolly informed her that the relationship between singing teacher and student was like that between a doctor and his patient.

"There must be no constraint between us, my lady, in these matters. Singing is, after all, dependent on anatomy, and it is only natural that from time to time, I must point out where the tension lies, for the sake of your art."

One afternoon, about three weeks after the lessons had begun, Dorothea was practicing taking deep breaths, while the comte stood behind her with his hands under her bosom, to determine if she was using her diaphragm properly.

"Een, out, een, out, yes, that seems to be correct. My felicitations, madame, on a great improvement," said de Blanchard.

Dorothea, totally engrossed in breathing as he directed, failed to see the drawing room door open.

"Exactly *what* is going on here?" someone said in a deadly tone, and Dorothea, whirling, saw that it was Sir Tate Bancroft. She had no trouble in recognizing this disheveled and wild-eyed gentleman as her husband, for he looked very much as he had on their wedding day three months earlier. His hair, badly in need of a trim, was in disarray; his cloak was flung casually over one shoulder; his buckskins and boots were sadly mud-spattered. In short, he could not have provided a more striking contrast to the elegantly clothed and coiffed comte.

At the expression in Tate's grey eyes, she wished to sink through the floor. That he should find her in such a compromising situation! She hastily removed herself from the comte's arms.

"Why, Sir Tate! I did not expect to see you here!"

"Apparently not."

"Oh, this," she waved vaguely at the comte. "This is not at all what you might think. This gentleman was but giving me a lesson in singing."

"An extremely odd singing master. I should say he looks more like a damned caper merchant." Tate's mocking gaze raked the comte from his pomaded locks to his glossy Hessians.

The comte stiffened. "I have called men out for less than that, Sir Tate."

Tate stared at him. "Called out? Of all the impertinence! Really, Dorothea, you promised me your discretion and you plunge me into a duel with a singing teacher? How very droll." He laughed mirthlessly and moved a step closer to the comte. "And as for you, my fine-feathered songster . . ."

"Tate, you're back! Thank heaven you are safe!" Adriana opportunely interrupted from the doorway, then flung herself into his arms.

"A., you look wonderful! And much more like my skinny twin than you were when I left." He held her away from him at arm's length for a moment, as though feasting his eyes, then hugged her to him once more. The resemblance between the two was particularly striking now that Adriana had lost the plumpness of pregnancy. Thea had never seen her stranger of a husband so relaxed and happy.

Adriana broke free and sparkled up at her brother. "You'll never guess, Tate, I have had twins! Aggie is in her element."

"Ah, A., I'm so happy for you and Nick. Does he know?"

"I wrote to him directly, but, of course, I've not heard anything." There was a brief moment of silence. Neither dared to mention where Sir Nicholas Laidley might be when news of his wife's delivery reached him. Suddenly remembering that they were not alone, Adriana exclaimed, "And have you met the comte? He has rendered invaluable service to me, and to your wife. Monsieur le Comte Henri Philippe de Blanchard, my dear brother, Sir Tate Bancroft."

Under any other circumstances, Thea would have found the astounded expression on her husband's face most amusing, but somehow, she could see little humor in it now.

"Service?" Tate faltered.

"Yes. 'Twas he who saw me safely home the night I was brought to bed, and now he has been teaching Thea to develop her voice. She has a perfectly lovely voice, in case you didn't know it."

192

"Yes, I have heard her sing," he said, flashing Thea a look which brought back the memory of her unfortunate experiment with Mathilde's guitar.

"Well, it seems I owe you an apology, sir," he said with a jerky bow, but his face still looked thunderous, even as he said the conciliating words.

The comte merely inclined his head and then returned his attention to Dorothea.

"I can see that once more I am *de trop*, now that your husband is returned, madame. Did you have a pleasant journey, sir?"

"Yes," barked out Tate.

"And did you have far to come?"

"Far enough that I am eager for my bath and board and bed," Tate answered evasively.

"Then I shall be gone. Until the next time, my lady," de Blanchard said. Under Sir Tate's blistering scrutiny, he gave Dorothea's hand its customary kiss and walked out.

When the door had closed behind the comte, Tate turned his scornful grey eyes on his wife. She felt shaken by the judgment she read there, but knowing his censure to be groundless, she raised her chin and returned his look with at least an outward appearance of calm.

"Well, madam," Tate finally flung at her. "I might have known that you would deceive me thus!"

Adriana laughed nervously. "Don't be absurd, Tate!"

"The comte comes here solely to instruct me in music," Thea countered simultaneously, stung by the injustice of the accusation.

Ignoring his wife, Tate addressed himself to his sister. "I do not mean that frippery comte," he said disdainfully, "though perhaps he should be included in what I can only call a practiced deception. When I contracted marriage with this young woman, she was no better than an ape-leader—a pallid, mobcapped, timid nonentity of a spinster. Now, I find this . . . this . . . Circe!" he exploded, sweeping his hand toward Dorothea and her new finery.

Adriana gurgled with laughter. "I think that what you mean is 'Penelope,' " she said, looking over at Thea as though hoping to find another to appreciate the absurdity of the situation. But Dorothea only stood mute with anger and pain, while her husband's tirade continued.

"And now, against all my expectations, I encounter her here in London, rigged out in the height of fashion!"

This proved too much for Adriana. "The height of fashion? That just shows abysmal ignorance, Tate Bancroft. This dress is far too simple to be all the crack. But Dorothea was as stubborn as a mule and refused to allow Mademoiselle Arlette to concoct something more *à la mode*."

She waved a disparaging hand toward Dorothea's muslin gown, which, although severe in line, was of a lovely pale green which became her admirably.

"I bow to your superior knowledge, but she does seem to have picked up the current mode of dalliance quickly enough. With my own eyes, I witnessed her encouraging advances by an ogling Frenchman. And under your roof! My God, Adriana, I never took you for a totty-headed idiot!"

At last Thea was moved to speak in her sister's defense, if not in her own.

"Adriana is no idiot!" she cried. Then, in an altered voice, she added, "If my appearance displeases you, I am sorry, but I did not dress with you in mind."

"That is quite evident," Tate growled, eyeing with

194

apparent loathing the door through which the comte had so recently departed.

"I might just as easily accuse you of deception, sir," Thea retorted. "I received a note not a month ago in which you declared, among other things, that you did not expect to return to England until the new year."

The baronet looked nonplussed for a moment at this counterattack and hemmed and hawed a bit about "an important mission for a fellow soldier," then turned on her once more.

"And what of my child, madam," he said, an angry spark rekindled in the grey eyes, "the child whom you promised to love unreservedly, and for whose sake you married me? Have you left her behind at the Hall to come kick up your heels in London? Or have you dragged her along on this unlikely adventure as well?" He stood, arms folded across his chest, while his fulminating gaze bore into her.

Under his censorious stare her own eyes fell. "She is with me, Sir Tate, but you don't understand . . ."

"Very true, I do not. Perhaps you can explain to my satisfaction why you felt the need to come to town, when the terms of our agreement were that you should stay at Bancroft Hall. Why, Aggie might have done as much and obviated this farce of a marriage."

Thea stood speechless with rage at his accusations. She grasped the back of the Sheraton chair for support, with white-knuckled hands. This was as bad as any upbraiding she had suffered at the hands of her cousin and, as she had under Miss Grayson's rake-downs, she began to feel physically ill. Apparently Adriana thought her brother had gone far enough as well, for she stepped into the fray on the side of his wife.

"That is quite sufficient, Tate. You would not have Thea think that you are a more exacting companion than that vicious Letitia, would you?" She went over to where Thea stood and gave her a quick hug.

"You have given her no chance to defend herself, so it appears that I must," Adriana said fondly.

Pulling the reluctant Thea along, Adriana seated herself on a chair and motioned them to sit on the sofa opposite. Both sat down as far as possible from each other, as though any physical contact would burn them. Neither met the other's eye.

Adriana directed Thea's defense at her brother's unrepentant head. "When your reason returns, Tate, you will acknowledge that Aggie could not have brought Martha, sickly and jaundiced as she was, to London," she chided gently. "And I needed Aggie very much at the time. Your daughter is now the picture of health and she owes it all to Thea."

"That does not explain why she felt the need to come trotting to the city," countered Tate, determinedly avoiding Thea's eyes.

"I take full responsibility for that," Adriana smiled and took Thea's cold hand in her own. "She came at my urging and not out of any impulsive notion of her own. I was, quite frankly, ready to die of ennui. After the initial fright of Dr. Collins' diagnosis and the worries of attempting to run the house and Harry from my bed were alleviated by Aggie's arrival, I quickly became bored to tears. Have you ever considered how you might fill twenty-four hours of a day, week after week, anchored to your bed? Sleep very quickly loses its charms when it is all one is permitted to do. As I had never been properly introduced to the *ton*, none of its members were about to come calling on me, particularly as I was in a most advanced stage of my delicate condition. I begged Thea to take pity on me, and when she did so, I quickly learned to love her. Here was someone with whom I could share confidences and talk about everything, from literature and politics to babies and husbands." She squeezed Thea's hand affectionately.

"As for her vastly improved looks, why I also take some credit, or, if you stubbornly insist, blame, for a small part of it. I derived a great deal of pleasure from dressing up my fair sister in a manner that befits her beauty and her station. You understand, of course, that I was at a stage of rotundity where my own appearance caused me nothing but embarrassment.

"Beyond my efforts, she is simply a lovely young woman. If you failed to see that earlier, you may blame your own shortsightedness."

Tate sprang to his feet and crossed to the window. In exasperation Adriana spoke briskly. "One would think you would be pleased that your wife is not the antidote you apparently thought her. And as for the comte . . ." she paused as Tate whirled to face them.

"Yes, A., as for the comte?" he quizzed her. "He, no doubt, possesses innumerable qualities that I, alas, lack."

"Not exactly," she smiled up at him. "But he does have the good sense to pay your wife the compliments her beauty deserves instead of heaping her with undeserved scorn."

"All right, all right, A. You have convinced me of my error, so give over."

He made a stiff bow in Thea's direction and flashed an apologetic grin that at once transformed the glowering man into a rueful boy. "I beg your forgiveness, madam, for any calumnies I was moved to lay at your door. At least no one can accuse me of trying to toad-eat you or win you over with gratuitous flattery." He extended his hand to her.

Thea's anger evaporated at the look of genuine contrition in her husband's grey eyes, and she shyly put her hand in his.

"I shall not ape your French friend," he said softly, still retaining his firm grasp on her hand, "but believe that my apology is sincere, and that I am grateful for the friendship you have shown my sister."

Adriana looked from her brother to Dorothea and back again and rose to her feet.

"I must go feed the babies, Tate. Do come up to the nursery in a quarter hour or so, and I will present you."

"Stay just a minute, Adriana. First there is a presentation which I must make to you." Tate flushed slightly and released Thea's hand. He did not meet the eyes of either lady.

Puzzled, both women stared at him, and the flush spread, while he ran one finger around his cravat, which suddenly appeared to be too tight.

"Presentation?" Adriana prompted.

"Actually, yes, there is a Portuguese lady I must introduce to your acquaintance. She is the widow of one of my fellow officers, Percy Smythe-Davies, who was killed at Vitória. Before the poor chap expired, he extracted my promise to escort her to England when I returned. The deuce of it is that his people here have not yet acknowledged the marriage." He seemed oddly shamefaced at this recital of his apparently goodhearted act.

"She is waiting in the carriage. I shall fetch her," he said brusquely and strode out.

Dorothea

Adriana and Dorothea exchanged looks of mystification.

"Well, he is certainly acting strangely," Adriana commented.

"I wonder what he means," Dorothea mused, "that the Smythe-Davies don't acknowledge the match. Sounds like a havey-cavey business to me, though I am in no position to throw stones."

"But that still doesn't explain Tate's peculiar behavior. He looked just like a little boy caught with his hand in the bonbons just before the dinner gong sounds. "Oh, shhh," Adriana cautioned. "Here they come."

Tate's return to the drawing room provided a stark contrast to his initial entrance. Clinging to his arm was a raven-haired beauty dressed from head to toe in jet black. But only the color was mournful. The black gauze bonnet, with its satin ruching and ribbons, was exceedingly dashing and set off the lady's green eyes to perfection. A Canezou spencer of black point lace failed utterly to conceal the low neck of the traveling gown beneath. And the slippers peeping out from under the frilled skirts were frivolously striped with black and white silk.

Dorothea took all of this in with her first glance. Her second fell on the stranger's countenance and caused her to catch her breath in dismay. This Portuguese widow could easily have sat for the portrait of Mathilde that adorned the gallery in Bancroft Hall.

Chapter 15

"Adriana, Dorothea, may I present Dona Maria Madalena Smythe-Davies," Tate said, his eyes riveted to the stranger's face.

"Dona Maria Mada . . . forgive me, but I can't seem to remember the whole," Adriana broke off with a nervous laugh.

"Maria Madalena," said the lady, fluttering her thick, dark lashes in their direction. "But you may call me Lena, as dear Sir Tate does. Circumstanced as we were, it seemed so *seely* not to do so."

"Indeed." An icy edge, which Thea had never heard before, crept into Adriana's voice. "But did you really travel all the way from the Peninsula without so much as a maid for chaperone?"

"Oh, no, of course not," Tate spluttered. "Her maid came along as far as O Porto, but then lacked the stomach for a long sea voyage. Fortunately, the captain of our ship was accompanied by his wife, who offered to act as chaperone. Then we came all the way from Portsmouth today. Poor Lena is exhausted by the journey."

"Poor Lena" swayed a bit, obligingly, as though to

illustrate the truth of his statement, but revived sufficiently to ask the identity of the gentleman whom she had seen coming from the house just before "dear Tate" had returned to the carriage.

"He looked most *gentil* and *elegante*. Is he, perhaps, a brother of yours, Tate? Naughty man, not to have mentioned him," she scolded playfully.

"Brother? That man-milliner? I should think not!" Tate exploded and the woman looked rather taken aback at the violence of his reaction. Nonetheless, she continued coyly, "Tate told me all about his delightful twin sister and also about his wife, and, oh, yes, how foolish of me, about you, Dona Dorotéia, as well. We've had days and days of *conversação íntima,* have we not, Tate?" She smiled dotingly up at the baronet.

Stung by the Smythe-Davies creature's pointed distinction between Mathilde and herself, Dorothea finally found her tongue. "That was the Comte de Blanchard, who has kindly been instructing me in singing . . . and some other things," she added with a half-smile. "Dear Philippe, he practically runs tame here of late." Out of the corner of her eye, she saw Adriana's eyebrows shoot up, but she was so nettled she didn't care.

"And speaking of things running tame around here, I must prepare you for another addition to the household. He goes by the name Lovelace," she quickly went on, forestalling another outburst from her husband. "I'm afraid he has become quite my pet. No, don't say a thing until you've met him, though strictly speaking, you, Sir Tate, have already done so."

She hastened from the room and sought out Lovelace, whom she found wallowing in a mud puddle behind the mews. "I promised to present you, and present you I shall. And please, Lovelace, if you love me, shove your muddy paws into her exquisite, fatuous face."

When she entered the drawing room with Lovelace in tow, she heard a most gratifying gasp of horror issue from the lady under discussion.

"B-but, you Ingles allow such feelthy brutes inside your houses? Oh, Tate, save me, he frightens me so." Maria Madalena squealed helplessly and took a tight grasp of her savior's arm.

Lovelace stood a moment in the doorway, then strolled over to sniff disdainfully at the hem of Madalena's gown. She made a dash behind the baronet to get away from the dog's inquisitive nose, which elicited a growl from the affronted creature.

"Don't worry, madam. He has bitten only one guest so far," Dorothea explained in dulcet tones. "I don't think you are in any real danger, especially with 'dear Tate' to protect you."

Tate turned and smiled indulgently at Madalena. "There, there, Lena, the beast is just trying to be friendly," and bent to demonstrate this with a pat to Lovelace's head.

At this closer inspection he suddenly recognized Lovelace. "It can't be. Surely this isn't the same animal you found dallying in the garden with vicious Letitia's pug?"

For the first time in her brief acquaintance with her husband, Thea heard him break into heartfelt laughter, all traces of bitterness and reproach wiped from his face. She stared at him, unable to take her eyes away, the transformation was so complete and so compelling.

"But why have you given him the name Lovelace? Don't you think it rather rich for his obviously mixed blood?"

203

"Tate," laughed Adriana, "you obviously haven't spent your time reading the same novels that your wife and I have. Lovelace was the seducer of Clarissa in Richardson's tale of moral turpitude, and Clarissa, let me remind you, is vicious Letitia's pug."

"How could I forget! Nasty little thing—almost as nasty as her owner," Tate said with a grin. For a moment, thought Dorothea, he looked very much like the youth in the portrait at Bancroft Hall.

Maria Madalena, obviously not following this rapid and idiomatic English, and not content with being ignored in favor of a dog, emerged from behind Tate and preened slightly. "Do you really permit this creature to run free in the house? In Portugal such a thing would not be permitted. I am terrified of such brutes and . . ." she began, but was interrupted.

The door flew open and Harry raced into the room. When he saw Maria Madalena standing there, his eyes widened, and he headed straight for her.

"Aunt Mathilde! You're back! They told me you never would come back, but I *knew* you would." He threw himself at her silken skirts and burst into sobs of happiness.

There was a moment of paralyzed silence. No one had the heart to disabuse the boy of his notion. When, instead of meeting welcoming arms, he encountered only a firm hand pushing him away with marked disdain, he himself was the first to speak.

"You're not Aunt Mathilde! Who are you? What are you doing here?" he said accusingly, and Lovelace echoed his sentiments with a rumbling growl.

"Now, Harry, don't be rude," Adriana admonished him, though her heart did not appear to be in it. "This is Dona Maria Madalena. She has come all the way from the war with your Uncle Tate, who, by the way, is standing right here, and you haven't even shaken hands with him."

Harry hung his head, embarrassed by his infantile mistake. Chastened, he turned to Tate. "Welcome home, sir. I'm sorry," he said meekly, and held out his hand.

Instead of taking the small hand in his own, Tate crouched down and gathered the small boy into his arms for an affectionate hug. "It's quite all right, Harry, no harm done," he said softly, and ruffled the boy's hair before letting him go.

Watching this exchange, Thea felt wonder at this evidence of yet another facet of her unknown husband. With a pang, she wished that he might evince the same affection toward her and Martha.

A glimmer of spirit resurfaced in Harry. "You won't make Aunt Thea throw Lovelace out, will you?" His pleading gaze went from Tate's face to Maria Madalena's. "He's my best friend ever, and I know Aunt Thea loves him, too, because she lets him go everywhere with us. She even let him drink champagne once at Bancroft Hall, at least that's what Adriana said, and, besides, when that putrid count called me a cabbage, Lovelace bit him on the ankle."

"Is that so?" Tate said, with an amused glance at Dorothea, which she found irresistible.

Maria Madalena chose that moment to utter a low moan and to pass a slender hand over her forehead in a feeble manner, while she spoke to Tate in a rapid undertone.

"Lena," Tate exclaimed anxiously, all consideration. "Whatever am I thinking of, standing about discussing that animal when you need to lie down and refresh yourself." His tone was solicitous as he asked her a question in what to Dorothea sounded like fluent Portuguese. Then he turned to his sister. "A., may I take her upstairs?"

"Of course, Tate, *fique à vontade,* as you say in Portuguese."

At these words, Maria Madalena's eyes flew open and she seemed to forget her weakened condition. "You speak *Português?*" she asked, surprised.

"Only a little. Not nearly so well as you speak English. Nicholas taught me, when we first met," Adriana replied modestly. "But do make yourself at home. And, Tate, once you have her settled for a rest, won't you join me in the nursery?"

"Of course, A., I look forward to meeting my niece and nephew."

Thea could not restrain herself. "And to seeing your own daughter, or have you forgotten her existence?" she put in acidly.

"I'm not likely to, seeing your frowning countenance. If it weren't for her, *you* certainly wouldn't be here."

"How kind of you to remind me."

" 'Twas you who started in with the sarcastic reminders, my dear wife," he retorted.

"Tate, dear," cooed Maria Madalena, "*could* you not postpone this . . . discussion until later. I believe I feel faint."

"Of course, Lena. Here, take my arm. Poor little thing, you look completely exhausted." With the Portuguese lady leaning gracefully against him, he slowly left the room.

Dorothea looked at the remaining three—Adriana, Harry and Lovelace, and shook her head in dismay.

"I don't know what to think," Adriana said. "It looks to me as if Tate has lost his mind."

"Or his heart," Dorothea said miserably.

"Well, I know what *I* think," Harry declared emphatically. The two women started and looked at him.

"I think she is a wicked witch disguised as Aunt Mathilde."

"You may be right, Harry. And I fear she has bewitched your Uncle Tate," Adriana said with a rueful smile. "Well, we shall figure out a way to break her spell, but just now I must feed your cousins. Do you want to come with me, laddie?"

"Lovelace, too?"

"Lovelace, too. His timely growl at Mrs. Smythe-Davies has quite won my heart. Come along, both of you. Thea?"

"Oh, I shall just stay here a moment or two to gather my thoughts. I'll be up soon."

Left alone, Thea began pacing the room, trying furiously to compose herself. Tate's reappearance had left her shaken, a physical reaction which she unhesitatingly attributed to anger. She was most unwilling to acknowledge that her turbulent emotions could have any other basis.

"He treats me with less courtesy than he would a stranger," she seethed, remembering his harsh words. "And how dare he accuse me of playing him false! Particularly when he shows every sign of deepest affection for that . . . that . . . witch, as Harry so aptly puts it."

The shelved plots of revenge that she had confided in Lovelace on that night nearly a month ago rose again to the fore, but this time they were directed at the porcelain countenance of Dona Madalena, whose resemblance to the dead Mathilde seemed to hold Tate in thrall.

She put her hands up to smooth her hair and was horrified to feel that it had escaped its pins and was falling about her face. She choked back a sharp laugh. I must be the one who looks like a witch, she thought, as with shaking hands she tried to tuck the fly-away tendrils up into their loose knot. It's no wonder my husband thinks me abandoned. I probably look the part.

She leaned against the mantel and rested her forehead against the cool marble surface. She felt nearly as hopeless as she had at Miss Grayson's. The only bright light in what seemed an uncertain future was the friendship and support of Adriana. The most frightening aspect of this new development was the uncertainty. It appeared that Tate was most attached to his "Lena" and there was nothing binding him to his second wife but the bonds of duty. If his affection for the Portuguese widow were allowed to blossom, as seemed Madalena's goal, it would be easy to declare the marriage null and void, a part of the unhappy past. She tried to find a morsel of comfort in this prospect, to feel that she might be happier without her enigma of a husband, but the image of his laughter when he recognized Lovelace, or the apologetic grin with which he asked her forgiveness, dimmed any such outlook.

Her gloomy reflections were interrupted by a knock on the door. Raising herself instantly from her dejected posture, she whirled to face the door. Was it Tate, returning to take up the battle where they had ended? Her heart thundered in her breast and she pressed her hand to her bosom in an attempt to slow its wild beating.

It was not her husband who entered the room, however, but the Comte de Blanchard.

"Ah, Madame Dorothée. How delightful to find you alone," he said, while his eyes darted about the room as if in search of someone else.

Puzzled at the reappearance of the comte and oddly disappointed that it was not her husband, Thea asked, "Comte, is there something I can do for you?"

"I only returned for some music I left behind in the, er, excitement, of your husband's return. Ah, yes, here it is, the Mozart duet."

"But I thought you had another copy of that piece."

"Oh, yes," the comte smiled apologetically. "Why, I do believe you are right. How absent my mind is today. It must be this heat, and your loveliness, which have sent my wits wandering. Oh, yes, and by the way, I couldn't help noticing that so very striking lady who came into the house with Sir Tate. I was afraid I might be interrupting your visit with other, more interesting company. But, I had an urgent need for this music, or so I thought, so found it necessary to impose. Do forgive me."

"But there is nothing to forgive," Thea said absently. "As you see, you have interrupted nothing."

"How very odd. I could have sworn . . ." he broke off, and a look of irritation crossed his handsome countenance. "But it is of no consequence, for at least I have had the ecstasy of seeing you again. *Au revoir*, once again."

"I shall walk you to the door, monsieur. Have you your music now? I would hate for you to have to make yet another trip back."

"It is right here, next to my heart, where I shall cherish it as something you have graced with your touch."

"Really, monsieur, you overwhelm me with your

compliments," she replied, as they reached the foyer, meaning every word. She gave him her hand to kiss, knowing that he would do so anyway, and hoping to hasten the proceedings. Unfortunately, the comte seemed to take this as a sign of encouragement, and he pressed his lips fervently to her palm, then lifted his melting eyes to her face. He then donned his curly beaver hat and walked out the door.

Dorothea stood in the hall for just a moment, the hand that the Frenchman had so ardently kissed pressed to her cheek, but her mind was hardly dwelling on romance. Why had the comte returned, she wondered, and on such a flimsy excuse? He had seemed inordinately inquisitive about Tate and Mrs. Smythe-Davies, even more than usual. Ah, well, she concluded, it is probably more of his absurd gallantry; the man seems irresistibly drawn to anything in skirts.

She turned to the stairs and a slight sound made her look up. With a start, she found herself gazing into the angry countenance of her husband, who stood on an upper landing and glowered down at her.

"Very pretty," he snorted, and wheeled to mount the stairs to the nursery floor.

Dorothea stood, appalled at having been spied upon and at the construction he put on what he had seen and heard. Seething with indignation, she stormed up the stairs, but by the time she reached the nursery, he was already inside.

Determined to confront him at once, she pushed open the door and went in. The picture that greeted her was not calculated to assuage her injured feelings. In addition to the expected scene of Tate, Adriana and Aggie with the twins, she saw Mrs. Smythe-Davies cradling Martha and chattering away in Portuguese with the delighted Seraphim.

Above the foreign conversation she heard Adriana talking to Tate about the twins.

"This little fellow is called Nicholas Tate. I'm sure you can understand why. As you see, he has our coloring, Tate, and the look of the Bancrofts about him, but I swear that he has already developed his father's sardonic air to perfection. He is always frowning at me as if to say, 'you idiot, you don't have the slightest idea how to mother a paragon like me,' and, of course, he is absolutely correct. Little wretch," she said, kissing him on his Bancroftian nose.

"And what do you call your little girl?" Tate asked.

Adriana looked quickly at Dorothea. They had often discussed this moment, and whether the chosen name would cause Tate pain.

Taking a deep breath, Adriana said, "I call her Mathilde Vitória."

"Mathilde Vitória? That has a good sound to it. I'm sure Mathilde would have been pleased that you remembered her," he observed with a striking absence of grief. "But why 'Vitória'?"

"As it turned out, she was born on June 21, the day Vitória was taken. And besides, I thought it sounded well with Mathilde," she answered, looking at him in wonder.

"Oh, Lena, you must come see these two. You'll never guess what they have named this doll—Mathilde Vitória," he called.

Mrs. Smythe-Davies fluttered over, still holding Martha. "Ah, *que amor*, what a little love, and the boy—how handsome. You must be very proud, Adriana. Your husband, he will be so happy when he sees them.

My own poor husband, he will never see his son," she said dramatically.

"His son?" Dorothea asked. "Do you mean to say you are *enceinte*, madam?"

"Ah, yes," she sighed, "but in *Português* we have a more poetic name for this condition, *dar à luz*, which means to give to the light. A lovely name for such a delicate state, don't you think? Alas, my poor, dear Percival shall never see his son," she said and drooped affectingly.

"And she should be lying down, as I instructed," Tate said fondly, all solicitation, "but no, she must come to see the babies, such a tender-hearted girl."

"But what were you doing on the landing?" Thea asked impulsively. "I had thought you coming from Mrs. Smythe-Davies, but she was here . . ."

"I merely went to fetch some trinkets I brought for the infants," he said, all fondness gone from his voice.

"Yes, see, Thea," Adriana broke in eagerly, "the darling rattles he has brought my twins from abroad."

"And for Martha?" she asked defiantly.

Mrs. Smythe-Davies' laugh trilled out. "Oh, it is so fortunate. We did buy three *brinquedos,* quite by chance. I insisted, you see, that he purchase something for Martinha as well as, as we thought, your baby. And we couldn't make up our minds among several. Just imagine—we took all three. How fortunate. I wouldn't want to slight this little *querida.* Oh, Tate, she looks so much like you—so very, very beautiful, your adorable *filinha.*"

"Do you really think so?" Tate murmured, and moved closer to peer at his daughter.

Dorothea squirmed uncomfortably. At last her husband was taking a proper interest in Martha, and it was only because that hussy had so beguiled him.

"If you will pardon me, I shall take Martha and feed her. She always fusses if she is not fed on time," Thea said primly.

"Oh, may I not feed her? It will be just like playing dolls!" Mrs. Smythe-Davies protested girlishly.

"But, you know how babies are. She might ruin your dress. And she *is* rather discriminating about who holds the bottle."

"I know we shall get along very well. If you will just get me the bottle?" the woman said in a cold, distant tone.

"Of course," Thea replied, in a repressive voice. When she returned with the bottle, she found the Portuguese intruder settled gracefully in the rocking chair, her black silk skirts arranged carefully for the greatest effect. She looked as though she were posing for a portrait of the Madonna; the only flaw was that the infant in her arms was disobliging enough to squirm. Tate hovered protectively nearby.

Dorothea handed her the bottle in silence and went with Adriana into the next room to prepare the twins for their naps.

A sudden exclamation, incomprehensible, brought her back into the nursery proper at a run. Mrs. Smythe-Davies, her face an unbecoming shade of scarlet, was scrubbing furiously at her gown with a handkerchief, while Tate stood by, holding the crying Martha.

"She, she . . . made *vómito* on my lovely gown. You have not trained her properly, Dona Dorotéia. It is all your fault," she pouted, every trace of sweetness gone from her voice.

"You obviously don't know the first thing about

babies, madam, and will be happier away from the nursery. Come, Martha. Did the foreign lady frighten you?" She wrested baby and bottle from Tate's hands and went back to the adjoining room, where Martha's cries settled gradually into happy gurgles.

"Martha, if there were ever any doubt, which there never has been, your performance today has made you dearer to me than ever," she whispered into the baby's shell-like ear. "What an inspired regurgitation, my best and only baby."

Adriana had left the twins to the care of Aggie and Seraphim. The two governesses were rocking the babies, their heads close together, deep in discussion, when Dorothea entered with Martha, and they did not look up at her arrival. She could not help overhearing their conversation as she gave Martha the last of her bottle.

"It is quite wonderful to have someone with whom I might speak *Português* again," Seraphim was saying.

"I'm sure it has been difficult for you, having no one around who knows your language," Aggie said soothingly.

"At the same time, there is something odd about Dona Madalena," the little Portuguese lady said. "I can't . . . how do you say . . . put my thumb on it, but there is something not quite right."

"She does seem excessively attached to Tate," Aggie observed. "But I suppose it's only natural, as he helped her to escape her own troubled land and brought her to England."

"Yes, and virtually without a chaperone. That makes me think, as well. I might expect such a thing of Dona Dorotêia, but a *Português* lady of good family? It is *escandaloso!* What could her family have been thinking of?"

Aggie came to Thea's defense. "I don't think Dorothea is so lost to all propriety as you do, Seraphim. She may not share your notions of comportment, but she has been raised as a lady."

"That is as may be . . ." the senhora began, but was interrupted as Thea cleared her throat to make her presence known.

Both governesses turned. "Ah, Dona Dorotéia," the senhora said, signally unembarrassed by her previous disparaging statements. "Your sister has gone to change her gown and asked us to tell you to invite Sir Tate and Dona Madalena to dine in an hour."

After her contretemps with Mrs. Smythe-Davies, the last thing Dorothea wished to do was to invite her graciously to dinner, but there was little else she could do. Skillfully patting Martha to slumber, she laid her in her cradle and went back to the playroom.

She was greeted by yet another affecting tableau. Dona Madalena was sobbing loudly against Tate's chest, and he was holding her tenderly in his arms in an attempt to comfort her. Dorothea had to lean against the door jamb to steady herself before she dared to speak.

"Forgive the intrusion," she snapped, "but Adriana wants us all downstairs for dinner in an hour."

Tate's arms jerked away from the lovely brunette as though he had been scorched. "Poor Lena" however, her back to the door, did not move a muscle, and with the sudden removal of the baronet's support, she tumbled to the floor with a helpless shriek.

"You *Inglês* certainly have strange ways of treating

215

a lady, I must say. You were never so disobliging on our journey, Tate."

The baronet was horrified and knelt to help her to her feet. "How could I have allowed such a thing to happen? If anything should go wrong I could never forgive myself. I'm the greatest beast in nature."

"I couldn't agree more," Dorothea fumed. "But even so, Adriana expects you at her dinner table." She turned on her heel and left the room.

Chapter 16

In her room, Thea sat on the edge of her bed and tried to compose herself to make some sort of plan for counterattack. It was apparent that Dona Madalena had her hooks into Tate and meant to have him, and that Tate's wife was, to her, a minor impediment.

There was a scratch on the door and she opened it to admit the dog, who came in and sat at her feet.

"Good evening, Lovelace," Thea greeted him. "I am always happy for your company, under any circumstances, but your growling at Mrs. Smythe-Davies makes you doubly welcome company. You and Martha have the good fortune of being able to express your views in your own inimitable fashions. I wish that I could growl at her or, better yet, mess her gown, but I'm afraid that might be viewed as terrible rudeness, not to mention *barbarismo*."

She smiled wryly at the dog, who thumped his tail loudly in response. "I just wish there were some way to bring Sir Tate around to our opinion."

She sighed and began taking the pins out of her hair. "Perhaps if I were to droop picturesquely and hang on his arm and his every word, I might be able to compete with her, but I find that role is not to my taste or in my nature."

Brushing out her sun-streaked auburn hair, she looked closely at her image in the glass. To her own mind she was not nearly so beautiful as the Portuguese brunette. If she had given any thought to her appearance, it would have been to dismiss any claim of her own to beauty. Her mass of hair, which she wished darker, hung almost to her waist; the hazel eyes, flecked with green, she would have exchanged for the full green of Madalena's, although her own were larger, more luminous and fringed with long dark lashes. There was a faint sprinkling of freckles across her straight nose, and a brush stroke of pink in her cheeks, which looked too bouncingly healthy. An interesting pallor would have been preferable. Next to the exotic ivory and ebony of Mrs. Smythe-Davies, Dorothea felt commonplace in the extreme.

"If I can't look like the picture of Mathilde, I can at least look my best," she said to the dog. "And try, though it will be most difficult, to keep my tongue in check."

Going through her small collection of clothes she gave silent thanks to Adriana for insisting she acquire a pretty gown or two. If she had had to appear at table in one of Cousin Letitia's hand-me-downs, she might just as well have raised the white flag in surrender. She took out the same jonquil silk she had worn to Lady Flemming's benefit. "If I can survive the ordeal of singing at the musicale and seeing Adriana through her confinement wearing this, surely it will get me through dinner," she murmured. She slipped into the gown and quickly dressed her hair in a loose style she had adapted from Monsieur Louis' handiwork.

Dorothea

When she descended the stairs to the parlor, the others were all assembled and waiting for her. Both Tate and Adriana looked up as she entered, and she was gratified to see a gleam of admiration in her husband's grey eyes.

"You look lovely, Thea, doesn't she, Tate?" Adriana began, obviously hoping to bridge the rift between them. Tate appeared ready to agree, when he was interrupted.

"Utterly charming," volunteered Mrs. Smythe-Davies in dulcet tones. "Although with such an odd shade of hair, one must choose one's colors with care."

"Yes, it's quite striking," said Tate in a bland voice. "Odd, I don't remember your hair being that copper color."

"It would be odd if you remembered anything about me, sir," Dorothea said stiffly.

"Never saw your own wife's hair? How very amusing," tittered Mrs. Smythe-Davies, as the quartet walked to the dining room. "In Portugal, of course, marriages are often arranged between a man and a woman who have never met, but, I assure you, once married, such intimate matters as hair color would never remain undiscovered. You English are so cold and formal."

Speaking in a voice colder and more formal than she had ever used in her life before, Adriana politely inquired when the widow would be joining her husband's family. "Will you be making an extended stay with the Smythe-Davies?" she asked.

Madalena cast a look of appeal at Tate, who seemed remarkably ill at ease.

"As a matter of fact, A., I was coming to that, You see, there is a bit of a problem with Percy's folks. It seems that they are not taking too kindly to having an unknown Portuguese daughter-in-law. Though surely once they have seen Lena, they could have no possible objection."

Madalena preened like a self-satisfied kitten and settled into her first course of turbot in a cream sauce.

"At any rate, here's the rub," Tate continued. "They refuse to have anything to do with her at all, the heartless wretches, until they have verified for themselves that the match is genuine. It is the most ridiculous thing. How do they expect to find regular records of such a marriage in a war-torn country? But for the meanwhile," he looked uncomfortable for a moment, then went on, in a rush, "for the meanwhile, I told Lena that you would, of course, be delighted to open your home to her, until such time as the Smythe-Davies accept her into their family." Tate drained his wine glass and promptly refilled it, without meeting his sister's eye.

Adriana and Dorothea sat frozen in their chairs.

"But-but, Tate," Adriana at last found the wit to protest, "we are so very crowded here. There is no bedchamber empty."

"Surely Dorothea has been here long enough. I don't believe you can claim your boredom as a reason for her remaining in London. I should think you have plenty to keep you busy with the twins. She can easily return to Bancroft Hall," Tate suggested.

"Never!" exclaimed Adriana. "You won't deprive me of my only sister, Tate. For she is that to me."

"Then let your sister sleep on a trundle in your room. You used to yearn to do exactly that often enough when we were young. Have a sister to giggle to sleep with. Then Lena may have *her* room."

"And where exactly do you plan to sleep, Tate?"

Adriana inquired, exasperated. "In the middle of the dining room carpet?"

"Oh, I shall not be here long. Only until I receive further orders, which could be tomorrow, or next week. Until then, I can sleep on the extra pallet in the butler's room upstairs."

Madalena looked from Tate to Dorothea and back again, but only murmured, "English marriages," with a sly smile and went back to her meal.

Dorothea sat mortified at this public declaration of the emptiness of her marital vows. Her wine glass slipped from her hand and spilled its contents over herself and her nearest neighbor, Mrs. Smythe-Davies.

"Do forgive me, ma'am, I seem to be all thumbs today," she stammered, trying to wipe claret from the other woman's deep blue silk gown.

Dona Madalena fixed her with a baleful eye, as if accusing her of spilling wine deliberately. When Thea returned her gaze with a defiant lift of her chin, the Portuguese widow's glance fell, and she turned her attention to the baronet. Thea, meanwhile, had a vivid memory of her confidences earlier in the evening with Lovelace. Well, she had messed Madalena's gown, though she would swear it was unintentional. Her amusement was short-lived, however. Her husband was discussing his immediate plans for Madalena with his sister.

"I have been thinking, A., that the best way to help Lena gain favor with Percy's family is to see that she is properly launched in society under our protection."

Adriana's expressive face reflected a combination of dismay and exasperation. "But Tate," she argued, "don't you realize that your own wife has not been 'launched in society'? The name 'Bancroft' hardly carries the cachet of an 'Alvanley' or a 'Brummel.' I never had a London season when I was a girl, and since my marriage there has been no opportunity. Nor did I desire it," she added in an undertone. "Besides, it has been only a few short months since Mathilde's death. It seems hardly proper to be gallivanting about."

Tate began on his third glass of wine and waved away her objections. "The Bancrofts may not be in the first stare of society, Adriana, but we can certainly mingle with that crowd. And as for Mathilde"—a shadow crossed his countenance, as he watched the deep red of the liquid in his glass catch the light from the candles on the table—"if I don't mind, why should society? After all, I am the one most affected, and it has nothing to do with anyone else. I feel quite a different fellow from the stricken animal I was. Why, the challenge of rescuing Mathil . . . I mean, Madalena, from penury by winning over the Smythe-Davies makes me feel quite young again."

He reached over and patted the widow's hand. "Not that we would ever let you be penurious, my dear. My home will always welcome you."

"You have made me feel so welcome already, Tate," she murmured, batting her lashes in his direction, then including the others in a sad smile. "He has told me so much about his beloved Mathilde that I feel almost as though I knew her. I see such, how do you say . . . parallels . . . in my own sad story. I only wish that Percy might have lived to see the *herói* Tate has been."

"That would have made Tate's heroics rather unnecessary, would it not?" inquired Thea, unable to refrain from this acid observation, but regretting it almost at once. For all the notice the others took of her, she might never have spoken.

"More than once I know I was a burden to your brother," Lena turned the full blaze of emerald eyes on Adriana, "but he never grew angry with me or treated me with impatience as others might have done. I can see why Mathilde fell in love with him—an English demigod, an angel," she whispered, letting her eyes fill with tears, which she then dabbed away with a lacy handkerchief.

"Hardly that," Tate said gruffly, with an embarrassed look at the others. "Just a good friend of Percy, who would never see his widow in danger or want."

In the middle of this touching exchange, Adriana looked at Thea and raised her eyebrows in patent disbelief. For her part, Thea did not know whether to laugh or cry at the absurdity of the situation. She found a very small morsel of comfort in the fact that at least Tate still had the grace to be discomfited by Madalena's outrageous flattery.

Any comfort was dispelled, however, by the turn that the conversation took after the removal of the fish course. As the fricandeau of veal was served, Madalena expanded on the perfidy of her husband's family.

"It makes my heart bleed, thinking that dear Percy's own father would try to, how do you say, *anular*, our blessed union."

"Annul." Tate supplied the word, then explained to the others, "The man is a monster. If he cannot find adequate documentation, he plans to annul their marriage. And with little Percy on the way."

"Is it so easy to *anular* in England? You must tell me truthfully, Tate."

"Annulment is easy enough, if the marriage has not been consummated. But in your case . . ." his voice trailed off, and Mrs. Smythe-Davies contrived to look coy.

"Then an unconsummated marriage . . ." She looked sidelong at Thea, "That can be set aside without difficulty?"

"Yes, if both parties agree. Now, enough of this talk of annulments. Let us instead confound their plans by plotting your social success. We will see to it that you are such a belle that the Smythe-Davies will be clamoring to claim you as their own." He raised his glass as though in a toast.

She clapped her hands gleefully. "If you can accomplish that, I will be your slave forever."

"Slavery is frowned upon in England, Mrs. Smythe-Davies, and I fear that my husband is being rather too optimistic," Dorothea said in quelling accents.

"Nonsense, Dorothea, why, we Bancrofts can accomplish anything, once we put our minds to it," Tate countered jovially, including her in the appellation.

"We Bancrofts?" Thea echoed, and subsided into silence at this indication that, against all odds, he actually thought of her as a member of the family.

"Now, tell me, A., is Almack's still the temple of exclusivity whose gates we must storm in order to scale the heights of the *ton*?"

Adriana looked panic-stricken. "Almack's?" she said, her voice sliding up to a squeak.

Tate ignored his sister's wide-eyed look of alarm. "Yes, Almack's. Did Nick number any of the patronesses among his acquaintance in his salad days?"

Adriana shifted uneasily in her chair. "I believe he was slightly acquainted with Lady Jersey, but . . ."

"Excellent. I shall call on her tomorrow morning and charm her into vouchers for all of our party for Wednesday evening."

"But Almack's is not open now, Tate. No regular assemblies are held until autumn," Adriana said, looking uneasy.

"But don't you remember, A.? There's to be a special ball there this week to celebrate the taking of Vitória. The patronesses have spared no effort to make the evening a memorable one. They sent invitations to all the ruralizing *ton* to return for the festivities. Why, there was a whole column about it in the newspaper this morning," Dorothea chattered nervously. She was astonished to see a look of great reproach directed at her by her sister.

"But what is this All Mox, of which you speak?" Dona Madalena simpered between bites. "Is it someone's home? So lovely and gracious as this?" She indicated the elegant dining room with a sweep of her fork. The vulgarity of this gesture was not lost on Thea and Adriana, but Tate was concentrating on his fourth glass of claret and missed it.

"It is a very commonplace assembly room, with indifferent decorations and insipid refreshments. Why, weak Bohea tea and lemonade are the strongest drinks allowed, and with their stale sandwiches, something more is required, believe me."

"Why, Tate, I never knew you to be an habitué of Almack's," Adriana exclaimed. "How did you learn so much about it?"

"Never set foot inside the place, or wished to, A., until now. I'm just repeating what I heard from my less fortunate friends who did. Sounded perfectly awful. But it is a necessary evil if Madalena is to win over the Smythe-Davies."

"But, if it is a dull place, why must we go?" Madalena asked, with the tiniest of frowns. "Though any place I go with you could not be dreary, Tate. Such a *heról*." The look she gave him dripped with worship.

Adriana choked on her food. "I find it exceedingly difficult to get used to the idea of Tate as a hero. But then, so would you if he had tied you to a tree and painted you blue." At Lena's stare of incomprehension, she added, "The teasing we are subjected to in childhood is not quickly forgotten."

Tate ignored both the fawning compliment and the sisterly setdown. "Almack's only value is the near impossibility of gaining admittance to its hallowed halls. There is a bevy of influential society matrons who have established themselves as a watchdog committee. Unless one of them disgorges the required vouchers, one cannot enter. Therein lies its charm."

"I still do not understand," Madalena protested.

"What Tate is too delicate to tell you, madam, is what all English ladies of a certain standing and age have learned at their mothers' knees. Almack's is the Supreme Marriage Mart of London, indeed of all England, where hopeful young ladies are paraded in front of eligible young gentlemen. Thus, the patronesses are really performing a task well-known in country circles: selecting suitable breeding stock," Dorothea said. "And, though Tate is correct in saying that your acceptance there guarantees your entrée into society as a whole, I think he has overlooked your recent bereavement." She looked closely at the widow and spoke in a tone gentler than any she had used so far in conversation with

Madalena. "Surely it would be all too painful for you to be thrust into the marriage mart. And if you are feeling delicate because of your condition . . ."

"Oh, la," laughed Madalena, "don't worry about *that*. Why, my mother went out dancing every night right up to the evening I was born." Perhaps aware of the shock in at least two pairs of eyes at this dismissal, she added hurriedly, "And as for dear Percy, why, he loved me so, I'm sure he would wish for me to be happy again."

"I see, well, then, there can be no further obstacle to attending Almack's," Dorothea said dryly. "If you feel Percy could have no objection."

"There is one thing . . . but . . . no," Madalena began hesitantly.

"What is it, Lena? Have you a question about how to go on in London society?" Tate asked. "We will do our best to help you, but you must understand that Adriana and I were raised in the country and seldom came to town," Tate offered.

"It is not easy to ask . . ." she stammered, lowering her long, dark lashes.

"Don't be silly. What are heroes for, anyway?"

"Well, since you insist, it is my wardrobe. I have nothing to wear to such a splendid place as Almack's. I should hate to disgrace you by my ragged clothes." She flicked a disparaging hand at her gown, which was more elegant and costly than anything either of the other two women had ever worn, if a little wine-stained.

"No one will have eyes for anything but your lovely face, Madalena," Tate gallantly assured her, "but you are right. If Adriana and Dorothea will see to it that you are properly outfitted, I shall pay the shot. Oh, and

227

get some things for yourselves," he added expansively, including his wife and sister in his magnanimity. "I plan to eat, drink and be as merry as possible on Wednesday night, though it is only Bohea and dry bread at Almack's. I intend to be the envy of every man there, with three lovely ladies in tow. Oh, speaking of men, have you seen anything of Robin Wynne lately? He should be in town and I'm most eager to see him."

"Wynne?" Madalena asked, looking a little pale. "Is that a common name in England?"

"Not common, exactly, but not rare either," Tate informed her. "Have you heard from him, A.?"

"Not a word, but then, he always was so desperately shy, I doubt he would have the courage even to write to a woman, much less come to call. Dear Robin, I haven't seen him in over a year. Thea told me he was at your wedding."

"Yes, though I had quite forgotten that."

"I shall never forget his great kindness in my most daunting hour," Dorothea said in passionate accents.

"Daunting? Don't be overly dramatic, Dorothea. It was no more frightening than signing a tenant lease, with Broderick officiating."

"Perhaps for you it might have been so, but to me it was a desperate gamble."

"Surely you have forgotten what your alternative was: living with vicious Letitia must, of course, have been the greater evil."

"That was what I thought at the time, but I'm beginning to think I was mistaken."

Tate, suddenly sobered, looked at her closely. "And have you forgotten the rigors of sharing a home with Clarissa?"

"Not at all, sir, but there are other rigors, more . . ." she broke off in sudden confusion and gave her attention to the syllabub that had just been served. For the rest of the dessert she was oblivious to the conversation around her, so overset by the emotion that was shaking her. When the others left the table for the drawing room, she pled indisposition and ran upstairs to the safety of her bedchamber, but realized almost at once that this was no sanctuary. From this night she had been displaced by Madalena.

"In more ways than one," she murmured to Lovelace, as she led him to the nursery and ushered him into Harry's bedroom. Then she fled to the small room where the twins and Martha slept soundly. Too distraught to care whether she awakened any of the three infants, she cradled the drowsy Martha tightly to her bosom. The baby yawned and peeked at her out of one eye before snuggling against her neck and going back to sleep. This prosaic gesture brought tears to Thea's eyes and she held Martha even more tightly. "I shan't give you up, Martha; they can't make me, 'anular' or no 'anular,'" she vowed under her breath.

While these promises satisfied her emotions, her mind was perfectly aware that she had no claim to Martha and that if Tate left her, the baby would be lost to her forever.

With a sigh of bitter regret, she patted Martha back down in her cradle and kissed her downy head. She went to her room and began removing all her possessions. In spite of Adriana's gifts, it still required no more than two trips for her to remove everything she owned from her former bedchamber. As she hung her new gowns in Adriana's wardrobe, she began running through her vocalization exercises in an attempt to calm her over-wrought nerves. She kept her voice as soft as she could as she went about the business of readying the trundle for the night, and wondering how many more nights she would be banished from her own chamber.

Chapter 17

Dorothea was tucking in the coverlet on the trundle bed when Adriana came into the room. In her activity and music, she had managed to set aside the cataclysmic events of the past eight hours, but Adriana's sympathetic expression brought everything back.

"Well, Thea?"

"Well, A.?"

"Tate has gotten me into some terrible scrapes over the years, but this distempered freak is the outside of enough! How could he be so blind about this . . . this adventuress?" Adriana said, throwing up her hands.

"They say that love is blind," replied Thea softly.

"Don't be daft. Love has nothing to do with the way she is using him for her own purposes. And now she is using us as well!"

"There must be something we can do to show him what she is," Dorothea burst out.

"Yes, but speaking from long experience, I can tell you that it will not be easy. What man do you know who accepts counsel in matters of the heart from his sister," Adriana sighed. "No, I can do nothing. It is entirely up to you."

231

"To me?" expostulated Dorothea. "But what can *I* do?"

"My dear sister, you are, after all, legally his wife, and as such you have a whole arsenal of weapons at your disposal that are not available to me. Nor to Madalena, as long as Tate is your husband. At least, not legally so," she added with a wry grimace.

"Adriana, your confidence is touching, certainly, but I'm afraid you don't quite understand. Tate looks upon me as a glorified—or perhaps not so glorified—housekeeper and nursemaid to his child, and not as a wife in any true sense of the word."

"If that is all he sees in you, then he's blinder than I thought him. My dear, you have nothing to be ashamed of in your appearance, although you continue to think yourself the dowd you may once have been. And furthermore, my brother is not as oblivious to your improved looks as you think. Why, that was the first thing he noticed—after the comte, that is—when he walked into the house. And then, this evening, I could clearly see that he admired you when you came downstairs to dine. And I can promise you, Madalena could see it, too."

"But how can I possibly compete with someone so like Mathilde?" Thea asked plaintively.

"The resemblance is only skin deep, Thea. Mathilde did not have one calculating bone in her body, and if I read the signals correctly, Madalena Smythe-Davies is *all* calculation. No, much as it pains me to say it, Thea, I must warn you that unless you can open Tate's eyes to the truth about that hussy, she will have him talked into an annulment before he even knows what is happening. Is that what you want?"

"N-no. Certainly not, there's Martha and . . ."

Dorothea

"Forget Martha for a moment. If there were no Martha in the case, would you also wish to end the marriage?"

"But Martha was the reason for beginning it! I cannot conceive of the situation having arisen if there were no Martha," Dorothea said evasively.

"I am asking you, Thea, directly and frankly: do you or do you not want Tate as your husband?"

"Why, I . . ." Dorothea whispered, hanging her head in embarrassment. "Yes, I do. With all my heart."

Adriana squeezed her hand. "I knew it. I was convinced that you were in love with Tate, whether you knew it or not."

"Me, love Tate? That is preposterous. I hardly know him, and he has nothing but disdain for me. Hardly a promising love affair."

"My poor, naive, darling sister. If you cared nothing for him, it wouldn't ruffle you in the least to see him at the mercy of Madalena. There are similar situations in the *ton* every day, and the wife turns a blind eye as a matter of course."

These self-revelations proved too overwhelming for Dorothea and she dissolved into tears. Adriana comforted her with a warm hug.

"There, there, don't give up. Do you really think that one paltry Portuguese *aventureira* can outwit two intelligent Englishwomen?"

"It's not exactly her wits she's relying on," sobbed Thea. "It's her wiles."

"Then you shall just have to polish up your wiles as well. My jobbernoll of a brother is going to come to his senses eventually, and when he does, his senses are going to tell him he is an exceptionally lucky man to

233

have you for his wife," Adriana declared in ringing tones.

"Y-you really think so?" hiccoughed Dorothea.

Adriana gave her a confident smile. "I know so."

"And I know that Sir Nicholas Laidley is far luckier in his choice of bride than my esteemed husband."

"How true, how true," Adriana said with a little curtsy. "Now, to start the campaign, let us plan your toilette for Almack's. It must send Tate reeling."

"Oh, do they allow only country dances at Almack's? I was rather hoping for a waltz." This time Thea's grin was impish.

"That's my girl. When all else fails, throw in the lowest of puns. Now, about Almack's," Adriana hesitated, then went on. "I hate to complicate your life with further worries, but if I don't tell someone else what danger lurks for me there I shall fly into a pucker."

Dorothea looked at her inquiringly. "What are you talking about, A.?"

"I hope that your sensibilities will not be greatly overset by what I am about to tell you. And you must promise not to breathe a word of this to anyone. Why, I didn't even tell Tate the truth of the matter, though he wormed enough out of Nicholas to have ample fodder for making game of me the rest of my life."

"Your secret is safe with me, of course, but what on earth could you have done that was so very bad?" Dorothea said with a smile.

"It is no small peccadillo, Thea. You know that when Tate was missing in Portugal, right after Father died, I was desperate to find him, and I ran away to seek him, with some maggot in my head about going all the way to the Peninsula if I had to. But what you don't know is that I took the precaution of dressing up in

234

Tate's old clothes, and it was as Adrian Bancroft that I was taken up in Nicholas Laidley's carriage on that stormy day. And having started thus, I was forced to continue the same. Poor Nick came to look on me as a younger brother before the awful truth came out. My, but he was angry." A faraway look came into her grey eyes, then she shook her head and laughed.

"So in reality I acted as Harry's tutor, not his governess, as Aggie thinks."

Dawning comprehension lit up Thea's face. "Adrian," she exclaimed jubilantly. "Cousin Adrian, the black sheep of the family, who was sent to America!"

Adriana grinned ruefully. "I see Harry has been sharing confidences. You must indeed be his friend."

"And that explains the boy's clothes I found in your wardrobe at Bancroft Hall!" Dorothea said with a considering look.

"Yes, Nick forbade me to bring them along on our honeymoon."

"That makes a good deal of sense. I doubt he wanted anyone to think he had married a young man," laughed Thea. "But I fail to see why you are flying up in the boughs now. All that is ancient history."

"Not ancient enough, I'm afraid. You see, Nicholas did not twig my disguise until we had come to London and he had presented Adrian Bancroft, young gentleman, tutor, and younger son of a baronet to the *haut ton*. Not only did I make an appearance at Almack's last year in my male guise, but I made a scene as well by insulting a lady, who deserved every word. In fact, if the coloring and accent are overlooked, I would say that Lena and Sophia could be taken for twins, much as I hate to debase the term. At any rate, Lady Jersey witnessed the whole, and may recognize me as that rude youth, Adrian. Then we shall be in the basket!" she wailed.

Grateful that it was her turn to be the comforter, Dorothea patted Adriana's shoulder. "Don't you worry, A., you shall also have a *grande toilette* that will baffle any percipient observers. You shall be so ravishing that no one could picture you as a boy. And we will embroider up that Banbury tale about how splendidly Cousin Adrian is doing in . . . now where is it he is supposed to be flourishing?"

"Philadelphia," Adriana said gloomily.

"Philadelphia—that all will be thrown effectively off the scent. Actually, I am glad you have told me. It will give me something to think about instead of Tate and Madalena."

"Speaking of Tate and Madalena, I must tell you the latest development. While you were up here singing, we could hear you from the drawing room. Modest little Lena let slip that she too is a singer of notable gifts. A soprano."

"A soprano, a prima donna no doubt, that fits. Good God, on top of everything else, that woman is turning me into a thoroughgoing cat!"

Adriana laughed. "Do you know, she didn't mention her singing until after Tate had told her who your singing teacher is. And there's something else."

"Yes?"

"Tate found out that she plays the guitar, and offered to send for Mathilde's instrument from Bancroft Hall for her to use. It is the most infuriating . . . I only tell you this to strengthen your resolve to fight, Thea," she broke off to say. "I hope your feelings aren't too wounded. I remembered what you told me of your experiment with Mathilde's guitar, and I just seethed."

"Poor A. All you have done tonight is to soothe and seethe, and all on my account. I thank you."

"You are most welcome. And now," Adriana yawned hugely, "let's get some sleep. That two o'clock feeding looms large in my future. How lucky you are that Martha sleeps all night." She snuggled down into her pillows and fell fast asleep.

Slumber did not come to Dorothea so easily, and when it finally did, she dreamed that she was fencing with Madalena. She could clearly see Tate standing nearby, cheering on his Lena and ignoring his wife! When she looked down at her fencing foil, however, she saw instead a large triangular weapon, which was rusty and blunt, while a similar contrivance held by her opponent was shining and razor sharp.

"But what is this?" she cried, struggling to hold the awkward metal object before her.

"Wiles, my dear Dona Dorotéia, my weapon of choice," Mrs. Smythe-Davies coolly informed her.

Whereupon Dorothea threw down her "wile" and fled, to the sound of their derisive laughter.

The next morning, Dorothea awoke with a start, not quite knowing where she was, or who the sleeper in the adjoining bed could be. Worse than that was the vague feeling of foreboding which hung over her, though she could not remember the cause.

She stretched and yawned, and snuggled back down into her bedclothes. Then she recalled the reason for her anxiety: Tate. Tate and Madalena, to be exact. Once this essential fact was grasped, further sleep was impossible.

She carefully slipped out of bed and into her wrapper and started for the door. But before she reached it, a muffled voice addressed her from the canopy bed.

"Remember, D., where there's a wile, there's a way," Adriana said, throwing back her own coverlet.

"Oh, Adriana, I tried not to awaken you. Lord knows you get little enough sleep these days."

Adriana gaped, rubbed her eyes, then gave a little laugh. "Oh, last night I was practically a lady, or, if you like, Laidley of leisure, compared to previous experiences. Both Nicholas Tate and Mathilde Vitória slept like angels, more or less. I was only up twice to feed them."

Dorothea grinned. "Only twice, and that's angelic? You are the one in the halo, to my way of thinking."

"Well, Dr. Collins may have been provoking in the extreme before my confinement, but I think he is correct in his advanced notions of maternal practices. Besides, didn't you know that breastfeeding is all the rage amongst ladies of fashion? I wouldn't want to lag behind the mode, now would I?"

"You ninny-hammer, as if the mode mattered a jot to you in anything."

Adriana struck a humorous pose. "As of this moment, I am a veritable slave to fashion, and so are you. Have you forgotten that we are going to rig you out in the very highest kick so that Lena sinks into obscurity beside your blazing beauty."

"Adriana," sighed Dorothea. "You are a hopeless romantic. It is absurd to think a new gown will make the slightest difference to Tate."

"You might be surprised, and if clothes make the man, just consider what they might do for an overlooked wife. In any event, you have nothing to lose . . ." she paused, and the two women chimed in together, "but your husband."

238

As if in response to their words, a knock at the chamber door brought Tate into the room.

"I was on my way out, but heard your voices as I came down the hall, so I knew you were awake. Though what a slugabed you are, A.! You used to be up with the birds, back home," he said, his glance flicking over the threadbare silken wrapper that Dorothea clutched at the neck.

"Well, I'm up with the owls, now," Adriana said ruefully. "Or rather, the nestlings."

"He has not the slightest idea of what caring for an infant entails," Dorothea said, bristling at Tate's teasing of his twin. "He just goes on his merry way, leaving the . . ."

"Babies to their mothers, as is only proper. Especially when the mothers in question are so in the modern mode," Adriana said emphatically, giving Dorothea a look fraught with significance.

"I am so glad to be back in England, if only for a short time, that not even my needle-tongued wife can irritate me," Tate said breezily. "Listen, A., I must get over to the Ministry first thing this morning, and then I am going to call on Lady Jersey and try to charm some vouchers out of her for the victory ball at Almack's."

Adriana shot a panicked look at Dorothea, but only nodded genially to Tate.

"And when may we expect the honor of your presence, sir?" Dorothea said awkwardly, hearing the ice in her own voice and hating it.

"Don't fret, madam. I shall trouble you with my company as little as possible, since you seem to find it so objectionable." He turned to Adriana. "I'll be back for nuncheon. I'm going to stop in at White's and see if I can locate Robin. But I shall be back early in the

239

afternoon to pick up Madalena. She is simply wild to see London and I have promised to show her the sights."

"Wouldn't you like to take Dorothea along, too, Tate?" Adriana suggested eagerly, looking back and forth at the two stiff countenances. "She has yet to see all that London offers, and you could get to know one another better."

"I think that my wife has more charming guides at her disposal, and besides, my curricle holds only two in any degree of comfort."

"I cannot go in any case, Adriana," Thea said with an artificially bright smile. "Have you forgotten that I have a singing lesson with Philippe today? And besides, I promised I would take Harry riding in the park, and that he might help me give Martha her bath. He, at least, takes an interest in Martha's progress."

"You see, my dear wife is so *à la mode* that she hasn't a moment to spare for her husband anyway. You must absolve me of all blame, A. Until this afternoon, ladies," Tate said, and strode out before either young woman could say anything further.

"He always did like to have the last word, the vexing, vexing man," spluttered Adriana. "But you mustn't let him put your back up. We are going to throw a rub in Dona Madalena's way if it's the last thing we do. Agreed?"

"Agreed, but . . ."

"No buts, my girl. This is war, our very own skirmish in the Peninsular war."

"But where is our Lord Wellington? We could use some heavy artillery on our side."

"We may lack a Wellington, but we have our comte, and a little judicious use of jealousy is worth a regiment of light horse."

"Speaking of light horse, I had best find Harry and get to Hyde Park. I must go, or he'll complain of me to Lovelace and then I shall be in trouble. I can't afford to lose two of my staunchest allies in this engagement." Dorothea gave Adriana an uncertain smile, and changed out of her wrapper into the rust-brown habit that she had worn only a few times. It had been one of Adriana's gifts, but since the advent of the music lessons with the comte, she had not had much spare time to spend riding with the boy.

Adriana looked her up and down with an approving eye. "It's too bad Tate isn't here to see you now, Thea. You'd take the shine out of Madalena for certain."

Thea merely shook her head modestly and left to collect Harry from the nursery. While he changed into his own riding clothes, she played with Martha and chatted with the two governesses.

Seraphim's praise of Madalena was, mercifully, more subdued than it had been in the first flush of excitement over having another *Portuguêsa* in the house.

"Senhora Madalena is delightful, of course, but some of the things she says are not quite *gentil*," Seraphim was saying to Aggie as Dorothea entered the room. "Still, it is *esplêndido* to have someone who can speak my language. Adriana tries, but her *vocabulário* is very small. But what a pity that she was not acquainted with the Conde and Condessa de Vasconcellos. Then we would have had so much more to speak of."

Seraphim's words were not likely to give Dorothea much pleasure, and she was delighted when Harry came out in his buckskins and riding boots and dragged her to the door. She bade a hasty farewell to the denizens of the nursery, and ran downstairs with the boy to the entry where the groom was waiting with Harry's pony, Harney, and Adriana's cob, Dolly.

As the two rode along Oxford Street to the entrance of the park, Thea felt the light breeze clear her brain of its haunting worries. It was a glorious day, sunny and warm, that held a promise of a hot afternoon. It appeared that half of London found the weather alluring, for Oxford Street was crowded with men and women of fashion, unusual for that time of day.

Not for the first time, Thea was grateful that she knew so few people in town. She and Harry and Lovelace could amuse themselve in blessed anonymity, without having to halt every few minutes to greet acquaintances. It did seem to her that some of the young bucks were remarkably rude, however, turning to ogle her as she rode by with their quizzing glasses stuck in their impertinent eyes. She was entirely unconscious of the striking picture she made in her severely tailored habit with her burnished hair pulled back in braids under her feathered, curly-brimmed hat.

They entered the park and proceeded down the ring, turning by the Serpentine and dawdling along on Serpentine Road, admiring the play of light on the waves of the lake. Lovelace was in ecstasy, following his nose along the side of the road in a perfectly innocuous fashion. Suddenly he received a challenge from an unlikely source, which ended Dorothea's idyll in an explosion of canine altercation.

At a particularly crowded section of the roadway, a middle-aged lady, dressed in crimson and puce, sat in an open carriage. She was obviously aping the mode set by "Poodle" Byng, the noted dandy who paraded a poodle as his fashionable eccentricity, for at her side sat an indulged specimen of that pampered breed. The small fluffy white creature apparently took Lovelace in instant dislike, for he set up a yapping that no self-respecting mongrel could ignore. To investigate this challenge, Lovelace leapt into the carriage, sending the lady into strong hysterics and her dog out the other side of the landaulet with Lovelace in hot pursuit.

Dorothea's first instinct told her to make a run for it, leaving Lovelace to fend for himself, but as this would doubtless lead to his apprehension by the park authorities, she reluctantly prepared herself to enter the fray on his behalf. She pulled Dolly up and dismounted beside the carriage, where the lady in question had progressed to sniffing her vinaigrette and calling for a constable.

Thea turned to Harry, who was nearly falling off Harney, he was laughing so hard.

"Harry," she said sternly. "Go after Lovelace this instant. Don't interfere if the dogs are actually fighting, but try to distract Lovelace, and send that absurd poodle back here." She did not hold out much hope that Harry could accomplish this mission, but watched the boy ride towards the circling animals with great uneasiness.

Before Harry could reach them, however, a tall gentleman scooped a hatful of water from the Serpentine and threw it over the two dogs. Lovelace, quicker in his reflexes from his years as a stray, ducked the shower, but the poodle got the full force of it, and ran whimpering back to the landaulet.

His mistress, whose face by now was the same shade as her gown, exploded in wrath at this maltreatment of her darling, as she called to the animal to sit beside her.

"Come, Bonbon, my poor baby. Come to Mamma."

Bonbon obliged, but then proceeded to shake himself dry all over the lady and her velvet squabs. It quickly became apparent that by this rash act he had forfeited his good standing with his mistress, for he was subjected to a heavy scolding. But the full weight of the woman's outrage fell on Thea.

"If it had not been for the behavior of your atrocious monster, my poor Bonbon would not have been subjected to this awful drenching. Why, he might catch his death of cold and it is all your fault, you wretched girl."

"I beg to differ, madam," responded Thea frostily. "If your animal had not had the audacity to bark threateningly at my party, my own dog would not have been moved to defend us."

The woman's gaze shifted to someone behind Thea and subjected this unseen personage to prolonged scrutiny. "And as for you, young man, if my Bonbon contracts congestion of the lungs, I shall hold you personally responsible. What is your name and direction, sir?" she demanded.

"Captain Robin Wynne, at your service, ma'am. You may reach me at the War Ministry, if the need arises."

Thoroughly vanquished by this highly placed defense, the woman directed her groom to drive on, but the two left standing together on the path were oblivious to her hasty departure.

Chapter 18

Recognition and redness flooded Captain Wynne's face at the same time.

"Why, Doro . . . that is, Lady Bancroft. I had no idea you were in town," he stammered out.

"Yes, in town, and in trouble." Dorothea answered, almost as nonplussed as he. She clung to her horse's reins, feeling as if every eye in the park were riveted on her. "Once again I must offer you my thanks for your timely support."

"In trouble? What . . . nothing has happened to Tate, has it?" he asked with a worried frown.

"No, no, I merely meant Lovelace's causing me problems here this morning. Tate is in prime twig. Prime. In fact he's here. I'm surprised he hasn't come across you yet. He said he would try to track you down at White's or the Ministry."

"Well, then, I imagine I shall be seeing him before he has to leave, and . . ." once again he flushed, "and perhaps more of you?"

"Oh, I do hope so," she said warmly. "I am staying with Adriana at present and I know she is eager to see you. Do please come to see us, both during and after Sir Tate's visit."

At her formality in naming her husband, Captain Wynne's blue eyes fastened on her own as if seeking an answer to an unspoken question.

She looked quickly away and spotted Harry trotting toward them, with Lovelace, unabashed, running behind. When the boy halted his pony in front of them and saw who Dorothea's rescuer had been, his eyes widened in pleasure. Drawing himself up into military bearing, the boy stiffly saluted.

"Captain Wynne, sir," he barked out. "Cornet Laidley requests permission to dismount, sir."

"Permission granted, you little scamp. Come here and give me a hug."

Harry looked about him in embarrassment. "Is that an order, sir?" he asked, visibly squirming.

Captain Wynne scowled fiercely. "It is."

Relieved of personal responsibility, Harry catapulted himself off his pony and into Captain Wynne's arms, while Dorothea watched in delight.

After a thorough hugging, Harry drew back. "Have you heard about our witch?"

"What witch?" the captain asked, quirking a dubious eyebrow.

"Our witch! Her name is Madalena and she is disguised as Aunt Mathilde. Uncle Tate brought her to our house. And Aunt Adriana thinks she has bewitched Uncle Tate, for I heard her say so to Aunt Thea, with my own ears."

"With your own ears? But don't you know that a good military man never trusts his ears alone? You must look for other evidence before reporting to your superiors," the captain solemnly instructed him.

"Aye, sir. I'll do that, and report back," Harry said, with a smart salute. He handed the reins of his pony to Captain Wynne and ran off to throw a stick to Lovelace.

Once the boy was out of earshot, the captain turned to Dorothea with a bemused expression on his face. "So there's a witch in the house, is there?" he asked.

Thea, to her own chagrin, felt her eyes fill with tears. "Though you may find it hard to believe, Harry is not so far wrong." She stopped, her throat swollen with emotion, and fished desperately in her habit pocket for her handkerchief. She pulled it out and dabbed furiously at her eyes.

The gentleman stood as if turned to stone beside her. He made, at last, one convulsive movement towards her, then stopped as if afraid of touching her.

"Won't you tell me about it?" he asked softly.

"It's really nothing that I can tell you about, sir. And what there is, I am sure Tate himself will tell you when you see him." She blew her nose prosaically and stuffed her handkerchief back into her pocket.

"Now, if you will excuse me, I must get back to Portman Square. Oh, and I should ask you, just in case Tate does not find you to ask you himself, if you would consider attending the victory ball at Almack's. Tate seems to feel unequal to squiring three ladies without some additional masculine support. He probably is worried that he will be stuck with a whole nosegay of wallflowers on his hands."

"You are too modest, my lady. He is more likely to be besieged by would-be partners. But, if it will make you feel more at ease to see a familiar face, I shall attend. I have a dining engagement beforehand, so I shall have to meet you there."

"Oh, thank you, Captain. You are a friend indeed. I shall look forward to seeing you again."

"And I, you, my lady." He threw her up into the saddle and called Harry back. Giving the boy a boost onto Harney, he stood rigidly by, watching as they rode away.

Harry chattered on about Captain Wynne and Dorothea nodded abstractedly until something the lad said echoed her own thoughts.

"Captain Wynne must still be feeling poorly from that musket ball he took. I'll wager he still has a terrible fever. I never saw him so red-hot. And when he looked at you he seemed sicker than ever. His eyes had that funny look about them, like Uncle Tate. Do you think they've both caught something?"

Confused by these percipient youthful observations, Thea challenged Harry to a race back to Portman Square. He gleefully responded by digging his heels into Harney's round flanks and getting a head start on her. They flew down Oxford Street with Lovelace bringing up the rear, scattering pedestrians in their wake.

When they arrived breathless at the Laidley townhouse, they found the comte on their doorstep. After she handed Dolly over to the groom, and helped Harry from his pony, Thea managed a winded laugh.

"Do forgive, Comte, but I did not expect you so early," she said as she led the way into the house.

The Frenchman murmured his usual graceful amenities, but kept a weather eye on the dog and Harry. For his part, Harry dragged along behind with Lovelace as though any contact with the gentleman might prove lethal.

Dorothea removed her hat in the foyer and tried unobtrusively to tuck her windblown hair back into its pins. Then, turning back to her companions, she attempted to bridge their animosity by recounting the race just concluded.

"Harry trounced me soundly, the rascal," she concluded with a laugh.

The comte obliged with a faint smile, but continued to regard the dog with noticeable apprehension and the boy with undisguised loathing.

"I think, Harry, that you had best go ask Cook for a treat. I'm sure the comte will excuse you."

"But of course," de Blanchard eagerly concurred, and watched, pleased, as Harry and Lovelace departed.

Thea gestured towards the room in which they conducted their lessons. "Shall we begin, Comte? Though I am afraid I'm sadly out of breath, still I think I can manage the *vocalises*."

"Your exercise has put roses in your cheeks and stars in your eyes," he said, leaning toward her.

"And your English is deteriorating, sir. What I have is dust on my cheeks and hair in my eyes. Now, the *vocalises*?"

"Bah, let us not bother with dull exercises today. I have brought, especially for you, a most romantic, passionate love duet for us to sing together."

He set the music on the wooden stand and started leafing through the piece. "You see, here, the lady sings of her hopeless love for the young man, with this trill that is completely heartbreaking. And my part, here, echoes her lament, and then we join our voices in an overpowering, delicious climax." He moved closer with every syllable of this speech, until he stood pressed against her side. "Does it not tempt you, madame, to abandon your tedious *vocalises* and unite with me in making lovely music?"

"You do tempt me, Monsieur le Comte, but I must refuse."

"Ah, but you refuse only in order to be further cajoled."

"Nothing so complicated as that, monsieur. It is a matter of pitch, and nothing more," she said, moving away from him and taking up the book containing the duet. "Look at that note, and that, and that! All far above what is comfortable for me to sing."

At this juncture, a dulcet feminine voice interrupted them.

"Do pardon me, Dona Dorotéia, for intruding on your *lição de música*, but I believe I left my fan in here." Madalena swayed into the room, her eyes glued to the elegant figure of the comte. De Blanchard put up his glass and eyed her appreciatively.

"May I ask what *música* you are working on today? I myself am most fond of singing." She smiled sweetly and looked pointedly at the music Dorothea held in her hand.

When the gentleman named the duet under discussion, Lena's red lips curved themselves into an "o" of girlish delight.

"But I have sung this many times with my late husband Percy. It is so beautiful a piece, so, how do you say, *apaixanado*, but poor Percy never could do it justice. These Ingles, so *insensível*. Do you not agree, Monsieur . . . Monsieur . . . ?" she looked to Dorothea in shy perplexity.

Thea sighed and made the requisite presentation.

"Mrs. Smythe-Davies, may I introduce Monsieur le Comte Henri Philippe de Blanchard. Comte, this is Mrs. Smythe-Davies, who is staying with us for the present."

"Comte," breathed Madalena, her eyes shining up at him.

"Madame Smite—oh these English names, they are so difficult," he said with an engaging smile.

"Please, call me Madalena. It makes everything so simple, yes?"

"And you must *both* call me Philippe. Few have called me that since I left France." The corners of his perfectly sculptured mouth curved down mournfully.

"Ah, yes, I can see you too have suffered in this dreadful war. I also have lost everything I held dear— my beloved husband, my home . . ." her mouth drooped, if anything, more pathetically than his, and a small tear swam in each emerald eye.

Thea looked sidelong at the gentleman, half expecting his dark eyes to be wet as well, but he apparently had not had as much practice in that art as his feminine counterpart. Suddenly it seemed to Dorothea that she was the only spectator at a skillfully acted tragical play, with two actors fiercely competing for the center of the stage. She decided it was time to ring down the curtain on the affecting performance.

"At any rate, as I was saying, Comte, this duet is really not suited to my voice and . . ."

"Oh, may I try to sing it with you, Philippe?" Madalena broke in. "It would be poignant, yet blissful, to blend my voice with a manly baritone, as I used to do with Percy. Poor, *querido* Percy."

"I would be transported with joy to do so, Madalena, but just now I am working with Madame Dorothée and . . ."

Madalena flicked a look at Dorothea. "I see. And is it the practice here for married ladies to 'work' *tête à tête* with young men?"

"When one is a serious student of the voice, ordinary social practices are set aside, and Dorothée is such a student. She has made remarkable progress in the short time we have spent together."

Madalena tittered charmingly. "If you are such a wonderful *mestre* as that, perhaps I could persuade you to take me as your student as well. *Meu Deus*," she said with a *moue* of impatience, "I must find something to fill my time until the Smythe-Davies come to their senses."

The Frenchman, baffled by her words, shook his head. Then he shrugged. "We shall see, Madalena."

Thea, weary of this banter, closed the music book with a snap. "Perhaps we should forgo the lesson today, after all. With my husband returned, the entire household is turned upside down and I simply haven't the time to lavish on my music, I'm sorry to say."

"As you will, madame, though it grieves me to depart after so short a time with you." As was his custom, he took her hand and kissed it.

As if to demand similar treatment, Madalena thrust her hand before the comte's face. The gentleman seemed a bit taken aback by the lady's forward action, but after an almost imperceptible hesitation, he put his lips to her hand as well, and left them.

There was an awkward silence until, with compulsory politeness, Dorothea asked her companion to sit down.

"I shall ring for nuncheon to be served as soon as Adriana joins us."

"Oh, but that will not be necessary," Madalena replied coolly. "I have already bespoke a light luncheon to be brought in directly." It was evident that the new arrival had no interest in wasting her considerable charm on Tate's current wife.

Dorothea flushed with indignation at Mrs. Smythe-Davies' presumption. "I do think it would be more fitting to wait for Adriana. She is, after all, your hostess."

"And yours," Madalena said with a distinct curl to her lip.

"She is also, let me remind you, my dear sister. And I am devoted to her happiness, not to mention that of her brother, my husband."

"Oh, don't try to cozen me, my lady. Your husband, he has confided everything in me, so you needn't play the devoted wife for my benefit. It won't wash."

"What won't wash?" Adriana's voice came to them from the doorway. "I do hope you are not discussing the merits of various fabrics, for I am sick of the topic. I have just spent an entire morning poring over issues of *La Belle Assemblée* and *Ackerman's*, and I shall scream if anyone so much as whispers 'jaconet' or 'crêpe de Chine' or even lowly 'muslin' to me. Indeed, all that reading about sleeves *en gigot* and *bouillonnée* merely made me hungry. Shall we send for luncheon?" she said, taking a seat next to Dorothea.

"Mrs. Smythe-Davies already has."

"Oh, has she indeed? How very . . . thoughtful of her."

Madalena, having little appreciation for the subtleties of English speech, smirked in triumph. Adriana smiled at her faintly and continued her discussion of finery.

"Now, ladies, despite my fatigue with the subject, I think we should take a look at these fashion plates together before Mademoiselle Arlette arrives. That is our modiste, Madalena. She is an excellent seamstress with a wonderful flair for color and design. I am sure you will be pleased with her work. Now, since you are going out to see the sights with Tate this afternoon, I think you should make your selections first, Madalena. We mothers have nothing pressing on our time except playing in the nursery with the babies."

Madalena was all enthusiasm for the task at hand, and by the time Tate returned to the house after lunch, she had already been measured for her Almack's gown, and sketched out what she had in mind for Mademoiselle.

"Success on all fronts," Tate announced gaily, as he came into the room. "The Ministry says I need not depart for several days, Lady Jersey was most accommodating about the vouchers for Almack's, and I unearthed Robin at White's. But it was the oddest thing. Convincing the reclusive Robin to join us at the Temple of Exclusivity was simplicity itself. Most unnatural behavior. I wonder what could have come over him since he was invalided out of the regiment. Poor fellow, perhaps civilian life has addled his brains."

"Or softened his heart," Adriana said with a glance at Dorothea. "Perhaps he is in the market for a wife."

"Robin? Don't be absurd. If a woman so much as smiled at him he would melt down into his Hessians in terror."

"This Robin, he is the Captain Wynne of whom you spoke before?" Madalena asked in an anxious tone.

"Yes, Robert Wynne. We only call him Robin as a nickname, an *apelido*," Tate explained. "He and I served together for ages in Portugal."

A look of definite alarm crossed Madalena's face, but she quickly pasted on her customary smile. "Oh,

Tate, I must show you the sketch of my *grande toilette* for Almack's" she said coquettishly.

Adriana seized the opportunity to speak out on the subject. "I think you will regret not having your gown more generously cut under the bodice. Sooner than you think, it will be too tight to wear, and I speak from experience. It would be a pity to have to set it aside so quickly."

"But I don't want to look like an *abóbora*," Madalena wailed, then added hastily, "any sooner than I must."

"You could never look like a pumpkin, Lena," laughed Tate. "Now let's see this dress."

Mollified, Mrs. Smythe-Davies took out the sketch. "It will be a *beleza*, an *encanto* of a gown, I am so grateful to you for letting me have it made."

"The pleasure is mine, my dear, and it will suit you to perfection. Such beauty and enchantment as yours is not often found at Almack's Assembly Rooms, or so I understand. My friends tell me that antidotes are more plentiful than nonpareils within those hallowed walls."

Madalena waved the drawing at him and the two of them huddled over it deep in animated conversation. Adriana and Dorothea shared an issue of *La Belle Assemblée* for the purpose of conferring with one another behind its oversized pages.

"I wonder why she is so interested in Robin Wynne," Adriana whispered, then followed this by an audible exclamation over the trim on a particularly unappealing ball gown.

"Perhaps she is starting a collection of soldiers, like Harry's leaden ones. Percy and Tate are not enough to make a set," Thea replied in a low voice. "Although," she added after remarking aloud on a grotesque turban surmounted by a stuffed bird, "it seems to me that she is more than interested in Captain Wynne. I would say that she acts decidedly uneasy every time his name is mentioned."

Adriana agreed with this interesting assessment, but further speculation was curtailed when Tate stood up and walked over to them.

"Well, we're off to explore Hyde Park and the Tower," he said with a grin. "Don't expect us until you see us."

"But what about dinner?" Adriana protested.

"Don't wait for us, A. We'll manage with a cold collation somewhere. But we will be here all evening. After all the afternoon's activities, I don't want to fatigue Lena by dragging her out to the opera or the theater. Must treat the poor thing with kid gloves, after all."

Dorothea thought privately that she would prefer handling the lady in question with bare fists, but judiciously refrained from saying so.

Tate took Lena's arm and started for the door, then paused and addressed Adriana once more. "Is a family evening all right with you, Adriana? We'll have all the babies and Harry, and even Lovelace, if he behaves himself. And with Lena, and Dorothea, of course, we can even make a little family music. That is certainly a novelty in our talentless family, isn't it, Adriana?"

"Sad, but true," Adriana said.

"And I nearly forgot," Tate said, stepping away from Madalena. "I have a surprise for you, Lena, that will delight all of us. Just a minute and I shall fetch it." He hurried out into the hall and returned with a leather case.

"Here you are, Lena. I sent for this for you to play for us. I know that Mathilde would have wanted it to be played by someone so like her."

Madalena beamed at him and opened the case. Dorothea did not need to look to see what lay inside. It was Mathilde's guitar.

Chapter 19

Adriana's hand shook visibly as she reached up to fasten her tiara more securely in her brown curls. The reflection that returned her frightened gaze did not appear to bolster her flagging spirits, even though her gown of silver tissue was very flattering, or would have been had her color been less ashen. For the first time in her life, Lady Laidley had been constrained to dip into the rouge pot, and the two red spots on her pale cheeks made her look like nothing so much as the famous clown Grimaldi.

She scrubbed at the offending color with her handkerchief and addressed Dorothea, who alone had accompanied her into the ladies' antechamber at Almack's for some final prinking before entering the "holy of holies."

"I don't mind telling you, Thea, that I am fretted to flinders about going in there. Whatever possessed Tate to come to this dreadful place? I hated it when Nick dragged me here as Adrian. And now I doubly hate it, knowing that Lady Jersey or any of a dozen others might recognize me and spread the delicious scandal all over town." She gave her head an angry shake, then, too late, remembered the tiara. Fortunately, it had stayed firmly in place. "Nick will be utterly furious with me for coming," she muttered, checking her headpiece's anchorage for a last time.

"There, there, A., don't fly into a pucker. You look entirely feminine and respectable. No one could ever take you for an upstart young man in that fetching rig," Dorothea whispered with a nervous giggle. Then she turned to inspect her own image in the glass, with more trepidation than she was willing to admit.

It was her gown that accounted for a large measure of her own uneasiness, having no past experience to haunt her. In all her twenty-odd years, Dorothea had never worn anything half so daring. She inwardly cursed herself for allowing Adriana and Mademoiselle Arlette to convince her that she should wear it. She recalled with a wry smile how Adriana had pronounced that if Tate's eye must rove, it might just as well be in Dorothea's direction. Now she only prayed that he wouldn't notice how the neckline of the pale apricot gown scooped to reveal the swell of her white bosom. She had been safe enough from his scrutiny when she had descended the stairs at Portman Square. He had been engrossed in conversation with Madalena, and Thea had clutched her silk mantalet over her *décolletage* like a shield.

Now, with the mantalet in the hands of the prinking room attendant, she inspected herself in the mirror with fresh discomfiture. She bit her lip, wishing fervently that the blond lace around her neckline had been added to cover rather than to display so much of her endowments. It was not only the bodice of her gown that gave her pause, however. Lace rosettes caught up the fall of the crêpe de Chine skirt, and revealed the filmy underskirt, which, in turn, revealed the outline of her limbs for all and sundry to see. I might just as well have dampened my drapery like an opera dancer, or be walking in naked, she thought wildly. She looked down at her feet and tried to take what confidence she could from the fact that they, at least, were unexceptionally clad in apricot satin dancing slippers.

Putting on a brave face for Adriana's sake, she said soothingly, "From what you have told me of Sir Nicholas, I don't believe he would care a rap if there *were* a scandal. Indeed, I shouldn't wonder if what he first loved about you was your unconventionality."

"Unfortunately, what society considers unconventionality in a young man is deemed scandalous in a young woman. And it was as the former that Nick knew me. And the Almack's crowd as well."

"And now all they will see is a lovely matron. Your secret is safe as houses," Dorothea assured her.

"Aren't you two ready yet?" Madalena said impatiently from the arched doorway. In her robe of rose silk, cut as low across the bosom as Dorothea's, and with matching pink flowers twined into her black hair, Madalena had little of the widow about her. Her only concession to her bereaved state was the black lace tunic that served to mold her gown more closely to her figure. As the woman tapped her pink kid slipper against the floor in irritation, Dorothea saw that Madalena did not share her qualms about the evening ahead.

"Tate sent me to tell you that it is nearly eleven, and we will not be admitted past that time," Mrs. Smythe-Davies said waspishly, then whirled and walked away.

"That would suit me down to the ground," Adriana moaned, but she gathered up her skirts and walked bravely into the corridor where Tate was awaiting them with his *protégée*.

Dorothea avoided any final glance in the looking glass, fearing that to do so would rob her of her tenuous poise. With her heart in her pretty, demure slippers, she went out to join the others. When she came up to them, she saw that Adriana was on one of Tate's arms and that Madalena was firmly clasping the other. This did not affect her nearly as much as the sight of Tate's broad shoulders. In his snowy linen and waistcoat, and his black coat of Bath superfine, she thought him by far the most striking gentleman in view. It did not escape her notice that the black satin breeches and stockings, *de rigueur* at Almack's, showed off his muscular legs to a nicety. From his waistcoat pocket hung an unusual garnet and pearl watch fob, the red stones making a splash of color against his black and white formal garb.

At Dorothea's approach, Adriana moved away from her brother so that he might escort his wife into the ballroom.

"Don't worry, Adriana," Thea said with a diffident smile. "I am perfectly able to walk into a room unassisted, even one as celebrated as this."

Madalena said nothing, merely clinging even tighter to the elbow of her gallant. Her expression of smug satisfaction was more than Dorothea could bear with equanimity, and she turned away. As she did, her glance crossed that of her husband and locked. She was transfixed by the intensity of his expression, which she found impossible to decipher, much less understand.

"Dorothea?" he said, his voice barely audible.

"Yes?" she breathed in reply.

He cleared his throat and in a voice devoid of all expression, continued, "You have lost your wrap. You'd best get it. There is no call for you to make an exhibition of yourself. I won't allow it. We are here, after all, to establish Lena's good reputation, and not to tarnish your own."

Anger flooded over her, made the more bitter because she had allowed herself to hope that he might be dazzled by the improvements in her looks. Instead he had as much as called her a member of the muslin company, and in front of Madalena.

Adriana, forgetting her own fears, came to Thea's defense. "Why, Tate Bancroft, I am surprised at you. Dorothea looks utterly divine tonight. Her gown is modesty itself compared with what others will be wearing, as you will see. Thea, let us go in together. And don't you dare cover up with that stupid mantalet."

Without a second look at the other two, Adriana and Thea linked arms and marched into the ballroom with a bravado born of anger. However, their confident facade crumbled almost at once when the first person they encountered was Lady Jersey. Sally Jersey, whom some wag had dubbed "Silence" because of her wagging tongue, was one of the more approachable of the patronesses. Nevertheless, she held a special terror for Adriana as the witness to her *débâcle* here two seasons before, and Adriana's grip on her sister's arm tightened convulsively as Lady Jersey addressed her.

"Why, you are Lady Laidley, are you not? I would recognize you anywhere, you are so like your young cousin. Such a remarkable family resemblance, I declare!"

Adriana and Thea exchanged looks, but "Silence" plunged on without waiting for a response.

"And how is your cousin these days?" she tittered, while she made play with her lavender fan, which matched her feathered headdress. "I understood from a mutual friend, Lady Arbuthnot, that the young scamp emigrated to America to seek his fortune. I do hope he is thriving. Such a good-looking young man, though a bit of an April squire."

Dorothea looked over at Adriana, whose mouth was moving soundlessly, and felt it incumbent upon herself to answer Sally Jersey's barrage of questions.

"Ah, yes, dear Cousin Adrian. I, of course, have arrived in the family too late to make his acquaintance, but from his letters, I feel that I know him intimately."

Madalena, moving gracefully ahead of her tall escort through the crowded room, caught the last of this. She turned back to him and demanded to know of whom they were speaking.

"You never told me you had a cousin in America, Tate. How *romântico!*"

When the baronet came up to them, he wore a roguish grin, but answered Lena's puzzled query with every appearance of seriousness.

"Ah, yes, Cousin Adrian. We do not often speak of him, you understand, as he has been the black sheep in our family. I fear that he left England under quite a cloud, but he has evidently turned quite respectable now. He's even married and become a doting parent. Yes, quite the pillar of rustic society now, our Adrian," he said, with an amused glance at his sister, who appeared on the verge of a swoon.

While Madalena took a modicum of interest in any conversation centering on a gentleman, she lost interest as soon as she heard that he was married.

"Tate," she pouted prettily, "are you not going to present me to this so charming lady?"

Recalled to duty, Tate made the introductions and began an affecting recital of Mrs. Smythe-Davies' misfortunes.

Dorothea

Lady Jersey forestalled a complete account with a flutter of her fan. "But I have already heard of the monstrous treatment she has suffered at the hands of her husband's relatives," she proclaimed. "I am convinced that so lovely a young lady cannot fail to be welcome in our ranks." Her attention span ended, she turned her restless eyes on Thea. "And speaking of lovely young ladies, Sir Tate, I have not yet been properly presented to your wife. I presume that this is she?"

Tate answered tautly that the lady was quite correct in her presumptions. "This is my wife, Dorothea."

Lady Jersey leaned forward to examine Dorothea closely. "You were a Sandham, were you not, my dear?" she asked.

"Why, yes, I was," stammered Dorothea, rather taken aback by the woman's knowledge.

"I thought so. Then you must be the young person who used to live with Letitia Grayson, who is a great good friend of Countess Lieven. What luck—they are both in attendance this evening. I'm sure that your cousin will be more than pleased to see you again," she crowed.

"I'm sure," came Dorothea's weak echo.

"Well, I shall send her your way when I see her. And now if you will excuse me, I must be about my duties. You see, it is the most thrilling thing. We are going to have a special cotillion tonight, with figures specifically designed to portray the maneuvers at Vitória. We call it the 'Wellington Rout.' I do hope you will all participate!"

There was a general murmur of acquiescence and the lady took her leave with a final flourish of her purple feathers.

"Fancy her remembering dear Cousin Adrian," Tate teased his twin, who flushed and looked exceedingly ill at ease.

"How odd that you have never mentioned him to me," put in Madalena, with a coquettish look at Tate.

Dorothea could not resist this opening. "We Bancrofts tend to keep Cousin Adrian to ourselves. He was such a rowdy lad, getting into mischief at every turn, that we don't like to bandy his name about with strangers," she said, deliberately stressing the last word.

Madalena did not bother to take exception to the term, turning instead to Tate with a devastating smile.

"It sounds as if they are playing a *valsa*. Oh, may we dance to the *valsa*, Tate?" she cooed.

"Of course, my dear. A., can you and Dorothea find places to sit and wait for us?" Tate said.

Adriana frowned her disapproval, but remarked that she thought they could manage. She and Dorothea watched in silence as Tate took the Portuguese lady in his arms and waltzed away.

"B-but, Adriana, shouldn't Madalena have asked permission from one of the patronesses before waltzing?" asked Thea. "I thought you told me that unless a lady asked permission first, she would be considered 'fast.' "

Adriana smirked ever so slightly. "That is very true. How remiss of Tate not to have asked beforehand," she said with a counterfeit sigh.

"Much as we would enjoy her being censured, A., it will only delay our getting rid of her in the long run," Thea warned. "If she comes to be labelled 'fast' it will hardly endear her to her prospective family."

"I didn't think of that," Adriana sighed, genuinely distressed. "Come, let's find Lady Jersey and talk to her on behalf of our guest before Lena and Tate are spotted dancing. Even if our plea shortens Madalena's stay by one hour, it will be worth the effort."

They ploughed through the stylish throng and easily located Lady Jersey by virtue of her lavender aigrette, which waved like a flag out of the group of grande dames.

"Excuse me, my lady, may we have a word with you?" Adriana said, tapping her on the shoulder.

Lady Jersey, all affability, replied, "Of course, Lady Laidley. Do you know, I feel as if I know you already, you look so very much like your cousin. Truly, the resemblance is remarkable."

"And, of course, like Tate," Dorothea contributed earnestly, hoping to muddy the waters. "Why, they could be taken for triplets."

Adriana nodded. "That's what everyone who knows all three of us always says," she proclaimed offhandedly, then plunged into her request, by proxy, that Mrs. Smythe-Davies be permitted to waltz with impunity.

"Hmm, it is rather irregular. I see that she is already doing so, but, just this once, I think I shall overlook it. After all, she isn't exactly the run-of-the-mill green girl, and the poor thing has suffered enough. Besides, we can't expect a foreigner to be knowledgeable about our little rules."

"Who has suffered enough?" someone demanded to know, in a voice all too familiar to Dorothea. It belonged, beyond the shadow of a hope, to her cousin Letitia Grayson.

A look of predatory delight came over the countenance of the ill-tempered old lady as she perceived to whom Lady Jersey was talking.

"Ah, Letitia," beamed Lady Jersey. "We were just

speaking of Mrs. Smythe-Davies. Has the countess told you the sad tale?"

"Yes, indeed," the small eyes glittered as she spoke. "A pathetic case. I feel quite overcome by her pitiable state."

Dorothea caught a glimpse of the pitiable Mrs. Smythe-Davies as she whirled past ecstatically in Tate Bancroft's arms. Oblivious to the others, Thea followed the couple with her eyes. Her absorption was broken by Miss Grayson's addressing her directly for the first time.

"Dorothea. Shouldn't you put some lace over your bosom? You quite put me to the blush."

Lady Jersey tsked at her friend. "Now, Letitia, you must not play the Puritan at Almack's, you know," she chided. "Especially when I heard you, not five minutes ago, give exactly the opposite advice to Lady Phoebe Robinson. Now where is that girl? She was right here just a moment since." She drew closer and confided, "Poor Phoebe is as flat as can be, and we were just advising her to eke out Mother Nature's lack of bounty by the judicious use of wadded cambric. Then she might be able to throw away her shawl. Such extremes of modesty are ludicrous in a lady of fashion, and I did not scruple to tell her so. Ah—here you are, my dear Phoebe."

The woman who came forward was substantially above normal height for a woman, but she was not so tall as to be grotesque. A few stray brown ringlets peeked out from her pleated turban, an adornment which in itself proclaimed to the world that she considered herself on the shelf. It appeared that she was not entirely resigned to her spinster state, however, for a frivolous heart-shaped beauty mark, very *démodé*, was glued to one heavily powdered cheek. It had the unfortunate effect of accentuating the fact that the lady was not a beauty.

Lady Phoebe's one really attractive feature was her eyes, which were sky blue, though their color was nearly obscured by her habit of fluttering them in a most mannered style. For the briefest moment, however, Dorothea looked straight into them, and was astounded to see that they were brimming with suppressed merriment.

After Adriana and Dorothea expressed the usual civilities, Lady Phoebe reciprocated in a high-pitched squeal strangely at variance with her angular features.

"Mercy me—so you are the two guardian angels who have taken in that poor little Smythe-Davies widow. You must have hearts of the purest gold!"

Since their heartfelt emotions were far from pure or golden, Adriana and Dorothea murmured polite demurrals, nonplussed by this ill-deserved acclaim. But Lady Phoebe would have none of their modest disclaimers.

"Yes, yes, I vow you have such enviable hearts," the lady insisted. "And unless I am much mistaken, here comes the object of your charity now. No, no, you must not think me clairvoyant," she warbled. "It is only that one rarely sees such raven hair in England. Besides, her companion closely resembles Lady Laidley, as befits a 'triplet.' "

It was Tate and Madalena who joined them presently, and Lady Jersey once again did the honors, presenting everyone who was unacquainted.

Tate forestalled her when she came to introduce Miss Grayson.

"Ah, but Miss Grayson and I know each other of old, do we not, Miss G? And how is Clarissa faring? I hope she has suffered no lasting ill effects from her adventures in my shrubbery last summer. We have often wondered about her fate, haven't we, Dorothea?"

Miss Grayson bristled. "Clarissa is very well, considering," she said tartly, giving Dorothea a look of pure venom.

"Considering she is mother to six of the strangest looking pups that we have ever laid eyes on . . ." Lady Jersey finished for her with a laugh. "And Letitia is too tender-hearted to drown them, as we have all urged her to do. So far no one seems inclined to adopt them, and there are far too many to fit their portraits on Letitia's calling card. Such a quandary."

Under Lady Jersey's quizzing, Miss Grayson flushed with anger. Tate sent a quick look of amusement at Dorothea, and in so doing, encountered the demure countenance of Lady Phoebe. His gaze was arrested and he stared at the powdered face with as much fascination as if he were admiring the loveliest of maidens.

To Dorothea's surprise, Lady Phoebe did not seem at all discomposed by this pointed scrutiny. She looked coy, and flirted her fan at the baronet in a manner more suited to a hardened coquette than a confirmed ape-leader. But she was not the only lady present who appeared to be acting in an uncharacteristic fashion.

In an unexpected burst of enthusiasm, Madalena exclaimed, "Oh, how I adore little dogs! May I have one of your babies, Miss Grayson?"

"Why, Mrs. Smythe-Davies, I should be delighted," Miss Grayson purred. "Such a request shows a remarkable sensitivity. Won't you accompany me to the refreshment salon and we shall discuss it at length. And then you may tell me more of your own sad plight."

"Of course," smiled Madalena, blushing prettily,

for all the world as though Miss Grayson were an eligible suitor. "I really should not dance too much anyway," she added with an arch look. She offered Miss Grayson one round white arm, proposing they seek out a quiet corner for a private talk.

Miss Grayson, glancing back, directed a malicious look at Dorothea, who felt her heart plummet. She had no doubt that Cousin Letitia and Madalena would waste little time before comparing notes about the circumstances and condition of Sir Tate's disgraceful marriage.

At the thought of her husband she looked about and was astonished to find him still deep in flirtation with Lady Phoebe. They were both chattering away like the oldest of companions, though to Dorothea their conversation conveyed little, if any, sense. Even Adriana seemed puzzled by the unlikely coupling, particularly when Tate did not even take notice of Madalena's departure.

"So, tell me, Lady Phoebe, do you sing like a lark?" he said playfully.

"La, sir, don't be a goose! I caw like an old crow. But please call me Sparrow—all my gentlemen friends do. They say it is because I twitter so preciously, though I suspect they only mean I am bird-witted."

"Now, don't grouse," Tate protested.

Suddenly Adriana exploded into a coughing fit that sounded well-mixed with laughter. "Why, Lady Phoebe, I have finally remembered who you are. It has been simply ages since I've seen you, my dear. I haven't been as fortunate as Dorothea here, who met with you as recently as yesterday, in the park. In the park, Dorothea . . ." Adriana said again, with a gentle nudge.

Dorothea wondered if Adriana had taken leave of her senses. She had encountered no one even remotely resembling this odd lady in the park yesterday. "Adriana, are you feeling quite well?" she asked anxiously.

"I feel wonderful. Really, I had no inkling that Almack's could be so much fun! Tate, come dance with me."

Tate replied with a bow and took his sister's arm to steer her onto the dance floor. Lady Phoebe watched the two of them move off with an enigmatic smile.

"Such dears, both of them. You are lucky to have them for your family. But, enough of them. Let us sit down and have a good coze. I want to hear all about you."

"But there is nothing to tell," Dorothea said, moving with Lady Phoebe to the hard chairs that lined the walls. "I'm really quite ordinary and my history much like any other's."

"I don't believe you for a moment, but I'll allow you the superior knowledge for now and switch the topic to Mrs. Smythe-Davies. I'd go bail that there is nothing ordinary about her."

"Hardly," Dorothea said dryly.

"And she doubtless has a very colorful history. Do you know, I have the oddest feeling that I have seen her somewhere before."

Lady Phoebe's affectations fell away for an instant and she looked into Thea's face without a hint of her earlier mannerisms.

"I scarcely think so. You have surely not been out with Wellington in the Peninsula, or have you?" Thea laughed.

"Surely not," the ungainly spinster said, gazing at Thea intently. "Can you imagine me as a dragoon?"

Suddenly recognition dawned on Dorothea. "Actually," she said slowly, her eyes widening in amazement,

"I rather think I *can*. After all, aren't you a very close connection of Captain Robert Wynne? I imagine that you have just as much sand as he does, not to mention *sang-froid*."

Lady Phoebe shook her curls, and the blue eyes twinkled. With a warning finger laid against her generous mouth, she whispered hoarsely, "Don't cry rope on me, my lady, else my goose, or should I say 'robin,' will be cooked."

Dorothea stared at her companion incredulously. "I shall not give you away, but what kind of rig are you running, Cap . . ." she started to whisper, but broke off abruptly when she found herself addressed by the Comte de Blanchard.

The Frenchman appeared, even to Dorothea's relatively untutored eyes, somewhat out of place in the plain, almost austere surrounding of the exclusive club. His rose satin breeches and gorgeously embroidered waistcoat were startling reminders of the more opulent age of the *ancien régime* in France.

"Why, Lady Bancroft," he murmured, his dark face wreathed in smiles. "How fortunate I am to find you sitting out a dance! Will you do me the great honor of finishing out this set with your humble servant?"

"I thank you, no, Philippe. I am rather fatigued and do not plan to dance for a while. But let me make you known to my new friend, Lady Phoebe Robinson, who is also without a partner at present," Dorothea could not resist saying with a twinkle. "Lady Phoebe, I might add, is an intimate connection of Captain Wynne, who served so gallantly in the Peninsula with my husband."

The brief look of consternation with which the comte had greeted Thea's suggestion gave way to a polite blankness, and finally was supplanted by an avid gleam of interest.

"Really? You are truly in the confidence of the so fearless and famous Capitaine Wynne? Such a loss of our gallant forces when the *capitaine* became *invalide*. I am told that he was one of Wellington's most trusted intelligence officers."

"Is that so?" Lady Phoebe said in her high falsetto. "I know little of such truly masculine pursuits. So, as to anything of that nature, well, you must simply ask him yourself. He is far too modest to boast of his exploits, even to me."

"You yourself are too modest, my lady. I'm sure you know much more of his feats than you reveal. And of his current pursuits as well."

"Current pursuits? But he does nothing now but read the newspapers and yearn for battle."

The comte's smile widened, displaying his small, perfect teeth. "And I do nothing but yearn for a dance with you. Come, my lady."

With a gloved hand he drew the still-protesting Phoebe to her feet. The fact that she was an inch or two taller than he did not seem to daunt the Frenchman at all. His smile did become a shade more fixed, however, as he took the large female into his arms and attempted to sweep her onto the dance floor. The effect of his gallantry was spoiled when Lady Phoebe's large satin slipper descended on his unprotected foot in its elegant, but low-cut evening pump. After a pained hop or two on the part of the gentleman, the two stumbled, then swung into the rhythm of the dance.

Fortunately for the captain, the waltz was nearly ended when they began, and after only a few minutes, he was escorted back to Dorothea by de Blanchard.

Adriana and Tate, returning at the same time, saw the comte and Lady Phoebe together, and grinned hugely.

"And are you rested enough to dance with me now?" the Frenchman began when he and his tittering partner reached Dorothea's side.

She looked over at Tate, whose good-humored smile somehow dimmed at the comte's words. Without really planning to do so she turned to the waiting de Blanchard, smiling and fluttering her lashes in the best Madalena tradition.

"I should be delighted, Philippe," she said, loudly enough for her husband to hear.

She gave her hand to her partner and allowed herself to be led off to the dance floor. The next quarter hour she spent parrying the gentleman's effusive compliments and giving thanks that the set was not a waltz. Even the brief meetings during the country dance gave the comte far too much opportunity to hold her much too closely. As she made her way down the set, she caught sight of her husband, frowning at her still, but she lost sight of him quickly and tried to put him out of her mind as well.

Her dance with Philippe left her agitated and nearly as fatigued as she had claimed. There was a glow in her cheeks that was not lost on the others when they returned to where Tate was engaged in hilarious conversation with Adriana and Lady Phoebe.

The Frenchman asked Adriana for a dance, and soon thereafter Dorothea found herself besieged by young men for the honor of partnering her. For the next hour, she never sat down, and when, exhausted, she looked about for the others, she saw only Tate and Lady Phoebe sitting together next to the wall, deep in discussion. She was still anxious to know why Robin was masquerading as the bombastic Lady Phoebe. When she approached with a tentative smile, both looked up and started slightly. Tate rose to his feet, and Lady Phoebe almost did the same, but remembered in time that she should remain seated, as befitted her age and gender.

"We were just speaking of your *cicibeo*," Tate said glacially, still maintaining an amiable smile.

Much of Thea's pleasure evaporated at his icy greeting. "You are determined to dislike the comte, Sir Tate, but I see no reason for this distempered freak. He is harmless."

"I wouldn't be too sure of that, my dear," said Lady Phoebe gently, then she patted the chair beside her for Dorothea to sit down.

Dorothea did so, but grudgingly. "I did not think that you too would turn against me, Capt . . . er . . . Lady Phoebe."

"I never would, Dorothea. You know that." Lady Phoebe, for the first time, seemed out of countenance. "It's just that the Comte de Blanchard looks a little smoky for my taste or comfort. For such a staunch foe of Boney he has some very peculiar friends." He turned to Tate. "I still don't think it's wise to allow him to run tame in your sister's house."

"Those are my sentiments, exactly," Tate said quietly. "But you don't know my sister or my wife at all well if you imagine that my opinion is worth a farthing to either of them."

Dorothea, looking from one to the other in exasperation, was amazed to see that both wore expressions of the greatest pleasure rather than the black looks their harsh words would have led her to expect. At this close range, however, she could discern that their smiles were forced.

"Well, I think you are both being too harsh on a man who has lost everything in this terrible war," she protested, carefully keeping her face as artificially gay as theirs.

"And I think you are blinded by his fawning flattery and seductive eyes," Tate muttered under his breath.

"Seductive?" she squeaked in outrage. "And just what do you accuse me of, Tate Bancroft?"

Lady Phoebe inserted herself into their altercation with a look of apology. "At the risk of being tiresome, might I suggest that you discuss this when you are alone. Don't forget, we are at Almack's, where gaiety and matchmaking are the order of business. Now, why don't you two stop pulling caps and dance with one another. As for me, I'm ready for my bed. After all, a Phoebe is not a night owl. I'll just find Sally and make my adieus."

"Fine," Tate spluttered, and taking Dorothea's limp hand in his, steered her into the swirling crowd.

At the touch of his hand on hers, Dorothea felt her knees and resolution weaken, and cursed herself for a fool. Drat that Captain Wynne, she thought furiously. The very last thing I want is to be embraced in a waltz in this very public place by my wretched husband. After the traitorous way her body had reacted to his insulting treatment when he had left Bancroft Hall on their wedding day, she did not trust her own instincts.

With a total disregard for her lack of enthusiasm, Tate encircled her waist with one arm and took her hand with his other.

"Smile, my dear wife. Everyone is watching us and

dying of curiosity about our mull of a marriage. Shall we give them something to gossip about?"

He drew her to him until she could scarcely breathe and whirled her across the floor. She was astounded to discover that whereas the comte's similar behavior only made her feel trapped and embarrassed, Tate's holding her so closely made her feel something quite different.

In a desperate effort to regain her emotional equilibrium Dorothea exclaimed, "I have heard many things of you, Tate Bancroft, but never that you were a dog in the manger."

Tate kept smiling down at her, but his words were like acid. "If you mean to imply that I envy the comte because you cherish a *tendre* for him, you are quite out. I wouldn't dream of interrupting your touching idyll. As long as you are discreet, of course."

"Oh, I am discretion itself, Tate darling. You have nothing to worry about."

"Fine, then shall we just enjoy our dance, preferably in silence?" snapped Tate.

"It would be my pleasure. When it is finished I suggest that you go and rescue your *protégée* from my cousin. I am sure that she will be effusively grateful and tell one and all that you are her knight errant."

She felt Tate stiffen and miss his step in the dance. Following the direction of his gaze, she saw that Madalena had already been extricated from Miss Grayson, by none other than the Comte de Blanchard. As they waltzed past Dorothea she saw what a striking couple they made. Both were dark-haired and dark-eyed, and built on more delicate lines than their English counterparts. Even their *toilettes* might have been designed with one another in mind: the brocade of the comte's waistcoat and his satin knee breeches so closely matched the rose silk of Madalena's elegant gown. They gave the appearance, as they swept along, of hanging upon each other's every word.

Despite her better judgment, Thea felt a pang of jealousy at the spectacle of de Blanchard assiduously flirting with Madalena. It was not at all like the icy rage that had consumed her when she had seen the same lady in Tate's arms, but it was enough to pique her vanity. Although she wisely discounted the majority of the Frenchman's compliments as ridiculous flattery, it was not pleasant to see him directing his gallantry to someone else—especially when that someone was Madalena Smythe-Davies.

Some of her chagrin was evident in her remarks to Tate. "It appears that the comte has already effected her rescue. Such an attractive couple. I so hope his gallantry won't supplant you in her estimation. He's so much more practiced at this sort of thing."

"He has certainly had the time and opportunity to practice—on you, among others. All those weeks of music lessons. And breathing exercises—ha!"

"Your Lena has been no sluggard at picking up his instructions, from what I can judge from here. He seems to be her newest knight errant, the role you enjoy playing no end."

"Oh, yes, indeed, no end. Just like this deuced dance."

"If it is so distasteful to you, I will contrive to end it, and without providing grist for the gossip-mongers. Oh!" Dorothea moaned, putting her hand to her head. "Do forgive me, Tate my darling, but I have the most terrible migraine." She looked up at him with glittering eyes. "Could you possibly carry on without me? I'm sure that Lady Phoebe will drop me in Portman Square.

I should hate to spoil your evening just because I am not feeling quite the thing."

Sir Tate's mouth looked grim. "Of course, I shall speak with Lady Phoebe while you fetch your mantalet."

"And you'd best tell Adriana. But do not let her leave on my account, I beg you."

"Certainly not. I do hope you shake your megrim before we arrive home. Poor little lamb," Tate said, then looking around to be sure that they were observed, he brushed his lips across her forehead. It was the merest butterfly of a kiss, yet it felt like a burning brand and rendered Dorothea motionless.

"I'm sure Lady Phoebe will join you directly in the prinking room. Good night, Dorothea," he said, sketching a light bow.

"Good night, Tate," she said quietly. She stood for a moment watching him walk away, then suddenly remembered her much-vaunted headache. With an obvious—and not entirely fabricated—wince of pain, she moved towards the arched doorway and lightly rubbed the spot on her forehead where he had kissed her.

Chapter 20

The very first question asked by Madalena at breakfast the next morning was whether or not any of the gentlemen she had met at Almack's had been Captain Wynne.

"These English names are so *dificil*," she said with the tiniest of frowns as she took her usual minuscule portions of kippers, eggs and toasted muffins. "I sometimes cannot comprehend when someone new is introduced. But I did not think that anyone of that name appeared among those with whom I danced."

"No, you are quite correct. Captain Wynne was certainly not amongst your dancing partners," Tate said. "In fact, I did not see anyone even remotely resembling Robin there last night. I shall have to ring a peal over the villain for playing such a trick on us."

"We didn't really need him anyway, as it turned out," Adriana said airily. "Once the comte pried Madalena away from vicious . . . er . . . Miss Grayson, the gentlemen simply swarmed about her. And Dorothea as well, until her head gave her grief. How lucky I was to be standing about in their company. All their rejected admirers fell to my lot."

281

"Don't be a goosecap, A.," Dorothea said firmly. "You know that you were mobbed yourself. Your Nick would have been pea green with jealousy, had he been there."

"Yes, and I noticed that you allowed that frippery man-milliner three dances, A.," Tate put in crisply. "That was hardly proper behavior in a sedate matron."

"Man-milliner? I don't understand, Tate," Madalena asked in pretty confusion. "Do you mean that Adriana danced with someone who makes *chapéus*?"

"He means the Comte de Blanchard, madame," Dorothea explained coolly.

"Oh, does that mean that Tate does not approve of the comte's so elegant hats?" Madalena persisted, her face clearly conveying her conviction that the English were an incomprehensible race.

"No, no! Hats don't enter into it at all," Adriana said with a sidelong wink at Dorothea.

Madalena shook her head. "It is of no importance. But the comte—I fear that one should not be flattered by his attentions. He has no discrimination whatsoever that I can see. Why, he even danced with Lady Phoebe!" Lena said, wrinkling her nose. "Now, Lady Phoebe is most *afável* and *simpática*, but so *feia*!"

Dorothea looked questioningly at Adriana, who mouthed the word "ugly."

"But Lady Phoebe and Miss Grayson, they are so warmhearted, not at all like most *Inglêsas*. They must be very rich, yes?" Lena observed with a sly look.

Tate, who had devoted most of his attention to his plate of eggs and ham, was finally stirred into speaking. "Well, I have often heard Miss Grayson described as warm, meaning plump in the pocket, but never as warmhearted. And as for Lady Phoebe, I can only say that she is a woman of deep mystery."

Adriana choked on her coffee and went off into a violent coughing fit. After ascertaining that her sister was all right, Dorothea deliberately changed the subject.

"So, tell me, Dona, are you actually going to adopt one of Miss Grayson's pups?" she asked wonderingly.

"But, of course," Madalena replied with a frosty smile. "Dear Letitia tells me that it is very *à la mode* for a lady to go about with a lap dog. She assures me that her animals are most gently and purely bred. Not like that disgusting *monstro*, Lovelace." She gave a slight shudder of revulsion.

This time it was Dorothea's turn to choke on her food. When she recovered, she found that the subject had again shifted. The others were discussing the plans for the day.

"Lena and I plan to spend the day at Richmond Hill and Hampton Court. Having heard of our Tudor monarchy she has expressed a desire to see the place where Henry VIII lived and Elizabeth I died. As a proper *Portuguêsa*, she admits to a certain skepticism about the abilities of our good Queen Bess, although she admires her taste in refusing to marry a Spaniard." Tate's grey eyes glowed with good-humored affection.

"It's true," Madalena chimed in with a trilling laugh. "Tate tells me *such* stories and I don't know what to believe. How could a poor, weak woman rule a country without the help of a big, strong man? And she managed to defeat the Spanish, too, though they were doubtless scum then as they are now."

Tate looked momentarily taken aback at this crude language, but under Madalena's limpid gaze his disapprobation evaporated.

"And tonight," he continued, looking round at all the ladies at the table, "when we return, we shall all go to Vauxhall for the masked rout. More victory celebrations, so I'm told, with great revelry the order of the evening. I depend on you to procure dominoes for all of us, A.," Tate said with a grin.

"Very well, but mind, don't dawdle on your way home. I have no wish to be up until all hours like last night. I have babies to care for, in case you have forgotten," Adriana said with a yawn. "And so does Dorothea."

At the mention of his wife and daughter, Tate's face hardened. "Don't worry. We'll be back in plenty of time. And we'll dine on the road, which will save your waiting for us. Come on, Lena."

The two left, gaily discussing the proposed outing. When the door closed behind them, Dorothea gave a humorless laugh.

"You see, Adriana, how miserably your schemes have failed. My breathtaking gown only set Tate's teeth on edge last night, and he is just as infatuated with Madalena as ever."

"It's early days yet, Thea. And I stoutly maintain that Tate's er . . . strong reaction to your appearance last night was actually rather heartening. If he truly cared nothing for you, he would not have taken you to task over your neckline. And speaking of necklines, how did you like Robin's *décolletage?*"

"Or Miss Grayson's advising him to amplify his meager bosom?" gasped Dorothea.

The two friends collapsed into laughter over Captain Wynne's masquerade.

"The irony of it all!" Adriana cried. "There I was in a quake for fear someone would unmask my scandalous

imposture, and along comes Robin Wynne, pulling the
same outrageous game, just for a lark. At least I was
forced into *my* perfidy by circumstances," she added in
mock self-righteousness.

"But what could have possessed him?" Thea asked.
"I tried to find out in the carriage, but as soon as we
were alone he shut up tight as a clam and would scarcely
speak to me. He is so quiet and shy—not at all what I
would envision a prankster to be."

"He is very shy, especially with women he admires, but he is also, or was, one of the most talented
and successful intelligence agents that England has ever
fielded. He is a master linguist, Tate says, and Tate is
no slouch in that department. Robin could pass with
ease as a Portuguese peasant, or Spanish grandee. But
his talent for mimickry has led him into many a scrape
as well. One time, when Wellington himself was to
inspect a convent for use as a military hospital in Portugal, Robin dressed up as one of the nuns and fooled
everyone. Wellington himself was heard to remark that
he was by far the best-looking sister there."

"He made a rather striking lady of fashion last
night, I must say," Dorothea mused. "But I had a hard
time keeping my countenance when the Comte de
Blanchard turned his charm on Lady Phoebe."

"Poor Robin," sighed Adriana. "He is really a sad
case. He is so consummately sure of himself in every
arena except romance. Well, enough of this lolling about.
Let us to the nursery and see if Martha has sprouted
another tooth. We shall just dispatch the footboy to find
us some dominoes while we busy ourselves with the
more interesting aspects of life."

Dorothea agreed wholeheartedly and they climbed
the stairs to the nursery in perfect charity with one

another. If, during the course of the day, Dorothea's thoughts turned to her husband and his *protégée,* she resolutely wrenched them back to the less painful affairs of the nursery.

After she put Martha down for her afternoon nap, Thea left with Harry and Lovelace for a ride in the park, but the day was positively sultry, and even the dog and boy did not seem up to their usual high spirits. If she had seen someone she knew in the park, she might have felt less oppressed, or so she reasoned with herself, but was careful not to specify anyone in particular. But, after all, it was not a fashionable hour for a turn about the row, and with a vague feeling of disappointment, she collected her companions and returned home.

When she looked in at the nursery after removing her habit and slipping into a dressing gown, she found Adriana, Seraphim and Aggie with their arms full of babies. She went to take Martha from the senhora, and for once that lady relinquished her charge with something approaching good grace. Still, the black eyes did not quite meet her own, and Dorothea wondered how she had once again incurred the woman's disapproval. As she carried Martha over to the window, she hoped that Seraphim wouldn't seize the opportunity to upbraid her for some minor offense, such as allowing the breeze to ruffle the baby's golden curls. Seraphim did follow her across the room but remained silent. As the uncomfortable silence stretched out, Dorothea finally spoke.

"Do you wish some conversation with me, Senhora?"

"Yes, Dona Dorotéia. I don't know quite how to say what I mean."

"I'll be patient. I promise that I won't snap your

286

head off." The senhora looked baffled by these words, so she continued, "I won't be angry. Is it something to do with Martha?" Dorothea queried.

"No, no, Dona, nothing like that." There was another pause, and then a rush of words. "It's Dona Madalena. When first she came here, looking so much like my Mathilde, I was *jubilosa*. But she is nothing like my Mathilde at heart. She tries to behave like a young lady of gentle breeding, but always there are tiny mistakes—small errors of grammar, words my Mathilde or her mother would never use. And then, too, she arrives with Sir Tate, without *acompanhante*, and goes about London the same way." The governess was becoming quite agitated and Thea, seeking to comfort her, patted the gnarled hand. "I do not want to say this, but I think Dona Madalena is an *aventureira*. She behaves very badly with Sir Tate. I think your sister should be rid of her."

Dorothea could not have agreed more that the widow was an adventuress, but hesitated to say so. "We shall be on our guard against her, Senhora, but Lady Laidley cannot evict her. And soon Sir Tate will be gone, back to the Peninsula."

The senhora seemed to derive some comfort, albeit cold, from this. She nodded briskly and went to help the others, and Dorothea was left to ponder her words. Madalena not the lady she purported to be! What could it mean?

When she met Adriana over a simple dinner of raised giblet pie, cheese cakes and buttered lobster, she eagerly relayed to her sister everything that Seraphim had said.

Adriana nodded her head vigorously. "I knew it! You and I spotted Madalena as an adventuress from the beginning. It is most heartening that Seraphim shares our opinion. So she doesn't quite speak like a lady. How strange that Tate hasn't noticed."

Dorothea smiled ruefully. "He is so dazzled by her emerald eyes that he doubtless is deaf to the niceties of her speech, or lack thereof. Besides, as fluent as Tate might be in Portuguese, he would not perceive subtleties like Seraphim. She is not only a native speaker, but she has also spent her whole life strictly supervising young gentlewomen. She of all people would notice significant slips."

"If only Tate knew what Seraphim thinks of his precious Lena," Adriana sighed.

Dorothea's mouth twisted bitterly. "But if we tell him ourselves, it will just make us look like spiteful old cats."

"I fear you are right, Thea. But, speaking of old cats, what do you think of Miss Grayson's taking up Madalena so eagerly."

"I thought my eyes were playing tricks on me. After all the times she accused me of being an adventuress, and once or twice intimating that you were just as bad, now she has been completely taken in by the genuine article."

"We must just hope that the lovely Mrs. Smythe-Davies herself makes an error which will give her little game away. Until then, all we can do is hold our tongues," Adriana said with a sigh of resignation.

"If there's any justice, she will soon be brought to book. In the meanwhile, let's go upstairs and make our preparations for Vauxhall," Dorothea said, pushing away her plate and rising.

"Very well, but wouldn't it be lovely if she were stripped of more than her *silken* mask when we reach the unmasking. Now that would be a victory to celebrate!" Adriana chuckled, her eyes brightened by the thought.

Buoyed by this unlikely possibility, they went to don their costumes.

When Tate and Madalena arrived an hour later they found Adriana and Dorothea already dressed and cloaked in their dominoes, the former in forest green and the latter in gold.

Tate had the grace to look a bit shamefaced at their late return.

"Sorry, A., but Madalena saw some swans on the river, and nothing would serve but she must stop and watch them from the riverbank. It was a lovely spot, I must say. Wildflowers grew everywhere and the sky was so blue. It was just like something out of *Midsummer Night's Dream.*"

"Why, Tate, how poetical! One might think that Puck himself had placed you under a spell," Adriana observed in an astringent tone of voice.

"Or whomever," added Dorothea crisply. "I would suggest that you get into your costumes so that we can arrive at Vauxhall before the fireworks and the pageantry begin."

"Fireworks!" Madalena said, clapping her dainty hands together in childlike ecstasy. "I adore fireworks! Oh, Tate, *vamos de pressa!*" She took him by the hand and led him quickly from the drawing room.

Dorothea turned to her sister as soon as the door closed behind them. "If you will excuse me, A., I think I shall run up and kiss Martha good night. In all honesty, after spending every evening in her pleasant company, I find leaving her behind to be rather unsettling."

"In all honesty, Thea, I think there is more reason for you to feel uneasy besides abandoning Martha to Seraphim! But, go make your maternal adieus, by all means. I've already tucked in my twins and prefer to sit a moment with my feet up before we leave for Vauxhall," Adriana said, stretching out on the sofa with a contented sigh.

Dorothea went up the stairs and down the corridor to the nursery, where she eased open the door. She quietly entered the large playroom, then, suddenly thinking that her mask might frighten the child, stopped by the door to take it off. The knot became entangled in her hair and she stood a moment silently struggling to loosen it. It was then that she heard an odd humming sound coming from Martha's bedchamber. The noise was unmistakably masculine in origin, and hideously out of tune, but by straining her imagination Dorothea recognized the melody as "The Turtle Dove."

She drew her domino cloak tightly about her so that it wouldn't rustle and tiptoed to Martha's doorway. There she saw Tate standing over Martha's bed, gently stroking the sleeping baby's cheek. He was half-crooning, half-humming the song she had heard.

Greatly moved by the scene, Dorothea stood motionless for a few minutes. Then the thought of Tate stumbling over her as she spied on the tender tableau sent her scurrying to her own chamber to await their departure.

Chapter 21

Madalena's enthusiasm for what she called *fogo de artifício* apparently lent wings to her feet. She managed to change into her scarlet costume and primp in a quarter of the time they expected of her. Soon the four were disembarking from the small boat that had taken them across the Thames to Vauxhall Pleasure Gardens.

As they approached the entrance to the noted place of revelry, which was well lit by hundreds of gaily colored lanterns, a figure disengaged itself from the crowd and came up to them. It was a gentleman clad in a domino of midnight blue, identical to that worn by Tate. When he took off his silken mask and bowed, they saw it was the Comte de Blanchard.

"How fortunate to meet with my lovely ladies from Portman Square," he said, somewhat breathlessly.

Dorothea, mystified, asked, "But how did you recognize us, Philippe?"

"Such loveliness as yours cannot be extinguished by a paltry piece of silk," the comte assured her.

"He probably bribed the footboy to find out the color of our costumes," growled Tate. "Are we going to stand about all evening out here, or go in and join the festivities? I, for one, am utterly famished! What with the swans and all, we quite forgot to dine. I'm looking forward to supping here on the shaved ham—as soon as possible."

De Blanchard offered Dorothea his arm, and she felt compelled by simple politeness to take it. As she did so, she could not resist glancing over at Tate. Though his eyes were concealed by his mask, she could see that his mouth was set in a grim line. When Madalena slipped her arm into his, uninvited, and asked when the fireworks would begin, his frown disappeared. He reached for Adriana's hand, and all three strolled off towards the tables they could see under the avenue of trees beyond. Thea and her attentive escort followed closely behind.

When they arrived, however, they discovered that all the seats were filled, and they stood undecided, discussing what they should do until there was an empty table.

"I shall go and look for some food for the ladies, and also try to find some more chairs. We can't have any of our beauties swooning from hunger, now can we?" the comte teased, bathing all three women in his enchanting smile, then walking off.

"Oh, Tate, do let's go find out about the *fogo*! I shall never forgive you if we miss any of it."

"But, Lena, I don't think we should leave Adriana and Dorothea unescorted. Vauxhall is not known for its respectability. Some most unsavory characters lurk about here at night, and they might be accosted."

"Oh, don't be a *bobo*, Tate! Who would accost them here, in full sight of everyone? Besides, they are both so very intrepid and *forte*," Madalena wheedled in a tone which implied that she possessed neither of these distasteful qualities herself. "None would dare molest them."

"She is perfectly right, Tate," Adriana agreed unexpectedly. "You run along and find your *fogo*, and we shall wait for you here."

Over Tate's protestations that he still thought it most unwise, Madalena dragged him gleefully away into a darkened path.

The two women, brave words notwithstanding, huddled together in silence for a few long moments.

"I do hate to be pudding-hearted, A., but maybe we should follow them. I feel exceedingly uncomfortable standing round like two lightskirts."

"Perhaps you are right, Thea. I can't think what could be keeping the comte."

In unspoken agreement, they began to edge toward the dim walkway where Lena and Tate had gone. They had taken only a few steps down the avenue of trees when they became acutely aware that someone was walking behind them. Linking arms, they walked faster, but whoever was shadowing them came closer nevertheless.

"Maybe it's the comte," Dorothea suggested hopefully and was surprised to hear the quaver in her voice.

"Well, whoever he is, he doesn't frighten *me*," Adriana said in a rallying tone. "And besides," she whispered, "I hear only one set of footsteps and we are two. We'd be a match for him—two such intrepid and *forte* women as ourselves."

To Dorothea's considerable alarm, her companion turned to confront the mysterious gentleman. Her consternation mounted when she saw his size, for he was taller than Tate or the comte, or Captain Wynne, and was dressed in sinister black from his domino hood to his booted feet.

"Sir, I demand that you identify yourself and state your business," Adriana stoutly proclaimed.

The stranger remained ominously silent, but continued walking toward them in a determined manner. He gave no indication of being the least bit daunted by the challenging note in Adriana's words.

To Dorothea, shuddering next to her sister, it was beginning to seem like a nightmare. In the flickering torchlight's eerie shadows, the stranger seemed close to eight feet tall as he loomed over them. She felt panic wash over her, but her fear was turned into pure shock at what happened next.

"Adriana," the gentleman said, softly but distinctly, and with disbelieving eyes, Dorothea saw Adriana throw herself into the masked stranger's open arms for a most passionate embrace.

"H-help!" Dorothea tried to cry, but her words came out in an inaudible croak. Gathering her skirts, she started to run for help.

Adriana's muffled voice arrested her flight just as she was about to round the corner of the shrubbery. "Thea, wait. It's all right! Come back."

Dorothea froze in her tracks, half convinced that Adriana had taken leave of her senses. A brief consideration led to the conclusion that such was highly unlikely, so she cautiously walked back to where Adriana stood in the arms of her would-be attacker.

"It's Nicholas, Thea. My husband, Nick," Adriana murmured ecstatically. "Nick, this is Dorothea, Tate's wife, of whom I have written you. Oh, Nick, you sapskull," she chastised him throatily, but there was no real anger in her voice. "Why did you not tell me you were coming? Surely the Ministry could have warned me."

"The Ministry insisted on the strictest secrecy. I am come to escort one of the French royal house down to the Peninsula. It is all very crackbrained, I grant you, even Wellington was rather taken aback when his invitation was accepted. But there is seldom much logic in war. However, no one must learn I am here, except Tate, who is to come with me when I leave tomorrow. There is a great danger in the business for all its absurdity. There are many Bonapartist spies who would dearly love this opportunity to assassinate the Duc."

"Tomorrow? So soon?" Adriana whimpered in dismay. Then getting a grip on herself, she said, "Then we shall go home at once. I don't want to waste a moment of your stay loitering about here."

"And so we shall," Nicholas agreed. "But you must tell the rest of your party you are indisposed. Perhaps Dorothea here would come home with you, to lend countenance to the story. Would you be willing to do so?" He turned and looked intently at his new sister-in-law. There was no mistaking the entreaty in the dark eyes, even in the semi-darkness.

"Certainly. You two stay here and I shall go make our excuses to the others."

Adriana and Nicholas made no demur, or any comment at all, having once again fallen into each other's arms. Dorothea hastened away, praying that she might find the others without any further incident.

She came into a sort of clearing, in the center of which was a large statue of a bewigged gentleman clothed in the style of the previous century. She paused, leaning with one hand against the cool surface of the statuary, and tried to catch her breath. A string of lanterns encircled the area, and their dancing light made the stone shape rather baleful in aspect.

As she stood there, bemused, suddenly she heard Madalena's sultry voice speaking softly but rapidly in Portuguese, just on the other side of the statue. The low masculine replies in the same tongue caused Dorothea to hesitate in calling out. Then the flow of Portuguese halted abruptly and Dorothea began to move toward the spot where the speakers had been. She soon perceived that the couple had not moved away, as she had thought. Madalena, unmasked, was wrapped in the arms of a gentleman whose own dark mask obscured his identity. They were locked in an embrace even more desperate and passionate than the one she had recently witnessed between her sister and Nicholas Laidley. Under Dorothea's shocked gaze, Madalena pulled back from the gentleman's eager arms and, in that moment, looked straight at Thea where she stood a few yards away. A satisfied smile tugged at the corners of the woman's mouth as she purred, *"Meu herói,"* and melted back into her lover's embrace.

Dorothea stepped back, then turned and fled back the way she had come, like a wounded animal. She stopped, panting and sobbing, and tried to gain control of her emotions, but was signally unsuccessful.

It had to have been Tate, she thought, over and over. Who else has such command of the language, or such an intimate relationship with the delectable widow? Who else does she call her *herói*?

Such reflections were not at all the sort to provide solace to her injured sensibilities, and she was still dissolved in tears when Adriana and Nicholas came across her.

"I couldn't find anyone and became a little panicky alone in the dark. Forgive me, A., I'm such a coward!"

"Don't be a gudgeon. We were mad to have allowed you to go by yourself. You must forgive us. You and I shall go together to fetch them. Nicholas, I'll see you soon, my dearest."

In answer, Sir Nicholas brushed Adriana's cheek with his hand and disappeared into the shadows.

"Now, let's go see what Tate and Madalena and the comte have been up to," Adriana said briskly, "and put on our little Cheltenham drama."

Dorothea nodded blindly and followed the other woman down the path until they emerged into a brightly lit pavilion, full of masked revelers intent on a good time. A small orchestra ensconced in a sort of open oriental temple played for the crowd of dancers under the flambeaux.

"There they are, all three together," Adriana cried, pointing.

Dorothea, with a great effort, looked where Adriana indicated and saw the scarlet of Madalena's domino, flanked on either side by the midnight blue of Tate and de Blanchard. Her head began to ache and she trailed behind Adriana with her eyes on the ground.

"Adriana," she said quietly before reaching the threesome. "Just tell them that I am the one with the migraine. It is perfectly true."

"Poor lamb. And here I am so wrapped up in my own good fortune that I failed to see it. Tate, Tate . . ." she called.

"Whatever are you two doing here?" Tate asked sternly. "You were to stay put where we left you. Though I do apologize for this age it has taken to get the food. What a crush!"

297

At this outrageous falsehood, Dorothea glared at Tate accusingly and he frowned. "And just what is your problem, madam? I trust no one assaulted your virtue in our absence?"

Adriana took Thea's hand comfortingly. "Oh, don't start in on poor Dorothea. She has a terrible headache and wants to go home."

Madalena's tinkling laugh rang out. "Poor Lady Bancroft seems very prone to these vapors, does she not? How sad for a robust gentleman like Tate to be saddled with an *inválida* wife."

Instead of eliciting a flirtatious response from Tate, her quizzing merely deepened his scowl and Madalena abruptly changed her tune.

"But then your sister and Dona Dorotéia will miss the fireworks and the *espectáculo* to celebrate Vitória. That will be a great pity," she said, her accented voice dripping with that spurious emotion.

"Yes, A., I hate for you to miss the fun," Tate added. "Surely we could find a quiet place for Dorothea to spend the remainder of the evening. After all, if last night is any indication, her headaches come and go with remarkable rapidity."

A note of pleading crept into Adriana's voice. "No, no, she must go home, and at once."

"But I can't let you go home alone. We shall all have to go," Tate pronounced firmly.

"Oh, no, Tate!" wailed Madalena. "You promised me we should see the fireworks. You promised!"

"Do not worry, sir. I shall see that the ladies reach Portman Square safely," the comte offered with his usual gallantry.

Madalena clapped her hands in delight. "Oh,

Comte," she cooed, "you are so *heróico* to sacrifice your pleasure so that I might have my heart's desire."

"It is nothing," the comte replied with a shrug, but Dorothea could see that he basked in Lena's admiring words. Tate, on the other hand, remained scowling.

Seeing him standing there, with his tray full of syllabubs, meats and punch, which had failed in their apparent purpose of proclaiming his innocence, Dorothea wanted to hurt him as much as his dalliance with Madalena had hurt her.

"Oh, Philippe," she said sweetly, turning her brightest smile on the Frenchman, "you are an angel to look after me. I must tell you sometime how deeply I value your . . . friendship."

"And I yours, Dorothée," he replied, gazing at her enraptured.

"Shall we go?" Adriana suggested with ill-concealed eagerness. "Dorothea is in a bad way, though she is too plucky to admit it."

"I can see that," Tate said bitingly, then he turned his attention to the waiting Madalena.

The Frenchman took the arms of his two charges and led them to the boat landing. When they reached the other side of the river, he skillfully arranged for a carriage and settled the three of them cozily inside.

"This reminds me of the night we met, Comte," Adriana said with a chuckle. "Though on the whole I am a good deal more comfortable this night than I was on that memorable occasion."

"Yes, tonight it is Dorothée's turn to suffer. If only I could take your pain all to myself, *ma petite*. I do hate to see beauty in distress."

Dorothea longed to scream at him that nothing would ease her aching head quite so much as a surcease of inane flattery, but managed to hold her tongue. Each cobblestone that the carriage struck sent an agonizing pain through her head and it seemed forever before they drew up at Portman Square.

De Blanchard gracefully alighted from the carriage and assisted the two women to descend.

"*Ma foi,*" he exclaimed, "it looks as if someone is having a party here. I have never seen your house so illuminated in the evening."

"I did not know you had ever come by at night, Philippe," Adriana replied flippantly. "Oh, we are quite profligate with our wax candles. Why, Aggie tells me it's one of my greatest faults. But I do like to have a little cheerful light in the evenings."

"But so many! Even in the master bedroom? It doesn't seem normal—perhaps you have been visited by burglars and even now your servants are tied up and your house ransacked. I *insist* on accompanying you inside."

"No, I assure you that there is nothing unusual going on," Adriana burst out. Then, bridling her anxiety, she went on graciously, "And though we are immensely grateful for your escort, we must bid you good night. Poor Thea is nearly asleep on her feet."

A look of great annoyance crossed the comte's handsome face. Did the man care so much that he was not to be allowed to play the hero? Dorothea wondered. It was but a momentary expression, however, which was quickly transformed into his dazzling smile.

"Then I bid you adieu, Lady Laidley, and I pray that you are better in the morning, *ma belle*." With a sweeping bow, he climbed back into the hack carriage and rode away.

Chapter 22

Adriana and Dorothea were admitted into the foyer by Smithson, who smiled from ear to ear when he saw who it was at the door.

"My lady, come in, come in! There is someone waiting for you in the nursery, and from the way he has been prowling back and forth, I was worried he would wear a path in the carpet!"

Adriana did not wait to hear any more, but dashed past him up the stairs. Dorothea tactfully held back, not wishing to intrude on the tender reunion. Then, upon reflection, she decided that she had better remove her sleeping things from the master bedroom forthwith.

Slipping past the nursery door, which was discreetly closed, Dorothea entered the master bedroom at the end of the corridor. There she hastily gathered up her nightdress and dressing gown from the small wardrobe which Adriana had made over for her use. Quickly bundling up her things, she started for the door. As she reached for the handle, however, it swung open towards her of its own accord, and Sir Nicholas Laidley strode into the bedchamber, masterfully carrying his wife in his arms.

301

At this vision of nuptial passion, Dorothea was paralyzed with embarrassment. Trying to make herself as inconspicuous as possible, she said, "Pardon me," in a tiny voice and began to edge by them.

Adriana, almost as nonplussed as Thea, would not allow her to leave just yet.

"Wait a moment, Thea. You must be properly introduced to my husband, now that you can see each other. Nicholas, put me down at once! You are causing this poor girl agonies of embarrassment, not to mention your poor wife."

If anything, this plea only caused Sir Nicholas to tighten his hold, and to raise his dark eyebrows in mock surprise.

"And I thought you were shameless, Adriana. At least *I* must be, for I can't help but think that *I* can meet Dorothea well enough as I am." He inclined his head slightly. "Very pleased to make your acquaintance, Lady Bancroft. You must excuse me if I do not take your hand. Both of mine are full."

Dorothea, much diverted by his lordly tone and Adriana's discomfiture, began to feel more comfortable. For the first time she was able to take note of his appearance. He was not eight feet tall as she had thought in the darkened path at Vauxhall, but he was well over six, and of a powerful physique. His complexion was dark and weathered, but not at all harsh, especially when he looked lovingly at his wife. Even as these thoughts crossed her mind, the etched lines in the countenance gave way to a broad grin.

"If you and my imp of a wife are as close as she has written me in her reams of letters, you are fully accustomed to her distempered freaks. Such a minor matter as catching her in the very act of being carried off to bed will be as nothing."

"As to that," Thea said airily, now totally at ease, "it happens all the time."

Adriana spluttered, "Dorothea, what are you saying? Are you trying to drive a wedge of suspicion between Nicholas and me?"

"Oh, I seriously doubt that anyone could fit a wedge or anything else between you, situated as you are," Dorothea said with a chuckle. "But being the paragon of tact that I am, I shall now withdraw."

"But where will you sleep?" Adriana protested. "You know as well as I do that all the chambers are full!"

"Don't worry about a thing. I shall find a place. Good night, A., Sir Nick," Dorothea said, moving out the door and shutting it quietly behind her. Warmed by the glow of their happiness, she hummed a little to herself as she went down the corridor and realized that her headache was utterly gone. With this realization came the memory of what had caused the aching to begin with. Once again she felt a pang, as she recalled in vivid detail the sight of Madalena and Tate kissing fervently by the statue.

Madalena's infamous conduct quite offset any privileges she might claim as a guest, thought Dorothea. Then and there she decided to move back into the bedchamber which she had given up to the widow.

Why should that unscrupulous witch enjoy splendid isolation in the prettiest bedroom in the house while I, the "wronged wife" if you please, have no place to lay my throbbing head, she argued with herself, ignoring the fact that her head was no longer giving her pain. That she caused me to suffer in the first place is sufficient reason to dispossess the scheming minx, Dorothea muttered, and threw open the door to her former domain with a flourish.

The ambiance had changed to a degree that she found hard to credit. Madalena's heavy scent permeated the air and jewelry, clothes, and powder jars were jumbled together on the mahogany dressing table. Although Thea was no demon for cleanliness, she judged the havoc to be inexcusable. Her anger spilled over into action and she ran to the window, throwing it open to air out the room. Then she grabbed up all of Madalena's things she could find and threw them into the wardrobe. She would have preferred to chuck them out the window, but refrained on consideration that doing so would only lower her to Madalena's level.

By the time that Dorothea had a wash and changed into her high-buttoned nightdress, she felt much better than she had ever since Madalena had first arrived at Portman Square. As she snuggled down into the soft bed, and pulled up the feather-light cover, she gave a sigh, if not signifying complete contentment, then at least of having a bit of her own back.

Despite her minor sense of triumph, Dorothea spent the next hour tossing and turning. The nagging vision of Tate with Madalena kept haunting her and she was unable to dismiss it from her mind. At last she threw back her coverlet, took the taper from the dressing table, lit it, and made her way down the hall to the nursery to look in on Martha.

The emotional chaos which was so intimately affecting the elder members of the household was completely absent in the nursery. Martha lay sleeping placidly on her stomach in her little bed, and Dorothea knelt down on the floor to catch a glimpse of the sweet face.

The sound and the candlelight disturbed the infant, and she raised her head to stare blankly about her. Then with a little mewing sound, she lowered her face to the soft blanket which lined her bed and closed her eyes without further ado.

Dorothea watched, envious of the ease with which Martha slumbered, and conjured up the memory of the scene she had witnessed in that very room. In its way, seeing Tate acting more fatherly toward Martha was just as disturbing as the later interlude with Madalena. Taken together, the two episodes were devastating in their implication. For the Vauxhall business meant that annulment was a real possibility, while that in the nursery destroyed any hope that she would be allowed to keep Martha with her if the marriage should end.

Martha stirred again in her sleep, which brought Dorothea out of her unhappy reverie. She stood and stretched her cramped limbs. Then, sadly, she gave the warm little back a pat and returned to her reclaimed bedroom.

Once again she crawled beneath the sheet and this time sleep was more forthcoming. She had just drifted off into a formless dream when she was roused by the sound of voices conferring in hoarse whispers outside the chamber door. Even in her drowsy state, she could easily tell that the speakers were Tate and Madalena, and that they had consumed a great deal of Vauxhall's famous arrack punch before returning home.

At last the conversation ended and Madalena came into the room carrying a flickering candle.

Dorothea thought it best to reveal her presence before Madalena came into the bed and discovered her, so she sat up and spoke.

"Madalena. It seems we are bedfellows tonight."

The jerk of the hand that held the candle sent shadows spinning violently about the room. Madalena stared at her dumbly for a moment, benumbed by liquor and shock. When at length she found her tongue, it was in scornful accents that she replied.

"You must be making game of me, Dorotéia. This is *my* room, and I don't recall asking you to share it with me."

"I'm afraid you must just, as we say in English, lump it, Lena. I allowed you to displace me out of necessity, and now I am moving back—out of necessity."

"And what is this necessity of which you speak? Eh?" Madalena demanded harshly, too intoxicated to pretend amiability.

"That is none of your affair."

"Bah, I spit on your 'necessity.' You are just jealous because you saw me tonight in the arms of . . ." she broke off with a sly laugh. "You only wish to make me *incómoda*. Well, I shall tell Tate how ill you have treated me and *you* are the one who will be sorry."

"Tate has gone to bed and so should we. Now, if you cannot stomach sleeping here, perhaps you should try the sofa in the sitting room," Thea said wearily, all her sense of triumph drained away.

"Very well, I will go to the *sala de estar*. But I warn you, tomorrow I will have Tate . . ."

"Please, Madalena. Tomorrow you may have Tate jump through your hoops to your heart's content, but tonight all I want is to go back to sleep," Dorothea said, turning over and covering her face in a marked manner.

She could hear Mrs. Smythe-Davies thrashing about in the depths of the wardrobe, searching for her things. Then there was a sound of splashing from the water basin, accompanied by a steady stream of mumbled

Portuguese imprecations, or so Thea gathered from their quiet explosiveness.

Madalena finally made her grand exit, slamming the door with a final vehement exclamation, leaving Dorothea to lie, tense and still, trying to forget the Portuguese widow's odious conduct.

After another half-hour of fruitless reflections, she scolded herself heartily, and thumped and plumped the pillow with an unladylike wish that it were Madalena's face. Then she snuggled once more under the bedclothes, resolving once and for all to put all such unsettling thoughts aside until morning.

Her eyelids had just closed when she heard the door open once again. No doubt Madalena has changed her mind after testing the lumpy cushions on the sitting room sofa, she thought sleepily. Hoping to avoid any further confrontations, Thea feigned slumber, keeping her breathing slow and measured.

When the person crossing the room stumbled over the footstool at the end of the bed, the resulting curses were not in the language or the voice she expected to hear.

"What the deuce is that thing doing there!" The words were English and the voice was Tate Bancroft's. He moved around the bed in the darkness until he stood very close to where Dorothea lay, trembling.

"Ah, Madalena," he began in a slurred fashion, "I am in flat despair! How could I ever have rushed pell-mell into this ridiculous charade of a marriage!"

In stricken silence, Dorothea kept telling herself that it must be another nightmare.

"It was in every way a mistake," he went on, "but I was despondent, and I believe, very near suicidal with grief over Mathilde's death. Now it seems incredible, but such was the case. Marriage appeared a reasonable solution to my predicament over Martha. I gave no thought to the future because I hoped I would have none. My one thought was to greet death bravely," he said with a grim laugh. "Lord knows, I tried hard enough to do just that, but the damned French just weren't obliging."

Dorothea shuddered at his words, which confirmed her worst fears.

"Well, perhaps my instinct for self-preservation was stronger than my wish for self-destruction. At any rate, here I am."

As if to properly illustrate his statement, he sat down on the edge of the bed. Dorothea could feel the mattress sink down with his weight, but still could not move or speak.

Apparently unperturbed by her lack of response, Tate continued. "Yes, here I am, indeed. Nothing has turned out as I had planned. I find myself, against all odds, alive and well, and legshackled to a woman who has taken me in extreme dislike."

He shifted slightly on the bed, and Thea sensed rather than saw the gesture of despair as he ran his fingers through his hair. And still she could not collect her shattered wits enough to speak.

"It's the very devil of a coil," he went on. "The worst of it is, that I find her . . . well, never mind. Perhaps you are right about my seeking an annulment. I'm beginning to think it is the only logical way out of this painful mess."

It appeared that the silence on the part of the woman next to him disturbed him, for he leaned forward so that she could actually feel his breath on her cheek.

"Ah. Madalena, *minha amiga querida*, you have seen how my wife comports herself with that damned Frenchman. I felt like wringing his dandified neck, and hers as well. Is she so totally lost to propriety that she carries on a flirtation under the very nose of her husband, albeit in name only?" he added bitterly.

"And you, sir," burst out Dorothea, "are you so utterly lost to decency that you lurk about in the middle of the night in the bedchamber of, as you obviously think, a lady who is not your wife in name or in any other way?" Overwhelmed by her fury, she sat bolt upright in bed and nearly collided with the stunned gentleman.

For a long moment there was no reply, then he spoke in a voice dripping with sarcasm.

"Well, well, well, my darling wife. I do hope that you have enjoyed your little game."

"Well, well, well, my faithful husband, I think you will rue yours. Crawling into Madalena's bed in the dark of night in order to whine about the shortcomings of our marriage—which was your idea, I might add—is despicable." She was so racked by chills of emotion that her voice quavered. "Oh, how I long to slap your face, if only I could find it in this confounded dark."

"That is remedied easily enough, Dorothea my sweet. Here." He groped until he found her hand and placed it against his cheek.

"Now, slap away, madam. I suppose that in your view I deserve it."

The bleakness in his voice made her falter for a second, but then, recalling his words to "Madalena," she brought her palm across his face with a resounding blow.

"Now I think it is only sportsmanlike to allow me

to exact punishment for your imposture," he said in an ominous tone.

She reached for his hand and held it to her cheek. "Fine, here is my face. Though how you could call it sportsmanlike to strike a woman I don't kno—" She never finished her indignant sentence. Placing his hands on either side of her face, Tate drew her to him and covered her lips violently with his own, which stopped her protestations in mid-syllable. She struggled with all her strength against him, but found herself being lowered back against the pillows. Against her will, she felt herself stirred by his kiss as she had once before, which only made her fight even more determinedly to free herself.

Then she thought of his plan to annul their marriage, which would lose her not only her husband, but her daughter as well. If yielding to him ends in consummation, annulment will be impossible, she told herself, and for a brief space of time allowed this notion to take possession of her mind and body. With a passion which shocked her by its intensity, she returned his kiss. But then cold reason returned like the slap she had dealt him earlier. His bitter words to "Madalena" showed her the futility of her hopes that he loved his wife, and a loveless marriage, consummated or not, was hardly the path to happiness.

"No, Tate," she said with as much force as she could muster, and stiffened in his embrace.

"Why, who could fault me for being in my own wife's bed? If you deny me, Dorothea my dear, it constitutes a clear case for annulment. Is that what you want?"

Once more his mouth descended on hers, and once more she felt herself caught in a whirlpool of emotion that threatened to carry her into its depths. She floated for a moment, savoring the blissful sensation of his lips, and tried to put everything and everyone else out of her mind, including Madalena.

It was not Madalena, however, who was haunting Tate's thoughts. As he put his hands to the buttons of her nightdress, he murmured disjointedly into her ear, "*Minha esposa adorada. Eu te amo*, Mathilde."

All romantic illusions dispelled, Dorothea said the only thing which could bring him to his senses.

"Nicholas is here. You must both leave on the morrow. Something about accompanying French royalty to Spain."

As she had calculated, years as a military agent caused him to sit up and demand, "Nick, here? Why on earth didn't you tell me this before?"

"You've hardly allowed me an opportunity, now have you? After all, you were the one who started this . . . discussion. I never thought of it, you made me so angry."

Tate flung out of the bed and started for the door, but was halted when Thea called to him to wait.

"Really, Tate, I am certain that Nicholas has other things on his mind tonight besides military matters. Surely you can leave him alone with Adriana until morning. Just because *our* marriage is an empty shell, doesn't mean that *theirs* is."

"So that is why you are sleeping in here," he responded in a wooden tone.

"It seemed the most expedient thing to do, under the circumstances. They hardly needed me sleeping alongside on the trundle bed," she said dryly.

"No," he answered shortly, then paused. "I'm sorry I was so beastly to you, Thea, and sorry that I got you

311

into this bumblebroth. Perhaps I should have left you with Miss Grayson. At least she never offered violence to your person, as I did. Please forgive me. I expect it was too much arrack punch."

"I expect so."

"I shall probably be gone by the time you awaken tomorrow," he said, coming back toward the bed. "Nick is ever one for crack-of-dawn departures. Could we shake hands and part as friends, Thea?"

"Yes, nothing would make me happier," she whispered, not trusting her voice to speak aloud.

"Nothing?"

"No."

"Then here is my hand on it." She felt his hand, warm and strong, find hers and a sob rose in her throat.

"I would give a pony for one dratted candle so I could see your face. From your voice I can't judge whether or not I am forgiven. I would hate to lose my life in the war with you on my conscience."

"You have nothing to reproach yourself for, Tate. Whatever pain you have given me has been more than made up for by the family you've given me in Adriana, and her twins, and . . . Martha."

"That's not much of a testimonial to marital bliss, but I suppose it is better than the implacable hatred with which you regarded me before."

"I have never hated you, Tate. How could I?" she said, her voice breaking.

There was a sort of convulsive movement in his hand, as if he were drawing her toward him once again, then thought better of it.

"Well, I guess this is good-bye again. We always seem to meet only to part. What a ridiculous way to run a marriage."

312

"Ridiculous," she repeated, faltering.

"We shall have to make some changes if . . . when I come back," he said gruffly, and withdrawing his hand, moved away.

"Tate, I . . ." she started to say, but her words were lost in the sound of the door shutting.

Feeling utterly bereft, Dorothea buried her head in her pillow and burst into tears. After a while, her sobbing dwindled into hiccoughs, but she was so upset that sleep was impossible. She dragged herself out of bed and crossed to the window, where she leaned out and drank in the cool air, with some notion that it might calm her hopelessly tangled emotions.

But even in this she was thwarted. In the small park across the street, by the dim illumination of the gas lamp, she descried a solitary figure pacing up and down. She had no trouble in recognizing the man as her husband. Even as she watched he flung himself onto the metal bench and buried his face in his hands as though in great despair. He looked fully as despondent as when she had seen him that first day so long ago in the rose bower at Bancroft Hall.

His air of desolation smote her conscience. How can I be so selfish as to hold him to a marriage which brings him only further misery, she reflected miserably. In the rose bower, all I wanted was to comfort him, and all I have done is to bring him more unhappiness. Well, he shall be gone tomorrow, and time alone will tell what his return will bring. And then I shall have to face the situation without flinching and, perhaps, give him his freedom.

With this painful decision made, she tore her eyes away from Tate's huddled form and gazed distractedly into the dark recesses of the little park. She was startled to see that another man was standing there in the shadows, motionless. Her first thought was that he might be a mohock, one of the roving villains who attacked those foolish enough to venture out alone in the London streets in the small hours of the night. She was about to call down to her husband to warn him of the possible danger when he stood up and came into the door which lay beneath her window.

For a quarter-hour or more she watched intently to see what the menacing figure would do, without taking her eyes from the place she had seen him. At the end of that time her vigilance was rewarded. The man, peering about him with the utmost caution, moved into the street. He shaded his eyes against the lamplight and examined the Laidley townhouse with marked interest. As he stood there, Dorothea saw him twirl a quizzing glass which swung on a cord of some sort from his wrist. It was a graceful gesture, and one that told her his identity as surely as if he had shouted his name into the square.

It was the Comte de Blanchard.

Chapter 23

When Thea awoke the next morning, her eyes fell upon the creweled canopy above, and for a few brief moments she forgot all that had happened since she had last slept in that bed. She stretched languorously, lingering in a hazy realm between sleeping and waking. Then her gaze took in the bookcases that flanked her bed. In place of her collection of novels culled from the bookroom downstairs, she saw a collection of tasteless trumpery acquired by Madalena on her excursions round London with Tate.

All residual drowsiness was thoroughly dispersed by the memories which came crowding in. The frivolous trinkets rendered her miserably wide awake.

A sudden knock at the door made Dorothea start with an absurd surge of emotion, thinking that Tate might be making her another visit, this time by daylight.

"Who's there?" she said, her heart pounding erratically in an absurd mixture of hope and fear.

" 'Tis Annie, my lady. I've your breakfast tray."

Dorothea, feeling exceedingly let down, bade her come in.

Annie briskly entered, chattering endlessly as she

came. "You nearly slept the clock round, you have. Though you're not alone in that accomplishment, I must say."

"I've no appetite at all this morning, Annie," Dorothea said listlessly. "Just take it away like a good girl."

"Now, now, madam, I daren't take it straight-away. But look, I've brought you a letter—perhaps that will whet your appetite!"

Despite the fact that the only previous letter she had received from her husband had been a study in recrimination, Dorothea snatched the folded sheet from the tray in all eagerness. But the handwriting was unfamiliar, and again her face and her hopes plummeted.

Annie set the tray down on the night table and put her hands on her hips in an attitude of obstinancy.

"I'll not permit your ladyship to skimp on meals. Sir Tate himself made me promise faithfully to take care of you proper. Why, 'twas the very last thing he said before departing this morning. He stood there with his eyes heavy with sleep, and so groggy that it was almost comical. 'Take care of my wife and daughter, my girl,' he says to me, 'and I'll bring you a little something home from the Peninsula.'"

"Just remember that the last 'little something' that the master brought home for our delectation was Mrs. Smythe-Davies, Annie. Unless you want a Madalena of your very own, I wouldn't raise my expectations too high," Thea said with a laugh. Nevertheless, the servant's account of Tate's parting words affected her greatly.

In a distracted stated she rose from her bed and drew on her dressing gown, allowing the sealed note to flutter unopened to the floor.

Annie, clucking, picked it up and handed it to her.

"And don't forget to read this," she admonished before marching out the door.

"I won't," Dorothea called after her, but she did not fulfill her promise immediately. Instead she sat watching the steam curl upward from her coffee and tried to piece together the puzzle that was Tate Bancroft. He seemed to her an admixture of contradictions: tenderness and sarcasm, humor and disapprobation, wisdom and gullibility, indifference and passion. Try as she would, she could not fit these diverse elements into a whole picture of the man. Who was the real Tate Bancroft and what would a future with him hold for her? That is, she amended unwillingly, if there is to be a future with him, which is by no means a certainty.

She sighed and took up her cup of lukewarm coffee. Just then Lovelace nosed his way past her door and presented himself to his mistress with a hopeful eye on her neglected slice of ham and congealed mound of eggs. She checked the doorway to make certain that Annie was nowhere about, then placed the tray on the floor for his pleasure.

"I daresay it is just as well that Tate is gone, Lovelace," she said bleakly as she stroked his inelegant coat. "After all, were he here, dancing attendance on Madalena and enacting bedroom farces with me, I think I should go mad within a fortnight. No, surely it is better this way. Still, fool that I am, I shall miss the vexing creature. Lovelace—stop that!" she cried, becoming aware that the dog had finished the eggs and ham with great dispatch and had turned his attention to the letter that she had unconsciously shoved under the plate.

She extricated the greasy remains of the letter from his jaws and smoothed it out with a sharp reprimand. Lovelace slunk away with a chastened air as she broke the wax seal and opened the page. Her eye quickly went to the signature at the bottom: Robert Wynne. She raised her glance to the top, exceedingly curious as to what the shy captain had to say to her.

Dear Madam:

I have something of the utmost importance to discuss with you at your earliest convenience. To this end I ask that you and Adriana come with me for a carriage ride this morning, away from prying eyes and ears. I apologize for the unfashionable hour, but this will suit my purposes best. If I do not hear from you to the contrary, I shall come by for you at eleven o'clock.

Your obedient servant,
Robert Wynne

Dorothea mulled over the contents of the mysterious letter as she pulled on her clothes and brushed and braided her hair. What matter could be of such import as to prod the bashful Robin to play the cavalier to not one, but two ladies? After carefully picking up the tray and dipping the silver fork into the scanty remains of her egg, she left the whole on the chest for Annie. Then she hastened to find Adriana to show her the invitation.

Her sister was still sitting in bed, finishing her own breakfast and looking rather mournful. She brightened at seeing Dorothea and greeted her affectionately.

"You know, perhaps Tate was right about Robin," Dorothea said playfully. "Maybe civilian life *has* addled his brain."

318

"Give over joking, do, and tell me what you are talking about."

Dorothea produced the cryptic note and Adriana read it with great interest.

When she finished her perusal, she looked up with a frown of concentration. "Depend upon it," she said firmly, "if Robin deems this matter to be important, he is not exaggerating. He is a gentleman of his word, despite his occasional escapades. And I for one am glad of a diversion today of all days."

"Oh, A., in my wonder over this Robin business, I quite forgot how wretched you must be, having seen Nicholas for so short a time."

Adriana smiled, a faraway look in her grey eyes. "Even one night is better than none at all. And, what about you, Thea?" she asked gently.

"What do you mean?"

"Well, I don't mean to pry, but you must know that Nicholas and I could overhear something of what was happening in your bedchamber last night, or should I say this morning. After all, there is only the dressing closet between the two rooms. We were not so lost to reality that we could fail to notice there were voices coming from your chamber, one of which was Tate's, and the other of which was definitely not Madalena's."

Covered in confusion, Dorothea stood up and went over to the window. It was bad enough to have lived though last night's bitter charade, but to have been overheard was unbearable.

Before she could frame a coherent response, Adriana went on. "We could not make out what was being said, nor did we wish to. But, oh Thea, I long to know if you and Tate are truly man and wife," she ended in a rush.

More than anything, Dorothea wished that she

could answer that they were indeed. It even occurred to her to tell Adriana that such was the case. Not only would it make Adriana happy, but if it came to an annulment, her sister's testimony to that fact would stand in her favor. But she couldn't do it.

"I'm sorry if you have imagined a rapprochement between Tate and me. What you overheard was merely another brangle," Dorothea whispered, flushing deeply. "How I envy you your happiness with Nicholas." She whirled from the window and returned to Adriana's side.

"Don't waste time envying me. Now that he has gone, and Tate as well, you and I are equal in our loneliness and anxiety." She patted Thea's hand, and they each sank into separate gloomy reflections, until interrupted by a knock on the door.

"Excuse me, my lady," Annie trilled, breezing in. "But Mr. Smithson sent me to tell you both that the Comte de Blanchard is come to call. La, what a nonpareil he is," she added with a simper.

"You may tell the comte that we will be down presently," Adriana said in quelling accents. "And do try not to drool on his waistcoat. He would take that very ill indeed and it would do you no credit in his magnificent black eyes."

The irrepressible Annie exited with a laugh.

"Well, here is another diversion sent from heaven! Now, mind, there must be no mention of Nick's visit," Adriana said, throwing on her dress as she talked. "I shall have to contrive to look and act in my customary manner. Please nudge me if I should slip and smile like an idiot."

When the two women, properly if hastily dressed in their light muslin morning gowns, descended the stairs and entered the small drawing room, they found that Madalena was with the Frenchman. She had apparently taken it upon herself to welcome him on behalf of the household and was regaling him with a lively description of the elaborate entertainment she and Tate had witnessed at Vauxhall after the others had left.

"Ah, Philippe, it was so *lamentável* that you missed all the fun because of that Dorotéia. It was so very diverting! There were actors on horseback who played out the drama of the entire battle of Vitória. The noise and confusion was so overwhelming, I quite clung to Tate for protection. I was such a little *boba* at first. I couldn't tell which actor was meant to be Wellington and which the King of Spain. But of course, I didn't need telling at the end because, of course, the player who triumphed was Wellington. But what a grand *expectáculo* it was!" Madalena exclaimed.

The comte acknowledged the arrival of Adriana and Dorothea with a graceful bow, but Madalena was undeterred by their presence and babbled on.

"And then came the *fogo de artifício*. Such a *maravilha, uma beleza!* Never have I seen anything to approach it. And, listen to this, there was a French lady, an *acrobata* called Saqui, who climbed a rope to the very top of the fireworks *plataforma* and then descended surrounded entirely by fire. It was a thing *incrível*."

"Not half so incredible as *her* bad manners," Adriana said to Dorothea in a low voice.

Madalena was still not finished. "And every time a rocket went off, I squealed and jumped about until Tate told me that I reminded him of a green cavalry horse. Can you imagine? A green horse! I was most insulted and scolded him soundly for saying such a thing of me.

You wouldn't ever call a girl a horse, would you, Philippe?" She gazed limpidly up at the comte, who rose to the occasion magnificently.

"I would sooner die than to say so ugly a thing to a lovely woman," he pronounced in his deep baritone.

Adriana could not resist this opening. "But you both misunderstand completely. I am certain that Tate would consider comparing someone to a battle mount to be the highest form of flattery. Why, you should have seen Pegasus—now there was a real beauty: swift, strong, and utterly dependable when the going was rough. I would be honored if Tate judged me to be as wonderful as Pegasus."

"You *Inglêsas*, you are so droll, are they not, Comte? Although I must admit that some of the ladies I have met here do look remarkably *equina*. Like that Lady Phoebe," she snickered, but stopped abruptly when the gentleman did not join her merriment. "But where is Tate this morning?" she asked, as though suddenly aware that he was not in the room. "We were up until all hours last night, but he should be awake by now."

Dorothea exchanged a worried look with her sister. After the way the comte had lurked about spying on their house last night, she felt instinctively that Tate's departure and, of course, Nicholas' visit, must be concealed from him at all costs.

With a leaf taken from the Portuguese widow's book, she glided up to de Blanchard with her lips posed in a tiny pout. "Ah, Philippe, do forgive me, but I am fagged to death this morning and just cannot face a lesson today. I was up so late with . . . with Martha, that my throat is as raspy as glasspaper. And, besides, I am engaged to ride with Captain Wynne in a short while."

Dorothea

The man was none too pleased at this development. "But does your husband not object? I was under the impression that he, shall we say, looks askance on your having *beaux*."

"Captain Wynne is nothing of the sort! He is, in fact, an old, old friend of my husband. Besides, Adriana is going with us."

Madalena laughed shrilly. "This Captain Wynne is a man of odd fits and starts, it seems, Philippe. First he told Tate that he would meet with us at Almack's and then he broke his promise. And now Tate himself is breaking promises. He agreed to take me to Tattersall's this morning and has turned into a slugabed instead. I hope that you do not prove equally unreliable?" she said with a rapid flutter of her dark lashes in the gentleman's direction.

For once, the comte appeared to be unmoved by this coquetry. He looked as though his mind were elsewhere, and Dorothea, watching, prayed it was not dwelling on the more interesting business of Sir Tate's sleeping so late, or Adriana's wasting so many candles.

Madalena looked irritated at his lack of attention. "Don't you remember, Senhor, you promised to sing with me. That *dueto de amor* which is too *difícil* for Dona Dorotéia," she said in a faintly waspish tone.

"Too high, *not* too difficult," Dorothea corrected, under her breath.

Adriana rose to her feet. "Fine, then, you two enjoy your singing, and Thea and I will go give the babies a bath," she said, taking Dorothea by the arm and pulling her across the room. As they shut the door, they saw that Madalena and the comte were already engrossed in the music, or whatever. Their heads were bent over the page so closely that his perfectly ordered curls brushed her artfully tumbled locks.

Adriana and Dorothea spent the next half hour with the children in the nursery. As always, Harry delighted in Martha's enjoyment of her bath and the baby's gurgles were echoed in his own exclamations of pleasure. Though as a general rule he loathed soap and water, he joined in enthusiastically for the sake of splashing Martha in a gentle water battle in the huge tin tub.

After Adriana finished feeding the twins and all three infants were dressed and handed over to Seraphim and Aggie for a morning walk in the park, the two sisters returned, rather reluctantly, to the drawing room and paused outside.

"I don't hear any singing, do you?" Adriana whispered.

"Maybe the comte realized he had met his match and beat a hasty retreat, though it is not like him to leave without kissing every feminine hand in the house," Dorothea chuckled. "Somehow I feel that the act of doing so gives him the strength to go out into the cold, cruel masculine world."

"Shh," Adriana said. "Listen, they're talking. What *do* two rogues talk about, I wonder."

For a few moments they stood silent, listening to the murmuring voices coming from within. It seemed to Dorothea that the cadence and flow was not that of English. She looked at Adriana in puzzlement.

"Aren't they speaking—"

"Portuguese," Adriana finished for her. "And most fluently, too. It appears that the Comte de Blanchard has hidden his linguistic talents under a bushel. Most intriguing."

"Exactly," Dorothea agreed quietly, but her thoughts

were in wild disarray. If the man spoke Portuguese, why had he troubled to deny it? This question was quickly pushed aside by a much more personal consideration. If the Frenchman spoke Madalena's language, he could as easily have been the man whom Dorothea had seen kissing her at Vauxhall. That this was also highly unlikely she failed to admit to herself, in the first flush of giddy hope before her wild conjectures were interrupted by Adriana.

"It all looks havey-cavey to me, Thea. I've a mind to demand an explanation here and now."

"No, I think we should play his little game along and see what he is up to before he senses we are suspicious of him. Come on." Dorothea put her hand to the knob and eased open the door.

Madalena stood with her back leaning against the comte's broad chest. Her head was thrown back on his shoulder, in a strikingly voluptuous attitude, and she was gazing deeply into his eyes. His arms encircled her, with his hands pressed against the high waist of her low-necked gown.

"Ontem, eu tive qui dormir na sala de estar," Mrs. Smythe-Davies said plaintively, her bottom lip thrust out. *"As mulheres da casa não me gustam."*

"Mas porque ontem? O que que foi ontem á noite extrordinário?" de Blanchard asked as he bent to lay his cheek next to hers.

"Não sei, não, mas aquela Dorotéia—"

Recognizing her name, Dorothea had no desire to be gossiped about, even in a language she didn't understand. She cleared her throat loudly from the doorway.

"Ah, Philippe, I see you are checking Madalena's breathing," she said innocently.

". . . out, een, out, een," the comte said abruptly,

as if in continuation of an interrupted sentence. "Yes, you are breathing very well. Such enviable control of your *corps*. Most impressive." Only then did he look up and "discover" that Adriana and Dorothea had arrived.

"But ladies, how delightful that you have come back before I had to leave. Madalena has surprised me greatly with her superb skills."

"Skills? Oh, I collect by that you mean *singing* skills," Dorothea said, lifting one eyebrow in emphasis.

"But of course, what else could I mean?" he answered with a faintly offended air. "And we shall soon be ready to astound you both with our, now how did you put it in your picturesque tongue, Lena? Ah yes, a *dueto de amor*. And, speaking of *amor* . . ." he turned to Adriana. "Am I to infer from the glow on your cheek that you have received news today of your noble husband? I do hope he is well?"

Adriana's glowing cheek paled. "Why, no. I have heard nothing to speak of."

"Come, come, my lady. You must not trifle with me. I am a man of noted *discernement* and it is clear to me that you are *très agitée*."

Dorothea, seeing that Adriana was, as he had pointed out, greatly agitated, plunged back into the conversation and steered the comte away. "If you will be so kind as to excuse us, Captain Wynne shall be here at any moment to take us up in his carriage and we must make ourselves presentable. We must, er, fetch our bonnets and parasols, and do all kinds of silly feminine things. Surely you know, Philippe, that these things take time."

The mention of time and the impending visit by the Captain made Madalena exclaim over the lateness of the hour. "This is just too bad of Tate! I shall send

Smithson to awaken him. Surely he has slept long enough, even if we did not get to bed until *madrugada*."

She swept out, leaving Adriana and Dorothea regarding each other with something near to panic. If de Blanchard learned that Tate had left so abruptly, and without a word to his *protégée*, he might piece together his various bits of observations and deduce something much too close to the truth, thought Dorothea.

"Pray forgive our hurrying you off like this, Philippe," Dorothea said, taking his arm once again and propelling him into the foyer. Adriana said nothing. She merely opened the door and stood by like a silent sentinel with a fixed smile on her face. "You see, we do have this other engagement, and since you are practically family, I know you will not take offense at our plain treatment of you."

The gentleman was disobliging enough to dig in his glossy heels on the very threshold and begin a lengthy recital of his appreciation for the honor of running tame in their family. It was when he began enumerating the reasons for his overwhelming gratitude to them that Madalena's screech split the air.

"Good-bye, Philippe, until tomorrow," Dorothea blurted out, and Adriana shut the door in his handsome, startled face.

As the two women followed the sounds of Madalena's hysteria, Adriana quickly told Thea what the comte and the widow had been talking about in Portuguese.

"She was complaining that she had to sleep in the sitting room last night, and that we don't like her. He was just asking why last night was out of the ordinary when you broke in. Thanks for being so quick-witted. Where Nick's safety is concerned, I am reduced to a blithering booberkin."

Their conversation halted when they arrived at the breakfast parlor, where Madalena had cornered the hapless Smithson.

"Gone? Without telling me? It is *impossível*. *Meu herói* would never do that to me," Madalena was crying as they came in. She whirled on them accusingly. "This, this *cretino* tells me Tate has left. It cannot be true," she wailed, dabbing at her eyes with a dainty lace handkerchief.

Her audience was not moved.

"I'm afraid it is quite true," Adriana said coldly. "And, by the way, Madalena, it is not the custom here in England to insult our servants. Please apologize to Smithson at once."

Madalena's green eyes shot sparks of defiance. "I will not! The man is but a servant and of no importance. I—Maria Madalena—will never *pedir desculpa* from such a one." She stamped her foot in outrage and flung herself down on a chair.

Adriana just stared, dumbfounded at this rude behavior, then shrugged and turned to speak to the butler. "Please accept my apologies, Smithson, for Mrs. Smythe-Davies' inexcusable bad manners. That will be all."

"Of course, my lady, thank you," Smithson said with a bow. Then, looking vastly relieved to escape, he scuttled from the room.

Dorothea tried to calm the angry widow with a civil explanation. "Tate was called away in the night, Madalena. You wouldn't have him neglect his duty in order to bid you adieu. You of all people should understand that he had no choice. It was, after all, through his strong sense of duty that you were brought into our lives, madam."

Madalena fixed her eyes, shining with tears, on each of the two by turns. Then a sullen expression settled over her features and she stood up in a marked manner.

"It is easy enough to see that without my champion, I am not welcome here. But I don't have to stay and suffer your enmity. I have been offered a home for as long as I wish with someone who truly appreciates my misfortunes." She smoothed out her plum-colored skirts like a self-satisfied cat preening after a bowl of thick cream. "With a dear *amiga* like Letitia to succor me, I need not feign affection for you two *frígidas* a moment longer. But just you wait until Tate comes back and learns how abominably you have treated me. You will regret this day, believe me," she sneered and flounced out.

In stunned silence, Adriana and Dorothea watched her dramatic exit. The instant the door closed, however, they joined hands and danced a spontaneous little jig round the table until lack of breath forced them to collapse into chairs.

"I—I don't care how Tate upbraids us when he returns. Nothing, *nothing* can tarnish the memory of this glorious moment," panted Adriana.

"Not only are we rid of Mrs. Smythe-Davies, but she is seeking sweet refuge with Cousin Letitia, of all people. What heavenly bliss!" Thea gasped out, and they both exploded into whoops of laughter.

Chapter 24

Dorothea and Adriana's hilarious celebration was interrupted by a masculine voice.

"May I share your joke? It must be uncommonly good." It was Captain Wynne, who smiled broadly as he came up to them.

"I am sorry to intrude, but Smithson told me where to find you and I told him I could see myself in."

"No, no, you don't intrude, Robin. Come, sit down," Adriana said, wiping the tears of laughter from her streaming eyes.

"Mayn't I hear the cause of all this merriment? I dearly love a good jest."

"Well, I'm sure it is most improper of us to tell you, but . . ." Adriana's twinkling grey eyes found a responsive sparkle in Thea's. "It's about Mrs. Smythe-Davies. It is only that she is leaving us—our 'hearts of purest gold' notwithstanding—because she greatly prefers the companionship of . . . of . . ."

Thea finished for Adriana, who had gone off into gales of mirth, "Cousin Letitia. Madalena is persuaded that Miss Grayson is a *much* more amiable, generous creature than we are."

Captain Wynne looked thunderstruck. "You must be making game of me!"

"No, no, I assure you that every word is true," Dorothea said with an unaffected smile.

He let out a long sigh of relief. "How glad I am to learn she is removing from your home. I thought it most inconsiderate of Tate to thrust her upon you. And besides, I . . ." he broke off uncomfortably.

"Besides you, what?" prompted Thea.

"It is nothing that need concern you, now that she is gone. But how delightful to picture Mrs. Smythe-Davies and Miss Grayson *tête à tête*. You know, a dear friend of mine, Lady Phoebe Robinson, is intimately acquainted with Miss Grayson. I can't help but feel, based on Lady Phoebe's perceptions, that Miss Grayson and Harry's 'witch' will be prodigiously well-suited."

"Oh, Robin, you jackanapes! What have you been up to now?"

"Only some unexceptionable, genteel social calls, Adriana. Very like this one," he grinned.

"From your note, I gained the distinct impression that this call was not merely social, Captain Wynne," Thea put in.

"No," he answered, his face suddenly sober. "As a matter of fact, my tiger is walking my team of cattle in the square. I hope that neither of you objects to a high-perch phaeton?"

"Not at all! I'll go get our bonnets and we can leave directly," Adriana said. She left the room almost at a run, still very much the Adriana that Miss Grayson had found so hoydenish.

After Adriana's departure, a silence fell, until Captain Wynne stood and put out his hand to help Dorothea to rise. "I trust that you, as well as Adriana, know something of the work in which Tate and Nick are engaged?" he said solemnly.

Thea nodded, looking closely at him. What could he possibly be leading up to? But before she could question him, Adriana came back, her own simple straw *bergère* hat thrown carelessly over her disordered brown curls. "Here you are, Thea, shall we go?"

Dorothea hastily donned her chip bonnet and tied the green ribbons under her chin as she walked out to the waiting carriage. It was a most elegant equipage, with a glossy wine-colored finish and two high-bred chestnuts in the harness.

Robin helped the ladies into the lofty seat, then clambered up himself, making a large third in the cramped space. He cheerfully dismissed his tiger and, as soon as the lad released the ribbons, steered the meddlesome team into the traffic on Oxford Street.

The two ladies sat quietly until the tricky turn into the park had been deftly negotiated. But as soon as they emerged from the narrow intersection into the broad carriage way, Adriana could contain herself no longer.

"All right, Robin, now what is all this secrecy about?" she demanded, turning impatiently to the gentleman.

Captain Wynne, keeping his expression blandly affable, as befitted a gallant on a pleasure jaunt with two ladies, answered her in a low voice.

"Both of you know, of course, that your husbands are involved in dangerous but vital missions in Portugal and Spain on behalf of the War Ministry?"

"Yes, Robin," retorted Adriana. "Believe me, we are well aware of the danger and difficulties they face.

Indeed, those worries are seldom out of our thoughts. But we do know how to keep our own counsel."

"That is what I am counting on. You see, I am doing similar work here in London, though under much more comfortable circumstances."

"B-but what about your injuries?" Thea blurted out.

"They really were very minor and incapacitate me not at all. But they did provide a convenient excuse for me to be 'invalided out' and restationed in London."

"But what possible good can you do *here*?" asked Adriana, a puzzled frown on her face despite her best efforts to counterfeit nonchalance.

"London is full of *émigré* Frenchmen who profess loyalty to the Bourbons, but who are actually in league with Bonaparte. Often these people gain *entrée* into the highest levels of society, where they are able to gather valuable information. A gabbling general's wife here, a pot-valiant subaltern there. What they have to tell could be most instructive to the enemy."

"But what has that to do with us?" Adriana asked.

Dorothea forestalled his reply. "It's Philippe de Blanchard, is it not, Captain Wynne?"

"I'm sorry, Doro . . . Lady Bancroft," Robin said gently. "It is. We think he may be a Bonapartist spy. And," his voice faltered slightly, "I have a favor to ask of you. I wish to enlist your aid in determining if it is so."

Adriana looked ready to explode. "If de Blanchard is what you say and has done anything to hurt my husband or my twin, I shall personally lead him to the gallows," she proclaimed.

Dorothea turned to her. "Adriana, you must hide your anger, as difficult as that may be, else we shall

334

accomplish nothing. If the comte should see you thus he will surely know that the scent is up."

Captain Wynne agreed. "Now, tell me, has the Frenchman ever said or done anything which would bear out our suspicions?"

Thea frowned. "Yes, many times. In fact, A. and I already harbored doubts about him." She told how the comte was continually asking questions about Tate and Nicholas, and how she had seen him from her window watching the house in the dead of night.

"You never told me that," said Adriana in shocked accents.

"I'm afraid it slipped my mind until just this moment, A. It was just last night that I saw him."

"Last night? You mean when Nick . . .?" Adriana's voice rose in a high squeak of alarm, but she was shushed by the other two. After fidgeting nervously for a few moments, she hissed, "Don't forget about the Portuguese."

"Portuguese?" Captain Wynne echoed.

"Yes, the comte speaks Portuguese with ease, and he specifically told us ages ago that he did not know a word of the language."

"That sounds most promising," Captain Wynne said with an approving nod. "I commend you for already catching him out in one lie. I've every confidence that you can work wonders where we have failed. Just remember what an effective intelligence agent Delilah proved to be."

"But what do you want us to do, short of cutting his hair or impaling him on our crochet hooks, which would give me a good deal of pleasure," Adriana whispered vehemently, the light of battle still in her eye.

"No, no, nothing as drastic as that," laughed the

gentleman. "For now, it shall be sufficient if you art-
lessly let slip a few tidbits of crucial information about
Wellington's strategy. It shall be totally false information, of course," he hurriedly assured them when he
saw their horrified expressions. "The comte will believe
what you tell him if you ascribe your knowledge to
letters from your husbands."

He paused while he guided his horses round a
couple of carriages standing at the side of the pathway
before continuing in the same light tone. "I think it had
better be Lady Bancroft who does this, Adriana, for I
fear your emotions would betray you. You face is like a
mirror of your thoughts and the comte is not a fool.
Besides, there is an *on dit* in circulation that the Bancroft marriage is a little . . . er . . . shaky. That should
work in our favor." He addressed Dorothea without
quite meeting her eyes. "You see, *you* might tell de
Blanchard these things as if you were angry with Tate
and complaining of his neglect, whereas all the world
knows that Adriana and her Nick are simply reeking of
April and May. No one would believe her if she pre-
tended that Laidley is treating her ill."

"You are quite right," Dorothea said stiffly. "How
fortunate that my situation lends itself so admirably to
your plans. What do you suggest I tell him?"

"Drop into some conversation that Wellington is
fatigued by the Iberian heat, and has no plans to storm
the French garrisons which remain in Spain at San
Sebastian and Pamplona. Say that he intends to wait
until further victories are won in Germany before
campaigning any further."

"Very well," Dorothea said, then considered a moment. "Perhaps I could embellish it by saying Tate is
engaged in foxhunting with Wellington in the mean-

while. I'm told my husband is a bruising rider and fully worthy of keeping up with the peer on the hunting field."

"Sounds most convincing. Do be sure and mention as well that the Earl always wears the sky blue and black of the Salisbury Hunt. Details help, you know."

By the time the phaeton drew up in front of the Laidley townhouse, Dorothea was well-versed and well-rehearsed in the part she was to play, and Adriana was resigned to staying out of the way.

To her surprise, Dorothea found her role as the wronged wife all too easy to fall into over the next few days. She had no trouble prattling on and on about Tate's neglect to the unsuspecting Frenchman at every opportunity. There were two aspects of her new role which did prove difficult, however. First of all, it was impossible for her to judge whether or not the comte's sympathetic attention was in fact but a camouflage for espionage. And secondly, whether the man was a spy or not, she found it increasingly difficult to keep him, physically, at arm's length as she tearfully confided all Tate's alleged perfidies and bogus plans.

One afternoon, soon after she had entered the conspiracy with Captain Wynne, she squirmed under the comte's consoling words and groping hands during her voice lesson.

"Poor little Dorothée. So alone and *désolée*. This Bancroft monster doesn't deserve such a one as you, with your blazing hair" —he brushed his lips against her braids—"your adorable little ears" —he nibbled at her earlobe—"your . . ." but before he could finish his catalog of her charms she drew away, chattering of Tate's failings as a husband.

"And I can't imagine when the odious wretch will

trouble to return home. He protests that Wellington himself requires his presence, though from what I can gather it is merely to be master of the hunt. They evidently plan to pursue nothing but the fox until well after Christmas. Don't you think it is disgraceful for a man to be away from his wife and daughter, especially at Christmas? Particularly a man like Tate, who needn't involve himself in this awful war at all. It isn't as if he were a pauper, a younger son dependent on the army for a living."

The comte's eyes held an arrested expression. "But I was told that the late Sir Walter Bancroft had died without a feather to fly with, except for the manor house."

"Oh, when he died that was indeed the case. But though his own pockets were to let at the time of his death, Tate's father made some exceedingly farsighted investments, which have turned Tate into a regular Golden Ball," she said airily. "That is another reason why my husband has no excuse to linger on, hunting foxes in the Peninsula. He should be back in England managing his capital instead of allowing the burden to fall on me." She sighed and contrived to appear as beleaguered as any giddy female might as this plumper passed her lips.

De Blanchard regarded her with, if anything, increased devotion and avid interest, and started to gather her into his arms, but Dorothea once more evaded his embrace and changed the subject.

"And, do you see anything of Mrs. Smythe-Davies of late, Philippe? We have quite lost sight of her, immured as we are with our infants. Are you still giving her singing lessons?"

The comte's eyebrows arched in surprise. "Then you have not heard the news?"

"What, has she been accepted by her late husband's family?" Dorothea exclaimed.

"No, the poor girl has had an accident. It seems she was tripped by Miss Grayson's dog and tumbled headlong down an entire flight of stairs. Of course, in her interesting condition, such an accident could have but one outcome. Your cousin feels so terrible that she is talking of settling a substantial sum on Madalena by way of recompense for the child she lost."

"You had best warn Mrs. Smythe-Davies that Cousin Letitia is wont to do a lot of talking and very little settling," Thea said tartly. "But do convey my condolences. She must be heartbroken over her loss."

"Yes, why at the rout last night at Lady Martindale's, she could dance only six sets, she was so affected. If you could have but seen her sitting there, cuddling her odd little lap puppy, it would have torn at your heartstrings."

"I dare say."

Suddenly the door burst open and Adriana flew into the room. "Oh, I didn't know you were here, Comte," she blurted out. "Thea, could you come upstairs immediately?"

"Of course A., what is it?" she asked, worried by the wild look on her sister's face.

"It's the children. Do come up as soon as you can." Without a backward look, Adriana vanished as quickly as she had appeared.

The comte started for the door, then stopped. "Have I done something to offend Lady Laidley? She has seemed angry with me these last few days."

Preoccupied by Adriana's brief appearance and her evident distraction, Thea answered without thinking.

339

"Oh, I daresay she is just worried that my friendship with someone like you somehow imperils her brother's happiness. But nothing could be further from the truth."

He looked affronted by her bluntness and she made a hasty explanation.

"I mean, of course, that my having a *tendre* for you would not bother Tate in the least. He just doesn't care."

This served to soothe the man's ruffled feelings and he took his leave, pausing only long enough at the hall pier glass to straighten his cravat and set his hat at the correct tilt.

Dorothea watched him and wondered briefly how she could ever have thought him at all attractive. Then, recalling Adriana's anxious face, she hurried upstairs.

Instead of Adriana, it was Senhora Seraphim who met her at the nursery door. The old woman was carrying Martha and led a bewildered Harry by the hand.

"It is *difteria*. We must go, now, before Marta and the *menio* are *infectados*."

Stunned by this news, Dorothea tried to move past Seraphim into the nursery, where she could see Adriana standing by the twins' cradles with a stricken expression on her face.

"Adriana, can this be true? Diphtheria?"

"Yes. I—" Adriana began, but tears overtook her and she broke down into sobs.

Miss Whitesley came into the room from the adjoining chamber, bearing cold compresses. "It is diphtheria, right enough. Both Seraphim and I have seen it before, and had it ourselves. So did Adriana when she was a lass. But I brought her through it and will do the same for the twins. Now you just get Harry and Martha out to Bancroft Hall. We'll launder all their clothes to rid them of the infection and send them out later. Just go. Now."

"A., I . . . I . . ." Dorothea stammered helplessly.

"No, don't come in," Adriana said in an unsteady voice. "I shouldn't even have gone downstairs and Aggie has thoroughly upbraided me for doing so. I know what it is you wish to say. And I love you, too."

Thea's eyes prickled with tears, but catching the senhora's measuring look she fought to get her emotions under control

"Very well, come to see us as soon as Matty and Nick are well," she said evenly, then taking Martha from Seraphim, she marched downstairs.

They all piled unceremoniously into the family traveling coach, with Lovelace riding atop with Jem and Annie. The dog's presence was a sop to Harry, who otherwise refused to climb into the carriage. At first Thea found the boy's resistance to the journey difficult to fathom, for in general, he was very well-behaved with her. But once the carriage began to move through the London streets, the lad's reluctance became perfectly understandable. Almost immediately he turned a sickly shade of grey and was sick all over the seats and the baby's only clean blanket. Terrified that he might be contracting the dread disease they were fleeing, Thea looked pleadingly at Seraphim, who was calmly wiping the cushions with a large sensible handkerchief.

"Wh—what are the symptoms of diphtheria, Senhora?" she asked in a determinedly offhand manner.

Seraphim, to Dorothea's astonishment, smiled and patted her hand.

"This is not *difteria*, Dona. Don't worry. Little Harry is only *enjoado* by the motion. Mathilde was

341

exactly the same as a little girl. *Meu Deus*, but she used to make a mess of her father's coach."

Before she quite realized it, Thea returned her companion's smile. To her surprise, she felt nothing but a sort of poignant regret at not ever having known Martha's mother.

"Happily, Senhora Seraphim," she said, giving the gnarled old hand a squeeze, "it seems that Martha has inherited her father's iron constitution then. For this swaying has only rocked her to sleep."

Harry whimpered and put his head on her shoulder. "There, there, Harry, now try to get some sleep. Just close your eyes and think of the fun we shall have at Bancroft Hall. We have a little horse about Harney's size, and a pony cart. Oh, I just know we shall be as merry as grigs."

She stopped talking and sang a lullaby. Under the spell of the music, Harry's eyelids gradually closed, and they rode along in silence for most of the afternoon, refraining from speech lest they awaken the children. The sympathetic looks which the two ladies exchanged from time to time were a far cry from the hostilities that had marked their journey in the opposite direction weeks before. This irony did not escape Dorothea and she rested her head back against the squabs with a wry smile as she watched the dusty hedgerows roll by.

Chapter 25

Once she arrived at Bancroft Hall life seemed to exist on several levels for Dorothea. On the surface she was the cheerful mistress of the manor, conferring with the servants, playing with Martha, and entertaining Harry as she had promised. But at the same time, her mind was far away from the elegant Hall and the flowery meadows and sparkling streams she wandered past with the little boy. Night and day she fretted over what was happening in Portman Square and worried about the fate of the tiny, vulnerable twins. Still another portion of her thoughts lingered in the Peninsula with Tate, praying that he was safe and trying not to dwell on what might happen when he returned.

She felt truly isolated in the quiet of the country. Adriana and Aggie were so involved with the care of the sick babies that neither apparently had time to write. And there was no word from Captain Wynne to indicate whether or not the false information she had planted had done its office.

In an effort to bury these troublesome thoughts, she would snatch an hour or so whenever she could to practice her singing. Sometimes Harry would sit with her as she did so, playing with his toy soldiers or paints as he listened. Lovelace too was a frequent audience, though he would insist on an occasional howl of his own, which would result·in his immediate banishment to the stables.

One evening nearly a week after their return to Bancroft Hall, Dorothea was practicing her *solfeggio* exercises in the small sitting room which had been Mathilde's favorite place. Somehow, after all her vivid, bitter encounters with the living Madalena, Tate's first wife had faded into a pretty child who offered no particular threat to Dorothea's happiness. The frilly sitting room, with its antique dolls and frothy mementos of a foreign girlhood, was no longer upsetting to the young woman who stood at Mathilde's wooden music rack and ascended the scale.

"Do, re, mi, fa," she sang, supporting her breath as the comte had taught her. It was supremely satisfying to feel how the sound reverberated properly in her head and how it drove out all other concerns from her mind. She broke off as Lovelace pushed the door open and entered the room.

"You know, Lovelace, de Blanchard may be a spy and a dandy and many other undesirable things, but he is also a first-rate singing teacher! How ironical that the same person who might be doing grave injury to Tate has done wonders for me. Life is certainly unpredictable," she sighed, then stretched and yawned. "I am a deplorably lazy creature today, and feel like shirking on my practicing. Let's get Martha and Harry and go for a ride! Would you like that?"

Lovelace was all enthusiasm, dancing on his hind legs and trotting at her heels up the stairs and through the nursery door.

"Seraphim, is Martha awake?" she called gaily. "We want to visit the old mill today and . . ."

The playful flow of words was cut off as she saw the grim expression on the older woman's face.

"I was just coming to tell you, Dona. Martinha, she is sick."

"Now, Seraphim," began Dorothea wearily, "we have been over and over this before. Just because Martha has a light cold is no reason she cannot enjoy the sunshine with us in the cart."

"It is not a cold, Dona. It is . . ."

Gripped by icy fear, Dorothea did not stay to hear the end of the sentence, but walked numbly into the adjoining room, where Martha's cradle stood.

She leaned over the little bed and saw that Martha lay listless and still, her small neck swollen to nearly twice its normal size and her breathing laborious.

Seraphim came and stood beside her, and together they gazed down on the sick child.

"Diphtheria?" breathed Dorothea.

"Yes."

"I shall send at once for Dr. Hawk. And instruct Harry to sleep in another room with Annie. Then I shall be back."

"But Dona, there is no need for you to expose yourself. I myself am safe from the *doneça*. I contracted it years ago when the condessa had it. Let me take care of Martinha by myself."

"Nonsense. I am her mother and my place is with her. It will take the both of us to nurse her properly," replied Dorothea dully. Without allowing Seraphim any further argument she left to make the arrangements, taking care to stay a safe distance from those with whom she had to converse.

When Dr. Hawk arrived, he took one look at Martha's swollen throat and confirmed their worst fears. He was a cheerfully plump gentleman whose natural buoyancy had sustained him through the myriad small tragedies of a country practice. He tried to calm the agitated mother and governess as best he could, but the only advice he could offer was to keep the baby cool and clean, and to give her broth and brandy whenever possible.

The two women followed his instructions slavishly, staying at the child's side by turns. For the first week, she grew steadily worse in spite of their efforts, and the rattling sound of the infant's breathing terrified Thea and threw her into a further quandary.

Almost from the first she had debated about writing to Tate about Martha's condition. On the one hand, he was so far away, and there was nothing he could do to help the child even if he returned. It would only add to his worries. But, on the other hand, it was something he should know. That he had grown fonder of the child he had once spurned was evidenced by the scene she had witnessed in Adriana's nursery. And as her father, he deserved to be informed that the baby's life was in danger.

She had finally dashed off a quick note to her husband, via the Ministry, and one to Adriana, informing them both of the situation and wishing Adriana's twins a speedy recovery. Before she could change her mind, she gave both missives to Robert to post and went back to her nursing vigil.

Gradually Martha's condition improved. The membrane that threatened to close off the tiny throat began to recede and the fever to cool. After little more than a fortnight, the doctor pronounced that the child had evidently escaped the serious complications that might have resulted from the infection. He assured them that she was over the most dangerous stage of the disease, and no longer contagious.

After he had left, Dorothea and Seraphim stared at each other, too relieved to speak. Then the latter turned away, her shoulders heaving.

"Why, Seraphim, you are crying," Thea said gently, placing her hand on the black-clad arm.

"I was so *assustada*," sobbed the tiny woman, "so terrified that we would lose Marta, and I couldn't bear it, after Mathilde . . ."

"And now, because of your care, Martha will live."

"And because of you," Seraphim declared, as she swung around to face Dorothea. "Mathilde herself could not have cared more tenderly and faithfully for her *criança*. Indeed, she probably would not have done it at all. She was always so delicate, she could not have borne it. But you, madame, you are now truly the *mamãe*."

"Then that makes you the true grandmother, Seraphim. And Martha is lucky to have you." It was an odd occurrence to feel so close to the Portuguese governess, and Thea just stood for a moment savoring the exotic sensation.

At last she spoke. "Now, if you will excuse me, Senhora, I believe I shall have a nice long soak in my bath before the dinner gong. For the first time in weeks, I can look forward to both."

She grinned as she left the room and danced down the corridor to her own chamber, so happy at Martha's recovery that she didn't care who saw her undignified behavior.

Annie arrived with the bath water and Thea spent

the next half-hour reveling in her joy and the soothing warmth. It felt as though her body were cleansed of all the knots and worries of the past fortnight.

When Annie returned to help Thea brush out her heavy hair, she brought a letter that had just arrived from London. This time she recognized the writing as that of Captain Wynne and she tore it open with shaking hands. As she read the opening line, Dorothea pressed her hand to her heart, thinking at first that the captain was writing to tell her bad news of Tate, but such was nowise the case.

Dear Lady Bancroft,

It is my painful duty to inform you that the person whom you and your sister were kind enough to shelter in London has been exposed as an adventuress. As you know, when I first had occasion to meet Mrs. Smythe-Davies, as she called herself, I had a strong feeling of having met her before. But as she had been, of course, much younger, and had used a different name when I was numbered among her acquaintance, I was not certain that I was correct. I will spare you the details of my previous experience with her, but suffice it to say that she quickly threw me over for a wealthy officer of the 6th, and the last I had heard of her, she was living in a grand style under his protection.

I was also given pause by the fact that Tate brought her here and installed her with you and Adriana. It did not seem possible that this "Madalena" could be the same person I had known years ago as "Maria." Still, nagging suspicions persisted.

It was when I heard her perform a duet with our friend de Blanchard at a musicale recently that all my remaining doubts were dispelled. However she might have changed in appearance, name and manner, her singing voice remains the same as when she drew me under her spell as a callow young cornet.

Acting on my conviction that this was indeed the woman I had known, I went to the Smythe-Davies and, with my information, they were able to look into the matter through an agent in Portugal.

They have learned that the woman, Maria Madalena de Andrade, was already married to her, shall we say, business partner, when she inveigled Percy Smythe-Davies to the altar. Her claim upon the family is therefore totally invalid.

Oddly enough, even after the story became known, Miss Grayson staunchly stuck by her *protégée*, defending her fiercely against all these "false charges." Evidently Maria Madalena herself saw the handwriting on the wall, however, because she has disappeared from Miss Grayson's home and hearth, and no one has seen her since.

Interestingly, the Comte de Blanchard has also dropped out of sight. It was deucedly frustrating, as we were nearly ready to arrest him for espionage.

The last time he was seen in public our friend Lady Phoebe had a fascinating chat with him about the successful storming of the garrison at San Sebastian. He looked positively apoplectic at the news, but Lady Phoebe kindly offered him her smelling salts and asked if his cravat was tied in the "waterfall," or "the noose," which is all the rage.

But enough foolishness. You should know that I have also written about this unhappy business to Tate. I know it will not please him to learn he has been duped by a woman, but it is infinitely better he knows the whole. I told him he was mad to overlook his lovely wife by chasing Mathilde's shade, and now I am proved doubly right.

I hope this letter finds you well. Your happiness and health are precious to me.

Your humble servant,
Robert Wynne

At the very bottom of the page there was another lengthy scrawl, as if in haste:

I have just this moment received word from Tate, saying he will be returning to England very soon. Now that Pamplona has been invested, and Wellington is preparing to cross into France, Tate's fluency in Portuguese will no longer be required. I should probably have let him surprise you with his news, but having seen something of how matters stand between you, I thought you would appreciate being forewarned. Tate has been posted to the Horse Guards in London where it is highly likely he he will remain for the duration of the war.

I hope that this news will bring you the happiness you deserve. There is also other

happy news to relate: Adriana asked me to tell
you that the twins are on the mend and she
will write as soon as possible.

Robin

This letter awoke in Dorothea such a mixture of
exhilaration and trepidation that she had to read and
reread it several times before she knew whether she
required a glassful of champagne or a bottle of smelling
salts. The twins were well, Madalena unmasked and
Tate on his way back to stay.

After one final perusal of the scribbled words, she
rang for Robert and requested that he bring a bottle of
the best champagne in the cellar on the instant.

"I suppose, my lady, that you also wish for me to
fetch the dog?" suggested Robert, with a perfectly straight
face.

"Yes, of course, Lovelace must be here, and Senhora Seraphim I think, if Martha is asleep."

"Very good, my lady." he said, backing solemnly
away, but before he had even left the room, Seraphim
herself scuttled past him and ran up to Dorothea in a very
agitated manner.

"Seraphim, what is it? You look beside yourself.
Do sit down!"

She took the elderly lady's arm and gently pulled
her down onto the brocaded sofa next to her.

"Now, tell me, what is the matter?"

"I received a letter, from London, with such news!"
Seraphim said, her mouth drawn into a tight line of
distress.

"Oh, dear," Dorothea said, half to herself. "I had
forgotten how fond you once were of her. How could I

ever think you would find her predicament a cause for jubilation, as I do."

Senhora Seraphim glared at her with icy hauteur and moved herself as far away from Dorothea as the sofa allowed.

"But I suppose that being fellow countrywomen must count for more than I had thought. Surely I would not feel so sympathetic as you toward a woman who had pulled the wool over so many eyes."

Seraphim turned to her with shock and outrage clearly etched on her face. "Pull the wool over . . . would you please explain what that means?" she said in a shaking voice.

"Flummoxed, cozened," Dorothea explained, looking hopefully at the woman sitting rigidly at her side. "After all, even *you* suspected that the woman was something of a fraud."

"*Uma fraude?* You tell me that the Condessa de Vasconcellos is a *fraude? Nossa, Senhora!*" Seraphim roared and leapt to her feet.

"The Condessa de Vasconcellos? What are you talking about?" Dorothea cried, aghast at the gulf of misunderstanding which yawned between them.

"My letter from the condessa," Seraphim articulated slowly, as she might to a child of limited intelligence. "She and the conde are in London, on their way here to see the *bebé*, and she has been taken ill. Why, her writing was so *trémulo* it barely looked like her hand. She asks that I come to her and take care of her until she is fit to travel here. They speak no English, you see, and have need of me. Now that Martha is nearly well, I feel that I must go to the condessa."

Dorothea almost laughed with relief, but managed

to contain herself. Seraphim looked as if she were ready to cry once again.

"Yes, it is only right that you go to your condessa. Forgive me for the confusion, I was thinking of something else. We were talking at cross purposes entirely."

"But to whom were you referring, if not to the condessa?"

"Why, to Madalena. She has been unmasked as an adventuress. Her marriage to Smythe-Davies was not valid and she has disappeared, as we say here, under a cloud."

Seraphim said nothing, but, taking a quantity of black bombazine skirt in either hand, she curtsied deeply towards the amazed Dorothea. Then, with her head still bowed, she spoke in a muffled tone.

"My lady, please accept my meager apology for the harm done by that evil woman to your family. I am humbled to think a *Portuguêsa* could do such a thing."

Dorothea helped the old woman to stand erect. "You have no need to apologize to me. There are rogues and scoundrels in every land and one cannot be held responsible for them purely because of a shared birthplace. Besides, she has brought no lasting harm to my family," she said, though under her breath she murmured a fervent addendum, "I hope." Then she continued: "Now that Martha is safe, you can go with a clear conscience. Now, let's get you packed and off to London. I know that the sooner you join them, the better you will feel."

Seraphim looked grateful and hurried away, leaving Dorothea to order the horses for the journey. In a very short time, she was waving good-bye from the nursery window, holding Martha up to the panes so

that Seraphim could have a last fond look as she went
by in the carriage.

After the coach was out of sight, Dorothea stayed
with the baby for a while, playing with her and telling
her of the meeting that would soon take place with her
two maternal grandparents.

"And they must be very, very anxious to see you,
little one, if they would journey so far, in wartime, in ill
health, to make your acquaintance. But speaking as a
totally unbiased *madrasta*, I believe is the correct term,
I can tell you without reservation that you are well
worth the trip."

Martha did not seem overly worried and merely
batted like a kitten at the crocheted balls hanging over
her bed. Dorothea kissed her and left her to nap.

After closing the nursery door with skilled maternal stealth, Dorothea went to the small sitting room to
seek some quiet and the nearly forgotten solace of
practicing. Since Martha had fallen ill, she had had no
time to devote to her music. The days had passed in an
unhappy blur of nursing and rest.

She leafed through her music, trying to decide
where to begin after so long without so much as a scale,
then suddenly she remembered the letter she herself
had received, which lay folded in her bosom. In all the
confusion and excitement over Seraphim's letter and
departure, she had not had a chance to mull over the
contents of her own missive properly.

She took it out and unfolded it, and once again
read the disturbing words. As she looked over the
postscript, a shiver of emotion passed over her. This
was soon followed by another and then another, until
Dorothea felt a *frisson* of alarm.

She felt her forehead, which was burning hot. Then,

putting her hand to her neck, she gingerly probed with a knowledge born of nursing Martha. The telltale lumps that her fingers discovered made her sink against the back of the chair, quivering with apprehension.

The chills, the fever, and the swelling on her neck, all signaled the start of what Seraphim called *difteria*.

Chapter 26

Dr. Hawk, having looked into Dorothea's throat, frowned and shook his head.

"It's diphtheria, all right. Your own diagnosis was correct, I'm sorry to say. Now we must find someone to take care of you properly. Who amongst the servants has already had the disease?"

"Seraphim is the only one I know of, and she has left. As for the others, I don't know." Her voice sounded hoarse as she replied, and her throat felt worse with each swallow.

"I shall make inquiries, and if there is no one with immunity on your own staff, I shall send someone out from the village to act as nurse. A pity I haven't a wife, for then I could volunteer her services without further ado, but as I haven't any, I shall just have to beat the bushes for someone suitable. In the meanwhile, don't you worry about anything except getting better. Annie will faithfully look after little Martha, and Harry has struck up quite a friendship with your head groom, Joseph, or so I'm told. He'll have a wonderful time in the stables whilst you recuperate up here. A better time than you will have, I can promise you," he added with a rueful smile.

Dorothea tried to return his smile, but could only manage a very weak imitation.

"Would you be kind enough to send word to the Conde and Condessa de Vasconcellos, Martha's grandparents, who are at Grillon's Hotel in Albemarle Street, in London. They should be told that I am ill so that they will not arrive and be exposed."

The effort of such a long speech exhausted her, and she sank back against the pillows of the bed and closed her burning eyelids.

The doctor did not disturb her with any further attempts at conversation. She heard him move about the room for a few moments, then the click of the door as he let himself out of the bedchamber. When the door closed she started up, only to fall back again at the pain which shot through her at this abrupt movement. It had suddenly occurred to her that a message should be sent to Adriana, and to Tate, if possible. The doctor was gone, however, and she felt unequal to crossing the room to the bell pull to summon a servant to send after him. Besides, she reflected, lying back once again, what would be the use of sending such letters now? Adriana has troubles enough of her own, and as for Tate . . . She shied away from the painful notion that Tate might even welcome the news. Losing a wife to diphtheria was, after all, much less scandalous and complicated than discarding her through annulment.

She shut her eyes and drifted off into fitful slumber. When she opened them again, darkness had fallen and the room was dimly lit by one candle. In her feverish state even the light of one taper was dazzling, as it flickered over the high canopy bed and plainly carved furniture. Her gaze slowly traversed the room and came to rest at last on a woman sitting quietly in an armchair by the low fire in the grate.

"Who-who's there?" she weakly queried, and the figure arose and moved towards the bed.

"I am come to nurse you, as a special favor to Dr. Hawk," said the woman as she walked across the room.

Dorothea passed her hand over her eyes, convinced that she must be delirious, for the figure and voice alike were those of Miss Stevens, the vicar's sister whose last visit at Bancroft Hall had been the disastrous dinner party.

"Miss Stevens?" Dorothea whispered wonderingly.

"I really think that if we are to be closeted here for the next fortnight, we should drop the formalities, don't you? Call me Cora," came the brisk reply. "I took the liberty of installing myself in Tate's old room across the hall. How convenient that you do not use the master bedroom, as there is no near chamber I could use that is so handy as Tate's is to this."

Dorothea wondered if she might be dreaming and surreptitiously pinched her own arm. Miss Stevens, seeing the resulting wince, leaned over her solicitously.

"Yes, I remember how painful it was to talk when I had diphtheria as a young girl. Of course, I was but a child at the time, but these things do remain with one," Miss Stevens said with remarkable affability. She then minced over to the chest, where there was a tray with a brandy decanter and a single glass.

Dorothea watched, growing more bewildered by the second, as the lady filled the glass to the very top and brought it over to her.

"Now, Dr. Hawk left strict instructions that you

are to imbibe as much of these spirits as you can, to fight the poison of the infection."

She handed the glass to Dorothea, who struggled to sit upright without spilling the contents. Taking a tiny sip of the golden liquor, the girl felt as if fire were streaming down her throat.

"Now I know why Martha screamed every time we gave her this vile stuff," Dorothea choked out. "It burns like the very devil."

Miss Stevens grimaced. "Just because one is ill does not give one license to speak profanely, Dorothea."

"Yes, ma'am," she said meekly, trying to hand the glass back so that she might lie down.

"No, you must drink more," said Miss Stevens, waving away the glass and fetching the decanter to fill it once again. "That is not enough to help."

"Oh, but . . ."

"No buts, my girl. I am in charge of you now and I say you must drink."

Dorothea obediently took another swallow, and to her surprise, found that the fiery sensation was much less pronounced. Encouraged, she forced herself to drain the glass and gave it back into Miss Stevens' mitted hand with an air of faint triumph. Then everything started whirling about in a most disconcerting manner.

"I—I believe I am a little bosky, and so hot, and . . . and sleepy," she murmured.

"Most satisfactory. Dr. Hawk will be pleased that I carried out his instructions so well," twittered Miss Stevens, shaking her ringlets in an oddly coquettish fashion.

There was something about the woman's tone that puzzled Dorothea, as it seemed to explain why Miss Stevens had offered her help. But she was far too woozy to grasp what it was, so she gave up and fell back to sleep.

For Dorothea the week that followed drifted by in a fog of fever and pain, strongly flavored with brandy, but at the end of that time, she began to feel substantially better. Miss Stevens did not hesitate to claim all the credit for her improved condition, though in a rather indirect fashion.

"Yes, Dr. Hawk," she purred, when that gentleman had exclaimed over Dorothea's having so light a case, "I think I have discovered my calling in life—I am just a born nurse." She fluttered her sparse eyelashes at the startled physician.

"Yes, you have done well enough with Lady Bancroft here," Dr. Hawk replied calmly, then turned his attention back to his patient.

"Well enough?" croaked Miss Stevens indignantly. "Why, I have worked my delicate fingers to the bone. And, let me assure you, I was not bred to such menial tasks," she added, her voice rising steadily in pitch and volume.

Something in the blank stare of the doctor's mild blue eyes and the curl of the patient's upper lip must have alerted the lady that she had lapsed, for she cleared her throat and paused before going on. When she did speak again, it was in a well-modulated voice. "But I have been perfectly delighted to have this opportunity to aid Dorothea in her hour, or should I say, week, of need. No sacrifice is too great for such a noble purpose."

It had long been obvious that the woman's purpose was far more matrimonial than medical in nature, and Miss Stevens' simpering only underscored this. Still, Thea reflected, the spinster had taken prodigiously good care of her, whatever her motivation.

"And I shall always be grateful for the sacrifices you have made on my account, Cora. If it weren't for you, I would have been in the basket," Dorothea said warmly.

Miss Stevens received her due with an arch smile, glancing sidelong at the doctor to see if he was taking in this testimonial to her capabilities as ministering angel.

Unfortunately for her, the doctor's attention lay elsewhere.

"Now, Lady Bancroft. You must pay strict heed to what I have to say. Although you are over the worst of the infection, and the pseudo-membranes have receded from the throat, you are still very much in the contagious stage and must not receive visitors for another week at the very least. I will permit you to see your baby, as she herself is safe from another episode of the disease. But definitely not Harry, nor anyone else who has never had the infection. Is that clear?"

"Yes sir," she murmured, filled with joy at the prospect of holding Martha once again. She thanked the physician for his efforts, and as soon as he left, sent Miss Stevens for the child.

But when the woman returned, she was empty-handed and open-mouthed. "You'll never, *never* guess who has arrived at the village inn!" she said in a dither of excitement.

"Really, Cora, I don't care about the comings and goings in the village right at the moment. I just want to see my Martha, and not exchange tittle-tattle."

Miss Stevens sniffed. "I'll have you know my 'tittle-tattle' concerns Martha, intimately."

"Whatever do you mean?" Dorothea exclaimed, staring at her.

Dorothea

"The persons who are arrived at the Cat and the Fiddle are none other than the child's grandparents, the Portugee count and countess. They sent a messenger over to tell you that although they have no wish to disturb you in your illness, they do wish to see the baby."

Dorothea put her hands wearily over her face. "The Conde and Condessa de Vasconcellos are here?" she faltered. "But didn't the doctor notify them to stay in London? Or did I just dream asking him to do so?"

Miss Stevens drew herself up and glared at Dorothea. "I am sure that Dr. Hawk did write to them. Dr. Hawk is a most reliable gentleman, I do assure you."

"I'm not vilifying the good doctor, Cora," Dorothea sighed. "I'm just greatly perplexed that they have come, knowing that there is serious illness in the house." She brightened. "But Seraphim told me that the condessa had diphtheria long ago so she, at least, I shall be able to meet with safety. Would you be so kind as to pen them a note for me, Cora, explaining the situation once again. Or better yet, ask the doctor to speak with them."

Any excuse to seek out the company of the eligible physician was a welcome task to Miss Stevens, and she flew out of the room with remarkable speed for a woman of her years. Dorothea, for her part, lay in bed filled with frustration at her inability to welcome Mathilde's parents properly to Bancroft Hall.

It was several hours before any further word reached her. Darkness had fallen when Miss Stevens came in, glowing with important news.

"Dear Dr. Hawk. He took me along to see the conde and condessa. What perfectly charming people! So refined—I was quite surprised. Why, the condessa

363

was wearing a gown of the loveliest Levantine silk, with Spanish puffed sleeves and . . ."

"Please spare me the details of their finery and tell me what they are like and what they said," Dorothea burst out.

"But how can I tell you what they are like without describing what they wore?" protested Miss Stevens, genuinely puzzled.

"But what did they say about the diphtheria? Have they both had it, after all?"

"As a matter of fact, neither of them has. That old Portuguese servant must be all about in the head. But, oh, I nearly forgot, *she* was not with them."

"How can that be?" Dorothea said with a deep frown.

"It seems that she fell down a staircase at Grillon's and injured her lower limb severely enough that she had to stay behind. They left the condessa's abigail to look after her. I was so impressed by that generous sacrifice—to do without one's personal maid, and for the sake of a servant, too."

"She has been with the family for these twenty years, Cora," Dorothea replied, "and she raised their only child, now lost to them. I cannot think that they regard her in the light of a common servant. But tell me, was her leg actually broken?" Dorothea looked at Miss Stevens with great concern in her countenance. At Senhora Seraphim's age, a broken leg might prove extremely dangerous.

"No, no," exclaimed Miss Stevens, obviously eager to move on to more interesting topics. "It is but a severe sprain. She should be able to travel within the week. But in the meanwhile, about the child . . ."

"Yes?"

"Well, Dr. Hawk suggested that, since neither of them is immune to diphtheria, it would be best if they did not come into the house. Then the condessa had the idea that they come every morning and take Martha with them in their carriage, either back to the Cat and the Fiddle, or for a ride about the countryside. It seems she has a consuming desire to acquaint herself with our superlative scenery, and such a plan would serve both of their goals to a nicety."

"B-but were you able to communicate all this to them? I thought they spoke no English! That's why Seraphim went to London in the first place."

"La, that Seraphim! She must have just been making excuses to go gallivanting off to town on her own. I have the same problem with my servants all the time. Why, just the other day Lucy insisted she be allowed to go all the way to London in order to match the ribbon on my new sarsnet gown. Foolish girl, doesn't she know that if anyone is going to town to shop, it shall be me? Why, I have an eye for color that is unsurpassed."

Dorothea glanced at the cherry and puce colored ribbons which adorned Miss Stevens' frilled morning dress. "Unsurpassed," she echoed faintly. "Now, Cora, do be a dear and bring Martha to me now. I think that a session of playing with her will be superior to the strongest of medicines, and infinitely preferable to that revolting brandy."

Miss Stevens agreed and brought the baby to her. With Martha crawling about her bed playing peek-a-boo and other fascinating infant diversions, Dorothea sank her concerns about the conde and condessa and Seraphim in her joy at being with her daughter once again.

At mid-morning the next day, Dorothea heard a

carriage rumble past in the drive below, and she dragged herself to the window to see what she could of Martha's grandparents. From that distance she could make out nothing of the features of the couple as they descended from the rather shabby chaise. The condessa's face was completely concealed by a thick black veil, presumably mourning for her daughter, and she was wearing a black gown of voluminous cut which revealed little of her person. As for the conde, he appeared to be somewhat taller than she had anticipated, though still slight by English standards. It was difficult to ascertain what he wore, as he had a black cape tied round his shoulders, but she could see that his breeches, waistcoat and jacket were all of black. She was a little amused to observe that he affected a powdered wig dressed in a cadogan, a style long since *démodé* in England, but apparently still fashionable in the hinterlands of Portugal.

Miss Stevens came out of the door, carrying Martha, and met them on the broad marble steps. The condessa took the child into her arms, a little awkwardly, it seemed to Dorothea, watching anxiously from above, and climbed back into carriage. Before the conde could follow, Harry emerged from the stables with Lovelace at his heels and went towards the chaise at a dead run. Frustrated by her inability to intervene, Dorothea watched as the boy and the dog flung themselves across the drive to where the conde stood.

Her mortification increased a hundredfold when she saw the gentleman distinctly recoil from the animal in fear. Harry, ignoring everyone but Martha, climbed directly into the vehicle in a most determined fashion, followed hopefully by Lovelace. Miss Stevens interceded at this crucial juncture, speaking to Harry with a severe expression, and sending a groom in to drag out the dog

by the scruff of the neck. Lovelace squirmed about in
the man's grasp, but was unsuccessful in his attempts to
escape, as he was ignominiously borne off to the stables. Harry himself did not budge from his seat inside
the coach, and after Miss Stevens stood arguing with
him for a space of time, she gave up and let the boy
stay where he was, throwing up her hands in vexation.

After the carriage pulled away, Dorothea returned
to her bed, wearied by her efforts, and full of conflict-
ing emotions. *If only I could have seen the touching
scene at closer quarters, both to witness the condessa's
felicity and to prevent Harry's rudeness,* she thought
with a sigh. But, then, feeling vertiginous, she settled
herself back into bed for a nap and resigned herself as
best she could to a passive role until the doctor released
her from quarantine.

During the next week, a new pattern was established in the routine at Bancroft Hall. Each morning,
the conde and condessa would arrive in state for their
grandchild and, inevitably, Harry. Every day their
excursion was a longer one, until it became commonplace for them to be away for several hours. Thus
Dorothea was not at all concerned when one afternoon
they had not returned the children by the time Miss
Stevens came into Dorothea's room with a dinner tray.
Indeed, if anything she was pleased at this evidence of
the pleasure they took in the baby. These sentiments
were unconsciously echoed by Miss Stevens, as she
watched Dorothea eat her potatoes *duchesse*.

"How delightful that the condessa and her charming husband take so much pleasure in the company of
little Martha. I myself wouldn't know what to do with
children for such extended periods of time," said Miss
Stevens.

Dorothea replied, rather indignantly, "Martha has such a sunny disposition that she is really no burden at all!"

"Yes, but Harry is quite a handful, and he has taken them in extreme dislike, though he still insists on accompanying them each and every day. I'm sure he is quite beastly on these little forays."

"Then why on earth does he want to go?"

"Some farrago of nonsense about protecting Martha. He has become very attached to her."

"Protect her? From her own grandparents? What a bacon-brained notion that is! If only I could talk with him and get that maggot out of his head," exclaimed Dorothea. "But then, I suppose he must find them a little frightening, with their foreign accents and black clothes. And that veil—does the condessa never put it off? I would think that for a child it would seem especially ominous. Still, I can't go on letting him be rude to them."

"Well, you will be able to tell him so very soon now. Dr. Hawk, as you know, has said that you will no longer be contagious after today. And so I told the conde this morning when he came for Martha. He looked quite overcome with emotion at the good news, quite overcome."

Dorothea nodded absently and sipped her tea in silence, nervously pondering what it would be like meeting Mathilde's parents on the morrow. Her ruminations were cut short by a sharp knock on the door. Miss Stevens, muttering about never being left in peace, went to open it and found Parker waiting in the hall.

"There's a letter for the mistress. 'Twas brought by a very ragged urchin, who *said* he was sent by the conde." Parker's expression said he found this doubtful in the extreme. "I thought that if it were from them, my lady, I should bring it right up."

Dorothea, seized by a fear that the conde's carriage had met with an accident on the road, rose from her chair and reached eagerly for the paper. Opening it hastily, she read:

Dear Lady Bancroft:
  By the time you receive this letter we will have reached our destination and have the children well-concealed. If you try to find them it will be the end of both of them. If you wish to see them returned unharmed, we require that you dip into your so ample capital for 30,000 pounds in ransom. It will do you no good to deny that you have access to these funds, for we know full well that your husband has given you control of his fortune in his absence.
  You must leave the money in a satchel under the stile by the crossroads of the Bath road and Rosemary Lane by midnight Wednesday.

For the first time in her young life, Dorothea Sandham Bancroft swooned and crumpled to the floor, the unsigned letter fluttering down to land beside her.

Chapter 27

For the hundredth time, Dorothea raced to the drawing room windows, thinking that she had heard the clopping of a horse's hooves on the drive. For the hundredth time, she was disappointed. The graveled semicircle was still as empty as the cherrywood cradle upstairs.

"Whatever could be taking that Joseph so long!" she exclaimed in frustration to Miss Stevens, who sat doing needlework with irritating calmness. "And all the menservants—surely they should have learned something by now!"

Miss Stevens lifted her needle and snipped at the silken strands with her scissors. "Don't forget. Joseph had to ride all the way to London, and though his horse was swift, it is still a long journey. Besides, perhaps he was delayed at Adriana's, for some tea or other nourishment."

"I hardly think Joss would hang about drinking tea under the circumstances. After all, his was not a social call—arriving posthaste to tell her that her little ward has been kidnapped, as well as her niece." Dorothea's voice broke and she gripped the back of a finely carved

371

chair to steady her emotions. "Surely she will have sent Joseph, or someone else back to us in a trice. Oh," she burst out passionately, "if only Tate were here. At the very least, he could arrange for the ransom to be paid, and at the very most, he could apprehend these criminals and bring them to justice. I can do neither." She looked stonily out the window.

"What a pity that both Dr. Hawk and my brother are from home," Miss Stevens went on phlegmatically, "else I am sure that they would be equal to the occasion. Though my poor brother does have a bad cold just now and wouldn't be fit to rush about in the night air. How often I've had to scold him for driving about the parish without his cloak. I do hope he remembered to take it with him on his drive to Brentley. He holds the Brentley living, in addition to this one, and must confer with his curate in residence there from time to time. As for Dr. Hawk, his housekeeper told Annie at the market that he has been called to a most difficult confinement over Denham way, the new Marchioness of Burleigh, I believe. Poor Dr. Hawk, having to work so hard and no wife to welcome him home."

"Someone's coming!" was Dorothea's only answer to this arch little speech, as she headed for the door. In front of the house she met the returning men, torches in hand, whom she had frantically dispatched hours before to scour the countryside.

"Peter, Toby, Edward, did you learn anything?" she asked, trying to discern their expressions in the wavering light.

"Nothing," answered the foremost member of the dispirited procession. "No one at any of the posting houses or inns or neighboring estates noticed them going by. Those two just vanished into thin air! Why, not even the dog here caught a whiff of them," he said, patting Lovelace, who looked every bit as done up as the men.

"Nonsense, these people are villains, not ghosts, and we shall find them. We must find them," she said vehemently, then broke off as she noticed how weary they all appeared.

"Well, there's no sense in looking further tonight. Go get some rest and we'll start searching anew at dawn."

"Yes, my lady," they answered as she turned back to the house. Her feet were leaden and her head spun with fatigue, but all she could think about was tiny Martha, crying for her, and feisty Harry, trying to "protect" the baby from the counterfeit conde and condessa.

Miss Stevens met her at the door, and it was a measure of her own tiredness that she watched Lovelace lope past into the foyer without her usual objections to his coming indoors.

"You must get some rest, Dorothea. You'll not help the children by collapsing through lack of sleep. Don't forget that you have not fully regained your strength," she said with a yawn as she folded up her embroidery and stuck it in her work bag. "I'm going to bed and suggest that you do the same."

"I couldn't possibly sleep, but you go ahead. Perhaps Joseph will return and . . ."

Miss Stevens shrugged. "Suit yourself, but it's a most foolhardy way to meet a crisis," she said, then walked off, leaving the young woman to her tormented, helpless reflections.

The night dragged by and Dorothea paced endlessly over the house, passing through the drawing rooms, sitting room, dining and breakfast parlors, library, and all the other rooms, oblivious to their splendors. The clock was striking six and the dawn faintly lighting the eastern sky when at last she heard the sound she had been awaiting so desperately: the crunch of a trotting horse on the gravel in front of the house.

This time she was not disappointed: it was Joseph, the head groom, who slid from the saddle in great exhaustion.

"My lady," he began breathlessly, "is there any word on the children's whereabouts?"

"Sadly, no, Joss, but Adriana, how did she take the terrible news?"

"She is most distressed and—but here is her letter." He drew a folded paper from his greatcoat pocket and waited quietly while she read it.

Dear Sister,

Tate is to return here on Wednesday morning (that's today, thought Dorothea with a start) and I will send him to you directly when he arrives. Meanwhile, there is little I can do but wring my hands. I have no access to my capital, either, and I doubt that our pin money combined would satisfy these rapacious vermin who have our children.

Try not to despair, Thea. Harry is as tough as a little nut, and surely no one could be such a monster as to harm Martha. Besides, Tate will surely come in time to set things right.

Would that I could come to you myself, but a nursing mother encumbered with twins is hardly the stuff of heroic rescues.

In haste,
Your loving sister,
A.

"I pray you are right, A.," breathed Dorothea. "If Martha is hurt I . . ."

"My lady," Joseph said gravely, "is there aught else I can do?"

"Just go and get some rest, Joss. You have done more than I can adequately thank you for already. When you have rested, perhaps you might join in the search with the rest of the men. They shall be going out again very soon."

"Whsst, I'll go with them now. I'm that angry over them snatching away the little laddie, not to mention the wee lass, that I don't feel sleepy at all," Joseph said with a shake of his leonine head.

"I know, I feel exactly the same. Ah, here they come now," she said, as a rumble of masculine voices was heard.

When the group of heavy-eyed men straggled to the doorstep, she issued crisp instructions, then returned to the house to resume her lonely vigil. All morning and afternoon she wandered about, her face pale and taut, but still no trace of the children or their kidnappers was found.

At Miss Stevens' adamant insistence, she did manage to swallow a few bites of dinner and drink a glass of wine. Under the influence of the latter, combined with the lingering effects of her illness and the strain of her vigil, she fell sound asleep sitting in the nursery rocking chair. Her head was pillowed on her arms resting on the rail of Martha's empty bed.

It was several hours later that the nursery door was flung open, and she looked up, groggy from sleep, to see her husband stride into the room.

"Tate!" she cried, rising from the chair and moving toward him out of an instinct to find comfort in his arms. Something in his face checked her impulsive movement, however, and she stood gazing at him without a word. The candle he carried revealed a scowl instead of the sympathy she had expected. Their eyes locked and then he spoke.

"How, how could you have let this happen? Good God, the only reason I married you was to take care of Martha, and now you have allowed her, sick as she is, to be carried off by perfect strangers," he growled.

"First of all, Tate Bancroft, your daughter is completely recovered, and secondly, these 'perfect strangers' posed as Mathilde's parents, and most convincingly. Dr. Hawk, Miss Stevens, *everyone* was taken in by their imposture. How could any of us be expected to recognize the Conde and Condessa de Vasconcellos? From what I could see of them from my window, they certainly looked authentic enough."

"From your window?" Tate shouted at her. "Do you mean to say that you never even met them, yet entrusted the children to them? What on earth could have possessed you?"

"Diphtheria, if you must know."

Tate looked thunderstruck. "Why did you not send word that you were sick, as you did when Martha was ill?"

"What good would that have done, with you off in Spain or wherever. Besides, you told me in no uncertain terms that you did not wish to be burdened with domestic trivialities," Dorothea said, her voice quavering in a manner which infuriated her.

He looked intently into her face so that she lowered her own eyes. "And you judged that your serious, perhaps fatal illness would be trivial to me?" he asked softly.

"Isn't it?"

A knock at the door prevented his answering and Parker bustled into the room, looking most overset with excitement.

"Sir Tate, you must come down immediately. It's Seraphim. She is returned, but in such a state!"

Without waiting for further explanations, Dorothea and Tate raced downstairs side by side. They found Seraphim lying down on the sofa in the large drawing room. Her clothes were ripped and muddy, her hair unbound and flying wildly to her waist and, most incredible of all, her feet were bare and filthy.

Kneeling next to her, holding a glass of what appeared to be brandy to the woman's lips, was the vicar, Mr. Stevens.

"Seraphim," cried Dorothea, rushing up to her. "What has happened? Where have you been?"

Seraphim took a reviving swallow of spirits and pushed away the glass before answering. "Excuse me, Dorotéia, but I must make my explanations in Portuguese to Sir Tate. It is so much easier and faster for me."

Tate silently took up a post next to her and Seraphim rattled off what seemed to Dorothea to be an unending stream of Portuguese. The only words that she could make out and comprehend were not likely to ease her mind: "Marta," "*menino*," "Madalena" and "Conde." Just when she thought she could bear the suspense no longer, Tate straightened up and spoke to the vicar.

"Where exactly did you come across her, Stevens?" he barked.

"She was on the Brentley road, marching resolutely towards Bancroft Hall, though it was a distance of

377

at least ten miles. She told me they were being held in an unused cottage near a cart track, and that she followed the track to the road. She took a chance that she needed to go west to reach home and followed the moon. What a plucky woman!" he said, his eyes shining with admiration.

"I must know exactly where to look for this cart track, Stevens. Come and tell me what you can whilst I load my pistols," Tate said curtly, and the two men left the room.

As soon as the door closed Dorothea leaned over Seraphim. "Please, Senhora, tell me at once what is going on. I thought you were in London with an injured leg."

Seraphim gave a bitter laugh. "I don't know what lies those two *impostores* told you, but there is nothing wrong with me except a few cuts on my feet. As soon as I arrived at Grillon's I was bundled into a hack chaise and taken captive. They blindfolded me and took me far into the country to the little *casinha*. And then when they brought the children . . ."

"The children! Have you seen the children? Are they all right?" Dorothea said, her words tumbling out.

"Yes, they are fine. Little Harry is giving those scoundrels *muitos dificuldades*, bless him. And Marta is well enough, although she keeps calling for 'mama.' I hated to abandon them, but it was the only way to get help. There was no other choice open to me but to leave them there with the conde," Serephim said, her eyes filling with tears.

"The conde! But I thought he was an impostor."

"He is an impostor, but he is also a genuine *conde*, a French *conde*."

Dorothea caught her breath. It wasn't possible.

But even as she thought this, she realized that it was all too true. Everything pointed to the man Seraphim accused: the false Conde de Vasconcellos' eccentric wig to cover his hair, his cape to conceal his figure, his arrival, timed to coincide with Dorothea's illness and, above all, his conviction that Dorothea held the strings to the Bancroft purse. She remembered, with a sick feeling gnawing at her vitals, how she herself had told him that she managed Tate's capital. There could be no doubt: the man who had stolen away the children was none other than the Comte de Blanchard. But the woman?

Before she could even frame the question, Senhora Seraphim spoke and confirmed her suspicions.

"Madalena—she was the *condessa falsa*. How ironical, you were right after all about the writer of my summons to London being *uma fraude*."

"Then it is de Blanchard and Madalena who have Martha and Harry?" she asked dazedly.

"Yes, the *diablos*. And she a *Portuguêsa!*" snorted the woman.

"But how did you get away from them?"

"I saw my chance while those two were quarreling. Marta and Harry were both asleep, for the entire night, if God wills . . . I climbed out the window and came down a tree. Ha! They left the window unlocked thinking an old lady like me could not do such a thing. Then I just followed the track to the road and followed it until I encountered Mr. Stevens. Such a man *intrépido*. He drove his little *carreta* as swiftly as a coachman."

"How far is it to where they are holding the children?" demanded Dorothea.

"About two hours' drive, though I think Sir Tate will be there in less, but then, he is much younger than

Mr. Stevens and his horses are fresh from the stables and . . ."

Dorothea did not wait to hear the rest. She leapt to her feet and ran for the stables, where she arrived just as her husband was climbing into a racing curricle. Without a word, she hitched up her skirts and placed her foot on the step.

"The last person I need along on this errand is a sick woman. Get down," Tate snapped, taking up the reins.

"I am no longer sick, and I have as much at stake in this as you. Besides, you can't meet them alone. Remember that there are two of them."

"I won't be alone for long. I told Joseph where to look and he will be following as soon as he can summon the men."

"That will take precious time and *they* won't be traveling in a curricle with a team of blooded horses. Face it, Tate, you do need me along. Let's go." She stepped into the vehicle determinedly and sat down on the cushioned seat next to him.

In grim silence he maneuvered his team out of the stable yard and guided them round the drive and down the long avenue to the highway beyond.

They jounced along in utter silence for a full half-hour. At last Dorothea ventured to speak.

"H-how fortunate we are to have moonlight," she said hesitantly.

"Oh, yes, we are fortunate indeed," he retorted in a most sarcastic tone, "having our daughter and Harry stolen away by two blackguards, and tearing along at a breakneck speed on a potholed road with only the moon and this paltry lantern for light."

An involuntary shudder ran over Dorothea at his

bitter words. How often she had dreamed about how he would treat her when he returned, but this was worse than any of her nightmares.

"And here you sit, shivering, without so much as a shawl! Did you think we were going on a pleasure outing?" he continued in the same biting manner.

"I was afraid you would leave without me if I took the time to fetch a shawl. Besides, I'm not cold. If I'm shivering it is only because I am overwrought. Though chasing after enemies in the middle of the night is commonplace to you, it is not for me," she said dryly.

"Especially straight from a sick bed," he added, and she thought his tone was little softer, but couldn't be sure.

"I think there is a carriage blanket under the seat— look and see."

She bent and found the woolen cover, which felt heavenly to the touch as the cool night air rushed by.

"Put it round our legs. I'm rather chilled myself after my ride out from London," he directed her.

She gingerly lay one part of the blanket across his legs and draped the rest over her own lap.

"This is no time to be missish, Thea. Tuck it in."

She reached across him, and grasping the blanket, pushed her hands under his muscular thighs. Despite her best efforts to the contrary, she shuddered again, though whether from the cold or from his touch she couldn't judge.

"You are still cold," he said. "If I did not need both hands for the ribbons I'd put an arm round you, but as it is . . ."

"I'm fine, really," she said hastily, but just his suggesting such an act made her feel warmer.

By the time they came to the posting house, The

White Hart, the horses were fully winded. Tate pulled them up in the yard of the inn and shouted to the ostlers to hitch up a fresh team immediately. Then he disappeared inside the building.

Dorothea sat huddled in the seat, watching the ostlers' skillful handling of the horses and trying not to think of whether Seraphim's escape had been discovered as yet. She set these fruitless worries aside as Tate rejoined her carrying a bundle.

He handed it to her, saying, "No one was willing to part with a shawl or pelisse, so you'll have to settle for a gentleman's greatcoat and beaver hat. Who knows, perhaps such attire will bamboozle our friends at the cottage into thinking that they have *two* stout gentlemen with whom to deal."

"Ready, sir," the ostler called up, and there was a clink of coins. By the time that Dorothea had buttoned the greatcoat snugly about her, they were on the open road once again.

As the lights of the inn receded in the darkness behind them, Dorothea's courage started to give way to an acute case of alarm. "H-how much further do you judge it to be?" she finally managed to blurt out.

"Perhaps another half hour to where the cart track cuts off to the right. I dare not take this rig up there, however, lest it overturn. We'll tie the horses to a fence and proceed on foot. Would that I had thought to buy you some stout boots from someone back at The White Hart. Unless I miss my guess, you are undoubtedly shod in some of those ridiculously thin kid slippers."

"If Seraphim could walk the distance barefoot, I am fully capable of getting there in my slippers," she said, her indignation driving away her fear for a moment. Then worry came flooding back. "Oh, Tate, do you think they would hurt the children?" she cried.

"De Blanchard is *your* bosom beau, my dear. What do *you* think?" he replied acidly.

"And Madalena?" she flung back. " 'Twas you who first put Martha into her gentle arms, or should I say clutches."

She bit her lip, fighting to keep from throwing in the subject of his own episodes in Madalena's arms. No matter how satisfying it would be to so indulge herself, gratuitous sniping at her husband would not help Martha and Harry.

Tate, seeming to read her mind, spoke in a low voice. "There is no point in quarreling now. There will be plenty of time to assign blame and trade insults after the children are safe. Now we must make our plans."

"I have an idea," Thea said, her brain racing. "I shall knock on the door with my hat pulled down over my face and tell some Banbury tale of my carriage overturning on the cart track. You yourself said such a thing might happen, and dressed like this, they'll take me for a strange young man idiotish enough to attempt the lane in the dark."

"A very strange young man," murmured Tate. "But no, I shall go to the door myself and just train my pistol on that reptile de Blanchard when he answers the door and . . ."

"No, Tate. What if the children are about? No, mine is the better plan. They would recognize you instantly, but they won't expect to see me in the guise of a man. They'll open the door to me, and while I engage them in conversation, you shall wait in the shadows with your pistols. I'll ask de Blanchard to come to my aid and then you can overpower him."

"Very well," he agreed grudgingly. "But I shall be very close by with my pistols at the ready."

A building loomed up by the side of the road.

"Ah, this must be the mill. Stevens said that the cart road was about a mile farther on."

In mounting tension they passed by the old mill and scanned the dark lane for the sign of a cart track. Another quarter hour brought them to the turning point. Tate steered his team round the corner where the track led off into the darkness and edged them to the side of the two ruts, overgrown with weeds.

"We are in luck, there's even a handy hedge to secure the reins," Tate said in a rallying tone as he climbed down. As he busied himself tying up his horses, she clambered down and stood nervously fingering the hat which was to complete her disguise.

From the floor of the carriage he took a coil of rope, then reaching under the seat he brought out a box, from which he withdrew a brace of pistols. One he stuck in his breeches' waistband, the other he cocked and kept in his hand.

"We shall leave the lantern here, to show the men where the turnoff is. Besides, there is no need to illuminate our approach to the cottage. They would see we are but two."

"Yes, I shall just tell them that my carriage lantern broke in the accident. Robin told me that details help when one is constructing a lie," she said, trying to bolster her courage.

He made no answer, apparently intent on finding his way down the gloomy path. Behind him, she came against a rock and stumbled. She would have fallen but for his reaching for her as she pitched forward.

"Here, we'd best proceed together," he whispered, placing an arm about her waist.

Held snugly to his side, Dorothea plunged forward with an odd confidence. They strode along together without further conversation until they espied a cottage, set well back from the track, its windows glowing faintly.

"Seraphim said there were no other houses—this must be it," whispered Tate in her ear. "Are you ready?"

"Ready," she stoutly echoed, tucking her hair up under her hat and checking that the greatcoat was securely fastened. She bent over and felt with her hands to make certain that no telltale muslin showed at the bottom of the coat. Satisfied, she stood up and squared her shoulders.

"Good luck, Thea," she heard him hiss and felt his lips brush her upturned, icy cheek.

With a herculean effort, she whirled away from him and marched toward the cottage door, her heart beating a loud tattoo.

Chapter 28

Thea knocked boldly on the oaken door with a fist that was stiff with cold and fear.

"Hello, is there anyone at home?" she called hoarsely, hoping that for once her contralto might pass for a tenor.

As she stood there, she could tell by the shifting pattern of light through the window that someone was coming to the door.

It opened a crack and a masculine voice said brusquely, "What do you want?"

Dorothea had no trouble recognizing the accented baritone as the voice of Philippe de Blanchard. She kept her head bowed away from the guttering candle he held to the crack in the door and spoke in a sort of gruff whine.

"Pardon, sir, but my gig came to grief down the lane. I hit a confounded pothole and broke a wheel, and the cursed lantern, as well. I'm looking for someone to help me set it back aright."

"Why, whatever were you doing in the lane at this time of night? It must be almost midnight! How do I know you are not a highwayman?" challenged the comte, still sheltering behind the door.

"Why, I . . ." Dorothea spluttered, trying desperately to think of something. "It's my sweetheart, sir. You know how it is. We were just looking for a quiet place to . . ."

Her words must have struck the proper chord, for the Frenchman threw open the door.

Dorothea dared not hazard a look at the face she had come to despise, for fear that he should see her own countenance. She found what satisfaction she could from noting the dismal state of his breeches, which were rumpled and dirty—surely a trial for the fastidious Philippe.

"Ah, you need not say more, my boy," the comte was exclaiming in a confiding manner. "I, too, was young once. *Les femmes*, the ladies, they do lead one into trouble, *n'est ce pas?* I myself know all too well. And now your sweetheart, she's mad as a hornet, yes? Don't worry, I shall help you. Madalena, *ma chère* . . ." he called over his shoulder.

Madalena glided into view, dressed in a filmy nightdress of periwinkle blue, edged with white swansdown, and revealing in the extreme. Thea was sorely tempted to throw off her disguise and scratch the woman's eyes out, but she saw that there was little she could do, a lone female, against these two arch-villains. She swallowed her violent impulses and resigned herself to continuing as planned.

The comte appeared to be searching for a lantern as he continued his explanation to Madalena. "This fellow needs my help, Lena. And as long as I am out, I might as well do that other *petite chose*, that other little task. After all, it is nearly midnight," he said with emphasis. He lit the wick of the lantern and Thea drew farther back, outside the spill of its light.

"But what shall I do if the children wake up, Philippe?" Madalena protested shrilly. "You know that I am helpless with them and that Seraphim just snarls at me, the old *puta!*"

So the senhora's escape has not been detected, thought Dorothea, her spirits lifting at the news, but the comte's next words sent them plummeting once again.

"They won't wake up," he assured Madalena. "There was enough laudanum in the baby's milk to make her sleep until noon tomorrow. And as for Harry, if he should give you any more trouble, tell him that he shall get the thrashing he so richly deserves when I return."

He started, as if suddenly remembering that a stranger was listening to his words, and he addressed Dorothea in the guise of an exasperated parent.

"Our children, they are such a trial. Don't rush into parenthood, my boy. Take my advice. You can run into more trouble in a desolate lane than an overturned carriage." With a leer that made Dorothea feel intensely ill, he handed her the lantern of punctured tin, then closing the heavy door, instructed her to lead the way.

They had not gone more than a few yards when Tate stepped out from the bushes and blocked their path.

"Stop where you are, de Blanchard," he hissed, but the comte did nothing of the sort.

Instead, he shoved Thea roughly out of his way and she fell to the ground as he tried to dart past Tate and down the path. In the scattered light of the lantern, which had tumbled down with its bearer, Dorothea saw the two figures meet in shadowy combat, but the light was too uncertain for her to discern which man was her husband and which her enemy.

389

Realizing that there was little she could do to help Tate, and fearful for the children, Thea whirled and ran back to the cottage. Just as she reached the door, a shot rang out and she stopped, paralyzed with fear. Then it flashed through her mind that if Tate were hurt, or worse, it was up to her to rescue Martha and Harry.

She wrenched open the door and flew inside, just as Madalena came rushing down the stairs. The sight of the Portuguese woman who had tried to steal her husband and who had literally stolen her daughter spurred Thea to action. She intercepted Madalena before she reached the door by the simple expedient of taking hold of the long black hair and pulling for all she was worth.

"What the devil do you think you are doing, you little . . ." Lena began to scream. Then Thea's hat fell off, causing the green eyes to narrow in fury. "Dorotéia!" she screeched. "How did you get here? Where's Philippe, what have you done with him?"

Dorothea ignored the woman's frantic questions. "More to the point Madalena, or whatever your name truly is, where is my daughter? Tell me at once or I'll pull out every hair on your head."

The woman struggled briefly and fiercely to free herself, using some tricks she had doubtless picked up in her colorful Peninsular career, but Thea had the advantage of size and determination. Lena was fighting only for herself, while Dorothea fought for her beloved child.

At last she managed to pinion Madalena's arms. "Where is she, you witch?" she panted.

"Upstairs," spat out Madalena, "with that hellcat, Seraphim."

"Oh, I think not. Seraphim is resting comfortably back at Bancroft Hall. I'm sure she is chatting with a magistrate by this time. And now, madam, I will need your belt."

"I'll see you in hell, first," snarled the woman.

"Do what she says, Lena," Tate's voice said sternly from the doorway, where he leaned wearily against the jamb. "And don't expect any help from your lover. He is not only unconscious, but tied hand and foot."

"Ah, Tate, *meu herói*," Madalena cried in a honeyed tone. "It was all Philippe's idea! He forced me to help him. I would never do anything to hurt you." When Tate remained still and unresponsive, not even meeting her eye, her pleading became more desperate. "Let me go free, Tate. Let me go and I'll never trouble you again. I'll go to America and start a new life, just like your cousin . . . what was his name . . . Adrian?"

"Save your breath to cool your porridge, Lena," Tate said dispassionately. "And give Thea your belt." He stood silently watching as Dorothea took the belt and tied Madalena's hands behind her to a heavy chair.

When she had finished, he came over to her. "And now, shall we find our baby and her champion?"

"Yes, oh yes," Dorothea said, and together they mounted the rough stairs. Near the top, Tate stumbled slightly, but he quickly recovered his balance. They went down the short corridor to the first door, and Tate turned the key which was in the lock. He pushed it open and stepped forward, and an object flew through the darkness and struck him in the shoulder with considerable force.

"What the deuce was that," Tate grunted.

"Uncle Tate, it's you!" came Harry's voice from the corner of the small room, then Harry himself hurtled into Tate's arms. "I thought it was that awful Count fellow, and I wanted to draw his cork with Martha's bottle. I've been planning it all night. Of course, I'd rather have used a Congreve rocket, but the bottle was all I had," he said modestly.

"Well-planned and well-launched, my boy. Wellington would have been proud of you. But you need not worry about the count anymore. He is going straight to prison for this little venture, and some others, equally dastardly."

Dorothea had not stopped to discuss this or anything else with Harry. She went straight to the box where her stepdaughter lay sleeping. By the light of her candle she inspected the baby. She was vastly relieved to see that, despite the powerful drug she had been given, Martha looked rosy and healthy and her breathing was regular. Dorothea said nothing. Setting down the taper with shaking fingers, she gathered the infant in her arms. Then burying her face in the baby's soft neck, she burst into ragged sobs of relief.

"Why is Aunt Thea crying, Uncle?" Harry piped up.

"I cannot tell you that, my lad. If I live to be a hundred I shall never understand women," she heard Tate say behind her. "Now that everyone is safe, she is transformed from the plucky comrade-at-arms into a watering pot. Why do females fuss when everything turns out exactly as they wish?" He paused, then exclaimed, "Listen! Do you hear anything outside, Harry? A military agent must have excellent hearing and a quick brain, as well as a good aim," he said, rubbing his shoulder where Harry's throw had landed the bottle.

Dorothea listened intently and in the near distance she could hear the sound of horses' hooves, the chink of harness, and a staccato series of barks which could only have issued from Lovelace. She also heard, to her relief, the sound of men's voices.

"It sounds like, why it sounds just like Joseph! And," Harry jumped up and down excitedly, "dear old Lovelace! Have they come after me, too?"

"Yes, Joss, and Lovelace, and about ten other men," said Tate, peering out the small window. "They searched for you all day yesterday and today, but they had no luck until Seraphim escaped and told us where to find you. All they must do now is to escort your captors to the nearest magistrate."

Harry didn't wait to hear the end of this explanation. He exploded from the room and down the stairs, calling, "Joss, Lovelace, here I am!"

"Shall we go down, Dorothea? Frankly, Madalena is such a Circe that I suspect she might try to work her wiles on the men."

"And in that nightdress, her chances of success are excellent," Thea said with a wry laugh. "Perhaps I should insist that she put on my greatcoat, if it is all right with you to so cavalierly dispose of your gift. It is not nearly so becoming as what she has on, but . . ."

"No one could compare with you in that coat, doing battle for Martha. You looked magnificent, like nothing so much as an avenging goddess," Tate said with an intensity that caused her to look away.

"You forget, sir, I have seen the Elgin Marbles in town and know full well what your average avenging goddess is wont to wear. It is definitely *not* in the greatcoat line," she said with forced playfulness, following him down the stairs.

The scene that greeted them in the room below brought semi-hysterical laughter bubbling up in Thea's throat. Madalena sat stony-faced on her chair, as Harry and Lovelace circled her playing "catch the stick." Nine men stood bashfully about ogling Madalena, while Joss tried in vain to send them outside to search for the count.

When he saw Tate and Dorothea, Joss gave a large sigh of relief.

"Oh, Sir Tate, it's glad I am to see you both. The laddie said you were upstairs with the wee lass. Is everything in prime twig in that quarter as well?" At Thea's happy nod he turned his attention back to Tate. "And where's the French scoundrel, sir? I trust you haven't allowed him to escape?"

"No, no, Joss, nothing like that. He's trussed up tight as a bagged pheasant, under a convenient tree out there. When last I saw him, he was insensible, though he may have recovered his wits by now. I'm afraid I shall need your help to bring him inside," Tate said, moving to the door.

Harry skipped ahead of him. "Did you draw his cork, Uncle Tate? Did you darken his lights and mill him down proper?"

"I can't think where you have picked up this execrable boxing cant, Harry. Would you have any idea, Joss?" grinned Tate.

Joss shrugged his denials and followed the others out.

Left alone with Madalena, Thea quickly removed her greatcoat and flung it over the woman's shoulders. She would have liked to cover Madalena's head as well, but stopped short of that. The Portuguese woman said nothing, just sat in a cold, furious silence, glaring at Dorothea. When Tate led the comte through the door, however, she let loose with a stream of invective that caused even those two war-hardened gentlemen to stare.

394

After letting her vent her spleen for a few moments, Tate cut her off with a few curt words in her own tongue.

To Thea's surprise, this had the effect of causing Lena to break into mirthless laughter and, happily, English.

"You *idiota*, as though I could ever have taken you seriously. You were even stupid enough to believe I was *grávida*. How I enjoyed watching you worry over my condition, when I was no more delicate than your own great cow of a wife! How I've laughed at all of you!"

This time it was the comte who interrupted. "Madalena, *cala boca*. My ears are beginning to ache. It was bad enough to have been forced to endure your off-key soprano, but this screeching is even worse. Have pity on my ears, *s'il vous plaît*."

Madalena looked daggers at the Frenchman and settled into a prolonged sulk.

Dorothea could see that one of the comte's eyes was nearly swollen shut, and a small trickle of blood had dried beside his lip, but her pity was not roused by his plight. Still holding Martha tightly, she went over to where the comte stood. In her towering anger, she longed to do or say something that would wound him as much as he had wounded her through Martha. But she could think of nothing but a feeble insult.

"You despicable excuse for a man," she spat at him. "How low you are, to take advantage of the country that has sheltered you, and to betray the trust of people who offered you their friendship." She could keep her anger in check no longer and lifted her free hand to slap him across his no-longer handsome face. But she stopped her swing only an inch short of his cheek, ashamed of herself for taking advantage of his helplessness.

He smiled sardonically down at her, his eyes glittering with unfathomable emotion. "Ah, *ma chérie*, is that any way to treat an *intime ami*, or perhaps I should say a *former* intimate friend. I can understand your jealousy when I was so fickle as to run off with Maria Madalena, but you were never one to have such a hard touch. Your caresses were much more gentle when we spent those long hours together in your sister's house. Besides, 'twas you who brought me to this pass. If you had not told me those lies about your husband, no one would have suspected I was not what I seemed. And if you hadn't flaunted your control of your husband's fortune in my face, I'd not have thought of holding the *fille* to ransom when I found our glorious cause was all but lost. So you have only yourself to blame, *ma belle*."

Tate sprang forward and would have knocked the Frenchman down, but Thea blocked his way.

"We've been through enough tonight, don't you think? Let me just get Madalena dressed and we can all go home," she said, and was surprised to see the bleak look that replaced the anger in her husband's grey eyes.

Oh, no, she thought, he believes that what Philippe said was the truth, or close to it. But she had no time to brood over this. Tate escorted the comte outside to where the men waited and she helped the sullen Madalena put on one of her black "Condessa" gowns and took back her greatcoat. Then she walked with her charge out to the hay cart brought by Joss and watched as Madalena was none too gracefully hoisted into the hay beside the glowering Frenchman.

Tate beckoned to her, and then helped her up to sit beside Harry and climbed up to take the reins. Joss and the rest of the men piled on behind and they rode in silence down the rutted track until they reached the curricle, where the lantern still burned.

Tate saw that Dorothea and the children were installed on the curricle seat and went back to confer with the men. Lovelace took the opportunity to leap from the hay cart onto the ground, and then scrambled up into the curricle. Dorothea was too exhausted to protest, so she merely pushed him to the floor of the vehicle and tried to spread the greatcoat and blanket over all of them.

She was beginning to feel numb from the strain of her sleepless vigil and the night's nerve-wracking adventures, and was barely aware of the curricle's jostle when Tate swung up beside her. With Harry on her other side, Martha nestled in her arms, and Lovelace stretched across her feet, she found that the carriage was significantly shrunken in size compared to their earlier journey.

When the curricle lurched forward and turned about on the highway, Harry stirred restlessly on the seat, and Dorothea remembered his illness on the ride from London. She prayed that he might not become what Seraphim called *enjoado*. She reached over and stroked his head affectionately.

Tate, noticing the gesture, asked quietly, "Is there something amiss with Harry?"

"Not yet, but the lad is not a great traveler," Thea said in a low voice. "He gets dreadfully ill in a closed coach, but I think he will be fine in this open rig, won't you, my lad?"

Harry just groaned and buried his head into her skirt. "I think he'd be all right if he could just go to sleep. I know he must be exhausted," Thea said.

There was a stiff silence, and then Tate said, seemingly with an effort, "Perhaps if you were to sing to him it might do the trick . . . sing that song I heard you sing once at Bancroft Hall, 'Turtle Dove.' "

Thea was fluttered by his request, not knowing whether to be flattered or pained that he remembered how she had sung so long ago in Mathilde's boudoir with such disastrous results. But the suggestion seemed a good one, regardless of the emotional underpinnings, and she began the song, haltingly at first. Soon, as always, the music swept her away, and her vibrant contralto filled the night air. By the end of the second stanza, Harry was asleep, and the man beside her had lost his rigid posture. Indeed, wedged next to him. Dorothea discovered how very insubstantial a barrier a muslin skirt and skin-tight stockinette pantaloons were between two impinging limbs.

She kept trying to surreptitiously move her leg away from Tate's, but each time she did, it seemed to do no good whatsoever.

In the silence that followed the song, she tried valiantly to stay awake, but her head drooped lower and lower, until, without her knowing it, it rested on her husband's shoulder.

Chapter 29

As Tate pulled the team to a halt at The White Hart Inn, Dorothea awoke with a start, and instantly raised her head from his shoulder in great confusion.

"Are we going to change back to our own horses?" she asked, her voice thick with sleep.

"No, we are going to stay the night," he whispered back and descended. A few minutes later he came back out and took the baby from her arms.

"We were lucky—we secured the last two rooms, though they are not the grandest of accommodations," he said, as he helped her down, gave her Martha, and reached for Harry. She saw him stagger slightly under the boy's weight, but he straightened and walked before her to the building.

"And the landlord has arranged to fix us a tray of cold meat, cheese and bread. I, for one, am like to starve to death."

They trudged into the entrance and up the stairs to a door near the end of the corridor. Tate pushed it open with his foot, and Dorothea saw a small pallet and a cradle in the dimly lit room beyond.

"Now, we'll just put Martha and Harry to bed, and

have our dinner in the other bedchamber," Tate said matter-of-factly.

Dorothea, startled, glanced up at him.

"The public room is scarcely a place for a lady," he said as he lowered Harry onto the pallet and pulled the blanket up around him. "Besides, it is high time we have a serious talk, and we can't do that through the keyhole," he said, opening the door which led to the adjoining room and holding it for her with an expectant air.

Dorothea, rendered utterly nerveless by his words, kissed the sleeping Harry and Martha and tucked them in, then walked past her husband into the other bedroom with Lovelace at her heels.

The chamber, though simple, was brightly lit and a small fire had been started in the grate to take the autumn chill from the air. The landlord, a portly, ruddy-faced man, had just brought the platter of cold viands and was pouring out two glasses of wine. A chambermaid, looking very sleepy, was passing a copper bed-warmer between the sheets of the large bed that occupied the center of the room.

When Thea entered, still wearing the greatcoat over her shoulders and beaver hat, the landlord eyed her askance, but bowed himself out, telling them to ring if they should require anything else before retiring.

Dorothea studiously averted her gaze from the bed and went straight to the fire, as did Lovelace, who threw himself down with a large sigh and went promptly to sleep.

Tate came up behind her and gently eased the greatcoat from her. At his touch, she trembled and turned away, hoping fervently that he might not perceive her agitation. "A serious talk," after all, could mean only one thing: the moment she had dreaded had arrived—he wanted to tell her he was seeking an annulment.

Looking wildly about, trying to keep from bursting into tears, her eyes fell on the sleeve of her gown, and she was shocked to see a dark red smear on the pale jaconet muslin.

"Blood?" she gasped, then looked reprovingly at Tate.

"Er, yes, well . . ." he began, "I did sustain a small wound, but I didn't want to give that damned Frenchman the satisfaction of knowing it."

"Tate Bancroft, you sit down and take off your jacket. Let me take a look. Why on earth didn't you tell me?"

"You had your hands full at the time," he said with a wan smile, lowering himself onto the rustic stool by the table. "And besides, it didn't bother me much then. I was rather busy, myself. But the cold air has made it rather stiff."

"And driving several miles in an open carriage, and carrying Harry into the inn and any number of other little activities cannot have done it much good," Dorothea said tartly.

She eased him out of his ruined jacket while he loosened his limp cravat. Against the white cambric of his shirt, the stain stood out in ghastly contrast, and Thea felt a momentary queasiness. Willing herself to be strong, she helped him unfasten the row of tiny buttons, then slid the shirt off and threw it to the floor. The angry gash was ragged and painful looking, but, as he had said, it did not appear to be deep or serious.

She started searching about the room for water and

a cloth, and turned back to find Tate's grey eyes following her every move.

"Exactly what do you plan to do to me?" he asked, quirking one eyebrow in mock trepidation.

"I'm going to wash out that wound and bind it up. But I can't find any clean cloth. And what I wouldn't give for some basilicum powder!" she said, wringing her hands.

"In the Peninsula, I often saw women tear up their petticoats to bind the wounds of their men, but then, *they* were camp followers, not respectable matrons," Tate suggested, an imp of mischief dancing in his eyes.

"My experience thus far tonight does not make me feel the slightest bit matronly," Thea snapped back. "And as for camp followers, I rather think I've had my fill. But . . ." She modestly turned her back and, unfastening her petticoat, let it drop to the floor.

"Yes, well," Tate said, clearing his throat several times and not meeting her eye, "speaking of camp followers, I . . . I . . . offer my humble apology for foisting one on you and Adriana."

Dorothea, concentrating on ripping up her linen undergarment, did not reply.

Tate looked at her, then faltered on. "It's just that, well, Percy was my friend and . . ."

"And the fact that his grieving widow was the image of the young wife you still mourned blinded you to her, shall we say, faults," Dorothea said astringently. She folded some of the soft strips of fabric into a sort of sponge, and dipped it into the water basin, then vigorously scrubbed at the wound.

Tate winced and eyed her reproachfully, but she ignored his gaze as she wrapped the arm in another long piece of petticoat and tied a knot to hold the makeshift bandage in place.

"And it certainly took you long enough to see her faults, even when you had ample opportunity to scrutinize her at close quarters, as you did by the statue at Vauxhall."

"Vauxhall? I don't take your meaning, I'm afraid. But I suppose I was blinded to Madalena's insincerity because I felt so deucedly sorry for her, especially when she was increasing, or said she was. I hoped that by pampering her, I could somehow make up for leaving Mathilde when she faced her travail and . . . death." His voice dropped to little more than a whisper, while Thea stood by, absently winding the remaining fabric into an exceptionally tight ball.

"But there is something I must tell you, Dorothea, about Mathilde. Something I did not fully understand until tonight, when I stood in the darkness and watched you stride up alone to confronte de Blanchard. Suddenly I realized that Mathilde could not have done such a courageous thing. You once said that she must have been brave to leave her parents for a foreign country. But I think that, to her, it was all a lark, something out of one of the *romances* she used to read. She was really just a child, a little girl, and though I loved her to distraction, I was only a boy. Now"—he lifted his eyes to hers—"I am a man."

Dorothea swallowed convulsively and riveted her eyes on the ball of linen clutched in her hands.

"I have learned my lesson, however," Tate went on with a grim look, getting to his feet. "Madalena taught me well. One cannot hope for second chances in life or fully make amends for past failures."

As in our marriage, thought Dorothea miserably.

There can be no second beginning. She set the ball of linen down on the table and carried the basin of water back to the chest. Then, quivering with emotion, she walked back and stood in front of the fire.

"Dorothea, there is something else I am honor bound to tell you as a gentleman and an officer," Tate said gravely.

"Y-yes?" she stammered, wondering what other confessions were left for him to make.

"It's just that, standing as you are, with the fire beyond you, and your petticoat wrapped about my arm instead of doing its ordinary office, your gown appears the merest gossamer, and does nothing whatsoever to conceal your . . . er charms. I thought it my duty to inform you."

Dorothea felt a blush envelop her from head to toe and dove for the nearest chair. "Shall we eat or do you want to stand about quizzing me all night?" she said severely.

Tate grinned at her and sat down again. "I am yours to command," he laughed.

Dorothea speared some food from the platter and laid it on her plate, very much aware that Tate was watching her with a puzzled expression.

"What in blazes did you mean about my 'scrutinizing' Madalena at Vauxhall? All I remember scrutinizing that evening was an overabundance of fireworks and some crazy Frenchwoman flying around in the middle of them," he said, helping himself generously to the meat and cheese.

For a moment, Thea regarded him with uncertainty. Then, taking a deep breath, she asked him pointblank if he had kissed Madalena in the Dark Walk.

Tate held up a hand as if to ward off her accusation

and a look of amusement came into his face. "By no means, madam. Why I was so starved that when we overtook the comte on the path, I asked him to take Lena to ask about the confounded fireworks. Then they came back and helped me carry the food. And, now that I think about it, when you and Adriana came along you were most vexed with me. It all becomes clear," he chuckled.

"Yes, it's perfectly clear that those two vipers were already intriguing together," Dorothea said, feeling very ill at ease under his teasing glance.

Her words wiped the smile from his face. "And by the by, Thea, just what did dear Philippe mean by all that gammon he was pitching back at the cottage? Calling himself your *intime ami*," he spluttered.

"I'll have you know that I was only acting according to the instructions of your friend Robin Wynne, feeding false information to a suspected spy. I couldn't exactly confide my little stories in him while slapping his face at every turn, now could I. Though he certainly deserved it," she added emphatically.

"Ah, yes, Robin, I was coming to him," Tate said, then stopped to drain his wine glass and fill it again from the bottle. "Robin Wynne is an excellent fellow, and my closest friend."

"Yes, Robin is a dear man, but what has that to do with . . ."

"Let me finish," he said, slapping his hand down on the table. "This isn't easy to say, and I would rather just blurt out the whole and get it over with," he said awkwardly.

Properly chastened, she subsided into silence.

"You must be aware . . . it surely is apparent to you that . . . Robin is deeply in love with you."

She started to protest, but remembered his injunction to allow him his say, and closed her mouth.

"You see, Thea, I have been thinking it over and have decided it would be best if I step aside, so to speak, so that you and Robin could make a match of it. I don't want to stand in the way of your making a proper marriage based on love, instead of this patched-up affair based on my selfish desire to avoid the responsibility for my own daughter. Even that basis is no longer valid, you know," he said, looking toward the room where Martha slept. "I want to be a good father to her. I pray I can be a better father than I have proved to be a husband." He threw down his napkin and started pacing back and forth in front of the fire.

Dorothea sat, bereft of speech, watching him. She was just as bewildered as she had been the day she had met him in the rose bower and he had made his abrupt, unorthodox proposal. Then, as now, she did not know what to make of his words. Was this merely a ploy to salve his conscience when he cast her off?

"Just say the word, Thea," Tate said softly, halting in front of her. "Just say the word and I shall start the annulment proceedings. It's up to you."

But Dorothea could not say any word at all. She sat silently and fixed her gaze on the flickering fire, as if it would counsel her.

"But you say nothing, nothing at all! Does that mean you have no *tendre* for Robin?" Tate demanded, coming up to her.

"Oh, Tate, I cannot think straight, much less talk to any deep purposes tonight," whispered Thea.

"Then I shall do the talking for both of us. Stand up," he ordered in a peremptory tone.

She dazedly arose and he reached for her left hand.

Then he twisted the ring, her mother's wedding band, off her finger and put it into his pocket.

Dorothea's eyes prickled with tears. Was this how it was going to end, then? But before she could wrench away her hand, she felt a cool circlet slide onto her ring finger. Full of wonder, she looked down and saw a strange new ring, wrought of white gold, and set with a finely cut garnet and pearls.

"There was a brooch that belonged to my mother, I used it as a watch fob. I asked Adriana to have it remade into pendants—one for her, and Matty, and Martha, and a wedding ring, a *proper* wedding ring, for you," he said softly.

She gazed at him, desperately trying to understand. "For me?" she echoed.

"Yes, you see I felt it was time we ended this sham of a marriage," he said with a frown.

"Oh, Tate, I shall give you an annulment if that's what you want," she exclaimed, unable to contain her tears any longer.

"Time we ended the sham," he continued, ignoring her tearful outburst, "and began our marriage, my love."

He cupped her face in his hands and drew her toward him, and she dissolved into his embrace with a joy she thought she had forever lost. When their lips met, Dorothea felt dizzy from passion, well mixed with relief and exhaustion, and clung to him even closer for support.

Unfortunately, Dorothea's outcry had awakened Lovelace, and he took violent exception to his mistress being so physically abused by a man who was all but a stranger. He leaped, rather unsteadily, to his feet and prowled around the oblivious couple, growling in a marked manner.

Completely unaware of the disapproving canine's outrage, Tate suddenly lifted his mouth from Dorothea's, and swept her off her feet into his arms, in a pose highly reminiscent of the embarrassing moment when Dorothea had surprised Adriana and Nicholas in their bedchamber. He turned and, carrying her, started toward the bed.

"Tate, wait, there is something I must ask you," Dorothea said in shaken accents.

"Oh, Lord, I hope you don't require any lengthy explanations of marital duties and pleasures," he said with a rueful laugh.

"No, I think all will be made clear without benefit of words, sir," she said with a blush. "My question is this: don't you think it is time we put Lovelace in the other chamber?"

"I couldn't agree more," Tate said, and he proceeded to do so with alacrity, much to the dog's chagrin, and Dorothea's delight.